Maverick of the Cloth

by
Norman Nielsen

**Edited and Cover Design
by James Van Treese**

Northwest Publishing Inc.
5949 South 350 West
Salt Lake City, UT 84107
801-266-5900

Copyright © 1993
Norman Nielsen

Northwest Publishing Inc.
5949 South 350 West
Salt Lake City, Utah 84107
801-266-5900

International Copyright Secured

ISBN #1-880416-94-8

Printed In the United States of America

DEDICATION

To my soul-mate . . . Lady Ann . . . the other half of my full circle . . . wife, lover, confidante and best friend.

To my son and daughter . . . Gregory and Jennifer . . . light beings . . . each on an earth mission extraordinarie.

iv

Although this MAVERICK OF THE CLOTH, and the people close to him are composites of the real, the imagined, the possible, the book is fiction.

Wherever, in the opinion of the author, names and locales might be interpreted otherwise, they have been disguised to preserve privacy.

PREFACE

"MAVERICK OF THE CLOTH" dramatizes that a religious expression which is dull, drab and divisive is a turn off. Its archaic language, portrays a counterfeit God. Takes us on a dead end guilt trip.

Mike Matthews begins to realize that to be a spiritual mentor is a most awesome responsibility because it touches the eternal human spirit.

Driven by his insatiable curiosity, he does the whole nine yards of graduate school, theology and classical languages. He becomes convinced that, at least for him, adequate preparation for spiritual mentoring goes beyond academics, degrees and pious sincerity.

He feels that personal doubts, struggle, adversity and suffering are also essential teachers.

Thus, it is only after reaching his late 40's, following successes in other careers, that he commits to being a spiritual mentor. Not as an ecclesiastical clone, nor papermache saint perched on a pedestal.

Certainly not as a huckster portraying a Las Vegas type deity while setting the hook in followers' bank accounts.

It is his mission to lead a church which is more concerned about people's hurts and healing than the height of its spires and the capacity of its pews. He earnestly hopes it will be a spiritual wayside service station where all ages, genders, races and creeds feel at home and equal.

Each reader of "MAVERICK OF THE CLOTH" will decide if Mike succeeds.

TABLE OF CONTENTS

Chapter

Chapter 1

Parsonage Brat to Street Tough

Sprawled on the gravel of the railroad yard, Mike Matthews felt the jagged rocks tear through his shirt.

His nosebleed was seeping into his mouth. He was getting sick to his stomach. Worst of all was the searing pain in his crotch from being kneed.

"How the hell," he asked himself, "did I get into this mess?"

On the edge of passing out he remembered.

This was his first day in a different school. He was in a new town. With his parents' approval, the teachers had pushed him ahead a year.

He'd already covered the subjects in this fifth grade, and now he was a sixth grader. A couple of years younger than most of these kids.

"I'm about the same size," Mike noticed, "but I don't know if I'll ever be able to make friends here. They all know each other. Grown up together. Their families have lived here forever. I'm an intruder. Why did my dad have to go and move?"

Mike's dad was Reverend Paul Matthews. He had decided to move from a church in Kansas City to a smaller parish in Lakeville, Wisconsin.

"These are tough times," Reverend Matthews had explained to Mike and his younger eight year old sister, Judy.

"Many of our church members have lost their jobs. They

can't afford to pay my salary, and it costs more to live in a big city.

"In a smaller more rural area I won't have to drive my car as much to visit sick and shut-in people. Also we can have our own garden. Your mother will be able to can vegetables and fruit. We'll raise chickens and buy meat directly from the farmers.

"Also, Michael, it'll be easier for you to get better paying odd jobs. Besides, your mother and I are concerned that you're getting into some bad company with that neighborhood gang of yours."

Slowly Mike was beginning to focus. Times were tough. The depression of 1933 was predicted to be worse than '32.

But he hated to leave Kansas City. Although he was only ten, he had a job delivering papers and selling magazine subscriptions door to door. He was saving money for a used bike he'd fallen in love with. Now he'd have to forget about that, and on top of everything else he'd have to say goodbye to his German Shepherd puppy.

Mike had pleaded with his father. "I'm going to miss my dog and the shorter winters. And you and I won't be able to go to any more Kansas City Blues baseball games. I won't be able to swim in the big pool at the park anymore."

The truth was that Mike was going to miss his friends the most. He'd been elected captain of his gang, and they were getting the reputation of beings kings of the neighborhood.

Of course, Mike's pleading was useless. Here they were in Lakeville, Wisconsin, and Mike's worst fears, it seemed, were being realized.

The Matthews lived on the wrong side of the tracks. The neighborhood of smaller, cheaper homes. Close to the railroad yard and two small factories. Uptown was across the river. The fancy stores were all there.

Sure enough the parsonage was right next door to the small church. "Everybody in town will know I'm the preacher's kid," Mike knew. "They'll expect me to be different. Better than anyone else."

"Shit! It's gotta happen. I'll be tested by some kid who

thinks he's tough."

It started in the cloak room. The bell had just rung ending recess. Everybody was hanging up their outside clothes. Suddenly this big bully shoved Mike into a coat hook and grabbed his cap.

The kid was a giant. Right off the farm. He seemed about two years older and at least twenty pounds heavier.

"Here you are city slicker," he teased. "You want your cap back preacher's kid? Just try, sissy."

He kept taunting Mike, dangling his cap just out of reach. "I'll fight you for it, pansy, down by the railroad yards after school."

That's how this fight had started. Mike remembered now as his opponent stood over him teasing him with his cap.

The guy's friends were circling around them. Now they were shouting their jeers: "Pansy! Sissy! Preacher's kid!"

True, Mike was the new preacher's kid in town. But he was no ordinary preacher's kid. These guys didn't know about his many hours of boxing and wrestling lessons.

His teacher in the parochial school had been his coach. He was a tough immigrant from the old country.

Mike didn't know how he'd gotten away with it, but he stayed after school to take boxing and wrestling lessons. His parents thought he was tutoring in geography and spelling.

Fortunately, Mike got in the low 90's in those subjects, but he'd have been ranked in the upper 90's in self defense. He learned some tricky wrestling holds and became the best boxer in his class.

Mike had learned his lessons well. He knew that fast feet, bobbing, weaving, feinting and jabbing could frustrate a stronger opponent. He learned how a guy could set up his opponent for a finishing shot to the jaw by a fast combination of lefts and rights to the body and head.

He had also learned good sportsmanship.

"You never pick on somebody smaller than you," his coach taught him. "In fact you don't pick fights at all. But you do learn to protect yourself. You never hold and hit. You don't hit below the belt or when a guy is down. And you never mix boxing and wrestling. You agree beforehand, with a toss of a coin if necessary, which it will be."

"Sure," Mike thought, "that's why I'm in this mess now. I thought this guy would fight by the rules. His friends tossed the coin, and I won. So naturally, being smaller, I chose boxing. I figured this guy is a tub. Out of shape, and probably can't box worth shit."

Sure enough, Mike had quickly caught him with two lightening left jabs, cutting his lip. Then he'd doubled him over with a right to his flabby gut. Mike was just ready to move in for an uppercut when the guy caught him in the balls with his knee.

Bent over with horrible pain, Mike was sent sprawling with a looping haymaker flush on his nose. No wonder it seemed to everyone that the fight was all over.

However, what they hadn't counted on was Mike's courage. His coach had also taught him something about heart and determination.

"When you think you can't go on," he had said, "there's reserve of power like a second fuel tank on a car that you can switch to. If you believe in yourself. If you have real determination."

Mike reached down and drew on that reserve now. He snatched his cap out of the bully's hand. At the same time tripped him with a scissor lock on his leg.

Before the guy could recover, Mike was on his feet. Just as his tormentor got up, Mike caught him with a combination of lefts and rights. Then "boom!" Nailed him with an uppercut to the jaw.

Now it was all over. Mike backed off, giving the kid a chance to get up. But he was done. His one eye was turning black and blue. His lip was bleeding, and he was sniveling something about having had enough.

So, as the bully's friends helped him to his feet, Mike Matthews proudly put on his cap and headed for the parsonage.

Chapter 2

Destined For The Pulpit

"Now I am in for it," Mike thought. "I never know how my folks are going to react when I get into some kind of trouble."

"If only they'd listen to my side of the story. If only they'd be consistent."

Mike quietly opened the back door and stepped into the small hallway. He wiped the blood off his nose with his handkerchief as best he could, and hung up his cap.

He caught the delicious odor of meatballs and freshly baked pie. But the minute he walked into the kitchen he knew he was in trouble.

He was late for one thing, and that was a sin in the Matthew's household.

"Where in the world have you been, Michael Matthews?" his father demanded. "I suppose you had to stay after school your very first day for getting into trouble.

"Oh, I see, you've been fighting again. Swollen nose and torn shirt. Get on upstairs and do your homework. When you've finished you can go to bed for the night. There'll be no supper. You can just think about what a poor example you've been.

"How do you expect me to talk from the pulpit about love and being Christian when my own son can't behave himself? We'll get at the bottom of this tomorrow."

Judy gave Mike a wistful, sympathetic look as he retreated to the stairs. Mrs. Matthews didn't say anything, but Mike could tell she hoped he was all right.

He was terribly hungry. The peanut butter and jelly sandwich and apple he'd had for lunch were worn off hours ago.

Otherwise he didn't mind so much being alone in his room. Time to think. He didn't feel he'd done anything wrong. Only defended himself. But he sensed that as long as he lived here in Lakeville he'd be held up as a model by his parents.

"I love my mother and dad," Mike thought to himself, "but I'm so tired of them telling me that I was born special. Destined for the pulpit like my father.

"That's what they've been drilling into me for as long as I can remember. I was barely old enough to grasp the meaning of my mother's words when she would tuck me into bed and say the prayer 'Now I lay me down to sleep,' and then tell me that I was born as a gift from God.

"She would say, 'When you were conceived in my womb I promised God you would be given back to him. You would be his servant.'

"She would go on to say, "I made an agreement with God that if you, as my first born, were healthy and strong I would dedicate you to the Lord. I promised that you would be a minister like your father.'

"Mom," I would ask, "what does womb and conceive mean?" That was enough of a mystery for me to handle."

From his earliest recollection Mike felt he had a wonderful mother. Her first name was Kirsten, but Reverend Matthews never called her that. It was always 'Mom' or 'Mother' and 'Dad' between them.

Mrs. Matthews' life was her husband, children and parishioners in the church. Especially the lonely, the ill, the needy.

Above all, she had this passion that her son was born to be a servant of God. Gradually Mike began to figure out why.

She was very devout. Her parents had immigrated from the old country where pastors were absolutely revered.

Mike learned how this adoration carried over to America.

Typical of so many, his grandparents arrived in this new country penniless. They settled in the Midwest. Staked a homestead claim. Worked hard. Saved. Were frugal, and raised seven children. They survived blizzards, drought and hordes of grasshoppers to become successful grain farmers and land owners.

After acquiring a farm for each of their children they retired to a small prairie town. They got a white frame church built and hired a pastor to hold services, and conduct weddings, baptisms and burials.

Mike had learned that the most important person in the prairie towns of early America was not the banker, the land owner, the teacher. It was the preacher.

He had the best education. He was a college and seminary graduate. Represented God. Knew the final word on almost every subject. He was holy. Could do no wrong.

He was at your side at the most important times of life. When you were born, married, had children of your own. Were ill, hurting, dying.

Little wonder that Mike's grandmother had this high ambition for one of her two daughters to snare a pastor. The five brothers stayed on the farm, but as soon as Kirsten was old enough off she went to a small church sponsored private college.

It was there that she met Paul Matthews newly graduated from the seminary and ordained. The steeple bell of the simple prairie church peeled joyfully and long following their wedding; and in the spring of 1923 they sealed their pledge of dedicating their son to the Lord.

Solemnly they wrote his name on the baptism certificate . . . Michael Charles Matthews.

"Oh, how I have hated that name," Mike thought as he leaned over his desk trying to get his geography and arithmetic homework done.

"Why couldn't I have been called John, or George or Pete like most of my friends. No, I had to be called Michael Charles. A first name that means something about archangels.

"Imagine! Me, an angel, when it seems I am anything but

an angel.

"On top of it I got saddled with a middle name of royalty. Charles, after King Charles of England. All I want to be is a commoner.

"And of course," Mike went on talking to himself, "my last name reminds everybody of one of the writers of the New Testament. I can't do anything about what my parents call me. I suppose that'll always be Michael, or Michael Charles, but out on the streets and in school it's going to be plain Mike.

"And as far as that business about being dedicated to be a servant of God, don't I have a choice? What if I want to be a wheat farmer like my grandfather, or fly airplanes, or be the head of a company or build buildings. Who says I have to be a minister?"

It was getting dark out. Mike was having trouble seeing the lines on his notebook paper as he finished his last arithmetic problem.

"Easy stuff," he thought. "I've had all this before. But now comes the hard part. Darn that teacher. She said we only had two days to get ready for this assignment of a three minute talk in front of the class. It was supposed to be an exciting experience or a most important memory in your life so far.

"God, how I hate to get up in front of people and talk. The last time I was shaking so bad I couldn't hold my notes still. I got all red in the face, and I could hardly swallow 'cause my mouth was so dry.

"Darn! I'd better start making notes or I'll never get through this."

So Mike started making his list. In a devilish mood he wrote down "Girls!"

"Yeah, I could talk about my first girlfriend. Her name was Romona. I remember bringing her a valentine and begging my mother to take me to her home so I could play in her playhouse.

"Then all of a sudden my love turned to hate because I found out she had another boyfriend. I couldn't believe it. Thought I was the only one. It hurt so bad I felt like bawling.

"But then I remembered what my dad had told me. Boys were strong. They didn't cry or show feelings. If they were sad they sort of wore a mask covering it up. Boys were expected to be tough. Be leaders. Know the right answers to complicated questions. Be hard workers. Make a mark in the world and provide for a wife and family."

Mike was really in a devilish mood now. Thinking about girls reminded him of another first experience.

That had been only about a year ago when he was nine. "Michael Charles," his mother announced one Saturday, "I've made arrangements for you to stay with some friends of ours while your father and I go shopping. They have a son your age and a daughter a couple of years older. They live out in the country. You'll have a good time and we won't be gone long."

"OK, Mom," I replied.

"Little did I know how exciting this was going to be."

"The girl suggested we play house. Her brother and I said we'd rather play 'ante-over' with the softball or 'kick the can'. But she won out.

"First thing I know, Mary said to her brother George, 'it's time for you to go out and play while Daddy and I make supper. Then we'll call you.'

"Well, she didn't make supper. She pulled down the shades. Locked the door. Took me over to the bed and started taking off her clothes. She said we were going to play doctor.

"I was terrified. 'Cause then she started taking off my clothes. Boy, did I get out of there fast. Ran looking for George. Never told my mother about that experience.

"Wouldn't that be fun if I told that story? Mike said to himself. "The teacher would be shocked. But I can't do it. I would be too embarrassed."

"I know," Mike went on remembering. "I could tell about my first day of school.

"I was only four and a half. Younger than most kindergarten pupils by a year. But I kept pestering my mother until she gave in. She got me enrolled because the teacher was a member of my dad's church.

"I'll never forget that morning. After oatmeal and dates with brown sugar, my father read from the Bible and prayed as always to begin the day.

"He said a special prayer for me, and wound it up with that reminder again: 'and help Michael Charles remember how special he is, the preacher's son, and someday he's going to be one.'

"I didn't like that part, but I was too excited to think much about it. Just climbed in the brand new 1927 Model T Ford my dad had bought and off we went.

"My teacher was wonderful. So kind. I liked doing the crayons and working on the alphabet which my mother had already taught me. Then it was nap time, and the most awful thing happened.

"I peed in my pants. I was 'mortified' as my mother would say. I'd been toilet trained and walking since nine months. But I had been too embarrassed to hold up my hand and ask to go to the bathroom.

"I just hung my head in shame when my father came to get me.

"OK, Mike, you can't tell that story either," Mike said to himself. "Now what?"

Slowly Mike went through his mental list of top experiences. He thought about how his father taught him to swim in the park pool.

Before immigrating, his father, while working as a fisherman apprentice, had learned to swim in the North Sea. He was a powerful swimmer and a good teacher. So Mike remembered how thrilled he was the first time he won a freestyle race the length of the pool.

There was also the thrill of getting his first bike. It was blue. Used, but newly repainted. Mike had traded in his scooter and paid for it with his own money saved from the paper route.

That was special. So was seeing his first airplane up close. It was a Ford Tri Motor at the Kansas City airport. That had only been a year or so ago. He'd never forget the feeling of amazement as that plane glided out of the sky and touched down to the roar of the crowd. Mike's only disappointment was that Charles Lindberg wasn't on board.

But it was the next day that Mike started making model airplanes and vowed that he would be a pilot in the air force.

There were other thrilling experiences. Mike thought about telling how he caught a fowl tip in the Kansas City Blue's baseball park. Afterward he and his dad went down on the field and one of the players autographed it. "Now, for sure," he vowed, "I'll be a professional baseball player."

Or he could talk about how happy he was the day he finally talked his mother into canceling his piano lessons. Mike had been a good student. That was part of the trouble as far as he was concerned. Because every time there was some special church program his mother made him play a solo.

"Michael Charles," she would say, "since you're going to be a preacher like your father you've got to know something about music. Maybe some day you'll have to play a pedal organ yourself for the hymns."

"No thanks," Mike thought. "I'd rather be playing ball than taking piano lessons. Besides that lady teacher is mean. When I mess up a piece or haven't practiced enough she raps my knuckles with her wooden baton."

That did it. Mike talked his mother into getting rid of the teacher by claiming she was mean to him.

"Oh, I know," Mike suddenly thought, "I'll tell about the day I had my tonsils out. That sure left a big impression on me. I'll bet I'm the only one in my class who had his tonsils out on the dining room table.

"Yeah! They had to come out because I had so many sore throats. But mom and dad couldn't afford the hospital room. So they had the doctor come to the house.

"The dining room table was covered with a fresh sheet. The overhead light was turned on, and I climbed on the table from a chair. The last thing I remember was that smelly ether held under my nose by the doctor's nurse. That evening I sat out on the front porch swing with Judy and my parents sipping ice water."

"Talk about being unique," Mike realized, "nobody in his class had lived in a parsonage.

"That would make a special story. I could talk about how dedicated my parents are. They really believe in what they are doing. They are proud to be serving the Lord.

"They never get the big head, though. The parishioners see to that in a way."

Mike could talk about how his parents were kept humble by being poor. Church members' reasoning went something like this: "He's a servant of God isn't he? We provide him with a free house. True, his salary isn't very large, but he gets those three altar offerings—Christmas, Easter and harvest time.

Little did they know how pitifully small they could be. The weather could be bad. Maybe a recent sermon had offended the big givers or there was a flu epidemic. Boy! Did the family ever tighten their belts then?

Never once though did Mike hear Reverend Matthew's complain. He lived by the Bible's words "Where your heart is there will your treasure be also." He truly believed he was called by God to be a minister and that his reward ultimately would be in heaven.

Thinking of rewards reminded Mike about the huge prize his parents received one summer. It was 1929 just before the great depression. Mike was six.

"I'll never forget," Mike realized, "the morning Dad called Judy and I into his study."

"I've got some news for you," he began. "Your mother and I are planning a trip for this summer."

"Oh, goodie!" I exclaimed. "Judy and I love trips, don't we?"

"Oh, yes. Could we visit Grandma and Grandpa?"

"No, this is a trip to Europe, and only your mother and I will be going."

"Europe?" I cried, "that's all the way across the ocean."

"Yes," Dad answered. "It is a long way, and we'll be gone all summer."

"What are we going to do?" Judy wailed. "Can we have our aunt come and stay with us?"

"No, Judy and Mike. Your mother and I have talked it over, and we've made some wonderful plans for you. Some very special friends of ours in a nearby town are managers of a church owned children's home. They've agreed to take care of you. They're very kind and they'll be really good to you."

"Children's home?" I cried. "That's an orphanage. They're mean places."

"That's how one of my worst summers began," Mike recalled. "I was so lonely. I tried to be happy for my father and mother. Especially Dad. He'd left home when he was only eighteen. Never saw his mother again, because she died very young.

"My dad returned to Europe for World War I as a machine gunner in the trenches for his new adopted country. But he'd never seen his brothers and sisters and father. So it was a wonderful treat, I knew, for them when the church told him he'd sold enough tickets to win a free trip for both him and mother.

"The harder I tried to accept the orphanage, the worse it got. I couldn't eat. Lost weight. They thought I was sick. I was. I was homesick.

"I remember seeing Judy once a week when they marched us hand in hand down the sidewalk of the little town to the big church for Sunday School. She seemed happy enough. Of course she was only four, and the manager and his wife treated her as their own daughter right in their home.

"Finally, I was moved from the small boy's department to a wing of older boys next to the headmaster who was a really friendly guy.

"He discovered part of my problem was taking my Saturday night bath supervised by nurses. I was embarrassed. After all, I was a boy. I liked the showers better with the guys, and somehow made it through the summer.

"Talk about an unforgettable experience! The day my parents drove up was the happiest moment in my life. 'Forever and ever,' I said to myself, 'I'll remember how awful it is not to have a home or mother and father.'"

As Mike finished writing his notes about the orphanage experience, he figured he would probably pick that as the most important event in his life to talk about.

But then he thought of one more that might be better. More unique. Combining several of his other important experiences. His bike, sports, adventure, happiness, as well as sadness.

"It was just after I got my bike," Mike recalled. "I talked Mom and Dad into letting me make a ten mile trip to the home of family friends.

"I remember they lived in a suburb. Mom packed a sandwich, apple and a couple of cookies and off I went. I had to promise I would telephone the minute I got there.

"It was a warm spring Saturday. Lawns were turning green and blossoms were everywhere.

"I felt so daring and grown up. I kept pumping away on the back streets. Took the paths through parks, and finally made my last turn on a country road just outside the city.

"I pulled over by a stream to enjoy my lunch. Down stream where the water was flowing faster, and the banks were farther apart, a group of boys were skinny dipping. They were swinging with a rope tied to a tree branch and diving into the swirling pool of clear, icy water.

"What fun!" I thought.

"Hey," one of the guys shouted when he spotted me, "come and join us. We're seeing who can swing the highest and dive the fartherest."

"Sure. Be right there."

"Within seconds I was taking my turn. I came up sputtering and paddling against the current when someone shouted, 'Where's Joe?'"

"He wouldn't leave without telling us. Look! There are his clothes on the bank."

"I sensed they were getting worried. Suddenly one of the boys screamed: 'Oh, no, look. Down there.'

"He was pointing downstream. Joe's naked, half submerged body, was caught between some rocks near shore. We all swam there as fast as we could, and pulled Joe to shore hoping he would be OK.

"He wasn't. It was scarey. He was so still and white. I had never seen a dead person before. We all started crying.

"I was the only one with a bike so I ran for my shorts and pedaled to the nearest house to call for help. It seemed like hours before the police came and then a fire truck.

"They turned Joe on his stomach and tried to get the water out of his lungs. But he was gone. Then I turned around as a car skidded to a stop by the bank. It was Joe's mother and father. They were sobbing as the police covered Joe with a blanket and helped the ambulance people carry him on a stretcher.

"That last mile or so to the home of my parent's friend was tough. But somehow I dried my tears and squared my shoulders and rang the doorbell.

"Michael Charles, wonderful to see you," the lady said. "Your mother has been calling. Is everything all right? You took longer than we expected and you know your mom. She was worried."

"Oh, everything is fine," Mike lied. "I stopped at a park to enjoy the flowers, a pretty creek and to eat my lunch. I'll call mom right away.

"Hello Mother, I made it OK. I'm just fine. No problems. It was so much fun," Mike lied again.

"Michael Charles, I'm so relieved you're all right. Maybe you could rest up and then start for home. And please be careful."

"I will, Mother. Thanks for the good lunch. I'm really enjoying my bike.

"All the way home I couldn't forget Joe being carried to the ambulance."

"Why do people have to die?" Mike wondered. "What happens to them? Why do they put people in a casket in the ground? Do they go to heaven? I wonder what it's like. I've heard the Bible stories of Lazarus and Jesus bringing him back from the dead. Why can't that happen to everybody? If heaven is so wonderful why do people cry at funerals?

"I remember it took me a long time to go to sleep that night. And I never told my parents about Joe, 'cause sure as heck they'd never let me go off on my own again until I was older. And I was in a hurry to grow up."

"I knew this was the story I should tell in my talk. I'll bet none of those other kids have seen a real dead person their own age. They'll think I'm something special now."

With his head spinning from all the memories relived, and a strange first day in Lakeville, Mike pulled the cord on the light bulb and went to bed.

Just then he heard the stairs creaking. He supposed it was Judy heading for her room.

There was a soft knock on his door, and a whisper "Mike! Mike! Are you awake?"

"Yeah, Judy, come in."

"I just wanted to tell you I'm sorry about your fight. Are you all right? Here, I brought you a meatball sandwich and piece of pie."

"Thank you, Judy. You're a sweetheart. Yeah, I'm OK. But you know Mother will miss this piece of pie. She'll know, and I don't want you to get into any trouble."

"Sure, she'll notice, but I have a hunch she won't say anything to Dad. She knows things didn't go right for you today. I didn't think she wanted you to go to bed hungry."

"Thanks again, Judy. See you in the morning."

"Good night, Mike."

17

Chapter 3

Iceberg River Raft

Reverend Matthews seemed to be in a better mood the next morning.

"Well, Michael," he said as they sat down for breakfast, "are you ready to tell us what happened yesterday?"

"I wanted to tell you when I came home," Mike replied, "but you didn't give me a chance."

"Now, don't get smart with me, Son."

"I guess Michael's right, Father," Mother chimed in, "we didn't really give him a chance."

With that opening, Mike just plunged in and told them the whole story.

When he finished, Reverend Matthews put his hand on his shoulder and said, "Michael, I guess we owe you an apology. I've always tried to teach you that you have a right to defend yourself. David did that with Goliath in the Bible. Remember? Maybe the kids will accept you better now that you've licked the big bully."

The next days at school did go better. Mike was even asked to join the softball game during recess. They stuck him in right field where nobody else wanted to play. But he felt he made a pretty good impression when he threw out a runner at home, and knocked in a run with a double.

On the third day in his new school Mike managed to stumble through his story about his bike ride into the country and seeing Joe's drowning. It got real quiet in the room. The kids seemed to be listening. A couple even talked to him about it after class. It seemed some of his classmates were friendlier now.

Mike also came to like the parsonage in Wisconsin. It was an old home. Simple. Comfortable. And the yard was big and wonderful.

Reverend Matthews convinced some landscapers, who belonged to the church, to donate a complete landscaping job to the property.

They planted shrubs, trees, annuals and perennials of most species growing in the Midwest. From spring to fall there were fresh flowers in the parsonage.

There was also a rock garden out back with a gold fish pond, a grape arbor and most types of fruit trees which would grow in this climate.

Back of the landscaped yard was a huge garden with rows of vegetables. To top it off there were more rows of strawberries, blackberries and raspberries. Of course all of this required a lot of work. Along with Reverend and Mrs. Matthews, Mike was the assistant gardener.

Most fall and spring days when it wasn't raining he would find a note on the kitchen counter with a list of chores for the day. After having a glass of milk and a cookie, it was off to work.

Sometimes Mike thought, "It's just a way to keep me out of trouble." But then he realized that his mom and dad also worked hard, and Judy helped keep the house clean and do the canning and laundry. They all took turns at the evening dishes, even Reverend Matthews.

"Your mother works so hard with all the baking, house-work and helping me visit the sick and poor people in our parish" Dad would say. "It's only fair that we help at home."

Mike actually enjoyed the garden work. It gave him a lot of satisfaction to see the beautiful lawn on a spring morning, the fragrant flower gardens. The blooming fruit trees.

Some of the work was boring. There were always weeds to pull. Vines to spray. Potato bugs to pick and drop in the kerosene can. There was spading, hoeing, cultivating, trimming, fertilizing.

The planting and harvest was the most fun, Mike thought. He would sit on the back porch opening pea pods and cutting the tops off radishes and carrots. He'd eat his share. It was the only way Mike liked vegetables. Raw. Couldn't stand the taste of most of them cooked.

When the Matthews caught up with the garden chores there was always the garage to clean out or the car to wash. One thing for sure Mike and Judy learned how to work, and the value of contributing to the family. They also learned how to be well organized and get their jobs done as soon as possible so they could go play.

A fun evening after homework was done, and supper dishes washed, was to make popcorn and fudge. Maybe listen on the radio to "Little Orphan Annie," "Major Bowes Amateur Hour" or "The Inner Sanctum".

Some evenings when Reverend and Mrs. Matthews had to attend church meetings Judy and Mike would get out the Carom board, or play Checkers or Old Maid cards.

Mike was getting restless now to get a job on the side and earn some money. So one Saturday morning he knocked on his dad's office door while he was studying for a sermon.

"Dad, can I talk to you for a minute?"

"Sure, Mike, come in and sit down. What's on your mind?"

"I would like to see if there is some way I could get a job earning some money."

"Well, Mike, we really need and appreciate your help here at home. I couldn't do all this work in the yard without you. The rest of the time you're in school, and you're too young yet to be hired for most jobs."

"I've been thinking, Dad, about a couple of things. Maybe I could get a job on Saturdays in that place I walk by to school where they sell cars and trucks. I've heard they need somebody to wash cars and clean them out before they sell them.

"Also, we have this potato picking vacation from school in the fall. Maybe I could get a job from one of the farmer church members picking potatoes for a week."

Reverend Matthews did some checking into Mike's ideas and that fall Mike got his first paying job since selling the magazine subscriptions in Kansas City.

The depression seemed to be getting worse. It was early October, 1934, and Mike was only eleven, but he moved out to the farm and got a job picking potatoes for a week.

Picking potatoes was torture. But good for building up the muscles. The wakeup alarm rang while it was still dark. There was a quick breakfast and then out to the field.

It was barely dawn when the workers started crawling on all fours shaking the plants and pulling the potatoes off the roots which had been dug up by machine. They pushed a wooden bushel crate ahead of them and it got heavier and heavier by the minute. By working twelve hours with a half hour off for lunch, it was considered good to pick a hundred bushels a day.

In Mike's six days on the job he hit that average. The farmer told him that was amazing for an eleven year old as he paid him the penny a bushel. One dollar a day. Six dollars plus room and board for the week.

Mike's hot bath at home that Saturday night felt especially good. He was bursting with pride as he put that six dollars in his own little bank.

Reverend Matthews also got Mike the car and truck washing job on Saturdays. That wasn't quite as grueling. He worked a ten hour day from 8 AM to 6 PM, and was paid by the number of cars he finished. Depending on the size, Mike could do eight or ten a day. They paid him twenty-five cents per car, so two to three dollars went into his bank every week.

The part Mike liked best was they taught him how to drive the cars and trusted him to move them to another place in the garage when they were clean.

Walking to his new school also turned into fun for Mike. It was about a mile. They went home for lunch so that made it about four miles a day.

Mike didn't mind the four miles. When it wasn't muddy or icy he would run to get in shape for sports. This would give him a few extra minutes too for shooting baskets in the gym.

It wasn't long before he found a short cut — a couple of back streets. A trail through a marsh, past the interesting store fronts of the little town. There was the drugstore hangout for the high school kids and finally the railroad trestle crossing the river.

It was on this run every day that Mike made his first new friend. His name was Ernie Johnson. They hit it off right away. They both liked sports. Ernie's family was a member of their church, but Ernie just treated Mike like an ordinary guy, not the preacher's kid. They liked to do the same daring things.

The railroad trestle over the river was one of their favorite challenges. They would wait until the slow moving freight came into view from the other direction on the single track. Then run like heck for the other side. The engineer would blow his whistle and shake his fist, but they always made it.

Except this one time. It was a different train, and the boys misjudged the speed. They got caught right in the middle. They thought of jumping, but the trestle was pretty high and the water was icy on this late fall day. So the boys managed to get hold of the ties and hung on underneath while the train rolled over the top of them. Fortunately it was a short train.

The icy water almost got them a couple of months later, however.

"Let's go rafting," Ernie announced one day on their run home from school.

"Go rafting? You must be nuts," Mike replied. "It's December and it's cold."

"That's OK. You see, what we do is go up to the power plant by the dam."

"You do what? You go on the river by the dam? The water is really steamy and fast there."

"That's the point. Because of the fast water in the middle what we do is take an ax and chop off a big piece of the ice by the shore, about twelve feet by twelve. We make a couple of long poles from the trees nearby and off we go."

That's exactly what they did. They were having a great time until coming to a bend in the river not far from Ernie's house. They got so busy trying to turn the raft that when it tilted they both slid off into the icy water.

Somehow both boys struggled to shore.

"Now what do we do, Ernie?" Mike asked through chattering teeth.

"Let's climb this bank and try to make it to my house," Ernie answered. "It's only a couple of blocks."

They were both soaked. Their jackets and boots were starting to get stiff as they stumbled into the back door of Ernie's house.

His mother almost fainted when she saw them, but she was a good sport. They told her the whole story, and it seemed to Mike that nothing Ernie did would surprise her. She promised not to tell Mike's parents, because he explained "my mother, especially, probably wouldn't let me out of the house for a month, except for school, church and my Saturday job."

In no time Ernie's mother got the boys some dry clothes and they were sipping hot chocolate and eating fresh baked apple pie. They promised never to ice raft again.

Mike's next best friend was Steve. Mr. Woods, his parents said he should be called. But Steve insisted on being called Steve. He and his wife were next door neighbors.

They were about thirty, and were not able to have children.

Steve was a great fisherman and hunter. There was nothing about the woods, lakes and streams of Wisconsin he didn't know. He was a dedicated conservationist and began to teach Mike everything he knew.

He loaned Mike his old "Field and Stream" magazines. So Mike learned what kind of lures were best for bass, northern pike and walleye. He found out how to put old coffee grounds on top of the moist black dirt in the garden to attract angle worms for sunnies and crappies.

Steve taught Mike how to make artificial flies for casting in spring streams for brook trout. He taught him how to take apart a casting reel, clean and oil it and put it back together. Mike also learned how to recognize the best shoreline or drop offs, how the weather and different seasons affected the depth of the fish.

Mike thought it was a thrill to sit in a fish house in the winter and watch a minnow bait swimming around while he waited for just the right second to spear the big northern pike through the hole in the ice. It was a highlight of Mike's week when Steve would come over and ask his parents if he could go fishing with him.

The two would take off on a spring or summer morning at the crack of dawn with their lunch packed and pulling Steve's boat on a trailer behind his car. Motors weren't permitted on the lakes they fished, so Mike learned how to row without making a sound. They'd cast and drift until they hooked a fish and then carefully lower the anchor.

Mike was in awe of Steve and his almost reverent attitude toward the beauty of nature. He would never keep a fish that was undersized. Even if it was close he would carefully remove the hook and toss it back. He taught Mike how to clean fish and take the bones out, and never keep more than was legal.

That first fall after meeting Steve was special. Mike couldn't wait to see if he could go hunting with his new friend. Steve had a wonderful dog trained for rabbits, pheasants and ducks, and Mike was hoping Steve would invite him to join him.

One evening after Steve's factory job Mike heard him talking to his parents in the kitchen. Mike was upstairs putting a model airplane together.

The door to his room was open, so he could hear them talking about the hunting season and Steve was saying, "Mrs. Matthews, you have a fine son. He's been a quick learner on fishing and I would be happy to teach him about the woods and safety and guns."

"I'm so afraid something will happen to him, Steve, but I know he really likes you and you have been so good for him. It was very hard for him to leave his friends in Kansas City, and you have been such a good neighbor and friend. Besides I know how careful you are, so I suppose . . ."

Mike never heard the rest, because he bounded down the stairs two at a time and almost slid into the kitchen.

"Mom, please let me go."

His first hunting outing was two weeks away. Several evenings after school Steve took Mike out to a field where he showed him how to hold a gun. How to put the safety on and off. How to sight the target and pull the trigger.

Then they would practice shooting at old cans on top of fence posts or throw them in the air.

Steve had a beautiful lightweight .210 gauge shotgun which he let Mike use. By the end of the two weeks he was still a little nervous but ready to go.

That first hunt was something. They were hunting white tailed rabbits in the woods. Steve's dog 'Max' was off like a shot when his master gave the word. His nose was twitching ninety miles an hour as he got the scent.

"How are we going to keep up with him?" Mike asked.

"Don't worry we won't have to. We'll post right here on the edge of this little clearing and 'Max' will bring that rabbit right back here. Now, this first time you just stand by me and watch."

Sure enough, a few minutes later they heard the yipping of 'Max' crashing through the brush. Just then here came the rabbit and 'boom' Steve had it. Mike felt kind of sorry for the rabbit, but Steve explained that everything they would hunt together needed to be thinned out in numbers or they would just die from freezing or starving.

Mike didn't get his rabbit that day . . . missed one, but there were other hunting trips for pheasant, quail and ducks. He even learned about squirrel and crow hunting with a .22 rifle, and always at the end of the day no matter how tired there was clean up time.

That meant first of all to feed 'Max' and then gut and skin the game and wrap it carefully to put on ice. Next they cleaned and oiled the guns and locked them away in the cabinet after double checking that every shell was removed.

The final chore was to clean their boots and scrub up before sitting down to a wonderful hot dish by Steve's wife. Now it was story time. Review the day. Recount the fun things which had happened. Sometimes tell a little fib or two.

Stretch a bit the distance of the shot, and have a good laugh about some of their misses.

Life was very good just then to Michael Charles Matthews. It was difficult for him to imagine how the coming years could be any better.

Chapter 4

Dull - Drab - Divisive

Mike was twelve, and already a ninth grader. "Sometimes he acts like twenty," Mrs. Matthews said.

"Well, Mom, if Mike acts old for his age," Judy would tell her, "it's because you're always reminding us we have to set an example."

"Does that really bother you, Judy?"

"Yes. Sometimes I wish we could just cut up like the other kids. But when we go to Sunday School or the youth meetings at church we have to be so careful what we say and do."

That was especially true on Sunday mornings.

Mrs. Matthews always sat in the third pew from the front on the left side. Promptly at ten minutes before the church bell rang, announcing services, Judy and Mrs. Matthews walked down the aisle with Michael immediately behind.

The children entered the pew first, and Mrs. Matthews took her place next to the aisle. Judy and Michael were always spic and span. Their clothes were freshly washed and ironed. Their shoes polished. They had to stand and sit at exactly the right times. Hold the hymn book properly and sing the songs. Above all they were to be quiet during prayers and the sermon.

One Sunday Ernie and his mother slid in beside Mike. The two boys started whispering and giggling during the hymns. Mrs. Matthews pinched Mike on the leg so they kept quiet during the prayers.

But right in the middle of the sermon, Ernie gave Mike a

jab and whispered: "Let's ask the Lord to keep us from sliding off the ice raft next time."

That did it. Mike let out a giggle that could be heard all over the church.

Suddenly it got very still.

Reverend Matthews stopped his sermon and glared at Ernie and Mike.

In his sternest voice, with his finger pointing at Mike, he said: "Will the two boys who are being so sacrilegious and rude as not to respect the house of the Lord leave this minute. You, my son. I'll deal with you when I get home."

There was no misunderstanding what that meant. Mike got his dad's belt on his bare ass and was sent to bed without dinner after another lecture about being an example.

Monday, in school, Mike caught up to Ernie in the hall. "What did your parents do?"

"Nothing much," Ernie answered. "My father doesn't go to church much. Just Christmas or a wedding or funeral. My mom told him what happened. He just gave me a swipe on the butt and told me to quit leading the preacher's kid astray."

Except for their frustration over being an example, the Matthews children felt pretty good about the religious atmosphere in their home up to this point.

The family always bowed their head to say "Grace" before meals. Supper was the main meal of the day, and they were normally together.

After the meal Reverend Matthews would read from a devotional booklet. He would try to explain the reading to the children, and encourage them to ask questions. Then he would offer a prayer. Frequently, he would mention each one by name and ask for something special on their behalf. It was also a time of sharing happenings of the day.

Occasionally, on Sunday evenings, they would gather around the piano in the living room and sing favorite hymns and folk songs.

Judy and Mike liked those times. They agreed that God came across as good and powerful. That he loved them, and

Jesus was a down to earth friendly person.

They had the impression that following him meant being kind to others, helping the poor and needy. Being honest and fair. No swearing. Behaving respectfully in church. Saying their prayers at night before bedtime.

Reverend Matthews, though very stern at times, also had a lighter side. When he had time he would take them on sightseeing rides through the countryside. Sometimes they'd all go on a picnic or swimming.

He also enjoyed his pipe in the study or a cigar after a Sunday dinner. Whenever someone had a baby or a wedding, they'd give Reverend Matthews a couple of cigars.

Mike always wondered if he missed the occasional cigar he slipped out of his dad's drawer. He'd sneak off to the loft of the garage and have himself a man sized smoke. Then proceed to get sick.

Reverend Matthews' human side also came through in his pleasure at having a glass of beer or wine with Mrs. Matthews at supper.

He brewed his own in the basement, and invited Mike to help with the bottle capper.

Mike was slightly puzzled though. "Dad, I thought we were in prohibition," he asked, "doesn't that mean drinking beer and wine is illegal?"

"Oh, not what I make," his dad responded. "Prohibition is just against strong liquor. What I make is mild table wine, and beer like we had in the old country.

"I grew up with this as a boy, Michael, and learned that, when it's mild like this, it's just a table beverage with a meal and good for you."

"Can I taste it, Dad?"

"Sure, son, I think you're old enough to understand."

Mike took a little sip of wine. "Oh, that tastes pretty good. It should. We made it out of our own grapes."

Then he took a sip of beer and almost gagged. "I hate that. How can anyone drink that stuff?"

It wasn't long before Mike discovered that his dad's wine wasn't so mild. Some of the corks popped in the basement, and he helped his dad clean up the mess. But Mike enjoyed sharing this lighter side to his father. He also felt that it taught him the difference between a meal time beverage and getting drunk.

This is why Mike was so shocked the day he came home from school and saw his father loading all the bottles, the crocks and capper into a borrowed trailer.

"Dad, what are you doing? Where are you taking all this?"

"Son, I'm hauling it to the dump."

"Why?"

"Because your mother and I have decided that this is not a good example for you and Judy or our church members."

"I don't understand, Dad. I can't see anything wrong with it. What made you change your mind?"

"Well, Michael, it's probably hard for you to understand right now. But your mother and I feel we have grown in our religious faith and are getting closer to the Lord. We feel the Lord has called us to be set apart. To be separate. To be holy. Not to be a stumbling block to any weaker soul.

"We believe," Reverend Matthews went on, "that the Bible commands us to be perfect examples as the Lord's followers. We are in the world, but we are not to be of the world. We are to separate ourselves from worldly things."

Mike didn't know for sure what his dad was talking about. But he was really surprised at what happened when his godmother came to visit them.

She was a dear friend of the Matthews. One of the finest Christian ladies ever. Her husband had recently died, and she went on a trip to Europe. She had picked up the European practice of smoking little cigars.

After supper, as they were all sitting in the living room, she lit up.

Mrs. Matthews, especially, seemed horrified. She rushed over to the windows and started pulling down the shades.

"What's the matter?" Mike's godmother asked.

"Oh nothing," Mrs. Matthews answered, "it's just that if any of our neighbors or church members walk by they wouldn't understand a lady smoking a cigar in the parsonage. They might think that was sinful, and we were being very hypocritical."

"Oh, goodness!" Mike's godmother replied. "I'll just put it out."

"No. No. You go ahead please and enjoy your cigar with your coffee."

Mike got a kick out of that scene.

But he was doubly confused when he learned that his dad had thrown out all of his cigars.

"Why did you do that, Dad?" Michael asked.

"Because, as I've gotten deeper into Scripture," he replied, "I've come to believe that smoking defiles our bodies. We're taught that our bodies are temples of the Holy Spirit, and we are not to put anything impure into this temple."

"That's a new twist," Mike thought to himself, "I wonder about all that horrible black coffee you and all the church members drink at those church suppers. That doesn't look or taste very pure to me."

For Michael, the mystery of the change in his parents to a far more strict and stern religious attitude was somewhat cleared up when he was invited to go with his parents to a Bible Camp just a few miles away.

Reverend Matthews had been one of the leaders in the state church organization to get this Bible Camp going. It was on a beautiful lake.

Mike loved that part of it. The kids had wonderful choose-up-sides softball games. All afternoon he could play ball, swim or fish. Mornings they had religious classes, including for children, since this was a family week.

The evening gatherings were something else. They had revival meetings. Mike had never been to a revival meeting. It was so different than regular Sunday church. He felt very uncomfortable.

The Evangelist, as he was called, stood up in front and waved his arms while everybody sang catchy gospel songs. That part seemed OK to Mike, but when the sermon began, this Evangelist was all over the stage.

He held the open Bible in his hand and the sweat rolled down his cheeks. His voice rose to a high pitch as he pointed his fingers at the audience and said they were sinners and needed to be cleansed in the blood of the lamb. He told everybody how Christ died for them and if they didn't accepted him as a personal savior they were doomed to eternal fire in hell.

He went on for about an hour about how the devil was out to get people. He said everyone needed to be freed from the evils of the world, to repent and be blameless in the eyes of the Lord.

Mike was scared. Especially when the lights were dimmed. The organist played soft music and sang a lilting song about "Softly and Tenderly Jesus is calling, O sinner come home."

The Evangelist then began to speak in a quiet voice inviting all to come up front and give their lives to the Lord.

"Won't you listen, dear friend?" he said. "Just thank the Lord that he has called you to be his own. Praise God, fellow sinner, that you have heard his word tonight. Tell him that you are ready to repent of your sins. Just raise your hand and come forward. We'll fall on our knees here together at the altar. Before God and man you can accept the Lord Jesus as your personal savior and take your stand as one of his followers."

"Boy, this is all beyond me," Mike thought. "I don't feel like such a sinner. I've smoked a few cigars and giggled in church, but I can't see going to hell for that."

Mike stole a glance sideways to the other side of the auditorium. There was his buddy Ernie sitting with his mother. He gave him a little wave and a smile. It didn't seem to be bothering him.

"He's probably thinking of our ball game today," Mike thought, "when he slid into home and beat those other guys from around the state."

The next night after the main revival meeting they had a testimony gathering. People who felt they were saved and going to heaven were asked to stay and stand up and tell about their religious experiences.

Reverend and Mrs. Matthews stayed so Mike had to also. He would rather have taken off to the camp store for ice cream.

"This testimony thing breaks me up," Mike thought. "It gives me the impression that there are different levels of being saved. It seems to me that these people think they are better than those who left.

"I have the feeling that there is a lot of pride here. I remember part of a Bible verse my mother had crocheted that hung on the wall of our kitchen: 'Pride goeth before a fall.' I wonder how that fits in here with all this bragging about being so holy."

Mike also recalled snatches of a sermon his father gave on a story Jesus told about a mustard seed. He said "This mustard seed is very tiny. And one of the things Jesus meant by his story for our day is that a person's faith can be small but very important. A child can be the most important thing in the eyes of God. You don't necessarily have to write out a big check for the church, or be a soloist in the choir or stand up and speak in front of people. You can express your religion in little unnoticed ways like being a true friend to somebody in trouble, or visiting a sick person in the hospital, or giving an honest day's work for your day's pay."

Mike never did do one of those testimonies or altar calls, as they were known. It wasn't for him, he decided. But he definitely felt that Bible Camp days, Evangelism meetings, and something he'd heard talked about called the "Pietism Movement," changed his parents in ways that affected him.

Mike wanted so much, for example, to join the Boy Scouts. He read the magazine "Boy's Life" regularly. He couldn't wait to see it at Ernie's house every month. He was eager to camp out, go on hikes and earn all those merit badges.

He talked to his father about joining. "Son," Reverend Matthews responded, "the scoutmaster is not a Christian. He's a very good person, but he doesn't profess to believe in Christ as his personal savior."

Mike was dumbfounded. Crushed. He couldn't believe it. "How could anything be better for me than being a Boy Scout?" he asked his dad.

"It's of the world, son, and we are called by God to stand apart from worldly things lest we be tempted to evil," was Reverend Matthews' answer.

That was only the beginning.

With school work and all the jobs at home, Mike didn't have a lot of extra time, but he asked if he could play a musical instrument rather than the piano. He was getting fairly good at piano, but hated it because whenever there was a program at church, he had to play a solo, or he and Judy would be asked to play a duet. Mike wanted to play the trombone, and he could get free lessons at school.

The Matthews gave in to this wish until the day Mike came home and asked "My teacher tells me I'm good enough now. Could I play in the school band?"

"We'll think about it Michael," his mother answered.

In about a week he got the answer.

"You can continue lessons, Michael, but your father and I have decided that this is a talent that should be put to work honoring the Lord. The school band plays some kinds of music and goes on trips which we feel is of the world."

That ended his trombone lessons. Next, however, there was a class play that Mike wanted to try out for. He had always been in the Christmas pageants at church and thought "Surely this will be all right." He couldn't believe it. They turned that down too, because it wasn't a religious play.

On a holiday from school Ernie asked Mike to join him for the school kid's matinee at the movie theatre. It was a cowboy and Indian film. They were starting to make movies for church programs too now so he figured that would be OK.

He asked his dad if he could go.

"No, Michael," Reverend Matthews replied, "we absolutely forbid you ever to go in the movie theatre. That's of the devil. They show pictures there about gambling and smoking, drinking and dancing."

The same turn down came when Mike asked to go to his first school party. He wasn't allowed to go because there might be influences that were not of the Lord, and they might play worldly music and dance.

More and more Mike rebelled against this expression of religious thinking. It seemed so negative to him. There was no happiness in it.

"Surely," he thought, "God didn't intend life to be this way. He must want us to have fun. The world is such a beautiful place and there are so many wonderful things to do outside of going to church. According to the Bible, God started things out in a garden with flowers, creeks and animals. Beautiful birds and butterflies. There must have been lots of fun things to do."

Fortunately, Mike had his pal, Ernie, to confide in.

One night when he stayed over at Ernie's house, they had a real confidential talk.

They had just turned out the light to go to sleep when Mike asked, "What do you think about our church and religion, Ernie?"

"Oh, I don't know. It's OK, I guess. I don't think about it much."

"Doesn't it bother you," Mike went on, "that there are so many different kinds?"

"I suppose," Ernie replied.

"Just think. Count how many different churches there are here in Lakeville. There's about twelve of them, and they're all claiming to be the only one."

"Yeah. That's stupid. If there is a God he's the same for everyone."

"That's right, Ernie. And how about all the different races and colors and nationalities of people through all of history? I'm sure God loves all of them the same."

"Makes sense to me," Ernie agreed.

"Sure God isn't going to condemn anyone to hell" Mike went on, "if they follow a different religious book than the Bible, or don't get baptized or have a different religious hero than Jesus."

"Mike, I agree," Ernie replied, "but you know what? I think you take all this too seriously."

"Sometimes I do, Ernie. But not all the time. I know one thing, if I were ever to be a preacher, which will never happen, I'd sure try to picture God and religion as inviting, and happy, and inspiring. Something to bring people together instead of starting fights and wars. Something to help us be a better person and live a more complete and useful life."

"You are absolutely right, Mike. But let's knock off the religious stuff for now, OK? Speaking of being happy, have you ever seen one of these?"

Ernie flicked his bed lamp on, and pulled a magazine out from under the mattress.

"Look at these juicy pictures, Mike."

"Jeez, I've never seen anything like this before."

"Look, Mike, here's good old Popeye from the cartoons with a big hard on being jacked off by Olive Oil. Now turn the page."

"Yeah, look Ernie, Popeye has his hand on Olive Oil's tit."

"Turn one more page, Mike. See? There's Popeye shooting the jazz from his cock all over Olive's bare belly. Doesn't that give you a hard on buddy? Doesn't that make you want to jack off?"

"Go on, Mike. It's easy. See, I'll show you. You just go up and down real fast with your hand. Like this. Oh boy, does that feel good. I've got an old handkerchief under my pillow. Here it comes. Wow!"

"Go ahead, Mike. Try it. It's good for you. Look at the pictures and you'll go off faster."

"I'm trying, Ernie. Oh, that feels exciting. How come it takes me longer?"

"You're just younger that's all. Keep doing it. You'll come."

"Wheeeee! Jeez, I came all over my pajamas."

"Doesn't matter, Mike. Here, use this handkerchief. It'll dry up fast. Now, isn't that better than all that heavy religious stuff? You'll really feel relaxed now. So let's go to sleep."

"Yeah, good night buddy. That was fun."

Chapter 5

Paycheck Time

Just as the school year ended in the spring of 1936, Mrs. Matthews received the news that her father had died from a sudden heart attack.

Mike was heartbroken, because he loved his grandpa so much. As a little boy he would let Mike sit in his lap up against his rolypoly belly.

He told him stories about being a master carpenter in the old country. How he came to this country and began farming and worked hard so he could leave a farm to each of his children.

Mike loved to smell his grandpa's pipe tobacco and hold his hand as they walked the two blocks to the post office for the mail.

They'd always stop at the general store. Grandpa would buy Mike a piece of candy and let him sit around the black stove while he and his cronies told stories about homesteading.

One of Mike's biggest treats came on Saturday night when Grandpa would take him by the hand to go to the vacant lot where they would watch the cowboy movie flashed on the brick wall of the general store.

Once Mrs. Matthews started to voice an objection about her son seeing the movie, but Grandpa just waved her aside. "Hush, Kirsten. This is fun for children. It will be good for him."

Mike was crushed when they lowered grandpa's casket

into the grave of the barren, windswept prairie cemetery. Mrs. Matthews was sobbing and so were Mike and Judy. Her five brothers and sister were also grief stricken. It marked the end of a wonderful parental home, since their mother had died several years before.

Most of the one hundred residents of the little town, plus farmers from miles around, turned out for the service and supper in the church Grandpa had caused to be built.

It was there, while eating and talking to all Grandpa's friends, that Mike's favorite uncle, Jim, put his arm around Mrs. Matthews.

"Kirsten, why don't you let Michael stay with us here this summer. He can live with us, and do some work around the grain elevator which I manage. He'll have such a good time with my sons."

Mike almost jumped out of his chair.

"Oh, Mother please! My cousins and I have been talking about this. I would miss you, but I would have such a good time. I would work hard for my room and board and Uncle would pay me a little toward my own shotgun that I want to buy. Please?"

Evidently Uncle Jim did a good selling job that evening, because next morning when Reverend and Mrs. Matthews and Judy left for the drive back to Wisconsin Mike was allowed to stay. Mrs. Matthews promised to send his work clothes and write to him every week.

So began a most memorable summer.

Uncle Jim's oldest son was gone all week, because he had a job in a neighboring town. But Pete, his other son, was just two years older than Mike and they were the best of friends.

They had their own little cabin in back of the main house. It had pretty curtains on the windows, a double bed, rocker with a lamp, a small desk and hooks on the wall to hang up their clothes.

The outhouse was a two-holer, and in back of the cabin Uncle Jim had rigged a shower with a big tank of water above it which was hooked up to the windmill.

It was blazing hot that summer. Sometimes the only way

to get to sleep was to grab an old blanket and lie outside under the stars. Mike felt like an early American settler.

"This must have been what it was like," he thought, "when Grandpa rode the wagons across the prairies."

Mike worshipped his uncle. He and Pete would sit around in the elevator office and listen to the farmers talk. They would always stay a while after weighing their trucks. That was so they would get paid for the exact number of bushels they had delivered, Mike was told.

Everything was new and intriguing to Mike. He watched as the trucks dumped their grain in the pit, and the right levers were pushed so the conveyors would lift it into the right bins. It would be terrible to make a mistake, and get the oats in with the rye or the corn in with the wheat.

Once in awhile Uncle Jim would invite Mike to ride up the two person elevator to the top. He taught Mike to work the ropes attached to pulleys so when they got up to the right platform in the elevator they would look down at the bins and tell if they were getting full. Uncle Jim also had to check for any mildew, or too much dust so that the elevator actually wouldn't explode in the heat.

The boys thought it was fascinating to listen to the one static filled radio station which carried the latest grain prices. Uncle Jim explained that this was how he knew when to sell the grain and make his farmers the most money.

Mike could tell Uncle Jim had a very important job. On his shoulders alone fell the responsibility of making the farmers a profit.

It was clear to Mike that life on the prairie farms could be tough. "It's been four weeks since we've had any rain," one farmer said.

"Yes, and I heard tell," added another, "that up north a piece, in the next county, it rained and hailed so hard that some farmers lost all their grain."

"What have you heard about the grasshoppers?" Uncle Jim would ask. "Which way are they moving out of Kansas?"

"Don't know," another replied. "Just hope they skip us. Two years ago the whole sky over my place got black with 'em. By the time they'd left my entire oats crop was wiped out."

There were a lot of laughs and many lighter moments too. The boys enjoyed watching the elevator cats chasing the mice. They also liked this one jolly guy who spit tobacco juice and always had a joke to tell. Most of them were about a traveling salesman who asked to be put up for the night and had to sleep with the farmer's daughter.

The men didn't realize Mike was old for his years. He got the drift all right, and what he didn't understand Pete explained to him later.

The feeling of being accepted and grown up came for Mike one day as Pete and he walked home with Uncle Jim.

"Could I try your chewin' tobacco just once?" Mike asked. "Just a little bit."

"Why, I guess so Mike. Every kid's got to grow up some time, and you appear ready. Just take off a little pinch there and put it in your cheek. When the juices come give a good spit. Like this."

"Man, is this something," Mike thought, "my mother would be horrified if she could see me now."

He wasn't prepared for how dizzy he got. It was something like smoking his dad's wedding cigars. He barely made it to the two-holer before heaving. Uncle Jim gave him a sly grin at the supper table when he passed up the fried chicken and gravy and just sipped at the soup.

Mike's first job for some banking money came the next day. Uncle Jim announced, "There's a carload of corn coming in and we have to unload it by hand into one of the bins by the track. All the conveyors are tied up."

"Mike," do you think you and Pete can handle it?"

"Sure, we can," Mike answered. Of course Pete had shoveled corn before.

The next day Mike worked harder than he ever thought possible. There was barely room for the two of them to stand on top of the corn in the freight car. They had big scoop shovels and a chute that went from the car to the bin.

There were over a thousand bushels of corn in that car and

the temperature went over a hundred in the shade.

They got down to their shorts and had to wear a mask to keep out the dust. With time out for noon lunch and water breaks, they worked ten hours, and it looked like they had hardly touched the corn.

The shower that evening from the cool well water felt like paradise.

"Mike," Pete asked, "what do you say we sleep later tomorrow, and do a little goofin' off and then work nights. I've done that before when it's been this hot. We can rig up lights, and it's a lot cooler."

"Fine with me," Mike answered. "I must have lost five pounds today, but I feel good now. By the end of the summer my shoulder and arm muscles will really be strong for football."

"Wait till we unload a coal car, Mike. That'll build up your muscles."

Mike thought the corn was tough. That was nothing compared to the coal car that came in the following week.

They worked again at night. They were so tired mornings, they could hardly walk, but they'd look at each other and laugh. Standing under the shower they could have passed for a couple of bums off the freight train.

The summer wasn't all work, however. They had some great picnics with other uncles, aunts and cousins. They'd clean up a corner of one of the pastures and have a fantastic ball game. Sometimes there'd be as many as twenty or thirty players.

The potluck picnic dinners were something. Always topped off with home made, churned ice cream, and apple pie. Before the day was over the kids would run to the swimmin' hole.

Actually it was an artificial pond in the pasture dug for the purpose of watering the cattle. It wasn't as fancy as the clear sand bottom lakes of Wisconsin. There were a few cow pies floating here and there, but they had a wonderful time.

There were other exciting adventures. Mike was introduced to some higher education in girls.

All Mike really knew for sure that summer in Nebraska was that he was stimulated by girls' bodies. And after that lesson about girls and sex from Ernie, he knew that having a hard on and getting it off was a wonderful feeling.

One Saturday morning after unloading coal all night, showering and having breakfast before going to sleep, Pete announced:

"Mike, how would you like to join us tonight for a picnic down by the river. We've lined up some girls. Got a cute hot number for you. She's noticed you and likes you. She's a little older than you. But, boy has she got nice tits, and does she ever like to neck."

"Wow, Pete, does that sound like fun."

"We'll get some wieners, buns and marshmallows and have a campfire. My dad said we could borrow Grandpa's Model T that's still in his barn. It's the latest four door with plush upholstery. And one of the older guys is getting a big jug of wine."

That was a night to remember for Mike. Six of them piled into the Model T. Elaine sat on Mike's lap and put her arm around him. Pretty soon they were kissing and Mike was getting harder by the minute. She took his hand and put it on her breast and he about went through the roof.

They floored that Model T like Grandpa never had and skidded around the gravel curves. The wine jug made the rounds and Mike was feeling a little dizzy by the time they got to the river.

The next morning Mike didn't remember a whole lot except the campfire. Roasting marshmallows. Finishing off the wine and necking on a blanket by the river. He was half asleep by the time they dropped Elaine off at her house, and the next day he had his first hangover.

Before he knew it, the days of August were almost over. There was a tearful goodbye, and Mike was at the train depot for his first train ride and home.

He was a deep brown from the prairie wind and sun. His shoulders were wider. He was starting to shave and the muscles in his arms were bulging. He had grown about two inches to 5'9" and weighed 155 pounds. As a thirteen year old he was entering tenth grade and eager to try out for the football team.

Mike was uncontrollably belligerent and angry when his parents declared: "Son we can't allow you to go out for the team."

"Why? I've had my heart set on it. You know that. I love sports, and I can't see how you could possibly find anything wrong with sports."

"Michael, the coaches are not born again Christian people. They'll have a lot of influence on you we don't agree with. The world will always keep trying to pull you away from the Lord, but we have to take a stand. We have prayed over this a lot, and this is the answer we believe is God's will."

"Well, I don't," Mike shouted. "To hell with God's will."

Mike made a beeline for the door to the stairs and his room when suddenly Reverend Matthews spun him around. He had his belt off and wacked Mike across his ass. Mike had no idea he was that strong and quick.

Reverend Matthews stuck his nose in Mike's face and said, "As long as you are under my roof you will do as I say. Don't you ever talk like that again in this house. Now go on upstairs and cool off. When you're ready to behave and apologize we'll talk about your future."

It was the last time Mike clashed openly like that with his father. He apologized, but was seething inside and grew more belligerent.

Mike confided in his friend next door, "Steve, what should I do? I want to play sports so much. I'll still have time for homework so I'll get good grades."

"Mike, your father and mother love you very much," Steve replied. "They think they're doing the right thing. They have their reasons for thinking the way they do. I respect them very much. Try to be patient. Maybe they'll change their mind on some of the things you disagree on."

Steve was a big help to Mike and on many fall Saturdays he had a good time on their hunting outings. He was also enjoying his high school classes, especially Art, Literature, and Shop. He was getting 90's and above in everything, including Latin. Most kids hated languages, but they came easy for Mike.

That year in high school Mike suddenly found himself in love. He had been noticing a certain girl for two years now. Her name was Sara. She was friendly, had a beautiful figure and had the prettiest smile. Her family must have been rich because she lived in a big house on the "better" side of town.

Mike made a special effort, in running to school in the morning, to be at a certain corner just at the right time so he could walk with her the rest of the way.

After school he would wait near her locker to see if he could walk home with her. Most of the kids who were not out for band or football or in a play would stop at the popular drugstore gathering place for a coke. Most of the time Mike didn't have any money so he had to pass.

But he got a real break when the drugstore owner needed some help at the soda fountain after school. He got to see Sara almost every day and it was fun making malts and cokes for the kids.

Pretty soon the first fall dance came up and Mike wanted to ask Sara if she'd go with him, but he knew he'd better ask his folks first. He had the money now so that was no problem, but he supposed they still felt the party would be worldly and he couldn't go.

Sure enough. Mike tried to explain it to Sara, but he didn't do a very good job of it. Surprisingly, she wasn't too upset. "Most of the kids aren't going as dates anyway," she said. "The guys are too shy to dance so we girls usually dance together until the last dance or two of the party when a few fellows will get up enough courage to try.

Mike had a very deep emotional feeling for Sara. It was painful not to be able to see her other than occasionally walk her home from school not to be able to ask her to a movie, a school play or party. She didn't belong to their church so he didn't see her at the church youth gatherings either.

Mike wished his parents would understand that she was a high class girl. Not like a few who were considered loose or fast. About the only thing she would allow is for him to hold her hand. Maybe one small kiss now and then. She was sort of considered by their classmates to be Mike's girl, but when he couldn't do things with her, she finally started to go out with someone else.

Mike was crushed. Couldn't blame her. But he missed her terribly. On top of not being able to go out for football he went through some very melancholy, depressing weeks.

At first Mike tried to compensate by getting into some hobbies in addition to school and his drugstore job. He painted some watercolors, built more model airplanes and had some good hunting outings with Steve.

After the hunting season was over Mike asked Reverend Matthews if he could get an old stove in the garage so he could build a workbench.

They found an old used one at the hardware store and the two of them installed it. Mike spent many enjoyable hours building his own jig saw with a rewound electric motor attached. His shop teacher helped him, and between shop at school and his home workbench, he made several bird houses for their yard. His best creation was a table lamp for his room, and a pair of bookends which he gave to his mother for Christmas.

Despite keeping busy he couldn't get Sara out of his mind. He tried to understand his parents, but couldn't. So instead of being surrounded by wholesome, healthy activities and the good kids in school, he gradually sought out some of the "no-gooders" and their rebel interests.

He started to smoke. He wore a pair of gloves so his fingers wouldn't smell or turn yellow from the nicotine. One of his classmates, who lived with his divorced mother, would invite him over when she was working and he introduced Mike to scotch and gin.

The two of them got into all kinds of trouble, but somehow managed to avoid a run in with the cops. They raided a farmers' watermelon field and barely got out of range before he came running after them with his shotgun.

Mike started sneaking in the local pool hall until one of the church members tattled on him for playing pool, swearing and smoking cigarettes.

After the Saturday evening drugstore job, Mike would slide into the back seat of the theatre. They let him in free because the movie was almost over. Before the lights came on, he would quickly leave and run all the way home so his parents wouldn't think he was late.

That Halloween, Mike and a couple of his friends broke into the high school principal's office, and smeared Limburger cheese over his radiator. The stench the next day was horrible.

Somehow he found out who was responsible and Mike was put on probation by both the school and his parents. On top of it all his grades were suddenly going into a tailspin.

All of this led to a serious session in his father's study. Mike thought his father realized that more punishment wasn't going to work.

"Son," he said, "what's happened to you? You've been such a wonderful boy and suddenly you've grown sullen around the house. You've taken up with some friends we don't approve of, and gotten into all kinds of trouble."

Before Mike could even think of anything to say, he went on, "Worst of all, as people start gossiping about the preacher's son, my ministry in the church is getting more difficult. People are saying that if I can't even control my own son how can I expect to be a good pastor for their young people."

There it was again, Mike thought, that insistence that he had to be a perfect model because he was the minister's kid. But he held it all inside, gritted his teeth and glared at the floor.

It got pretty grim and silent in the room. Finally Reverend Matthews said, "I suppose, Son, you're angry at your mother and me for not permitting you to go out for football and to attend movies and school parties. Is that it?

"Yes. That's right," Mike replied.

"Well, I'll tell you what we'll do. We've talked it over and we'll think about the football for next fall when you're in the eleventh grade, providing your grades come back up and you stay out of trouble."

That brought Mike a glimmer of hope. "How about the movies and class plays and things," he asked. "I like this girl, Sara, Dad, but I can't see much of her because you won't let me go to any of the fun events at school."

"No, Son," Reverend Matthews replied, "we can't compromise on the other activities. I preach on Sunday about not flirting with the world, and worldly pleasures lest we be led astray. The Lord has laid it on my heart to bear witness to his word, and I believe his word teaches us that although we are in the world we are not to be of the world. We are to be separate, and to be a witness to his truth."

Mike didn't know how to answer that. He didn't agree or like it, but the prospect of playing on the high school football team in the fall was encouraging.

"Dad," he responded, "I'll do my best to go along with what you and Mother want. I'll try to improve my attitude here at home. I'll work on getting my grades back up. You know I love and respect both of you, and I don't want to make your work harder for you."

Secretly he knew it was going to be tough. He couldn't understand how things like plays, school parties, movies and what he saw as just good clean fun could be sinful.

"I'll tell you what, Michael," his dad continued. "I heard there was a Saturday job open on Main Street working in a hardware store. It might even expand into after school so you could make more money than at the drugstore. You'll soon be old enough to get a driving permit; and they need someone to help with deliveries and picking up things that need fixing.

"I understand they also need a young man," he went on, "to help the owner and his wife keep the sidewalk clean, decorate the store windows and sweep out at the end of the day. Even help in waiting on people and maybe learning how to fix broken windows and repair old stoves.

"Would you be interested?"

"Definitely, yes I would," Mike replied. "I know which store you mean and they have lots of fishing and hunting equipment. I could save my money and get my own rod and reel and shotgun. They might even sell it to me cheaper if I'm working there."

With that Reverend Matthews got up from his chair, walked over and put his arm around Mike and gave him a kiss on the cheek. "I hope you know Michael," he said, "that I love you very much. I'm so proud of you in many ways, and I want you to grow up to be a fine Christian man."

Mike returned his father's embrace. "Thank you, Dad, I love you too. I don't want to make your work harder than it already is. I'll try to keep my part of the bargain."

As he left his dad's study Mike thought about this other side of his father. True, he was so strict and stern when it came to religion, but there was his soft, tender hearted, sentimental side.

"By example in our home, Mike realized "he has taught Judy and me to be grateful and helpful toward Mother. He has always made a point of having us help Mother with the hard tasks around the house. Dad has always been the first after each meal to put his arm around Mother, give her a kiss and thank her for the fine meal."

It was a surprise for Mike, that evening when Reverend Matthews was at a church meeting, that his mother came and talked to him as he was doing homework at the kitchen table. "Michael Charles, how did your talk go with Father today?"

"Pretty good, I guess. Didn't Dad tell you about it?"

"We haven't had a chance to talk yet today, he's been so busy."

"You say, it just went pretty good?" Mrs. Matthews asked, "You look so glum. Come on, cheer up."

With that Mike responded with a smile. "Yes, it was better than pretty good. He promised that I might be able to go out for the football team next fall if I had a better attitude here at home, got my grades up and didn't do things that the church members would gossip about. I'm really excited about the football and, oh, he said maybe he would help me get a job at the hardware store."

"Wonderful, I know you'd like that, son. I also have to tell you something else. You may have guessed that I know you've been smoking cigarettes. I found your pack in the dresser drawer under your socks when I put some clean clothes away. I debated in my mind a long time about this, but I decided not to tell your father."

"I appreciate that, Mom," Mike replied.

"I hope," she went on, "that you will give them up. When you're older that will be up to you to decide; but now you know it's not good for you and you want to be an athlete and the coaches won't let you smoke. So, as a favor to me, please give up the cigarettes. I promise you that I'll encourage your father to let you play football. You know, I'd rather you didn't so you won't get hurt, but I also want to see you happy."

With that Mike gave his mother a big hug. "Thank you, Mom, I do so want to be a good athlete, and it will help me get into a good college."

Mother lit up at the thought of college. "You know, Michael Charles," she said, "I have such high hopes for you. I haven't given up my prayer that some day you will follow in your father's footsteps and be a servant of the Lord in his church. Naturally that means that you will go to college."

The next day Reverend Matthews talked to the hardware store owners, and they said they would be willing to have Mike apply for the job. He stopped in after school. He was nervous as they asked a lot of questions. They said he would be considered along with others they were talking to.

It was about a week later that a call came to the house telling Mike they would like to hire him on a trial basis. He could work three hours after school every day, and Saturdays from 7 AM to 10:30 PM because all the stores were open Saturday evenings. With time off Saturdays for lunch and supper, he got in about twenty-eight hours a week and made three dollars a week. But that was a lot when a coke was only a nickel, and he made sure he passed the trial period.

Mike loved his job. There was so much that he learned about running a business.

He was taught how to fix broken windows and repair stoves in the back room. Helped unpack boxes of new merchandise and put it away. Swept out the store, and helped decorate the store windows.

They even let him wait on a customer once in awhile until he got good at it. Then he took his regular turn.

Chapter 6

An Education in Girls

Now that Mike had money of his own, he could buy a coke once in awhile at the drugstore hangout. He also managed by spring to pay for a new rod and reel. He even picked out a shotgun and asked if they would put it on lay-by until it was paid for.

Reverend Matthews was right about the driving permit. As soon as Mike had his fourteenth birthday, he got a permit, and learned to drive the hardware store's Model A Ford pickup. This was really fun. He couldn't wait to get out and make deliveries. The job at the hardware store made the whole year go faster, and his grades shot back.

Actually, one of the things Mike was thinking about now was that he wanted to go to college. He knew that was the only way to be successful. Besides, it would be a way for him to get away from the tight restrictions of his parents.

Mike knew the only way for him to get to college was to have good grades, and save money from the job. He knew he would need to pay his own way since his parents just didn't have the money.

Mike also knew that it would help if he was good in sports, because colleges gave good paying jobs to athletes.

A wonderful break came his way that summer. Because he was such a good swimmer he was offered a job as assistant lifeguard at the Bible Camp. He vowed to stay as far away as possible from those pulpit pounding evangelists, however.

Mike spent a week studying, working out, and taking tests from the head lifeguard in rules and procedures to follow in covering the beach.

The sun and the water did wonders to his body and mental attitude. He got to swim and dive a lot, and one of his duties was to patrol the outer limits of the roped off area with a row boat. He also gave swimming lessons.

By the end of the summer Mike was nearly black. His arms, shoulders and neck bulged with muscles.

Apparently he was attractive to girls too, because he had three terrific girl experiences that summer. One was with a daughter of some people who were from a neighboring city. They had set up their tents in the campgrounds for the summer. The mother and father drove back and forth every weekend and worked at home during the week. They left their daughter with an older male cousin to watch over her.

It wasn't long before the cousin and Mike were good friends, but he got to be better friends with the girl.

Following an afternoon at the beach on his off day he would go back to her camp with her. She had her own tent and they'd wind up in a heavy necking session. In no time at all he had her swim suit straps down fondling her breasts. He almost came in his trunks, but that's as far as they went.

Another girl, a couple of years older, he met by accident. Literally.

It was after hours at the beach and Mike was practicing diving off the high board. He thought everybody had left. Did a jack knife and forward somersault off the board, but as he hit the water he barely glanced off something. Didn't know what it was until he broke the surface.

But here this gorgeous girl was with a slight bruise above her eye, and looking dazed. He immediately reached an arm around her, and with a powerful side stroke brought her into the beach. By that time she was fine. Mike got the first aid kit and treated the bruise.

"Where did you come from?" he asked. "Didn't see you by the tower when I dove. Anyway the beach is supposed to be closed."

"I know," she said, "but I was watching you from the porch of my parent's cabin. I thought you looked interesting so I came out to join you."

"Sorry about the bruise. How's the rest of your body?" he asked with a wink.

"How does it look to you?" she shot back.

Both of them were feeling the chemistry. She had long black hair, and a fabulous body. Mike found out she was from Michigan and here for a couple of weeks with her parents who at the moment were at some camp meetings.

"Why don't I walk you back to your cabin" Mike offered.

"That would be nice. Maybe we could have a coke or something," she answered.

The something turned out to be a hot session on her bed. They just barely got around to the cokes before her parents returned from the meetings.

Just before the summer ended Mike had an experience that topped them all. He met this guy from around the lake who was from Chicago. He and his family spent the summer at their cabin. He was about a year and a half older than Mike, but because he was big for his age they hit it off well.

His parents had to go back to Chicago for the weekend so he invited Mike over to swim off their raft. There he met the most beautiful girl he'd ever seen. She was tall, slender, with long blond hair and a tantalizing pair of breasts. They bulged out of her swim suit.

"Who in the world is that?" Mike asked.

"Oh, her. That's just my sister," his new buddy said.

"Your sister? I'd like to meet her."

That took about two seconds. Her name was George-anne. They swam around awhile together and then lay on the raft talking and sunning.

"Are you ever dark," she said. "I wish I could get that tan. I have to be so careful with my light skin. Would you put this lotion on my back, Mike?"

Mike lingered over that opportunity as long as he dared.

"Anything else I could do for you?" he asked.

"Yes, matter of fact there is," she replied. "Why don't you

come back for a beach party we're having this evening. My brother has invited a girlfriend of his from the other side of the lake. There might be some others. Since I'm oldest, a freshman in college as a matter of fact, I'm supposed to be chaperoning my brother. Would you like to come?"

"Would I like to come? Try to keep me away. Can I bring anything for the party?"

"No, Mike, just your handsome self and your swim trunks, We'll have a campfire, some snacks and we'll manage to sneak some wine from my parent's supply. Maybe we'll even go for a little moonlit swim."

The party was a winner. There were only two or three other couples there. The moonlit swim turned out to be a skinny dip. Georgeanne and Mike spent most of the time kissing and fondling one another under water.

Pretty soon everyone else was gone, including Georgeanne's brother and his girlfriend. They were alone on the beach by the last embers of the campfire and just a towel wrapped around them.

"Where did your brother go?" Mike asked.

"Oh, he's probably in bed with that girlfriend of his up in the cabin. I'd better check. Want to join me Mike?"

They walked hand in hand to the cabin and got as far as the wicker couch on the porch. Within seconds they were all over each other.

Mike had never been totally stripped with a completely naked girl before. His cock was so hard he thought it would break in two.

The next thing he knew this older, sexy gal reached in her beach bag. She came up with a rubber which she deftly slipped on Mike's hard-on. Gently sliding on top, she guided him inside her warm, exciting moistness, massaging him with her flexing hip movements. In seconds Mike exploded with moans of ecstasy.

Suddenly, Michael Charles Matthews had come of age sexually. Interestingly, he never had a feeling of guilt. It seemed so natural and good. They had been careful about her getting pregnant. Mike couldn't understand how such a wonderful shared human experience, which didn't cause harm to anyone, could be anything but good.

There were other beach parties that summer but none to match this sensational first experience. He saw Georgeanne frequently, but always her parents were there.

Before Mike was ready August was winding down. The single most important thing to him now was, "am I going to be able to go out for football?"

He put the question to his parents and got a reluctant 'yes' as they signed the form required by the school. He was ready, he thought, only fourteen, but an eleventh grader and muscular, fast, tough , weighing about 160 and grown to 5' 10 1/2".

Mike had been running five miles a day on the beach. Sprinting. Dodging. Imagining himself carrying a football, because he wanted to play in the backfield. He wanted to play left half in either the single or double wing, or maybe even quarterback in the new T formation. So he had been passing a football to his friend Ernie at least an hour a day most of the summer at camp. Ernie had been out for football before, and made the junior varsity, so he helped Mike to know what to expect.

He wasn't prepared for that first week of practice, though. The coach had played for the University of Wisconsin and was lean and mean. He had them running through old tires layed out on the field. They did sprints up the bleacher steps. If they missed a block or tackle he would block or tackle them. Then order so many laps around the field.

It was still hot in the last week of August. 85 to 90 degrees. Every day that first week Mike had vomiting spells just like most of the other guys.

They practiced twice a day. Of course the scrubs who hadn't been out before got the oldest equipment. They also were tested by the veterans, but Mike gave it right back on the field.

It was their fourth day of practice. The scrubs were on defense against last year's varsity players. Mike was playing a defensive back and just nailed the star halfback with a crunching tackle.

As he picked himself up he said, "I'll get you buddy."

Later turned out to be in the locker room. As Mike stood toweling himself in front of his locker, this guy whipped by and shoved a fistful of hot massage ointment up Mike's ass. Mike was going to go after him, but the guy was surrounded by his buddies pointing and laughing at the rookie.

Besides, the ointment was starting to burn like heck. Mike went back in the shower and tried to get it cooled down with the cold water, but it didn't help much. Walking home would have been almost impossible with the friction adding to the heat. So, he heaved a sigh of relief when he called home and found that his father could come and pick him up in the car.

When Mike told his mother what had happened she was horrified, but she knew what to do. She chipped some ice from the icebox, and used some soothing lotion followed by talcum powder.

So it was that Mike, the football toughie, suddenly reverted to the treatment of a baby again.

The balance of the football season was a thrill for Mike. He made the second team, and got in enough quarters of varsity play to earn his first letter.

There were no more run ins with team members. They accepted and respected him as an important part of the team. They had three separate second team games, and it was especially thrilling for Mike that his father came to all the games. The highlight of that fall was breaking loose for his first touchdown, and actually hearing his dad screaming "That a boy, Mike."

That was the first time he had ever called him just "Mike".

After football Mike knuckled down to his after school and Saturday hardware store job again. His grades now were the best they'd ever been. He even took an extra class in typing because he was told it would help write notes and papers more quickly in college. He was one of only two boys in a class of about thirty girls, but managed to get the highest score.

Now that Mike had broken the sport's barrier with his folks, he got permission to try out for baseball and tennis in the spring. He became a sub in tennis, but easily made the baseball team because of all his sand lot play. So at the athletic banquet Mike received two more varsity letters.

Even though he was only fifteen, he was starting to think more seriously about college and life work. Mrs. Matthews, of course, still reminded him, though not as frequently, about her dedication of his life to God.

The summer of 1938 before his senior year of high school was critical, Mike thought, to start saving for college. He had been buying his own clothes and hunting and fishing equipment. But now he felt it was necessary to earn more money. So he passed up a second summer as a lifeguard and all the girl fun that went with it.

He was lucky to land a job working for a landscaper. The work was tough with long hours. They worked ten to twelve hours, six days a week. Mike's job mainly was to help load the dump truck with black dirt, gravel or landscape rocks. It was done by hand with a shovel.

By the end of the summer Mike was up another ten pounds. Taller and stronger, and he had managed to save sixty dollars out of the six dollars a week he earned.

He went back to early football practice and the guys said, "What happened to you? You look like you've grown two sizes."

"I have, I guess, but you have too. We should really have a good season this year."

They did. Mike played sixty minutes - both ways. Got a chance to run and pass a lot and they won all their games and the conference title. Both Reverend and Mrs. Matthews attended the football banquet and applauded as loudly as anybody.

"What are your plans now, Son," Reverend Matthews asked after they got home? "I know there are some colleges writing and wanting you to play football."

"I know," Mike replied, "but I want to pick a school where I can also get a good education. Besides, it can't be the most expensive, because I know I'll have to work my own way. And that's OK with me."

"You know, Mike, your mother and I would prefer your attending one of the fine colleges sponsored by the Church."

"Here it comes again, Mike thought. "The business about being a minister and studying religion. That's the last thing I want to do.

"What I'd really like to do, Mother and Dad, is go to a college where they also have a military program. It won't cost me as much and I would like to learn how to fly and be a pilot in the Air Force.

Much to Mike's surprise, his dad answered, "Mike, you've proven to us that you are dependable, hard working and smart for your age. I'm sure you'll make the right decision and we'll all pray about it. Incidentally, after the football banquet tonight, your coach told me that the coach of a fine private college in St. Paul, Minnesota will be in town next month and wants to talk to you."

"Is this a large university or a smaller college?" Mike asked. "You know the University of Wisconsin, where some of my buddies are going, would like me to play for them."

"I know, and that's a compliment, Mike. But this is a smaller private college by the name of Jefferson University. You might get more individual attention and have smaller classes at this school. You'd probably have a better chance to get good paying jobs and maybe even play more in the games right away."

All of this appealed to Mike. Especially when he learned from the coaches' visit that you really didn't have to take religion.

"The college," he said, "was originally founded by a branch of the church, and still receives some support from the denomination. But we are a general college with a broad liberal arts education."

"That appeals to me," Mike replied. "How about jobs and what are the rules about freshman playing?"

"If you're good enough to make the team you can play in our conference as a freshman. From what I've heard from your coach you'd probably earn a letter your first year. I understand you also have potential in baseball, so you might want to try out for baseball in the spring."

"I'd like that," Mike responded.

"Now as far as the jobs and the money part," the coach went on, "we could see that you got one or two simple jobs, like cleaning the halls in the dormitory or working in the cafeteria to pay for your room and board. Then we would help you get an academic scholarship to help pay your tuition. Our conference doesn't permit us to give strictly athletic scholarships, but we do have a student loan fund."

"How much more would I need for books," Mike added, "and some spending money?"

"I would say about two or three hundred dollars" the coach replied.

"I think I could save that much," Mike countered.

"Here, Mike, let me leave this application for admission with you. It tells you everything you need to fill out for the academic scholarship, and from what I have been told your grades are excellent."

Mike's decision was pretty much settled. After talking to some other schools, by graduation time he had been accepted at Jefferson University, in St. Paul, Minnesota.

"Now," he realized, "I really have to get down to business and get a better paying job for the summer."

First there was graduation. Mike didn't even ask his parents if he could go on skip day. He just went. They had chartered buses and went to Door County peninsula and spent the warm sunny day roaming the Lake Michigan beaches. There was a great beach party at dusk, and some of the kids had managed to secret a bottle or two of wine and gin along.

The bus ride home got pretty wild. Mike's eyes were on Sara most of the trip. He was so jealous he could hardly stand it because she was dating this other guy now.

But then one of the young chaperones started getting real friendly and Mike forgot Sara temporarily. This new first year teacher was only twenty-one.

She was good looking, and probably thought Mike was eighteen like all the other guys when actually he had just turned sixteen.

The bus was crowded and she wound up on Mike's lap. The lights were turned down in the bus and she could feel Mike getting excited. Nothing more than a little feel here and there happened, but it capped an exciting senior skip day celebration.

Graduation day turned out better than Mike thought it would. They had a baccalaureate service in the morning. The class had asked Reverend Matthews to speak. Mike was proud of him. He didn't get too sentimental and wasn't too long winded or strict.

Before the evening commencement Mike had the most fun of his day. Reverend Matthews had recently gotten a new car, and agreed to let Mike borrow it for a couple of hours in the afternoon.

He had managed to get one last date with Sara, since she and her regular boyfriend had broken up temporarily.

He picked her up at her lovely home in the fancy neighborhood. That was actually the first time Mike had met her father and mother. They promised to be back in plenty of time for the evening commencement.

"I like your car, Mike. How long have your parents had it?"

"Just about a month. It's fun to drive. I wish I could afford a car of my own."

"You will, Mike. You work hard, and you're good in school What are your plans?"

He told her about being accepted at Jefferson University, and planning to play football and baseball. She had never heard of Jefferson, and said she was planning to go the University of Wisconsin along with half the class.

"Where would you like to go this afternoon, Sara?", Mike asked.

"Why don't we drive around the lake out by the golf course. We could stop at that little resort on the other side of the lake and just talk and have a coke."

Mike was delighted at her suggestion. Naturally he had to show off. He spun the wheels on the gravel road and took off at about sixty miles an hour until they came to the peaceful, curvy road around the lake.

"I've missed you, Mike," Sara said touching Mike's hand.

She let him put his arm around her as she moved over closer. Mike had a lump in his throat as he realized how much he had always liked her.

"It's been agony for me, Sara," Mike explained. "You know I wanted so badly to be your steady boyfriend, but I told you how my parents got so involved in that strict, negative type of religion. They wouldn't let me go to the parties or movies."

"I know, what a shame," she replied, "that religion or someone's interpretation can separate people. We could have had so much fun together. I think we were good for each other. By the way, I heard some rumors about some of those escapades you were involved in out at the Bible Camp. I was jealous."

They stopped at the little store on the beach, got a coke and took off their shoes and went for a walk. It was very nostalgic, because Mike had a feeling this would be their last time together.

"What are you doing this summer, Sara?"

"We're going to spend the summer at our home up north, that is Mother and I. My father will come back once in awhile to run his business. What are you doing, Mike?"

He told her about just having gotten a job. "It's back at the hardware store, only now I'll be working full time—about seventy hours a week. I'm lucky to get a job. This will give me a chance to save enough, together with my football jobs and scholarship, to get through my first year of college. The spare time I have this summer I'm going to go running and throwing the football with Ernie."

Before they knew it their beautiful Sunday afternoon together was over. They walked back to the car, wrapped their arms around each other and slowly, tenderly kissed and said "good luck." Mike realized he may never see Sara again.

All he remembered from the commencement address on this beautiful June evening was something about '39 being the year of "The Wizard of Oz", a beginning of prosperity and war rumblings in Europe.

Before he knew it, the program was over and the class was reciting Edwin Markham's poem:

In an old city by the storied shores
Where the bright summit of Olympus soars,
A cryptic statue mounted toward the light
Heel-winged, tip-toed, and poised for instant flight.

"O statue, tell your name," a traveler cried.
And solemnly the marble lips replied:
"Men call me Opportunity. I lift
My winged feet from earth to show how swift
My flight, how short my stay -
How fate is ever waiting on the way."

"But why that tossing ringlet on your brow?"
"That man may seize any moment: Now,
NOW is the other name; today my date;
O traveler, tomorrow is too late!"

Chapter 7

Collegiate Sports Star

The summer was bittersweet for Mike. Bitter because of the long seventy hour work weeks, much of it monotonous.

Bitter because of missing Sara, knowing his childhood years with his family were about over.

Bitter too, because it seemed the time dragged so slowly, and Mike was restless for his next opportunity.

The summer was also sweet because it marked the end of negative parental restrictions which he didn't agree with. Sweet because of money saved. Sweet because of a goal reached, a bus ticket and trunk packed for Jefferson University.

Other joys of that summer were the long evening hours Ernie and Mike practiced passing a football together. Mike worked on his friend all summer to join him so they could share a dormitory room, play football and continue some of their devilish pranks together.

The good news came just a week before Mike was to leave and Ernie announced: "I'm joining you buddy. Just got my acceptance, and the coach has got us rooming together. Jefferson, here we come!"

College life turned out to be everything Mike had dreamed. At 175 pounds and six feet tall, with quick feet and a strong arm, Mike made the varsity and won a letter his freshman year.

They had twice a day workouts for two weeks before classes started so by the time the other students arrived they were pretty much adjusted. Also properly hazed, and initiated as freshman. Mike had to make the football captain's bed each morning for two weeks.

As the coach promised, Mike was given two simple jobs. One for board, and another for his room. He spent twenty minutes each day pushing a dust mop down the halls of one of the girls' dormitories.

What a treat that was. He had a chance to look over the field, but he had decided this year was going to be all sports, earning money in his jobs and good grades.

Mike's second job was to man one of the pots and pans scrubbing stations in the kitchen after the team evening meal. By the time the job was done it was seven o'clock and time to hit the books.

He liked his teachers. Took all the usual freshman subjects. Got B's and A's. His entertainment was mostly homemade. Very few of his friends had much money so when there was time to relax it was a bull session in someone's room, a walk down the street to the ice cream shop or a prank on some guy who was a stuffed shirt.

Mail time in the student center post office was also a daily highlight. Reverend and Mrs. Matthews were so faithful to write Mike each week. They would take turns. Tell him how proud they were that he was doing well. His mother would often include a clipping from some religious tract, reminding him of her pledge for his future.

By this time, Mike had coped with, and discarded, all feelings of resentment against his parents for their negative strict ways. He felt he understood them.

"They were products of their times," he thought. "I don't blame them. They gave their best to parenthood as they saw it, and there was never a doubt about their love for Judy and me."

Once in awhile a letter from home included a five dollar bill. Mike knew how much sacrifice went into that gift. Occasionally a package of homemade cookies arrived. They never lasted back to the dorm. The shouts would start at the mailbox, "Mike's got cookies, let's share!"

It quickly became apparent to him from classes, and rubbing shoulders with kids from all over the country that the church background of this college was poles apart from the negative, strict, pious atmosphere Mike had grown up with.

Chapel was once a week, and normally very inspirational with some outstanding speaker.

Mike even enjoyed a Comparative Religion class in the department of philosophy. It began to become clear to him as he had always intuitively felt, that God was revealed in religions other than Christianity.

Mike also discovered that the neatest students on campus were those who were well rounded, and had high values, but also enjoyed having a good time. When free time permitted, they'd go roller skating at an indoor pavillion, attend a school party or a movie.

Mike was starved to see all the movies he had missed. "Gone With The Wind" was at the local theatre three times during the year, and he went all three times.

Having been forbidden to go to high school dances, it was a special treat for him to learn how to dance to the music of the big bands like Sammy Kay, Guy Lombardo and Glenn Miller.

Before Mike knew it spring had arrived. The baseball team had been practicing batting and throwing indoors in the field house for a month. Now they could practice outside.

His biggest sports thrill of the year was their first conference game against an archrival across the city. The score ended four to one in Jefferson's favor. The headlines of the school paper the following week read: "Freshman Mike Matthews Wins Game With Grand Slam."

Spring also exploded with fragrance and color in campus lilacs, daffodils and tulips. On the lawns of the student commons, between classes, or after chapel and cafeteria times, the welcome warmth of the sun attracted dozens of students. Lovers holding hands. Friends sharing a blanket. Others cramming for finals or reading a letter from home.

It was on such a day, that Mike met Julie. He had just leaned back with his eyes closed on one of the lawn benches when he heard this melodic voice say, "Mind if I join you?"

He looked up and saw the sparkle and smile of one of the most attractive girls he'd ever seen.

"Please do," he said.

"Aren't you Mike, who runs the dust mop down the floor of our dormitory every day?"

"That's me. I hope I've done a satisfactory job for you. That job pays for my room so I can afford to be here."

"By the way my name is Julie, Julie Kelly," she announced. "I'm a freshman too, as I know you are. You see, I saw your name in the student paper about the grand slam. Sounds like you're quite an athlete."

"Nice to meet you, Julie. I don't know about being 'quite an athlete', but I've always loved sports. It's really what brought me to Jefferson. Mainly to play football and get a good education. I haven't done much but study and practice."

"How would you like to get in on some campus social life, Mike? I'm usually not this forward, but it's May Festival Lilac Time and there's a big sweetheart dance. The king, queen and attendants will be crowned. It's this Saturday — a girl ask boy thing — and I'm one of the candidates for queen, but don't have a date. I'd love it if you'd join me."

With that she tilted her head back and broke into a girl size giggle. "Whew! That's about the longest speech I've ever made. Certainly the first time I've asked a guy for a date. Hope you're not offended."

"Offended? How could I be? I'm just relaxing here for a few minutes before going to baseball practice. I open my eyes and see the prettiest girl on campus who invites me to the biggest party of the year. Julie, believe me, I'm honored. Shake! It's a date."

So began a torrid relationship for the final month of Mike's freshman year. They saw each other every spare moment. "It's a miracle," Mike thought "how many spare moments one can discover when you're infatuated and falling in love."

They spent late night hours at their private blanket parties in the campus arboretum. They strolled hand-in-hand between classes. Julie was Mike's biggest fan at the baseball games.

They made the student gossip column of the campus newspaper. "It seems that Jefferson's own Clark Gable - all books, all business, all sports and no girls for eight months has suddenly fallen head over heals for Princess Julie, crowned freshman queen at the Lilac Time Sweetheart Dance."

"It is true," Mike acknowledged. "I have discovered the girl of my dreams. Julie has even made me forget Sara and every other girl I've ever been with.

"Our relationship is so pure," he thought. "Heavy necking but no sex. Not that we don't have a powerful sexual attraction for one another. But it's as though we both feel we are destined for something special together always. And maybe it's because of how we were both raised, or the romantic culture of our times, or a code of 'nice girls don't and save yourself for marriage'. Or maybe it's all of this mixed with a fear of pregnancy. Perhaps that's what's keeping us just a fraction of a step away from a complete sexual relationship."

Their last night together, before splitting for the summer, was a special candlelight dinner at the best downtown restaurant. Then a quick clothes change followed by all night with a couple of blankets on the beach of a beautiful city lake.

Sunrise brought the dull ache of their frustrated desire, tearful goodbyes, and passionate promises of daily summer letters.

"I'd like you to read this, Mike, after we've each gone our individual ways," Julie said. "I ran across it in the library the other day. Maybe you would even want to keep it on your desk this summer as a daily reminder of how I feel about you."

With that she handed Mike an envelope. He couldn't wait. As he walked across campus he tore it open, and found a beautiful card with these words in her handwriting:

In India, when we meet and part we
    Often say, "Namasti", which means:
    I honor the place in you where the

Entire universe resides. I honor the
Place in you of love, of light, of truth
Of peace. I honor the place within you,
Where if you are in that place in you and
I am in that place in me, there is only
One of us.

There were dozens of romantic letters that summer. They even splurged on a long distance phone call per month. But gradually the daily letters became every other, and then weekly.

At first Mike used the excuse of time. After hitchhiking home for a brief visit with his parents and Judy, he returned to St. Paul where he had a ten hour, six day a week job with a contractor.

Ernie and Mike both were lucky. With help from the coach, they got a good paying job. The depression was about over, so Mike jumped from ten cents an hour to twenty-five cents an hour.

His first day on the job the boss handed him a shovel and pointed to an excavation for a small building.

"The horse drawn scoop," he said, "left the basement level two feet too high. Your first job will be to dig out the two feet."

It took Mike two weeks with a pick and shovel in the packed clay soil, but he got it done. However, the blisters, sore muscles and working out with Ernie cut into his letter writing time to Julie.

More importantly, he began to reflect on the implications of their relationship. He talked it over with Ernie.

"You know buddy, the way I feel about Julie, I want to marry her. I think she feels the same way about me. But I've got three more years of college, maybe graduate school, and no money. Besides I'm only seventeen years old."

"You've got a lot of livin' to do, Mike" Ernie responded. "You better sort out your priorities. You need to do some thinking."

"You're right, Ernie. Maybe we could just date through college like other people do and then get married."

"Makes sense to me, Mike. Give it a try."

"The only problem is," Mike replied, "I know darn well we'll get involved in a heavy sexual relationship, and first thing we know Julie will be pregnant. Then what happens? I'm not ready to be a father, for gosh sakes."

"Mike, I know you pretty well by now. You're determined to get good grades. You have to be good at whatever you do. We both know how much you love sports; and have to keep working at the jobs to support yourself. Maybe you'd be better off to break up now. It would probably be less painful, and if it's meant to be maybe she'll wait for you."

The last few weeks of summer were agonizing. Each letter from Julie, pledging her love and counting the days until their reunion, made Mike's decision more difficult.

Finally, he decided to talk it over with Julie. But not by letter or on the telephone. He asked her if she could come back to school a few days early on a weekend, so on a Sunday with a day off of football practice they could be together.

Their coming together was like they'd never been apart. She looked as beautiful as ever. Mike held her in his arms, in their private arboretum hideaway. They felt like they had discovered a little bit of heaven. They shared their lonely feelings of the summer, and talked about all the exciting times they could have together this school year.

It didn't make Mike's resolve any easier. But he knew what he needed to do.

"Julie," he began, "I've been struggling all summer with a decision about my future. I feel very responsible about having to work hard, get a good education, pay my own way through school and do something with my life which I feel is important."

"Mike, that's one of the reasons I love you, because you are so responsible."

"But, I need to tell you how I feel, Julie. I've got at least three more years of college and probably graduate school. If we keep going together I don't know how we can put off getting married before I'm solid in some career."

"What do you mean, Mike, if we keep going together?

We've both looked forward all summer to getting back together, and now it sounds like you aren't sure. I don't understand."

The tears were beginning for both of them as Mike replied, "Julie, this is the hardest thing I've ever had to do in my life. I love you and always will, but I can't ask you to wait for me. It isn't fair for either of us, most of all for you. As painful as it is, I believe we should let go."

"Mike, I don't understand. I never will understand. I love you. Please!"

"Julie, I can't go on with our relationship."

Mike held her for one long last moment, and then they walked back to the dormitory where Mike said goodbye.

A few days later he learned that Julie had moved out of her room, left school and returned home.

It was the next spring, the anniversary of their Lilac-Time beginning, that Mike learned from one of her girlfriends that she had gotten back together with an old home town boyfriend and they were engaged.

Ernie had one depressed roommate on his hands that night. Mike tried to be happy for her. He breathed a silent prayer that God would look after her and grant her a happy marriage with a husband worthy of her love.

Chapter 8

Call to Arms

College life wasn't the same for Mike again. He missed Julie terribly. But he immersed himself in study, work and sports.

He played football with abandon that fall. Then in his junior year Jefferson had a championship season - one tie, and no defeats. Mike had a couple of minor injuries, a concussion and a broken nose, but nothing to keep him from playing.

It was their final game. They were six points behind, and were on their own thirty yard line. It was Mike's carry over tackle. Ernie laid a tremendous block on the only guy who could bring him down. He broke for the sidelines, and thought he was home free. But suddenly was blind sided. Mike felt the ligaments in his knee give way, and the socket fully dislocated.

He was carried to the sidelines and hustled to the doctor's office. They put him out and got the knee back in place. There was no known surgery. So they put him in a cast and on crutches for several weeks. Mike was happy that the guys won the game. But his football career was over.

It was about a month later that they all suffered a much more cruel, tragic jolt to their joy filled college years. December 7th, 1941, and Pearl Harbor, changed their lives.

Mike's friends quit school left and right. Many were enlisting. Others were later drafted. It was like the end of the world for Mike when Ernie enlisted in the air corp after Christmas.

Mike wanted desperately to follow suit, and tried. But he couldn't pass the physical. He did everything he could to follow Ernie. He went through all the exercises prescribed to strengthen his knee, but it was impossible to disguise how stiff, swollen and sore it was.

He even tried the chaplaincy reserve as an assistant. The Navy had a program he thought he could get into. Since there wouldn't be combat, and with his background of going to a church founded college, and his father being a minister, Mike thought he might get into the service that way. No dice!

Meanwhile the letters were coming from his friends. Ernie wrote about getting his wings and flying combat missions in the Pacific. Mike sent letters to Ernie as often as he could, and shared how he felt.

"I'm humiliated and frustrated," he said. "You guys are over there fighting for our freedom and survival, and I'm sitting here in college safe and cozy. But it bothers me so much. The only guys left here, almost, are the 4-F's, the draft dodgers, and the cowards. When I circulate around the city I feel people are looking at me and thinking: 'Why aren't you in uniform?'"

Ernie kept writing back saying "You can't help it, hang in there, keep doing your thing and we'll have this war over in no time."

Mike was studying Milton, in English Lit II, so he made an attempt at a sonnet which got published in the college literary magazine. It was entitled: "To College Friends In the Service:"

> Sometimes in lonely, quiet, dreary hours
> My anxious troubled mind recalls again
> The happy moments that were ours, when
> We had not felt the sting of selfish powers.
> The flag that waved so high on freedom's towers
> Seemed there to guard each ivy-covered wall.
> Partings in spring brought tears, but in the fall
> Our joys were shared by stars and wind and flowers.
> O friends! Where are you now? And why this fear
> Of Death? They taught us nought of hate and war

That rends men's souls apart. Will you no more
Find joy 'mid scenes of youthful laughter here?
Can tears avail, O God, to bring them back?
I hear your answer, Lord, and kneel to pray . . .

Following intensive research, a Naval recruiting officer
told Mike about an assistant chaplaincy reserve program he
might get into if he took the right subjects through the balance
of his junior and senior years in college. So he took more
comparative religions, psychology, philosophy, and speech.
He also became very proficient in languages beneficial to the
study of theology like Latin, German and Greek.

The summer before his senior year in college, Mike even
volunteered to accept a job teaching vacation Bible School.

The minister was a graduate of Jefferson. He advertised
through the student personnel office for someone who had
some background in religious training to teach the parish
children.

The minister and his wife were going to be gone for a
month. The job also involved holding church services each
Sunday. Mike said to his personnel counselor, "No way can
I do that. I wouldn't know where to start. You'd better find
someone else."

"Just a minute!" the counselor replied, "You don't know
the whole story. This is in the far northeast corner of Montana.
It involves one small town church and another out in the wheat
country. When I say small town, I mean a gas station, one
grocery store, a grain elevator, a few houses, a school building
and a church. These people are only used to having services
every other Sunday."

"But I don't know how to conduct church and give
sermons."

"Nothing to it!" the personnel counselor assured him.
"The minister says his members would be happy with a few
hymns, a Bible reading, a prayer and he'll write out a couple
of sermons you can read. Give it a try. I think it'll be an
adventure you'll enjoy."

"Ok, I'll do it."

The latter part of May, Michael Matthews, college athlete, preacher's kid from Wisconsin, was chugging down the tracks in the great plains of Montana on a single passenger car freight train.

The counselor was right about the town. Mike stayed in the parsonage and cooked his own meals. He was able to do some running now, so every day at dusk he headed down the road for some exercise. The locals thought he was some kind of a nut at first.

Before long, he began to gain their approval. He taught their kids for two weeks in town, and two weeks out in the country. He covered all the grades, except sixth through eighth graders because they were working on the farms and ranches.

There were about twenty kids in school. It was up to Mike to run the whole day, but there were some pretty good materials furnished by the minister from the church publishing house.

When it came to the singing time of the curriculum, Mike even played the piano. Sometimes it was only with one finger but he got through the songs. Art time he was particularly good at. However, the kids thought he was best at recess when he taught them games and played with them.

The Sunday church service went OK too. There was a lady there to play the pump organ, and before the service they picked out some hymns she said the people liked. Everything was quite informal.

Mike picked a Bible reading either from the Sermon on The Mount, or the Psalms, because he liked poetry. His prayer was short and simple. Always thanks for blessings, hope for a swift end to the war, safety for sons, brothers and friends and a wish for a good crop of grain.

As for the sermon, that was really short. Mike read over the minister's written one, and decided he couldn't in good conscience read that. It was too theological for his taste, and he didn't agree with a lot of what he said. Some of it reminded him of the fire and brimstone of Bible Camp days.

Now Mike was in a pickle, because he didn't know what

to say. He had learned in speech classes though that the worst speeches frequently are those which are impromptu, rambling and long winded.

So he determined to try not to be guilty of wasting people's time with that approach. Therefore, he spent about six hours on Saturday seriously thinking what to say. Writing it out word for word, and then studying it before he went to sleep that night and again the next morning.

The twenty-third Psalm was the basis for his talk: "The Lord is my shepherd, I shall not want. He makes me to lie down in green pastures. He leads me beside the still waters. He restores my soul . . ."

Mike had the jitters when he walked to the lectern. "Good morning, friends," he began. "You're probably wondering why the sermon is coming to you today from the lectern rather than the pulpit.

"Let me explain. When I was a little boy my minister father would sometimes let me play in the church when he would leave the parsonage next door and go over to post the hymns for Sunday. He would open the altar Bible to the right pages for the readings. Then I was allowed to sit on the organ stool and pretend to be the organist, or take a place in the pew pretending I was a member of the congregation.

"My greatest fascination, however, was the pulpit. Once, when my dad wasn't looking, I walked the steps into the pulpit and tried to peer over the top pretending to be the minister.

"When my father saw what I was up to, he scolded me. Told me to come down immediately, and never do that again, because the pulpit was reserved for the appointed servant of God, he said.

"I never forgot that. Don't know if that is necessarily true, but I feel more comfortable over here at the lectern.

"I don't feel qualified to speak FOR God — maybe no one is. I am going to try to say a few words ABOUT God, from my limited learning and experience.

"My theme is: 'HE RESTORES MY SOUL.'

"I experienced this during the past week. Actually I felt this working with, teaching and playing with your children.

We stumbled through our lessons pretty well, and I hope they learned as much as I did.

"I hope they learned above all that there is a God who loves all of us, like the Psalm says. We all have our down times when we feel discouraged, lose our way, have troubles.

"I know I have. At times like this, I try to think about all I have to be thankful for. In spite of problems, it's amazing how much I have to be thankful for. And when I'm listing off those things, I can't be discouraged, I can only be thankful.

"Then something else happens. I feel like the writer of the Psalm that the Lord has restored my soul. I try to tell the Lord that in my own way; and as I do, I feel more of a spiritual inspiration, power, peace and guidance come into my life.

"You probably have the same experience — you men sit all by yourself on your tractor in the middle of a hundred acre field with nothing but sky, land and the distant horizon as your companion. But you do have another companion. The Lord is your shepherd and friend.

"And you mothers and wives. You probably have alone times also. Maybe you feel discouraged at times. You must get awfully tired of all the gardening, baking, mending and clothes washing. I believe your soul can be restored too by quietly thinking about all your blessings and being grateful.

"Well, those are my thoughts for today. I hope they might be of help to you during the week. Now let's all pray the Lord's Prayer together."

It seemed to Mike as he greeted each person afterward that they appreciated the service. At least no one fell asleep, and there were a few more people there the next Sunday.

He almost panicked one day the next week when he stopped at the country store. There was a fellow there who said, "I'm from the next town down the road. A hired hand died, and I'm looking for a preacher. I'm the local under-taker. Our preacher is on vacation, so I came over here thinking there'd be one here.

"Young man, they tell me you're pretty good with a prayer, and a few words. It looks like you're it."

"You're kidding!" Mike replied. "I'm not a minister. I'm

just a college kid barely turned nineteen. I'm not qualified to conduct a funeral."

"No problem! I am, and I'll help. It'll be real simple, because this man was a drifter. Nobody knew who he was. We tried to find out, but can't get a trace on him. Besides he hung himself in the barn, and some religious people think that's a mortal sin and won't have anything to do with giving him a decent burial. I've taken up a little collection. We'll furnish him a simple pine box and a spot in the pauper's corner of the prairie cemetery. How about it? Will you handle the religious part?"

"When is it?" Mike asked.

"I was thinking we'd do it tomorrow, if that's all right with you. I'll bring the body back in the hearse and we'll try to spread the word so a few people can help give the poor buzzard a proper send off."

Mike was terrified — couldn't believe what was happening to him. He realized his mother, of course, would have been proud as punch, but he was petrified.

That evening Mike was paging through some of the lesson books for the little kids Bible school classes the next day. He looked at some of the pictures illustrating the Bible verses, and suddenly felt calm and inspired. After a couple hours of writing and rewriting what he was going to say he felt better.

The next day when about ten people gathered at the open grave, Mike opened the Bible to where Jesus was talking about the lilies of the field, the birds of the air, the importance of just one person and said, "The first shall be last and the last shall be first."

He walked a few steps and picked a wild flower from the prairie grass. Holding it up, he said:

"We are here today to honor a fellow human being. We don't know where he came from or who he belongs to, but I think you would agree with me that God knows.

"The Lord talked about the lilies of the field, like this flower, being important. He said just one mustard seed was of value to God, or one grain of sand by the sea, or just one of those birds flying just now overhead.

"Jesus of Nazareth tried to teach the people of his day that everyone of us are important to God — that we all are in his care.

"I'm sure this fellow human being, whose body we are laying to rest today, was important to God. Somewhere there may be a friend, a relative, a son or daughter who misses him and doesn't know where he is. We are standing in their place wishing him well on his journey to a new life.

"I believe life goes on. It doesn't end here. Only changes. I'm not smart enough to know what it's like. Maybe nobody is; but I believe just like the seed blown by the wind and buried in the soil of this cemetery, we do not disappear. We change. Like this flower. So this man whom we lay to rest today will somehow live again in some form, some place, and some life which will be better than this one."

With that Mike placed the prairie flower on top of the simple pine box and asked the group to join him in the Lord's Prayer.

He stayed and helped the mortician lower the casket and shovel dirt back in the grave. There was something about that experience that made Mike feel he would never again be the same.

His month in Montana was quickly over. He returned to St. Paul and a job in a defense factory where he could feel he was contributing to the war effort. He worked a ten hour shift six days a week, and performed the same, small, boring task over and over.

The only thing to break the monotony was the morning, noon and afternoon refreshment cart. Mike felt he was going to lose his mind. Couldn't understand how human beings could spend their entire working lives on an assembly line. At least he decided that he would do almost anything else than be a factory worker.

He wasn't putting them down. If anything he learned to respect the job they did. It's just that he knew it wasn't for him.

Returning to Jefferson for this senior year normally would have been cause for a celebration. But Mike was still frustrated over not being able to get in the service.

The Navy officer he was in touch with now informed him that he would have to have some seminary training.

"That's the last thing in the world I want" Mike thought. "But I'm so determined to get into the service I'll do almost anything."

So he knuckled down to his humanities and Greek language majors. He also immersed himself in American and English Literature minors.

Mike was able to read Plato, Aristotle and Socrates as easily in Greek as English. Speech and creative writing courses had also become favorites.

Three part time jobs occupied Mike's free time, now that he was unable to participate in sports. He worked three hours, five nights a week stocking shelves in a supermarket, two hours weekday afternoons as a salesman in a ladies' shoe store, and Saturdays washing trucks in a bakery garage.

Mike was elected president of his class, was a member of the student council and graduated cum laude.

He also decided to apply to Emerson Theological Seminary in Boston, and was accepted. He figured maybe after a year or so, he could get into the chaplaincy reserve program.

Meanwhile he desperately needed to earn some money to repay his student loans and pay upcoming tuition at the seminary. The first part of the summer the football coach got him a job as a contractor's laborer. He made pretty good money, but it was boring.

Fortunately, about mid summer Mike got a call from one of the Montana farmers he had met the summer he taught vacation Bible School.

"Would you like to have a job for the harvest season?" he asked. "We'll teach you to drive a tractor pulling the combine. If you can come right now, I've got a job for you. You can work the flax fields first, move on into the oats and then the wheat fields last. I'll pay you eight dollars a day and room and board. I guarantee you won't have any time left to spend a dime, and I'll pay your bus fare out and back."

"I'll be there first thing Monday," Mike answered. "Thanks for the call."

Mike found it awesome to begin combining on a hundred acre field of grain at dawn. Cut a swath twelve feet wide and see the grain pouring out from the combine into the huge trucks.

It was hot, dusty and tiring. But they took a break mid morning when the farmer's wife and children delivered fresh rolls and coffee. Again at noon they reappeared with a complete hot dinner. Mashed potatoes, gravy, meat, vegetables, freshly baked bread and pie.

Once more in mid afternoon there was homemade cookies, coffee or lemonade.

At dark, with the sun setting on one side and the moon rising on the other, they shut down the machinery and headed for the farmhouse.

By ten o'clock, after a shower by the windmill, they sat down to a huge supper.

The farmer was right. There was no time to spend money. The only break they got was on Sundays. Even during harvest time, this farmer took the seventh day off as a day of rest.

On the days off, Mike would borrow a .22 rifle and a pickup truck, drive across the prairies trying to pick off pheasants or prairie chickens on the fly. There were hundreds of them, and once in awhile he got lucky.

His other diversion was to lasso one of the semi wild range horses, get a bridle on him and ride bare back across the prairies. Usually the horse would go wide open, with Mike desperately hanging on, until the horse tired. Then they'd trot slowly back to the corral.

The farmer boss was true to his word. After the harvest was over, he handed Mike the money for a bus ticket back to St. Paul.

"You've done a good job, Mike. Good for a city kid and a student. Understand you're going to go to the seminary."

"Yes, I'm due at Emerson Theological Seminary in Boston in a week."

"Goin' to be a preacher, huh?"

"No, not necessarily. I want to get into the service so badly. Because of a wrecked knee from football, I can't pass the physical. But I may have a chance to get into the Naval reserve as a chaplain's assistant. But they require some seminary training."

"Well, son, you'll do fine in whatever you decide. Here's the three hundred and fifty I owe you and another ten for a little extra. Good luck!"

On the way east, Mike stopped to visit his parents. They were empty nestors now since Judy was in college.

The Matthews were ecstatic over Mike's decision to enter the seminary. His mother particularly beamed as she wished him well. "Michael Charles," she said, "my prayers are answered. I told you that someday you would be a servant of God."

"Maybe so, Mom," Mike answered, "but perhaps in some different way than you imagine."

He had no idea what to expect at the seminary. For all he knew, the students took vows of chastity, no smoking, no drinking, lived in a cell size room, and either went to classes or studied all the time.

What he found was quite different. It was quite similar to college, except there were no girls. For the time being he didn't have an interest in or time for girls anyway.

There also were no organized sports. But there was a gym, workout rooms, showers, and tennis courts. A few of the guys also played some touch football on the college green.

Mike still couldn't do a lot of running but he could sure pass. So he joined them.

The first day he met an ex-jock like himself. Few of the other students had played collegiate sports. The two of them hit it off right away. Robert Mackay was his name. By the time their first touch game was over, Bob had caught everything within reach.

"You're quite a receiver, Bob. Where did you play?"

"In high school, it was a suburb of Chicago, and then on to the University of Illinois."

"How about you?" Bob asked.

"A small Wisconsin town by the name of Lakeville, and then Jefferson University in St. Paul. What brings you here?"

"For starters," Bob replied, "I'm not one of these 4-D's who suddenly announced they were going into the ministry so they could escape the draft. I couldn't pass the physical because of a football injury.

"I've got a bunch of friends who have died in the Pacific and Europe, and I want to be a part of this thing. The only way left that I've been able to figure out is to get into the chaplaincy program.

"What about yourself, Mike?"

"That's exactly why I'm here also. By the way, why don't we see if we could room together. It seems to me we have some things in common. Maybe we could help one another through this experience."

"Sounds good to me," Bob replied.

So began a close, long time friendship.

They shared a large corner room with a beautiful view. Attended mostly the same classes. Studied together late into the night. Shot some baskets. Played a few games of tennis, and frequently got into some very deep philosophical conversations.

Bob was a big help to Mike when he got a letter telling him that Ernie had been shot down and lost at sea. Mike was so depressed that he quit going to class for several days —just sat in his room and stared out the window.

"What's the matter?" Bob wondered. "You're acting strange, and you look terrible. Want to tell me about it?"

Mike broke down for a minute as he told Bob about Ernie.

"My very best friend, shot down over the Pacific. We grew up together. Pulled off every prank we could think of. Were teammates in high school. Went on to college and played football and roomed together. He's part of my life. I'll never see him again."

Bob was quiet for a time. Finally he laid a hand on Mike's shoulder. "I know it's tough, Mike. You're just going to have to let your grief and anger out. It's OK. Don't hold it inside.

"I know how you feel. I had a brother killed when the Marines landed on Okinawa. We got the news just before I came here to the seminary. My folks just about went to pieces, and I almost went crazy with grief. He was my hero."

"I'm sorry. Thanks for telling me."

"Tell you what, Mike, let's go for a walk down to the corner tavern and have a beer. It's a pretty good place to shoot the bull for a while."

"Good idea, Bob. Let's go."

Slowly Mike got it back together. He had to because the subjects were so tough. In addition to New Testament Greek, he was taking Hebrew. Although languages came easily for him, Hebrew was especially tough.

The other classes were also difficult, and some of them very dull. If he didn't spend an hour or two on each subject every night he couldn't keep up. There was loads of reading and many papers to write.

The quarterly exams were killers. Each one took three to four hours, and they had five or six of them. Sometimes two in one day.

There were courses in Biblical doctrine, the science of Bible interpretation, the technique of organizing and delivering sermons, plus the language classes.

They also studied psychology, counseling and church administration.

The toughest subject for Mike was church history. First of all, the professor was boring. And he was appalled to read about the church councils, the bickering between church leaders, and the fights over doctrinal interpretations.

"The dominance, rigid control and arrogance of some bishops toward downtrodden, poor peasants was enough to make your blood boil." Mike thought. "But the wars and crusades were the worst."

It seemed to Mike that the organized Christian movement deteriorated with its designation as "The Official Religion of the Roman Empire" by the Emperor Constantine in 325 A.D.

The numbers grew, and the political impact expanded, as did the systematized theology, and organization.

But Mike wondered, "Was it as dynamic, life changing, inspiring and spiritually vital as intended by the prophet-teacher from Galilee?"

True, the organized Christian church grew enormously wealthy. But the course in church history revealed that there were hundreds of incidents of decadent moral and ethical behavioral examples on the part of some clergy.

Conflicts between branches of the Christian church during the reformation weren't much better. Each side claimed an inside track to the only true God. Each denomination claimed to have the only correct interpretation of the Bible.

Bob and Mike talked, sometimes into the night, about their reactions to their classes.

"Frankly, many times I get disillusioned and depressed about being here," Mike began one evening.

"Why is that?" Bob asked.

"Well, I can't go along with the party line."

"You mean some of the dogmas, Mike?"

"Yes."

"For example?"

"I can't accept the teaching of main stream churches that the Bible is the only religious book through which God reveals himself."

"You're questioning something pretty basic, Mike. We're taught here as you know that the Bible is the only written revealed Word of God. If you can't subscribe to that, Mike, the seminary will never recommend you to be ordained."

"I know that," Mike replied. "And I'm not necessarily planning to be ordained. But when parts of the Bible endorse genocide, slavery, women being subservient to men, human sacrifice and Jehovah ordering the killing of an entire tribe, then I have a problem believing that all of it is God speaking."

"Mike, if you don't feel the Bible is word for word the revelation of God, how would you describe the book?"

"I believe the Bible is inspired," Mike answered. "It's inspired in the same way other great spiritual writings have been handed down generation after generation. I believe it contains a blend of a people's history, mythology, poetry, philosophy and spiritual insights. But that's also true of the Koran, or the writings of Buddha and Confucius.

"Let's stop there," Bob countered. "Do you go along with

the dogma of the mainstream church that Jesus was Divine?"

"Sure, I do. But, Bob, I believe others are too. Every civilization has had its Prophets, its Wisemen, its Shaman and "Keepers of the Secret," like the Polynesians, who were head and shoulders above the average in spirituality."

"Like who?" Bob asked.

"Like Mohammed, Ghandi, Socrates or Albert Schweitzer of our century, just to name a few," Mike replied.

"Speaking of Schweitzer," Mike went on, "I really like his description of Jesus of Nazareth. Remember he says, 'He comes to us as one unknown, without a name, as of old, by the lakeside, he came to those who knew him not. He speaks to us the same word: follow me? and sets us to the tasks which he has to fulfill for our time. He commands. And to those who obey him, whether they be wise or simple, he will reveal himself in the toils, the conflicts, the sufferings which they shall pass through in his fellowship; and as an ineffable mystery, they shall learn in their own experience who he is."

"I like that description too Mike," Bob responded. "But don't you think Schweitzer is defining Jesus as the one and only son of God in those words?"

"Not necessarily."

"Well, Mike, how would you describe how you think of God? I have to say I'm getting concerned about you. Your beliefs seem to be so different from what we're being taught here, and what I think I believe."

"Bob, I'm not saying you have to think the way I do. That's part of the strength of our friendship. We can disagree and still respect one another.

"But you asked how I conceive of God. I think of God as an intelligent, loving, infinite presence and creative power. I think this presence permeates this universe, including you and me and every human being.

"I think this is what all religious writings mean, including the Bible, when they describe our humanness as being created in the image of God.

"I believe God exists within each of us. I believe we can tune in to this spiritual connection through prayer, meditation and growing through life's experiences.

"I think we have a potential, a plan, as part of our genes, to fulfill our dream, to reach for the stars as it were.

"Some of us never see our image. Ignore it. Reject it. Never achieve wholeness. But the potential is there."

"Mike, you're very persuasive. I like the way you put things; but for the time being I'm going to have to go along with the historical, orthodox route. As you know, I definitely plan to make the church my career. Probably teaching.

"Meanwhile I share your hope that we'll quit barricading ourselves behind walls of isolationism and sectarianism.

"If you ever decide, Mike to go into the ministry I hope it will be through the mainstream church. You seem to be cast in the likeness of New England's Thoreau and Emerson of a generation ago. As you know, they were spiritual giants in colonial times and the Unitarian church.

"Organized religion needs more voices like that. Who knows. Maybe we'll all see things differently in a few decades from now."

Chapter 9

Having Everything and Nothing

Mike and Bob got their opportunity to practice some of their beliefs after completing two years of classes.

A prerequisite for graduation was nine months of internship in some church institution or parish, before completing the final year at the seminary.

Bob was assigned to a church in his home city of Chicago. Mike was designated for Fargo, North Dakota.

Most guys would have considered that the end of the world, but he was looking forward to the change.

However, before they could leave Boston, the war ended. It was August 15, 1945, and the six inch headlines proclaimed: "PEACE!"

The excitement was phenomenal. The celebrating was at a fever pitch, as it was all over the country. Bob and Mike took a bus downtown. They stood shoulder to shoulder on the streets. There were people hanging out of office windows. Everyone was hugging and kissing each other.

It was incredible. They were alternately laughing and crying. It went on all night.

Bob and Mike decided to visit the seminary chapel before going to bed. Kneeling to meditate about friends who had given their lives, they said a prayer of thanks. They asked God to help them be something worthwhile in the world in the way of healing and inspiration for the lost, the hurt, and the lonely.

The next afternoon as they left for their assigned parishes

they agreed to give this internship their best shot. "Maybe the chaplaincy service can still use some help though the war is over," Mike thought.

He was elated with the Fargo countryside. The duck, geese and pheasant hunting was fabulous. There was also a state college. He enjoyed mingling with college kids again including the ROTC units under the military.

He was asked to teach a course in comparative religions. His class was small, and he enjoyed the open discussions without a denominational overseer looking over his shoulder.

Life in the church parish was challenging. It was a church of over a thousand members. Mike was assigned to the high school organization which was typically half dead.

No wonder. The meetings were so dull he couldn't figure out why anyone would attend. As quickly as possible, Mike reorganized everything. Held a big rally party on a night that didn't interfere with a school event. Had records the kids liked. Lots of cokes and a carnival atmosphere.

The next week he invited to a meeting all who were counselors or would like to be, plus all students who wished to see a vital, fun and stimulating church youth group. Thirty people came with lots of ideas and discussion.

Out of that came goals determined by the kids, translated into programs and scheduling. By the time the year was up there were four hundred high school kids attending each week.

About once every six weeks the senior minister asked Mike to give the Sunday sermon. They had two services and by the second one things would go better. The second service was also broadcast on local radio.

Mike spent about twenty hours preparing for each sermon. By this time he was determined to try to share something of a spiritual benefit that was inspirational, applicable to daily life and not boring or long winded.

He was also determined not to read from a manuscript. So although it was written in essay form, he knew it well enough to have direct eye contact as he spoke from simple notes.

It was hard work. Part of the difficulty was not to offend

someone who was traditionally orthodox, including the senior minister. He must have walked the fine line OK, because each Sunday it was announced Mike was to speak, the church was packed with folding chairs added to the aisle.

A fourth of the crowd were teenagers and college students, and that made him feel good. Mike realized, from a lot of personal counseling with them, that they were faced with some pretty tough choices including the affects of the war on their lives.

The last sermon of his internship, before heading back to Boston, Mike called: "THE YOUTH WHO HAD EVERY-THING."

He wanted it to be special for the high school and college kids because that's who he cared mostly about. "Good morning!" he began. "I'd like to tell you a story today.

"It's a Bible story. You may know it as "The rich young ruler." I'm going to update the story a bit and tell it in my own way.

"This young man, whom I call 'The Youth Who Had Everything' was on his way early one morning to try to meet Jesus the Galilean. He'd heard so much about him.

"Accounts in the local news said he was a great teacher and prophet. Some people even said he performed miracles.

"The young man was curious. He was also looking for something more meaningful in his life. He wasn't quite sure what.

"He already had about everything. He lived in a fashionable villa. You might call him a suburbanite. He lived in the outskirts of Jericho where all the best people lived.

"He was wealthy. Wore the latest fashions in tunics. Belonged to the best clubs. Was a patron of the Arts . . . had studied in the best universities in Rome . . . was well versed in the wisdom of Plato, Socrates and Plutarch.

"He was admired by his peers. Had many friends. His parties were always the best. Anybody who was anybody came to swim in his pools and drink his wine.

"But something crucial was missing. It bothered him.

"When he met Jesus, with his friends, that day down by the sea of Galilee, he identified his gnawing emptiness this way: 'Good teacher,' he asked, 'how can I inherit Eternal Life?'

"Jesus liked him right away. The young man was handsome, spirited, talented, and forthright.

"The bond which developed between the two of them was mutual. The young man realized immediately that for one thing Jesus was no wimp.

"After all, the word was that this Jesus had been born in a stable. He had worked with calloused hands in his father's carpenter shop. After that, he had spent something like fifteen years in the desert and the wilderness grubbing out his own living.

"He endured the extremes of heat, and cold—the hazards of the desert—all the while getting in touch with himself, searching for spiritual truths and preparing for his life work.

"Just think, fifteen years! We get impatient with how long it takes to become an engineer, a doctor, a coach, a pilot.

"It was true, Jesus was no wimp!

"The young man also saw in him a person who was equally at home with a crowd or in a one-to-one situation. This holy man, it was reported, even loved a good party.

"When the wine ran out at a wedding in Cana, Jesus saw to it there was a fresh supply. They also said that, when one of his best friends died, he cried like everybody else.

"There was a calm and serenity about him. You could tell he was comfortable with all types of people—the Roman Governor, an army general, a farmer working the fields, a thief in jail, a prostitute on the street or these ruffian fisherman friends of his.

"The young man had heard many of the stories. The one that impressed him most, oddly enough, was the one about Jesus and the children—the new generation.

"Jesus had held a child in his arms and told the parents, the soldiers, Pharisees and Scribes of the temple: 'Let the little children come to me, and don't hinder them, for they are the Kingdom of God.'

"In other words, if you want to start learning about eternal life and spiritual truths, you might have to remove some of the clutter from your brain and soul. Set about your quest with the unsophisticated, inquisitive, open mindedness of a child.

"The Youth Who Had Everything got down to a one-to-one with Jesus. 'How can I find Eternal Life?' he repeated.

"Jesus gave him three clues. The first was, 'Keep The Commandments.'

"Immediately, the young man interpreted that as: don't commit murder, don't steal, don't have an affair with somebody elses' wife. The young man said, 'I know the commandments of Moses. I've kept all of them from my early childhood.'

"What he missed was this: Jesus wanted him to discover that keeping the commandments was primarily an internal attitude, not just external behavior. It's what you think and feel inside that counts most, because the 'Kingdom of God is within you,' He said. Religion isn't primarily a list of rules and negatives.

"The second clue which Jesus gave was: 'Go sell your riches and give the money to the poor. Then you will have treasure in heaven, and come follow me.'

"Again the young man missed the point. He didn't seem to understand that Jesus frequently talked in parables. Although the young man should have known this having himself also been schooled in the parable ways of the Hebrew and Aramaic teachers of his day.

"'Sell everything I have? That's nonsense. I can't do that.'

"That's what the young man thought. And I doubt any of us would do it either.

"But, you see, this isn't what Jesus meant. He wasn't saying that to be a Christian person you have to go around with holes in your shoes, patches on your jeans and a forlorn look on your face.

"Not at all! He was trying to illustrate that all of us have something we put first— something that is supreme in our life —central—a primary focus.

"For some it is to be popular, to be accepted by everybody.

For others it is power over others. It can be lots of money and success in some way or other. Or it can even be an addiction to something destructive to our inner selves.

"Whatever it is, Jesus was saying, if it's wrong get rid of it. If it's just OK, but dominating your whole life, then get your priorities reorganized.

"If you truly want to relate to the peace, the power, and tranquility of the Divine presence within and around you — give it priority.

"The third clue was akin to the second. Jesus said: 'Love your neighbor as yourself.'

"Now the young man was stumped. This prophet had really hit a sore spot. The young man knew how self-centered he was. He was a taker — not a giver. He was so locked in to being a receiver, always expecting what life could do for him that he was immune to the needs of others.

"His spirituality was crippled. Until he could let go and take a gamble he wouldn't make his big discovery that the Kingdom of God was within him.

"So the story of "The Youth Who Had Everything" has a sad ending. It says in the Bible that 'He went away sorrowful.'

"But you know what? So did Jesus, because he failed. Does that surprise you? Jesus failing. Sure he did. He wasn't always successful, no more than we are.

"Maybe there was a sequel we don't know about which the biographers didn't write in the Bible. Perhaps the sequel is today.

"Just imagine for a minute what a contemporary Jesus would say if he joined us on a street corner, or walked into one of our classrooms, or went for a ride in our car, or greeted us after a ball game, or hopefully was welcomed into our church on a Sunday morning.

"Do you think He would feel at home?

"What do you think He would say through the story I've told you today?

"It might be something like this: 'Young man or woman of today, are you really content? If not, why not?

"Are you troubled with the feeling that no one understands

you, much less your parents?

"'Are you over indulging in something that isn't good for you because you're restless and searching for something satisfying?

"'Are you afraid of the future? Worried about the affects of the war on your life?

"'What about your future? Do you plan to do something worthwhile with your life? Do you wonder at times why you are here, what it's all about?

"'Do you ask yourself if there really is a God who cares about you and loves you and needs you?

"'Let me tell you then, there are answers to your questions.

"Start by asking. Take one step at a time. Talk to your parents, for example. Maybe they aren't as dumb as you think they are.

"'Begin to communicate. Take off your mask. Reveal yourself to those you can trust. Talk to your friends, a counselor at school perhaps, your minister. Get a firm hold on your self-esteem.

"'Start being a giver. Get yourself out of the center of your life. Quit being a taker all the time. Figure out ways to share some joy, some help with others.

"'You might even begin with a younger brother or sister. That might shock them . . . but they'd appreciate it, wouldn't they?'

"'Take a few moments each day to be quiet and meditate. Cultivate a sense of wonder. Believe in miracles. You will discover things within yourself you never knew were there — like the presence, the peace, and power of God.

"'You are of the utmost importance to God. You too have a limitless potential. You are the future of this whole world — tomorrow's scientists, politicians, fathers, mothers, teachers, coaches, writers, artists, leaders.

"'You can shape not only our world, but the Kingdom of God, because the Kingdom of God is within you.'

"I'd like to close today with a poem by an anonymous writer. I found it in a small roadside shop while exploring the mountains of Vermont."

There stands before you a mountain.
You think it is an arduous climb.
But there is no surrogate glory.
'Tis your own choices that make you divine.
Your life consists of two options.
One is to reach for that glory.
The other is to circle the base.
Joy will lighten your burden
When you embark on your climb.
But to ever circle the base
Will only immortalize pain.

Chapter 10

Seminary Light Side

Getting back to Boston for his senior year, and seeing Bob again, was exciting for Mike. They both found the city's atmosphere of history, academics and culture tremendously stimulating.

These were times when Mike couldn't believe how full and varied his life had been since Lakeville, Wisconsin.

That was only seven years ago, and here he was only 23, in the fall of 1946, beginning his final year toward a Master's Degree in Theology.

He also enrolled at Harvard for a course in the School of Business. Immediately the class proved helpful, because it enabled him to get the job of managing the student bookstore at the seminary.

It was a student cooperative, and the job paid well.

His responsibilities included ordering and inventorying textbooks, supplies and a wide range of books of philosophy, theology, the arts and a smattering of contemporary novels.

Above all, his fellow students expected him to carry on the tradition of profitability, lower prices than the commercial stores, and a dividend check at the end of the year.

In addition to running this business, Mike had a full load of course work, was writing a thesis for the master's degree, and functioning as president of the student body. He had very little time for fun and games.

"This theological stuff is no snap," Mike concluded. "But

then, neither are the requirements of aeronautical engineering, architecture, law, business or medicine across the river at M.I.T. and Harvard."

Bob and Mike were also committed to staying in shape physically. With the aid of a knee brace, Mike could still play intramural touch football, half court basketball, tennis and softball. They also used the Sem gym for calisthenics about three times a week.

In addition to stirring up some competition among the ex-jocks, Bob and Mike held the title of number one pranksters.

They knew one of their classmates had recently gotten a speeding ticket. So they faked a phone call to him. Had him paged out of class. Bob pretended he was a reporter.

"Is this Jim O'Brien?" he asked.

"Yes. What can I do for you?"

"Mr. O'Brien, I'm from the daily news. I was going over the police records from last Friday, getting some profile information for a story. Are you the O'Brien who received a speeding ticket?"

"I guess so."

"What do you mean 'I guess so'? Are you or aren't you?"

"Yes, I am, Sir."

"Is it true you were clocked at fifty in a thirty zone?"

"I'm afraid it's true."

"Why were you in such a hurry?"

"I was late for class."

"Oh, you're a student, Mr. O'Brien. Which school do you attend?"

"I'm enrolled at Emerson Theological Seminary here in Boston."

"Oh, this is interesting. You're going to be a minister?"

"Yes, I am."

"What year are you in, Mr. O'Brien?"

"I'm a senior?"

"So, you'll be the minister of a church someplace in this country in the very near future?"

"Yes, I will."

"How do you feel about the speeding ticket as an example,

Mr. O'Brien?"

"Not very good."

"Mr. O'Brien, have you paid your fine yet? The records are not clear on that."

"No, as a matter of fact I haven't."

"Well, thank you, Mr. O'Brien, for your interview. This will make a very good human interest story. My supervisor will go for this . . ."

"Sir," Jim interrupted, "I didn't get your name, and when will this story appear?"

With that there was a loud click as Bob slammed the receiver down, muffling their laughter.

What a ball! Watching Jim tear to his room for some money and heading downtown. Every morning at the dormitory cafeteria his classmates watched Jim desperately scan the paper before eating. It wasn't until graduation that the pranksters dared tell him what they'd done.

Their prize accomplishment, however, was on the dull Old Testament prof. He always plunked his briefcase down beside his lecture desk, after marching down the aisle. When class was over, he would usually be occupied a few moments by students asking questions.

Bob and Mike thought, "The perfect time for our trick."

It was a beautiful spring morning. The Old Testament class was first thing. So immediately after class the two of them slipped across the hall to the janitorial closet where they had stashed their props.

While the professor was occupied with questions they slipped their props into his briefcase. A big red apple, two cut-out pictures from a sexy magazine—one a very curvaceous naked lady, and the other a muscular naked man. The clincher was a live, harmless, spring garter snake. To his tail they had fastened a label which read: "DIRECT FROM THE GARDEN OF EDEN!"

Their only disappointment was not being around when he opened his briefcase. Later, however, they learned that the old prof did have a sense of humor.

In one of his chapel talks he said: "I hope the senior or

seniors who staged my Garden of Eden surprise aren't quite
that creative in illustrating sermons in the parish."

For a diversion, Bob and Mike would organize a gin or
poker game. Stakes were half a cent a point, and payoffs were
made at the end of the semester. Also, as the budget allowed,
they would head for Fenway Park, and get a bleacher seat
behind the big net at a Red Sox game. Their best treat, once
a winter, was a ski trip to their favorite slopes at Stratton Mt.,
Vermont.

Otherwise, Mike's social life was a complete disaster. It
made no sense, but he was still carrying the torch for Julie. The
scar ran deep from their separation.

"This must almost be how a divorce feels," he kept
thinking. "The stages of grief, sense of failure, regrets,
loneliness are hard to handle."

Other than a half dozen blind dates, over the past six years,
Mike might just as well have taken a vow of chastity. It also
made him horny as heck, because he sure wasn't an undersexed
goody goody. His only sexual release all that time was either
a fabulous dream, or a quick hand job in the shower.

Bob had been fortunate to meet a wonderful girl attending
Wellesley. They planned to be married in June, before Bob
went on to graduate school at Princeton.

Mike's plans beyond seminary were still uncertain. He
was still open to the possibility of chaplaincy but he wasn't
making any progress getting through the physical.

Completing the senior year was quite a challenge.
Meanwhile, there was a thesis of twenty-five thousand words
to write. Also there were oral exams of up to two hours with
a professorial review board. They could cover everything
which had been studied during the four years.

A favorite diversion for a few of the students was a Friday
or Saturday night at a tavern near the Harvard campus. Over
a beer or two, Bob and Mike could talk for hours about their
plans for the future, and some of their impressions about profs
and fellow students.

They got into it pretty good one night.

"How do you think," Mike asked, "some of the members

of our class are going to impact the church life of America?"

"Not too good," Bob answered. "We both know that a few of these guys are here to escape the draft. That's a heck of a motive. A few others are here because they can't do anything else. Some just love this academic cocoon. If they didn't have to make a living, they'd love to stay in the ethereal haven of theory all their life."

"You're right," Mike responded. "I feel sorry for them. But I'm more concerned about the churches which get 'em. A few, obviously, are on an ego trip. They can't wait to put on a robe, turn the pulpit into a pedestal, and pontificate their profound wisdom."

"Yeah, that's one thing bothering me about going into the ministry," Bob countered "I don't want to be on a pedestal. I'd rather people didn't look upon me as having all the answers."

"I agree, Bob."

"I have no interest," Bob went on, "to aid the church in being a monolithic hierarchy. I just see myself helping others apply spiritual truths to everyday life and the problems of our world."

"Those are my sentiments too, Bob."

Before they knew it, the year was over. "I can't believe it," Mike said. "Where did these eight years of college and seminary go?"

Mike's thesis was typed and turned in. With the approval of his advisor, his topic was "The Theological and Practical Relevancy of the American Church to Teenagers."

He held his breath that the faculty committee might reject it for heresy or for being too liberal, but they approved it. He also passed his oral exams on a squeaker. The vote was three to two.

That was an ordeal! They sat for two hours, in an awesome board room setting being grilled by the professors. Mike felt he passed, with room to spare, on the objective questions. But on a few of the subjective questions, he had to fudge slightly— such subjects as: the literal inspiration of the Bible, the doctrine of the trinity, and the relativity of Christianity to other world religions.

Toward the close of the orals, Mike's advisor, who was on his examining team, asked: "Mr. Matthews, we have two final questions.

"First, who is one of your personal heroes?"

Without hesitation he replied: "Elroy Hirsch."

"Who is he?" his interrogator asked. "I don't think I've come across his name."

"Oh, he was an All American halfback at the University of Wisconsin. The best. They called him 'Crazy Legs' because he was so fast and shifty."

"I see. I guess we didn't make it clear," the professor went on, "we meant who is one of your religious or spiritual heroes?"

"Oh! I guess that would be Francis of Assisi," Mike replied, "the twelfth century Italian Friar, later canonized by the Catholic church."

"That's an interesting choice," the faculty interrogator commented. "Why is he your spiritual hero at this time?"

"Well, I would say it isn't because the Franciscan Order is attributed to him, because he really didn't try to establish any order or following. That was not his goal or ambition. He wasn't even a priest, but he was devoted to a sincerely spiritual life.

"I like him because he lived at a very difficult period in the hierarchy of the church. It was a time of oppression of the common people. Francis was a mystic, almost introvertive; but he genuinely loved people. He was only forty-four when he died; but I feel he achieved his dream."

"What was that, do you think?"

"To be an example of living spiritual values. To be of help to simple, common people, and live among them sharing their hurts, their oppression, their longings. I believe he accomplished that. He was almost an unknown who became a spiritual giant, I feel.

"I believe he emulated quite well the major life purpose Jesus is reported to have had when he began his career. He announced, as you know, 'The spirit of the Lord is upon me because he has anointed me to announce the good news to the poor. He has sent me to proclaim release to the captives, and recovery of sight to the blind, to set at liberty those who are oppressed, to proclaim the year of the Lord.'"

"Very well put, Mr. Matthews," the advisor responded.

"Now, we come to the end of the orals for you. We'd like to ask a final question: "What single recommendation would you make to the faculty as a priority for our consideration in future curriculum modifications?"

"I hope you don't mind, gentlemen," Mike replied. "I came prepared for this one. I have it written out. As you know, previous students at the Sem have told us you might ask this question.

"First, I would commend you for asking. I think that's being progressive. I also wish to thank you for your time, inspiration, and patience shared during these four years.

"Now as to my answer: what would I recommend for the future?

"My single recommendation is in two parts, A and B.

"A, is to add more subjects in the area of Practical Theology which will aid the future ministers of churches in America to understand today's issues; relate in a better way with our different strata of society; and perform more dynamic roles of leadership by example and teaching.

"B, is not strictly speaking a curriculum change, but it's related. I've been asked by the senior class to request a review of your consideration on one of our classmates.

"The word is out that he's not going to be recommended for ordination because of his poor grades in Hebrew and Greek. He's heartbroken. You know who I mean.

"As president of the senior class, I have a petition here signed by ninety percent of the students asking you to re-consider. We feel he has a lot of heart—deep feeling for people—would make some small parish a marvelous spiritual leader, where they could give a hoot less about Greek and Hebrew (pardon me!.) He could be another Francis of Assisi.

"Thank you, gentlemen for your courtesy."

The review board must have listened hard, because at the

graduation ceremony the student was listed as recommended for ordination. The class broke out in spontaneous applause when his name was read.

As for Mike, he wasn't ready for ordination. Still didn't know what he wanted to do. The chaplaincy program was not going to be possible. Going on for a doctorate occurred to him, but he ruled that out because he was tired of the academic cocoon.

He was thrilled to have his parents attend the commencement. His mother told him at lunch afterward that she alternated between a big grin and tears when the name, Michael Charles Matthews was announced as a graduate with honors.

They had a good discussion at lunch. It helped sort out some of Mike's reasons for not being a candidate for ordination.

Of course Reverend and Mrs. Matthews wondered why. His dad opened the subject.

"Do you feel like telling us, Michael, why you don't want to go on into the ministry? The senior minister in Fargo, where you interned, told us you were the best intern he'd ever had."

Mother chimed in, "Maybe you'd just like to take a little rest for a while. When the time is right you'll do the right thing. God will make it clear to you."

"Mother," Mike thought to himself, "you've really mellowed."

"Dad," Mike continued, "remember when you used to say in the pulpit that God needs people in the shops in the stores, on the farms, on the factory assembly line in the big companies, in government?"

"Yes, I remember, and it's true. I used to say that it can be much more difficult living a Christian life in those places than the pulpit."

"I agree with that," Mike replied, "and that's part of what I'm feeling right now. I just finished reading a book by a Quaker theologian on the subject of vocation. As you know the word from the Latin, means 'calling from God.'

"One of the things he said left a big impression on me. He wrote: 'There are so many exciting, demanding opportunities in this world representing a calling from God that it's a shame most men miss all of them but one.' I don't want to do that."

"What are you thinking of doing, Michael?" his Mother asked.

"I'm not sure, but I think I would like to live my life in about four or five different vocational chapters. Maybe something in a service related profession. Perhaps another in business and sales. Maybe another in government.

"Frankly," Mike went on, "I also don't feel qualified to be a minister of a church. I think I would need much more maturing and diversified experiences to be a spiritual leader of others. In working my way through school, I've had a lot of different experiences rubbing shoulders with people out on the street. They've taught me how tough it can be, and how difficult it is to make religion seem relevant.

"Let me ask you, Dad, do you feel the church of today needs to re-examine and improve on its relevancy to the changes and challenges of our post war world?"

"Your mother and I both feel that way, Michael."

"I'm happy to hear that. Say, you two have changed since I was a kid at home, haven't you? I hear you even have a TV set and enjoy a glass of wine at home now and then. You're actually watching those evil movies on TV you wouldn't let Judy and I see at the theatre?"

Before they could answer, Mike added, "That's OK, I was kidding you. I think it's great.

"But I do feel a little more comfortable sharing something else about how I feel about the posture of the church in today's society. It has something to do with why I'm not going to be ordained."

"What's that, Michael?" mother asked.

"I don't want to offend you; but this is how I feel after all these years of intense theological study and thoughtful research.

"I feel the church has strayed a long way from its source. I see it more concerned with systems, structures, and organizations than spirit and people.

"I don't think religion is a vital force in politics, international affairs, economics, business. I feel the church is not communicating as it should, or applying its message adequately among the youth, the poor, the racially disenfranchised. I think we have to do a far better job in the arena of social justice, and peace among nations.

"I believe, furthermore, that the church has been too negative. It is altogether too fragmented with hundreds of competing denominations all saying they are the only true way to God . . . to say nothing about other valid brands of religion around the world.

"I think much of our missionary work has been arrogant— more concerned with colonization than ministering to people's pain, poverty and spiritual needs.

"I believe God is revealed in experiences, and people beyond the boundaries of the Christian religion. I also think there is increasing opportunity in today's world, to do something spiritually meaningful in occupations other than the clergy. I need to take time figuring out where I fit best."

"I understand. That makes a lot of sense for you Michael," Dad responded, "and you know your mother and I are your biggest supporters. Thank you for sharing your thoughts with us."

Chapter 11

Payback Time

A challenging job offer was presented to Mike the day after graduation.

He was packing for a week long hiking-camping trip at Franconia Notch and the Appalachian Mountain trail in New Hampshire. Mike felt the fresh air, solitude and exercise would clear away the cobwebs in his brain.

Dreaming of trails, trout streams and lakeside campfires, he was suddenly paged over the dormitory loud speaker.

"Michael Matthews, will you please call the president's office."

He got through right away and was asked if he could visit with the president for a few moments.

Getting quickly to the point, the president said, "The president of your alma mater, Jefferson University, has heard you are not applying for ordination. He's checked with me and the faculty personnel committee. I have recommended you for the position of Vice President for Development at Jefferson."

"That's an honor, sir," Mike replied. "Thank you!"

"I suggest you call him immediately."

Mike did just that. They chatted for quite a while. Mike explained he was going on a week's camping trip and would give him an answer when he returned.

Bob was leaving for graduate school at Princeton, but Mike took a minute to explain his job offer.

"What do you think I should do?" he asked.

"It appears to me the job is tailor-made for you, Mike. You have an excellent touch with people. You're good at management and organizational skills. The class you took at Harvard should help, and you're looking for a way to be of help to returning service personnel. I think you'd be a natural for the job."

"Thanks, Bob, your opinion means a lot to me. I'm going to do some serious thinking about this while I'm on the trail in New Hampshire."

"By the way, Mike, what kind of a salary are they paying?"

"You know, I forgot to ask."

"That sounds like you, Mike, colleges aren't exactly known for their high salary scales. But don't be afraid to set your sights high. You're worth it."

Mike left his car, an old junker, at the parking lot near the campsite at Franconia Notch. It was only a short hike from there to the mountain trail.

The trail was exhilarating. The fragrance of spring. The fresh scents of virgin woodland flowers and fern. Newly budding birch. The sounds of silence, interspersed with the cardinal's mating call.

Each evening he camped by a stream or lake where he could fly fish. Regularly, he had fresh filet of trout with his dried pack food. The clear, ice cold water from the streams was his champagne.

At Mike's last campfire before heading back to Boston he decided to record in his journal a list of self helps for decision making.

The list evolved from his classes in Logic, General Semantics, and Psychology.

1. Take your time. Don't make an impulsive decision.

2. Get away by yourself. Let your mind be uncluttered by stress, and anxiety.

3. In tranquility and solitude, focus on the vibrations of energy from within. They are trying to transmit a message to you. In this state of consciousness you will find it easier to

tune to spiritual frequencies. Recognize that the mind is like a radio sending and receiving set. It is even capable, through meditation and prayer, to communicate with Divine energy.

4. Be true to your center. If you are aware of your major life purpose, ask yourself: "What decision will best serve that purpose?"

5. Try to identify the FACTS involved in the decision, not fantasies. Don't get trapped by a "false to fact" reasoning process. Be sure your premises are true.

6. Seek the counsel of at least one very close friend who knows you well.

7. Ask for the guidance of at least one or two qualified people.

8. Once your decision is made, Plunge! Don't look back. Full speed ahead!

Mike knew now what he should do. Accept the position. He got a satisfactory salary commitment from the president, so after his week camping he was on his way back to Jefferson University.

He loved the job immediately. His division of administration, under the president, covered the areas of: Student Admissions; Alumni Affairs; Fund Raising; Public Relations; Campus Master Planning.

Mike plunged in with abandon. He became acquainted with groups and leaders of the college family. Met with Board of Governors, Faculty, Student Body, Alumni, Existing Staff in areas of public relations, fund raising and student admissions. He tried to identify the power persons and prime movers, as well as staff weak spots.

As quickly as possible, Mike attempted to understand the educational credo of the college, its roots, its hopes and dreams as presently conceived for the future. He asked for written capsule statements by strategic college family groups.

Gradually, he compiled a statement of purpose, needs, goals, translated into staff and operating budget for the Development Program of the University.

The goals covered optimum student body size and geographic, cultural, academic mix; faculty size and salary scales;

curricula priorities; endowment needs and purposes, and finally campus renovations and expansion.

Mike was able to secure a retainer for a top local architectural firm. They agreed to prepare a conceptual rendering of campus and plant needs over the next ten years.

The financial requirements were set at twenty million dollars, and the Development Division's annual budget at $100,000.

When Mike submitted the program and budget to the president, his eyes bulged. Catching his breath, he said "We don't have this kind of money. Where do you propose getting it?"

"I promise you," Mike replied, "if you enable me with this budget, to hire the staff I need, we'll cover our budget and meet our fund raising goals."

"Congratulations, Michael! You've done a good job of planning so far. I'm going to propose acceptance of this program at next week's Board of Governor's meeting. I'd like you, subsequently, to present it to the Faculty, Student Body, Staff and the News Media.

"I'm going to stick my neck out and give you my unqualified support, Michael. If it fails, we'll both go down the chute; but with God's help I think we'll get the job done."

"Thank you, Mr. President. Let's shake on it!"

The next weeks were hectic. With recommendations from other professionals in the field, Mike hired a seasoned consultant who approved of what was done so far, and recommended they meet every other week.

With his assistance, Mike filled all his staff positions.

Carefully, he recruited key personnel for membership on the Development Council. The first person he recruited was a senior partner in the leading Advertising- Public Relations firm of the city.

He aided Mike's PR staff to prepare the graphics needed to sell the University and its program to other public, and council members.

With these graphics in hand Mike successfully recruited Development Council members from the top owner- management of the newspaper, TV-radio stations, and the finance community.

He was able to convince two CEO's of leading corporations to join the Council, in addition to a representative of the Mayor's office.

The coup was to enlist one of the state's Congressmen to serve on the Council. In turn, he got an OK from the Governor to be the main speaker at the college announcement gala.

It was held at the largest hotel banquet facility in the city. Every segment of the student body was represented. Band members heralded with trumpet fanfare the unveiling of development targets.

Captains of each men's and women's athletic team were at the head table, together with faculty heads of each department. The President and Dean of the faculty were at their best in their brief speeches. The Governor was exceptional, and the news media's coverage superb.

Mike's personal finale was an announcement he had been asked to keep secret from everyone, even from the President, until this moment.

"Ladies and gentlemen," he began, "it is my pleasure to announce the first gift of money for our development program. The donor prefers anonymity. The pledge is a "matching" gift. It's contingent on our raising a like amount over the next six months. The amount is $500,000."

The applause from a standing audience was heart-warming.

When the evening was over, the President shook Mike's hand. "Magnificent beginning, Son," he said. "Job well done! Now our real work begins."

Interspersed between the long, intense hours, there was one fabulous interlude for Mike. It involved the chairperson of the student division of the Development Council. Her name was Jane Carroll. She was a senior, the leading actress in every college play, a recent Miss Wisconsin and runner-up Miss America.

Her talents were dynamite. She was able to create a fever pitch of excitement, support and participation in the Development program from otherwise blase' students.

She also whipped up a pitch of excitement in Mike. Whenever he could, he went out of his way to attend her sub-committee meetings with students. Frequently, she would stop in the office to talk Development. He felt there was some other developing going on. Maybe a romantic interest.

It was spring, and Mike had been on the University staff for nine months. Jane was graduating. They met one day over a cup of tea in the student lounge, following her final Council meeting.

"What are your plans, Jane?"

"I'm off to New York. I've been invited to audition for an off Broadway play. It's a very small role, but a chance of a lifetime. Henry Fonda is the male lead."

"Wow! That is a great opportunity. You know I'm scheduled to make a trip to New York in the fall. I'm calling on national foundations. If you are in the play, and I just know you will be, I'd like to see it. Maybe we could have lunch together or go somewhere for dinner afterward."

"I'd like that," Jane replied. "The alumni office will have my address. I'm committed to staying in New York until I make it. Acting school will occupy most of my time."

"It's been fun working with you, Jane. Good luck, and I hope we'll connect."

"I hope so too. I'll make it easy for you to reach me. I'll send a card or two during the summer so you'll have my address and phone number personally."

Jane was on Mike's mind all summer alongside dollar signs, budgets, staff meetings, goal reviews and a myriad of successes and frustrations. Generally, however, the per-formance curve was up.

Mike's people contacts in the city on behalf of the Uni-versity were pyramiding. He became active in the Chamber of Commerce, Athletic Club, a Country Club and was elected to the Board of Directors of the downtown Kiwanis Club.

He was invited to give a key speech at the national convention of the churches originally sponsoring Jefferson U. Happily, the pledged budget support for the coming biennium was doubled.

Through staff, Development Council and Consultant input, major increases were also projected in fund raising areas of Alumni, Wills and Trusts.

Finally, he was ready for the fall trip to New York. Appointments were set with a number of foundations, including Ford, U. S. Steel, and Campbell Soup.

He was also scheduled to meet individually with a few wealthy and prestigious alumni who were chief executive officers or partners of Fortune 500 companies. Advance brochures and graphics had been sent to them.

As exciting as this prospect was, Mike was almost obsessed with the thought of seeing Jane again. She had mailed her address and telephone number. He had responded with a note saying he would call her.

He was met at the airport by the chauffeur of one of Jefferson's Alumni corporate greats. He was escorted in a Cadillac limousine to the New York Athletic Club where he stayed for two weeks as his guest. The next day they were scheduled for an hour's meeting in his office, followed by lunch in the executive dining room.

This was a heady experience for a young twenty-five year old fresh out of school on his first major career responsibility. But he loved it. Felt humbled by it all, but confident he would succeed.

First things first, however. He tried to call Jane, and learned that her phone had been disconnected and she now had an unlisted number. He felt crushed.

"Why are you so devastated?" Mike asked himself. "What is so important about seeing Jane? You don't know her all that well. After all she is busy. Has more important things to remember than seeing you. Why do you even care?"

He knew. It was because he was fascinated by her, and was terribly attracted to her. There was a magnetism about her that he couldn't and didn't want to resist.

Now it seemed he wouldn't get a chance to see her. But Mike wasn't going to give up so easily.

He checked with the desk and discovered that the play she

was in was still on stage. Her name appeared in the billing. The Athletic Club was successful in getting a reservation this his first ever evening in New York.

The play was great. Though Jane's part was small, he scarcely noticed anyone else, even the star, Henry Fonda. He sat there wondering how he could talk to her. There was no getting to her dressing room without an appointment, so he stood outside with the rest of the crowd waiting for the actors and actresses to leave.

Suddenly, Mike spotted her. She was on the arm of a young actor in the play. Before he could even wave, she and several of her friends were in a limo and gone.

Mike walked for blocks across Broadway, to Park Avenue and toward Central Park. He was feeling low. Finally he hailed a cab back to the club. Immediately checking at the desk thinking she might have left a call for him. Nothing.

Lonely and depressed, he went in the dining room for a late sandwich. Before going upstairs he checked at the desk once more. Again nothing.

Mike knew he had to get ready for an important meeting the next day, but instead thought about ways he could make contact with Jane.

Finally he decided he was going to send a dozen roses to her dressing room for tomorrow night's performance with a card, saying: "Congratulations! Loved the play. Missed you. Don't have your new number. Could you call me at the New York Athletic Club?"

In a pensive mood, he decided to sketch in his journal some of his thoughts from his first day in New York. It turned out to be a few lines of free verse. He called it: "The City Is A Lonely Place."

Gray walls, haunting shadows.
Angry horns, piercing whistles.
Staccato neons, mocking music,
Dispenser food, screeching wheels.

The city is a lonely place . . .

Nameless faces, frantic feet.
Puppet waiters, pushing peddlers.
Waxed dolls, probing youth.
Carpeted cages, despairing wishes,
Shattered fantasies, grinning actors.

The city is a lonely place . . .

Stunted grass, biting wind.
Hungry bird, misting rain.
Barren mailbox, muted phone.
Vacant room.

The city is a lonely place.

The next morning Mike felt better and was eager to get going. He worked out first in the gym, swam several laps and spent a few minutes in the sauna and steam room before breakfast. After catching up on progress back at his University office, he confirmed appointments for the week and reviewed notes for his noon meeting.

The meeting turned out spectacularly. He got a pledge for $50,000 a year for five years. More importantly, perhaps, he received advice as to how to approach busy, successful executives like the President of the U. S. Steel Foundation.

On a whim, and feeling like a love sick school boy, he got a ticket for the play again. He was feeling: "If I can't talk with her, I can at least see her; and maybe I'll get a chance to be in the right place when she leaves the theatre."

No such luck. The second night was a repeat of the first.

After picking up his messages at the club he almost sprinted to the elevator. Jane had called. Her message read: "Thousand apologies. Have a new number. Will explain. Sorry I missed you. Love your roses. Please call 10 AM. Could we have lunch tomorrow?"

He was ecstatic. Fortunately, though he had appointments all day, twelve to two was free. Hearing Jane's voice the next morning was a thrill. He caught her just as she was leaving for an acting class.

"Sorry, Mike, about the change in the phone number. I'll explain over lunch. It's so wonderful to hear from you. I can't wait to see you."

"I feel the same way, Jane. I've been planning all summer for this trip to New York."

"Mike, I've got to run or I'll miss the subway. There's a marvelous intimate French restaurant close to my acting teacher's apartment. Shall we meet there?"

She gave him the address and name of the restaurant. They agreed to meet in two hours.

Mike was there early, sipping a glass of wine in the intimate bar just inside the door. When she entered, it was like a golden sunrise on a spring morning.

She caught sight of him right away as he rose to greet her.

"Mike, how wonderful to see you again! We have so much to talk about."

They gave each other a hug. Just touching her hand gave Mike chills up his spine.

"Jane, this is the highlight of my trip. Let's find a table.

"You were right about this being a cozy restaurant. I love it."

"They have the best French soups here and marvelous salads," Jane added.

"Why don't you surprise me, and order your favorite for both of us with wine you'd recommend?"

With ordering out of the way, Jane asked, "How is your development program going? I've read all kinds of good reports coming out of your office."

"I'm pleased, Jane, with progress so far. You heard about the half million dollar matching gift. We're getting close to meeting that goal. I think after the Alumni fund program this fall we'll have it made."

"How are your appointments in New York going?"

"I've just had one with a highly successful entrepreneur alum. That turned out fabulously well. At two today I meet with the Ford Foundation. But, Jane, what I've enjoyed most is seeing you in the play. Sorry I missed you afterward. I should have made arrangements."

"That's my fault, Mike. Let me tell you what's happened in my life."

"Please, I'm anxious to hear how you're doing."

"The play is exciting. Even though my part is so brief, as you know, just to be on the same stage with Henry Fonda is a dream come true. It's leading to other contacts and offers, possibly TV and movies, which I'm considering. Plus, I'm really making good progress in my classes.

"But right now," Jane went on, "the most exciting happening for me is the actor I've been dating. We just decided to move in together. That's why my telephone number has been changed. He has an unlisted number. We'll have to work on that because I need to hear from my agent regularly."

Mike managed a smile. "That sounds wonderful, Jane. You seem very happy."

Mike's insides had just hit the skids.

"I had hoped to see her again before leaving New York," he thought. "But I guess that takes care of the romance possibilities."

Jane seemed to pick up on his mood. "How about you, Mike? Do you have time for any social life? Are you dating anybody? Excuse me, I'm getting too personal. You were the rage of the sororities, you know, when you hit the campus as VP. That's all I heard for a while. How handsome, brilliant, desirable you were. I couldn't wait to meet that Michael Matthews, and see for myself. They were right."

"Thanks, Jane. I'm flattered. No, I'm not dating anyone. I haven't had much time for a normal social life. But, if we could only clone you!"

"Gee, I never thought about that, but it's interesting. Who knows? Another time. Another place. I think I'm much like you, Mike. Hopefully, I've got a long term future in my career and I'm not ready to settle in to any permanent commitment yet. My friend and I have an open relationship. We may stay together. We may not."

"Jane, I'd like to see you again next time I come to New York. Maybe we can drop each other a line now and then.

Meanwhile, I'd like to toast your success. Here's to a gorgeous woman . . . to your talents, your future, your happiness, and our meeting again."

"Thanks Mike. I do want to hear from you. I'll write and give you my new number. Please let me know how the development program turns out. Who knows, I may be appearing in a play in Chicago or the Twin Cities. I'd love to see you then."

Mike had a devil of a time shaking off the vision of her contagious smile, the touch of her hand as they said goodbye.

But he hadn't given up hope.

His appointment with the Ford Foundation took the balance of the afternoon—to and from by cab in bumper to bumper traffic—waiting in the outer office for an executive who was running behind by at least an hour.

This was a new experience for him. Dealing with corporate and private foundations with a history of giving away enormous sums of money each year. The setting was somewhat ominous and foreboding. Very formal. Walnut paneling. An oil portrait of Henry Ford the only art.

He felt like he was in the outer office of a supreme court justice, expecting any minute he would appear in his black robe and escort him into the inner chamber.

"Mr. Matthews? Mr. Fairchild will see you now."

The receptionist's voice startled Mike back into reality.

Actually, the meeting went well. Mr. Fairchild acknowledged having read the preliminary brochures he mailed to him.

He was complimentary about the definition of goals for excellence in faculty quality, student profile and creative planning. It helped that he knew the admirable qualities of Jefferson's President and the reputation of the Consultant Mike had hired.

"The one thing you'll have to accomplish," Mr. Fairchild stated, "is to at least double the financial support by your alumni. You will find, Mr. Matthews, if you haven't already, that we, in the business of support to higher education, will only support those institutions whose alumni believe in and support their University."

"I understand, sir. This is top priority for our Alumni Fund this fall."

"Good! Get in touch with me when your fall drive is completed. At that time we'll take a look at your overall progress, and decide if we can fit our grant philosophy with your development needs."

"Thank you, sir, for your interest and time. I'll keep you informed and be back in touch. Meanwhile, I'll report what you said to our Alumni Executive Committee and our Development Council."

Mike's meeting the next day with the president of the U. S. Steel Foundation was quite a contrast. The setting of the suite of offices was very contemporary and upbeat in contrast to the Ford Foundation's formal academic mood.

He walked into Mr. Myers office and paused for a moment admiring it.

"Quite a view of the city, isn't it?" Mr. Myers exclaimed. "Good to see you Mr. Matthews. I didn't realize you'd be so young. You've accomplished quite a bit for your age. I've just been reading your pedigree.

"Do you like my office? By the way, excuse me a moment, I've got an urgent call to the bathroom. Got the runs. Something I ate at a party last night. Be back in a minute."

Mike couldn't believe his informality. But it surely made him feel relaxed.

The office was enormous—approximately thirty by fifty. The desk was very modern, a single pedestal glass topped desk with one piece of paper on it. It was the brochure Mike had mailed.

To one side of the room was an inviting, casual sitting area with a spectacular view of the UN building and the river.

"I see you like my office," Mr. Myers said, "sorry to keep you waiting. I feel much better. Let me take a moment to show you part of our art collection here in my office.

"You'll note it's all impressionistic work by contemporary artists. U. S. Steel believes in supporting all of the Arts. Our company knows how to produce steel, but we need architects, engineers, and artists who are capable of good design, who reflect the best in shape, form and color.

"Let's sit here in this comfortable area overlooking the city, Mr. Matthews. Can I get you a cup of coffee or tea?"

"Coffee, black, would be fine."

"Now, tell me, Mr. Matthews, how is your development program going? We are somewhat familiar with Jefferson University. I've done a little research and discovered a number of our executives graduated from your University."

"I believe, Mr. Myers, that our program is making good progress. You know we have a half million dollar matching gift announced at our big kickoff banquet. We have almost met the goal. We also have plans to double our Alumni Giving base this fall."

"That all sounds promising," Mr. Myers replied. I'm glad to see you plan to challenge your alumni. We take a hard look at alumni commitment before we support a college."

"Yes, I know most corporations do, and legitimately so. I also believe, through the key Twin City leaders we have recruited for our Development Council, that we will receive some sizeable commitments from local business, industry and foundation sources."

"What specifically would you like U. S. Steel to do at this time?"

Mike took a quick sip of coffee, and slowly gulped before answering.

"Mr. Myers, it would be of tremendous assistance to Jefferson's move toward a higher level of excellence, as well as a focus on our returning service personnel, if U. S. Steel would pledge a matching gift of a million dollars toward a new science building which we need very badly."

Mike took another quick gulp and went on. "I know we could match those funds from other corporations or foundations and be in the ground with footings in the spring. The building would of course be appropriately named as you wished."

"I like your optimism, Mr. Matthews. Why don't you put your proposal in a formal detailed written form, when you get back to your campus. Get it to me as soon as possible. I won't make any promises, but I will review it carefully and present it to our board."

"Thank you, sir. It's been a pleasure meeting you. Thank you for your interest and time."

He walked out on air and felt as though he floated down the elevator.

Mike felt a need to talk with Bob at Princeton,   so he put in a call for him and fortunately he was in his dorm room, working on a paper.

"Bob, how are you pal?"

"Mike, where are you this time? Seems like you're always traveling, or are you on campus?"

"No, I'm in New York. I've had some great fund raising appointments. But I've got the rest of the day and tomorrow free. Have you got time to see me?"

"What do you mean have I got time to see you, Mike? You know we'll always have time for one another. How soon can you get here? The trains run pretty regularly to New Jersey."

"I'll catch the first one I can get and call you from the station when I get in. I'm anxious to hear about your doctorate work, and I have loads to share with you."

In no time, it seemed, Bob picked Mike up at the station and they were settled in his room for an overdue update on happenings in their lives.

"I have one more year of class work on my doctorate," Bob explained, "followed by a thesis and orals. That will qualify me for those three stripes on the black robe."

"What then?" Mike asked.

"Not sure. I may work as a minister in a small town or suburban mid-American church for a while. Ultimately, I think I would like to teach."

"How about you, Mike? From your letters and develop-ment mailings, it sounds like you're super busy and doing a great job. Have you given any more thought to being a minister?"

"Not really. I've been too busy to give it much thought. Also, Bob, I don't really feel qualified. There are so many other things I want to do as well. I need to learn, grow, experience life in many more facets before I would feel qualified to take on the minister role."

"I think that's commendable, Mike. However, you would make a hell of a minister. There's the flip side to your position also."

"What do you mean?"

"If you wait until you have all the knowledge and experience it could be too late. We all have to start someplace. There would be no surgeons, engineers, dentists, artists, scientists if everyone waited until they felt they knew it all."

"I see your point, Bob. I'll think about it. But one of the reasons I wanted to see you was to share something else that's been going on in my life."

"What's that? Don't tell me. You're in love!"

"Close! There is a lady to whom I'm strongly attracted. Her name is Jane Carroll. She's a beautiful person, physically and every other way. Jane was chairperson of the student division of my Development Council. We spent a fair amount of time together, though I never dated her."

"However, I felt there was some chemistry there, so we wrote back and forth a couple of times when she graduated and left for New York."

"What is she doing in New York?"

"She's an actress. She's in an off-Broadway play starring Henry Fonda. I saw the play. Left several messages for her and wanted very badly to spend an evening with her. Finally she called and we had lunch. She explained that the reason she hadn't returned my calls sooner was that she had a new telephone number. She just moved in with an actor boyfriend.

"I was crushed. But I feel there still might be hope for me. So I'm going to keep in touch.

"Well, Mike, you've never been known as one who gives up easily. Hang in there. Now, let's go have a beer and something to eat."

"What are we waiting for?"

Mike's overnight stay with his ex-roommate was terrific therapy.

The two of them had a stiff workout in the gym. They even managed a pick up touch football game on the commons. That produced some good laughs when they discovered how rusty they'd become.

Mike returned to New York and was able to wind up the balance of his corporate appointments with a flourish. He felt fortunate to close on promises of several additional capital gifts and faculty grants.

Before heading for the airport, he called Jane, thanked her for the time together at lunch and reminded her about keeping in touch.

The highlight of Mike's second fall as Jefferson U's VP was the Alumni telephone fund drive Phonorama.

The efforts produced over $100,000, more than double the amount of the previous year.

The balance of Mike's year flowed smoothly. His staff met the matching U. S. Steel million dollar grant from other corporate gifts, and by spring the new Science building was underway.

Chapter 12

Career II

Jefferson's next brick and mortar goal in its development program was a new sport's complex.

The architect's work was completed and Mike and his staff and volunteers raised five million dollars in three months.

A bonanza was the commitment of three million from one alumnus and his wife. The sport's complex would bear their names in tribute to their generosity.

It was an emotional moment for Mike when he was called upon at the dedication to unveil the marble placard listing Jefferson's service personnel killed in the war.

He was painfully aware that his dear friend Ernie's name was on the list.

With another of his goals for Jefferson completed, Mike realized he was ahead of schedule at his alma mater. The challenges and successes were exhilarating. He had traveled most of the country. Covered the alumni banquet circuit addressing Jefferson constituents and friends.

Mike knew he had only one major personal disappointment. Though he had visited over dinner with Jane when she played Chicago, he felt his chances with her slipping away. They seemed all but gone when he received a note from her saying she was engaged.

He called her immediately.

"Congratulations, Jane. I wanted to wish you happiness and good fortune."

"Thank you, Mike. You are the sweetest guy I know. Aren't you tied up yet? I'm going to have to go to work on that with my friends."

"Remember, Jane, I told you that if you could only be cloned . . . do you have plans for a wedding date?"

"No. We're not in any hurry. Getting engaged was probably more my idea. I'm sort of old fashioned. I got to the point where I wanted a commitment. Otherwise I felt it would be better for me to move out."

"Promise to keep your cards and letters coming, Jane. Please let me know when you go on the road again and where."

"I will, Mike. You're a favorite friend. I wish I could talk to you more often."

"Take care, Jane."

"Goodbye, Mike."

There wasn't much time to feel sorry for himself. The next day the President asked him to drop in at his office.

Mike was shocked when he was told, confidentially, that the President planned to resign and take early retirement.

He said he felt things were going so well since Mike's arrival that he could do what he'd wanted to do for a long time—step down, maybe travel, teach and do some writing. He told Mike that he thought it only fair that Mike be the first to know, but asked him to keep it private until he could meet with the Board of Governors.

Two weeks later, after the board had met, Mike got a call from the chairman, James Bradshaw. "Mike, would you be willing to have lunch with me this week."

"I'd be honored, sir."

"Could you meet in our corporate board dining room on Wednesday at noon?"

"Yes, I'm free then."

"Good, just take the elevator to the top floor, and I'll meet you there."

The lunch was delicious and graciously served. and the setting was elaborate and very private.

They were barely into their lunch when Mr. Bradshaw

said: "Mike, I am informed that you know about our president's intention to resign and take early retirement."

"Yes, he told me."

"I asked you to have lunch with me because the executive committee of the Board of Governors has authorized me to talk to you about becoming the next president of Jefferson."

"Really? That comes as a complete surprise. What an honor!"

"We realize you are young, Mike, but you are a distinguished graduate. You've done an amazing job on Jefferson's Development Program. You have four years of graduate work behind you. You'll need a doctorate eventually, of course. The faculty will require that. But we can pay for your additional education. It's a formality anyway. We'll see that you are awarded an honorary doctorate meanwhile. I'm sure we can persuade our president to stay another year or so while you complete your Ph.D work."

"I can't believe it. You're right. I really am young. Only twenty-six."

"Please don't give me your reactions now, Mike. But we'd be pleased if you would seriously think about it. We believe you have the drive, the personality, the leadership qualities we need."

All I can say is: "Thank you, Mr. Bradshaw. I appreciate what you've said. It's very flattering. I've just never thought of myself as a college president."

"We'd appreciate it, Mike, if you would keep this strictly private, for now. The Board, as you know, is going to meet again in two weeks. Perhaps we could get a feeling of your response by that time."

"OK. I'll honor the need for privacy, and do my best to have an answer for you in two weeks."

Those were the toughest two weeks Mike had ever had. He referred again and again to his guide for decision making.

He had a long talk with Bob. Unfortunately he couldn't get away even for a day. But he went for long walks early in the morning. He found the serenity of sunrise time conducive for meditating.

With the two weeks nearly up, Mike made an appointment with Mr. Bradshaw.

"Sir," he began, "you can't imagine how flattered I am to be considered for the Presidency of Jefferson. A big slice of my life is at this college. You've bestowed a tremendous honor on me."

"Definitely deserved, Mike."

"Thanks. It's not easy for me to tell you that after carefully evaluating my career goals, I must withdraw my name from consideration."

"I'm very sorry to hear that, Mike. Would you feel free to share your reasons with me? Is it money? We never discussed monetary terms. The Board, I am confident, would also work out an acceptable plan for study, travel and sabbaticals."

"It's nothing like that, Mr. Bradshaw. I was sure you'd be more than fair on all those fronts. You see, my decision has to do with a philosophy of career goals I have chosen for myself. I have a mind set, or major life purpose, slightly different than the ordinary."

"Do you feel like sharing that with me, Mike?"

"Yes, I've decided I'd like to spend my time in several different career chapters. This has been one of them here at Jefferson. My contribution to our returning service personnel, and the field of higher education, has been fulfilling for me. But, I feel my next career chapter should be in the field of business."

"As sorry as I am to hear that you won't consider the Presidency of Jefferson, Mike, I want to wish you well in whatever you decide to do. Have you considered anything specifically yet?"

"No. I have a few projects to finish at Jefferson first."

"Would you please talk to me before you make a final decision? I'd appreciate it."

"Sure I will. And thanks again."

A shift in careers came to Mike more quickly than he anticipated.

He and James Bradshaw were having lunch again following a chamber meeting.

"Have you any definite decision yet about your future career direction?" Mr. Bradshaw asked.

"No, I haven't," Mike replied. "But I think the time is getting close."

"You're absolutely sure about the University position?"

"Yes, I am."

"I'd like to talk with you then about an idea I have. I'd like you to consider a position with Bradshaw and Associates. As you know, I'm chairman of the Board and CEO. We like to move people to the top positions from within our company. One of these days I will be phasing out of the CEO position. It's no secret that my president will probably move up, and one of his assistants will replace him."

"Your company surely has a great reputation in this city, Mr. Bradshaw."

"I'd like you to be one of our Vice Presidents. I've had a good chance to observe you in action. I think you would be a good choice as the top executive in a new division of Public Affairs we're creating."

"Thank you, Mr. Bradshaw. That type of position could interest me."

"I'd like you to understand, Mike, that this could be a position from which you could move up the ladder in our company. What I would like to suggest, if you are interested, is that you set up an appointment with our president. He will fill you in on the job description, goals of the division, staff, budget and salary considerations."

It didn't take Mike long, after meeting with the president, to make his decision. He accepted the offer and joined the firm after taking two weeks to ensure a smooth transition in Jefferson's Development Program. Mike was able to continue to do many of the same things he was doing now in the community. Occasionally, he traveled to other parts of the country where the company's product was heavily marketed.

He assisted the advertising division in embellishing the company image. Originally the firm was founded as an international distributor of grain and by-products. However, like many other companies, it was involved in acquisitions including various special foods and restaurants.

Bradshaw and Associates also sponsored a variety of community activities. A number of strategic local, national and international events were supported financially. It was vitally important that the company be favorably represented at those events.

This was Mike's challenging and exciting job. He plunged in with the same energetic planning and dedication he had given to the Jefferson U position.

It was now his privilege, instead of asking for grants, to make decisions dispersing philanthropy. Normally, everything he proposed was approved by the Board.

He had a budget of one million dollars to administer annually. His division was responsible for determining criteria for support—events which would not only enhance the company image, but be of meaningful value to people.

The high visibility of Mike's position led to his receiving a distinguished surprise award. The Chamber of Commerce and TIME, the weekly news magazine selected him as "One of 100 Young Newsmakers of Tomorrow."

He was the only selection from Bradshaw and Associates. The media thoroughly covered the award. Naturally, he was tremendously flattered.

Mr. and Mrs. Bradshaw were his hosts at a formal banquet extravaganza on a beautiful spring evening in 1950 as the presentation was made.

As they were escorted to a table of honor the Bradshaws kidded Mike. "We thought surely you'd be arriving with a gorgeous date. How have you escaped?"

"I don't know," Mike replied. "Maybe I've been working too much." He realized it was kind of dumb for him not to have invited a date. However, there was no one he was attracted to, and his thoughts that evening were with Jane. She had called when she heard about the announcement.

He was thrilled to hear her voice. Jane wanted to know all about his new job. She told him her professional interests were now focused on upcoming TV and movie roles. The bombshell for him came when she announced: "Mike, I just got married. Imagine! Me married."

Mike almost choked.

"Congratulations, Jane. I hope you'll be very happy."

He tried to be upbeat and light. "Does that mean we can't correspond or see each other now and then?"

"Not at all, silly. You're one of my dearest friends."

Mike's continued visibility in the city, and across the country, led to some very interesting encounters. It was common knowledge that he had graduated from Emerson Seminary and had a Master's Degree in Theology.

Frequently, he was asked why he had chosen not to enter the ministry.

"It gave him a chance to share his ideas about vocation. He found that the business world included many men who were restless and unhappy with their careers.

The most important thing to a number of them was not how much money they made, but being happy and doing something they felt was truly worthwhile.

Oddly, more and more ministers were also contacting him about being dissatisfied in their profession. Bob, who was now teaching at Princeton seminary, referred one such minister to him. Mike agreed to an appointment with him.

"What can I do?" he asked. "All of my life I wanted to be a dedicated clergyman. I prepared well. I love people and want to be of help wherever I can.

"It would appear you've arrived at the top," Mike commented.

"I know. The minister of a city church. On radio and TV. Admired, respected. People flock to listen to my sermons. But I've had it. I can't be all the things they expect of me, I feel fractured. Splintered in all directions."

"Maybe you just need a vacation," Mike suggested.

"No, I'm tired of being on a pedestal. I'd like to try something else in life. But that's not considered acceptable in my church circles. If you leave the ministry, they think you're either sick, lost your faith or had an affair with the organist."

"It's not a sin" Mike reminded him, "to be something other in life than a clergyman. You know that. There are many other ways to serve God. I've heard you preach. I've heard you tell people that maybe their most effective way of serving God is to be a terrific parent, or to be a   farmer, factory worker, secretary, executive entrepreneur.

"Yes, of course I know that."

"Maybe this phase of your ministry is over," Mike continued. "Why don't you ask for a sabbatical. Teachers do. Ask for some time off. Get away and think about it. You might come back refreshed. Or maybe it's time for a change."

Some of the men who came to see Mike were tied up in knots over stress. A few were taking themselves too seriously.

He shocked one clergyman out of his chair when he said, "Mr., you will just have to learn how to say, 'F. . k it!'

"You can't be everything to everybody all the time. You're only human. Why don't you figure out what phases of the ministry you can do best. Is it teaching, counseling, preaching, youth work, calling at the hospitals, working with children? Decide on what it is. Train volunteers or hire someone else for the other duties."

"That makes sense."

"Take some regular time off," Mike went on. "Nobody can work ninety hours a week for long, at least. Spend more time with your wife and family. Let it be known that you're unavailable at certain times, except for dire emergencies.

"Lighten up. Have some fun. Get involved in some hobbies and sports. Live a more well rounded life such as you preach about. Practice being more human. Quit playing God. People may see the spirit of God more clearly in you if you are more genuinely human. Don't take yourself so seriously. Work at not being a solemn stuffed shirt. You'll be more approachable and believable.

"Maybe it wouldn't even hurt you to have a beer once in awhile. Go to a play, a concert, a movie. Take your wife to a motel with a pool and have a ball. You'll be a better minister. And remember one thing for sure, you can't please everyone."

Mike listened to another clergyman with a drinking problem. The man knew what to do as well as Mike did, and he was doing it—seeking help. So Mike got him connected to Alcoholics Anonymous, and the road to sobriety.

It was equally troubling to Mike to listen to the turmoil of a young returned veteran, turned minister, who bordered on a sexual addiction. He had never messed with a woman in his parish; but it was a constant temptation.

He was frustrated in his sexual relationship with his wife. "Not an excuse or a reason," he confessed. "I'm the problem.

"When I'm giving communion," he went on, "and this sexy gal with the low cut dress looks up at me with dreamy eyes I get turned on. I can't help it.

"Or, I meet a good looking woman at a social gathering, married or single. She's got a great figure. She seems to be making a play for me. I start imagining what she looks like without clothes on, and how I can get her into bed.

"Whenever I am in another city, after meetings or appointments, I go off alone looking for the nearest sauna. I can be anonymous there, and get laid. What am I going to do? Maybe I should leave the ministry."

"Maybe you should," Mike replied. "But not necessarily. There's nothing abnormal or wrong about a strong sex drive. Be thankful you're not chasing boys or little girls."

"It took a lot of courage for you to come and talk to me. You know, of course, that I will keep what you tell me in strict confidence. I'm not going to run off to your bishop or wife."

"I know that. You spoke with a friend of mine also and he told me I could trust you."

"Good. Incidentally, how about a little humor in this heavy conversation? Have you heard the story about the four preachers who went to a retreat?"

"No."

"Well, one was a Catholic Priest, another a Rabbi, the others a Presbyterian and a Lutheran. They were involved in this therapeutic sharing session where they were instructed to let it all hang out, even tell about their most horrible sins.

"The Priest started. 'I've never admitted this to anyone

before, but when I get off by myself I love wine and drink until I'm blotto.'

"'That's not so bad,' the Rabbi said, 'my greatest sin is lasciviousness. I covet the body of every sexy woman I see.'

"'I've never had those problems,' the Presbyterian chimed in, 'but I have fought all my life with something worse. It's caused me all kinds of problems. I've asked the Lord to help me, but I just can't conquer my sin.'

"'Well, what is it?' they all asked, 'maybe we can help you.'

"'When I lose my temper and get terribly angry I cuss and swear something awful.'

"Now it was the Lutheran's turn. 'Gentlemen, I empathize with you brothers. I also have a major fault. My sin is gossip, and I can hardly wait to get out of here.'"

Mike's new friend shared a good laugh with him. The story was so close to home.

"Seriously," Mike went on, "you guys in the ministry also need a minister, a counselor. You need at least one true friend you can let your hair down with and trust implicitly.

"From your counseling training at the seminary, you also know that the first step in solving a problem is to acknowledge to yourself and maybe another person that you have a problem."

"Yes, I know that, but we didn't have much counseling training at the seminary I attended. it seemed to be mostly classical theology, Latin, Greek, Hebrew and dogmatics. Very little about the human side of being a minister."

"That's a real shame," Mike acknowledged. "but I do have a couple of suggestions. I have a close friend who is one heck of a theological professor you could talk to. You can trust him. We roomed together at Emerson Seminary. He's about as down to earth as they come. His name is Bob Mackay.

"Here's his address and phone number. I'll tell him you may contact him. OK?"

"Thank you. I appreciate this very much."

"Another suggestion. You referred a few moments ago to a poor sex life at home. Have you ever considered it might be because you are a poor sex partner for your wife?"

"No, I have to admit I haven't."

"Have you ever really communicated openly with your wife about how you feel? Have you asked her if she is sexually satisfied, or if there is something you could do that she would enjoy sexually?"

"Not really."

"This could be a good start in solving your problem. Perhaps you aren't fulfilled sexually at home because you're not helping your wife to enjoy sex thoroughly."

"Does your wife have a vibrator?"

"Oh, no."

"You do know what a vibrator is, don't you?"

"Sure."

"If you don't I can tell you where to get one. But what I'm getting at is that so many of us men in our generation are amateurs about sexual technique. Not that technique is a substitute for respect, tenderness and caring.

"But so many of us tend to be so macho that we think all that matters to the woman is how big your penis is. So it's slam, bam, thank you ma'am. We get it off, but they don't.

"Do you know if your wife has ever had a true orgasm?"

"I think so."

"But you're not quite sure. You would be if she did. Talk about it. Ask her what she enjoys. The truth is it's not the penis inside, but the caressing outside, including her clitoris, which helps a woman to orgasm.

"What I'd like to do is recommend a terrific sex counselor to you. Your wife and you should both go. This counselor is a woman. You may think that would bother you, but it won't. She's old enough to be your mother and has all the clinical training, true caring and street smarts to help you. Here's her name and telephone number. Will you call her?"

"Definitely! I can't tell you how much you've helped me. Thank you."

The inner satisfaction Mike received from helping these troubled clergymen was more than worth the time and effort. He began to understand a little better what some modern day clergymen were struggling with. It also caused him to shy farther away from entering the profession himself.

Meanwhile, he was enjoying his public affairs position. Mr. Bradshaw kept repeating that he was grooming him for the presidency. It appeared that he wanted him to think seriously about a step up and be prepared when it became available.

That opportunity did not materialize.

Chapter 13

A Many Splendored Thing

At this time in his young life Mike felt a keen, almost mystical, awareness of crossroad.

It was akin to the sensation Robert Frost, the American poet, felt when he wrote about "two roads diverged in a wood." He wrote about "taking the one less traveled," and concluded "that has made all the difference."

"It was as though life is saying to me," Mike thought, "Once you are committed to being an earth being on a pilgrimage, you will be confronted with a paradox.

"You will discover that it is not the destination which is the primary objective. The destination will change. Like the horizon, you will never reach it.

"What is important is the journey, the creative search. You will constantly be challenged to explore, to ask questions, make choices.

"Along the way you will encounter opportunities to listen to the tales of others, to watch for the pageantry, the pathos, the harmony and discord. Your soul will expand. You will learn and grow. You will wander, pursue, face crossroads."

A crossroad for Mike came in the form of a request that he accept an appointment to a post in the federal government. He was asked to be the assistant director of the United States Information Agency.

In his position of Director of Public Affairs for Bradshaw and Associates, he had attracted the attention of his congressman as well as the mayor. It was they who said, "The appointment is yours if you wish it."

It didn't take Mike long to say, "Yes."

He resigned his company position. Received severance pay and additional paid vacation time.

Mike found it fascinating to go through the security check with the FBI. He was aware of the probe being conducted of all his past history including college, seminary, jobs, friends and associations.

He felt it was particularly interesting to spend a day at a federal building in Chicago being interviewed by a number of investigators.

He passed that test. Approval now had to come from a congressional committee. Fortunately, it was unanimous. Now all he had to do was wait.

Mike decided to take some of his severance pay and play golf in Florida. He had discovered that golf was one sport he could play despite a gimpy knee. He loved the exercise, competition, sociability and being surrounded by the changing elements of nature. It also was appealing to take lessons and practice when time didn't permit playing. As a result he was down to a six handicap.

Mike took off for West Palm Beach. Played a number of courses there. Then moved up the coast to Stuart and Port St. Lucie. He entered a Pro Am tournament at Stuart Country Club, and fell in love with that area. Fewer people, not as many high-rises. Fabulous access to boating and fishing on both the ocean and intercoastal.

Most important, he was enjoying the people he was meeting. Was making some good friends with men who were fun to be around and loved the game as he did.

Most of them were not tourists, but local businessmen who had migrated to Florida. A few were native Floridians. They all were married, owned lovely homes, and were financially successful in a variety of enterprises.

Mike found himself thinking, "What a perfect place to live, get involved in some business. Spend the winters here, maybe nine or ten months, and have a summer home in New

England or even Hilton Head."

One evening when he returned to his rental condo and picked up forwarded mail, he recognized the handwriting on the pale blue envelope. It was from Jane.

He tore it open.

Dear Mike,

Writing to tell you that my marriage is over. My divorce was final yesterday. I am devastated. It is so painful, although I realize it is for the best.

I realize no divorce is caused totally by one person; but my husband developed a drinking and drug problem. It was a nightmare. When he was sober he was adorable. But when he was on pills and liquor it was like Jekyl and Hyde. He became violent and abusive.

I tried to help him. Pleaded that he seek help, that we go together to a counselor. It went on for over a year. I couldn't cope any longer. Thank God we didn't have children.

Mike, you've always been such a good friend. If you feel like it, could you call me? I need to talk to you. I feel lost, such a failure. How could I be so stupid to make such a mistake?

Fondly,
Jane

Mike called her immediately. "Jane, I just got your letter. It was forwarded."

"Where are you?"

"Florida."

"On business?"

"No, believe it or not, I'm just playing."

"That's different for you, Mike. Seems like you're usually working. Thanks for calling. This has been such a traumatic time, but I'm feeling better. Fortunately, I've had a chance to get some variety into this heavy scene, because I'm in between contracts."

"Jane, I'm sorry about the tough time you've been through. But, I just got a great idea which might be helpful."

"What is it?"

"I'm taking some time off between jobs. It's a long story. Tell you later. I've got this beautiful condo I'm renting on the beach near Stuart, Florida. Why don't you hop on a plane tomorrow for West Palm. It's not far. I'll pick you up. We can spend a few days together just having fun and talking. It'll do you good. You can share some of your trauma with a good friend."

"That's really neat of you, Mike. Are you sure you want to take on old sad face. I don't want to intrude on your good time."

"You won't be intruding. You love the sun and the beach, don't you?"

"Sure."

"Well, we'll go for long walks on the beach, swim, snorkel, and surf. We can go out for dinner in the evening. They have some great restaurants and super fresh seafood. We'll have time to talk about both our futures. I told you I'm also at a major change in my life."

"You're making it hard to turn down, Mike. I just don't want to interfere with your plans. I know how much you like to play golf. I do too, but I'm not very good at it."

"That's OK, Jane. I've been playing thirty-six holes a day. Made some great friends. I'll still get in a round or two. You'll want some time to yourself anyway."

"Incidentally, where am I going to stay?"

"I'll give you a choice, Jane. I've got an extra bed here in the condo. You can have complete privacy. Or I'll get an ocean front room for you in the motel down the road."

"OK, Mike, we can talk about that when I arrive."

"Great! That means you're coming?"

"You talked me into it. Give me your number. I'll call you back as soon as I get booked. You say I fly into West Palm?"

"Yes, you should be able to get a direct flight from New York."

"It's going to be so good to see you, Mike. Thanks."

Mike was so excited he hardly slept that night, thinking about all the fun times they were going to have. What a bonanza," he thought. Jane and I together, maybe for a week.

Nothing but leisure, sunshine, beach, surf and time to learn to know one another better.

"Who knows? "Perhaps there's still a chance for a romance between Jane and me."

Before he left for the airport the next morning, he got another phone call which almost sent him into shock.

It was his congressman friend calling to tell him that the appropriations bill to expand the United States Information staff had been voted down. His appointment was canceled.

The congressman was angry, embarrassed and bitterly disappointed, but there was nothing he could do about it. Some votes he had been promised didn't materialize.

So that was the end of a wonderful dream for Mike. To live in Washington. Learn some of the inside working of the federal government. Travel extensively. Meet fascinating people from all over the world. Hopefully, have an impact, however small, on the course of American postwar development in the fifties.

"So be it," he thought. "I'm not going to let it get me down. There are other opportunities, perhaps right here in Florida. I'll think about that later. Meanwhile I've got a fabulous week to look forward to."

The meeting between Jane and Mike at the airport was magnetic. The minute their eyes met there were intense vibes between them. She looked so fragile, but attractive as ever.

They gave each other a long friendship hug and a kiss on the cheek. Then it was off for the condo and the beach.

The minute Jane saw the condo there wasn't a choice.

"This is gorgeous, Mike. What a view! I can hardly wait to go for a swim and sun on the beach. If you're sure you wouldn't mind, I'd love to stay right here."

"Be my guest. Here's your room. Make yourself at home, and as soon as you're ready we can run right out the patio door and ride the surf."

The next days and nights were the most romantic Mike had ever known. They talked and shared. Laughed and cried, touched and danced.

In one week he was more intimate with Jane than he had ever been with any woman—mainly because each of them could be their own person with the other. They didn't feel a need to hide anything.

They felt equal. No one dominated. There were no games to play, no roles to fit. They were two people exploring each other.

By the end of the week, there was the feeling they were falling in love. They shared the sensation that love can be whimsical and temperamental. It seems to come when it pleases and fades away without warning.

They talked about how love comes and goes, perhaps times without number. But when it comes, they agreed, they should enjoy it and not be concerned about its departure.

They discovered that love between a man and woman is one of life's greatest experiences.

Jane and Mike felt drawn into intimate communion, not only with one another, but with the Infinite Presence—the Giver of love and life.

When the week was over they said goodbye at the airport, but knew it was only temporary. They sensed that their lives were now intimately and indelibly interwoven.

They had a lot of catching up to do. There were quick notes, and long letters. Mostly, there were long "getting to know you better" telephone conversations.

Jane was about to begin rehearsals for a TV play. They agreed that as soon as those rehearsals were finished, which should be in about a month, they would see one another again. This time, perhaps in New York.

Mike had told Jane about the fall through of the USIA appointment. She had also met a couple of his new friends in Florida, and encouraged him to look into business opportunities with them.

"One thing for sure," Mike thought, "my holiday is over. Time to get back to work."

Mr. Bradshaw heard about the USIA budget cut, and offered Mike's job back. But he felt it was time to move on.

Now that Jane and he were close, he was motivated more than ever to move into a business enterprise which was long term. More and more he was leaning toward an opportunity where he could own and manage his own business.

That opportunity came one day as he was talking with one of his golf buddies after a match. Dan Adams and Mike sat alone in the grill having a beer.

"Have you ever thought about the land development and contracting business, Mike?"

"No, I confess I haven't," Mike answered.

"That's what I do," Dan went on. I'm a third generation owner. The business has been good to me. It's fascinating, demanding and rewarding. We are probably entering into one of the most lucrative periods ever for land development and building in the state of Florida. Why don't you give it some thought, Mike?"

"It sounds like something I'd like to do. But what do I know about land and construction?"

"I can teach you. It's not that difficult to get started. You don't need to know how to build buildings. You hire professionals to do that—architects, engineers, field superintendents."

"You also need a good attorney firm, a top notch CPA, a major bank, and perhaps a joint venture investor. Above all, you must be a good manager of people, a selfstarter able to make tough decisions, and willing to put in long hours."

"I think I can do that."

"I'll tell you what I'll do, Mike. We could use another capable man in our firm right now. You seem to get along well with people. You appear to have moxie and street smarts. You certainly have a good education. Why don't you take a position with us for six months. Consider it an apprenticeship.

"Get your Broker's Real Estate and Securities licenses during off hours. The pay won't be huge, but it'll be adequate. After six months, if you want to stay in our firm and move up, fine. If you want to go on your own—our blessings."

"That's a fantastic offer, Dan. How much time do I have to think about it?"

"As much as you want. But I have a hunch you're the type who makes up your mind pretty fast."

"I usually do. But I have a very dear lady friend I'd like to discuss this with. I'm going to New York to see her this weekend."

It was April. Mike recalled the dramatic magic about spring in New York. Flowering trees, daffodils, tulips waving a colorful farewell to icicles and brown grasses. The plaintive cries of song birds welcoming newness of life. Even the Statue of Liberty seemed to have a smile on her face."

Jane and Mike shared their own magic also. She was free from rehearsals for the weekend. They joined the joggers in Central Park. Took the harbor ferry boat ride. Held hands at a favorite sidewalk cafe. Talked late into the night. Made love as though there were no tomorrow.

Over a romantic candlelight dinner at an intimate walk-up French restaurant, they talked about their career futures.

Jane's agent was trying to convince her to move to Hollywood. He said her future would be more promising there. "It's not clear to me what I should do," Jane admitted.

"I love the stage, but my teacher also feels I'll have many more opportunities in Hollywood. But New York is like home to me. You know my parents were both killed in a car accident when I was a sophomore in college, and I'm an only child. So my remaining family is an aunt and a cousin whom I don't know very well.

"I'd also be so much farther from you, Mike, if you decide to settle in Florida. You're leaning that way aren't you?"

"As you know, Jane, I've been offered this apprenticeship, I call it, in the development-contracting business."

"What a beautiful part of Florida, Mike. I love it. How do you feel about the company and the people you'd be associated with?"

"As far as I can tell, the firm is very successful, and has an excellent reputation. Most importantly to me, the people I would be working with are skilled, experienced and professionals with integrity."

"I suppose you've done some checking on them. You can be sure they've checked into your background."

"Yes, I spoke with a prominent banker who is not associated with their bank. I also talked with a couple of city managers as well as the executive director of the county General Contractor's Association. Also Dan Adams is on the Board of The National Organization. A contractor must have an impeccable record to serve on that board."

"Sounds good to me, Mike. Why don't you go for it?"

"I think that's what I should do, now that I have talked with you about it. I needed your reaction. Hope you'll come and visit me as often as possible."

"Try to keep me away. I love you very much. As soon as they finish shooting this TV program I could visit for a few days. Meanwhile, you can work hard, do your license courses and save yourself just for me."

Mike packed into the next six months a wealth of information and experience.

He took a crash course at the University of Miami and got his real estate and securities licenses. He met with city planners and planning commission members. Also attended a few public hearings.

Surveyors, engineers and architects taught him about land use plans, zoning ordinances and variances. He learned about building specifications, bid taking and negotiating contracts with subcontractors.

He was taught, on the job, about critical path scheduling of construction, quality control and inspections. He rubbed shoulders with the various trades people, and worked with interior designers and decorators.

He was especially intrigued by the marketing experts with Dan Adam's company, and spent time in their sales models. He also met with Dan's bankers and received a short course in "up front financing," "short term construction financing," and the "long term" mortgaging of property.

Finally, he observed attorneys, closers and title personnel working with buyers, and renters of homes and commercial buildings.

He discovered how rental properties could be built, or purchased, and sold for sizeable capital gains with significant tax write-offs. All under the umbrella of General-Limited Partnership syndications.

As Mike's six months apprenticeship came to a close, he realized there was an enormous amount of knowledge and experience yet to acquire. However, he also felt he had received the equivalent of a college education plus internship in this compact span of a few months.

Now it was decision time.

"Here I am," he thought, "at another major career cross-roads.

"Should I accept a lucrative offer from Dan's firm? Or, should I strike out on my own?"

Jane and Mike discussed this on the phone. She also was facing her major choice—stay in New York, or move to Hollywood.

Both of their decisions fell into place so simply. It was Christmas, their first together. They decided to treat themselves to a trip to St. Thomas.

They found a beautiful villa on the beach. Bought a miniature Christmas tree, and did their shopping with the tourists off the tour ships. Swam, danced and absorbed the sun.

A special treat was a Christmas Eve candlelight service of carols in a small native church. They sang "Hark the Herald Angels Sing" to the rhythmic beat and stomping feet of fellow worshippers.

Christmas Day was paradise. They had made arrangements to lease a thirty-two foot boat with captain and mate and go sailing.

The day was spectacular. The winds were gentle. The fluffy, white cumulus clouds occasionally turned to blue-gray and honored them with a gentle cooling shower.

They never left sight of land. Each new island was more beautiful than the last. At noon the captain anchored in a peaceful lagoon, while Jane and Mike snorkeled among millions of rainbow colored fish and magnificent coral. All too soon, the bell was sounding for lunch.

What a lunch! A gourmet meal prepared by the captain's girlfriend, and licensed mate. Champagne with fresh squeezed orange juice. The most marvelous fresh ocean fish they had ever tasted. The meal topped off with bananas foster—all prepared in the tiny galley.

How could life get any better? Unless it was the lazy afternoon in mirror image of the morning.

As they docked, it was sunset time—a ball of fire silently fading into a symphony of ocean, and a horizon followed by encores of delicate pinks, golds and reds.

Their souls were radiant with a reverence for life.

"Let's not go anywhere this evening," Jane suggested. "Why don't we stop at the resort deli and pick up some shrimp, cheese and a bottle of wine, and snack in our own cozy villa?"

"Sounds wonderful," Mike agreed.

"We could turn on some background Christmas music, light some candles and bask in the wonder of this day. I'm so happy, Mike. I feel so grateful and nostalgic. Besides, I have a small gift I'd like to give you."

The setting couldn't have been more romantic. Jane had found the most beautiful card designed by a native St. Thomas artist.

Inside she wrote, "Mike, since you've entered my life, I am a different person. That first week we were together in Florida I was guilt-ridden, struggling with failure over my divorce. You helped me accept that there's nothing more I could have done. With your help I got my feeling of self-worth back."

"Jane, believe me, I received more from you than I gave."

"You entered my life, Mike, when I felt like a fragile bird of the sea. Wounded and in pain. You helped me heal. Even the scars are gone. I'm able to soar and sing. Thank you. I love you."

Inside her gift box was a gold chain and pendant—a beautifully crafted, flattened, irregular gold piece. Attached, as in the foreground of a cloud, was a tiny gull in full flight.

"Jane, thank you. I'll treasure this forever. I love it, and more than ever I love you. But how did you sneak away from me long enough to find this marvelous surprise?

"That was easy. Remember, yesterday when I said I'd like to shop for some cologne and that probably wouldn't interest you?"

"Oh, that was it?"

"Well, Jane, I did a little shopping also when we split with the tourist crowds around. I had seen something in a shop window that I wanted to go back and look at. I like it, and more importantly I hope you will, because it's my gift to you."

With that he reached into his garment bag and extracted a gift wrapped box about 8" x 6" x 4".

"I didn't have time to get a special card. I saw you coming down the street and the clerk and I just barely got it wrapped and bagged. But it comes to you with my love, now and always."

Mike felt he was more excited than Jane as she opened the outer box, and found a smaller one inside cushioned by the confetti. It took just a moment, and there it was—a ring with a single diamond.

Her eyes started misting over in harmony with a cry of sheer joy. "Oh, Mike, is this what I think it is?"

They were in each other's arms hungrily seeking the moistness of their lips in union.

"My darling Jane, I'm hoping you'll marry me. I love you, want you, need you—to spend our lives together."

"You know how much I love you, Mike. I'm the happiest woman alive. Please just hold me for now. Oh, Yes! I want to be with you always."

"That makes my career decisions simple, Jane. Now that we'll be Mr. and Mrs. (though we agreed you'll retain your maiden stage name, Jane Carroll) I'll definitely go into business for myself."

"Wonderful, Mike! And I can commute, for the present, from New York."

"Let me refill our wine glasses," Mike replied. "Here's to us, Jane. Our first home together in Florida. Years of happiness . . . and a wonderful marriage."

"I'll drink to that," Jane answered.

Chapter 14

I Do!

Jane and Mike were married six months later in the floral decorated chapel at Emerson Theological Seminary. Jane had just turned twenty-five, and Mike but a half-dozen months from the magic number of thirty.

Following a champagne brunch celebration, the new Mr. and Mrs. Matthews drove to Mt. Desert Island, Bar Harbor, Maine.

Their honeymoon was storybook. A room in a quaint bed and breakfast overlooking the ocean. From white wicker lounge chairs on the porch, they enjoyed sunsets and returning heavily loaded fishing boats. A one day ferry excursion to Nova Scotia was memorable.

They went bike riding. Hiked in Acadia National Park. Toured the peninsula to Northeast and Seal Harbors. Attended the dinner theatre at Boothbay Harbor where Jane knew two members of the cast.

One golden, sunny afternoon, following wild strawberry picking, the honeymooners lay on a blanket at Cove Beach.

Embraced by a gentle breeze, the magnificent glacial coastline, and the shadow of Mt. Cadillac, they reminisced about their wedding and career decisions for the immediate future.

"I loved our private ceremony, Mike," Jane exuded. "I'm so grateful that Ashley Martin could be my Maid of Honor. She's been a good friend. We've been in a couple of plays together, as you know."

"Yes. She's a likeable, talented person," Mike replied. "I admired her ability in the one performance I saw where you were together. Also she and Judy had fun catching the bridal bouquet."

"Does Judy have prospects of marriage in the near future, Mike?"

"Not that I'm aware of. My sister is dedicated to teaching for the moment. She's working on her doctorate at the University of Wisconsin. But she's only twenty-seven—plenty of time."

"It was a treat for me to get to know Bob Mackay better too, Mike. I can see why he was your best man and closest friend. He's got a full professorship at Princeton Seminary now hasn't he?"

"Yes. He's a true scholar, but also street smart and down-to-earth. His students are lucky.

"By the way, Jane, didn't my dad do well. He tends to get long winded sometimes, but he kept it short, and I've never seen him happier.

"Yes, he was a sweetheart. And I love your mother, Mike. She was so cute when we said goodbye. Remember she told you: 'Take good care of her, Mike. You're a lucky man. Be as patient and loving as your father has been to me and you'll have a wonderful, happy life together.'"

"She's absolutely right," Mike responded. "And she said something else to you, Jane, which I didn't catch. I was kidding with Dad and Bob at the time."

"Oh! We talked about how she always calls you Michael and she told me how she had pledged your life to God. You've told me about that. She said: 'I always thought Michael would serve God in a church, like his father, and maybe he will. But Michael has helped me see other possibilities also.

"'He's already left behind some impressive footprints serving God in other ways. I know his business can be another way. I've learned that there are different ways of serving.'

"I agree with you, Mom," I told her. "I hope you don't mind that I call you 'Mom'."

"What did she say?"

"She said, 'I'd consider it an honor. I hope you will.'"

"To change the subject, Mike. I can hardly wait to see our beautiful new home."

"Isn't it going to be exciting," Mike replied. "It should be completed by tomorrow when we return. The interior designer you chose should have the basic furnishings in place."

"We were so lucky, Mike, "to have first choice in those fifty lots you contracted for with Dan Adams. And your architect did a beautiful job of minor redrafts of the floor plan.

"I'll have a chance to get us cozily settled in, before I return to New York for my last play commitment. For the present at least."

"I'll miss you, Jane, but I know how important it is for you to continue your career for awhile and as we agreed, I'll visit New York two or three times. You can commute home once every other week and pretty soon the summer will be over and we'll be together.

"Besides, I'm champing at the bit to get on with my business. You know it's going to be called "MATTHEWS ENTERPRISES, INC. with four divisions: Development; Construction; Marketing and Property Management; and Syndications.

"Before I left, I was able to select a real estate attorney, a CPA, architectural and engineering firm. I also appointed a vice president in charge of construction and linked up with a prominent bank. So MATTHEWS ENTERPRISES, INC. here we come."

Before Mike became too enmeshed in the maze of corporate details he wrote a credo for his company.

There was no doubt in his mind that he would make a great deal of money so his vocational ethic led him to define some ground rules in handling wealth, compatible with his primary life focus.

Mike felt the order and majesty of the universe cries out for the pursuit of excellence in any worthwhile endeavor.

He remembered a statement by a contemporary theologian by the name of Reinhold Niebuhr. From his continued reading of philosophy and theology since the seminary, he recalled a paraphrase from this writer:

"Nothing is worth doing that can be achieved in a lifetime; Nothing which is true or beautiful or good makes complete sense in the immediate context of time; Nothing we do, however virtuous can be accomplished alone . . ."

Mike believed that there is a higher consciousness and a Divine energy "which enables us to achieve." He believed "None of us succeeds alone. We are part of a passing parade.

"The past," he felt, "has contributed to our present opportunities. The people around us, family, friends and those with whom we work and love are vital to our accomplishments."

Naturally, as he stood on the threshold of a promising business career, Mike was aware of the words etched in the fiber of his soul from childhood by his mother.

"Michael Charles Matthews, you are destined to be a servant of God."

He felt he could indeed be a servant of God at this time, in this place, in this profession. He was determined to perform with pride and dignity in a role, thought by many to be slightly lower than a used car salesperson, to the benefit of people he served.

Therefore, Mike's credo included five basic principles: (1) Strive to give to all clients a quality of service in excess of payment received. (2) Treat employees, colleagues, and staff personnel with respect, fairness and consideration as members of the team, not as servants. (3) Reach for the highest levels of excellence in the treatment of land and its enhancement, with sound, useful and beautiful structures. (4) Because we are trustees, not landlords on this planet, reinvest in society in proportion to corporate prosperity a measure of time, service and dollars. (5) Practice not only the Golden Rule: "Do unto others as you would have others do unto you," but also the silver rule: "Don't let anyone do to you what you would not do to them."

Dan Adams drilled his "Silver Rule" into Mike during his apprenticeship.

He told him:

"This is a tough business. You should be fair, but you don't have to be a patsy. You are a person with dignity; therefore there is no virtue in letting people walk all over you or cheat you.

"Some will try. When that happens you'll have to do the same thing you did when you ran with the football in college— use a stiff arm".

"This proved to be one of the toughest lessons Mike had to learn.

The Credo of MATTHEWS ENTERPRISES, INC. was prominently displayed in the reception area of the offices. An attractive printed reproduction was shared with each new client and employee.

Mike also took an active role in the Chamber of Commerce, the local and state Contractor's Association, and the local Rotary Club. He also joined the country club where he had played as a guest of Dan's.

Selecting a church was an interesting experience. Jane and he ruled out the older, established, prestigious "name" churches and opted for a young nonsectarian community church.

He made a point of not disclosing that he had a Master's Degree in Theology. It was important to him to be accepted as a fellow human being in need of spiritual growth and expression, not for any label or pedigree.

He and Jane volunteered to be advisors to the church's youth program. When the kids learned that Jane was THE Jane Carroll, whom they had seen on TV, they were really impressed and couldn't wait to meet her.

The opportunity came very shortly. Jane came down for one of her commutes during the summer; and they partied with the teen group at a Saturday night pool and barbecue party as guests of one of the parents.

They all got a chance to get acquainted. But Jane was the star attraction.

"What was it like to be on the stage and TV? How is it living in New York? Do you think you'll ever go to Hollywood?"

Jane was bombarded with questions, but she enjoyed it. Everyone had a fun evening, and Jane and Mike felt good about gaining the confidence of the kids.

Mike managed to get away for two short weekends in New York. Otherwise he worked sixteen hour days developing his business.

He hired a mature woman, with a broker's license as an executive assistant. He also found a man with ten years experience in real estate sales to be his marketing director.

In addition, he established a line of credit, and purchased an outstanding piece of land with access to the inland waterway.

His purchase agreement included eighty acres with the possibilities of mixed zoning ranging from single family to medium and high density. He also had an option on one hundred more acres adjoining.

Mike's architect's firm did a feasibility study on the land. Results showed that population growth, combined with economic predictions and housing needs, would support three 100-unit apartment buildings and approximately the 150 homes for which the property was platted.

Following preliminary approval of financing from his bank, Mike proceeded with working drawings for the three story apartment buildings. Simultaneously, earth moving and grading work began followed by installation of sewer, water and utilities.

Landscapers developed an impressive, inviting entrance to the property. They also built two miniature lakes with fountains, a playground, two swimming pools, tennis courts, and a hiking trail.

Meanwhile, construction crews built an attractive apartment model which doubled as the sales office for both the rental units and custom homes.

Within weeks MATTHEWS ENTERPRISES, INC. was underway with the first apartment building. It was rented up before it was half finished. So the second and third buildings were started immediately.

The profits in the apartments were incredible. Largely because of appreciated land values reflected in the appraisals, the company was able to borrow 110% of the projected actual cost. The extra 10% amounted to approximately $150,000 per building on the profit and loss statement.

In addition, rents produced a handsome annual cash flow after servicing principle, interest, taxes and maintenance-management costs.

By the end of twelve months on the project, the three buildings were completed and 98% rented. The head of marketing and his associates had also sold seventy-five custom home building jobs.

The cashflow seemed enormous, and was. Mike's accounting firm told him he had already netted over $350,000. Nearly $500,000 was projected for the following year. It was almost embarrassing. Especially knowing that his dear friend, Bob Mackay, was only making $8,000 a year as a Ph.D professor.

Bob had two more years of education than Mike did. They were about the same age—just turned thirty in prosperous America, 1953.

It was time for a party and some thanksgiving.

Jane and Mike hosted the corporate staff, subcontractors, tradespeople, architects, engineers and key city professionals. A marvelous party was held at the country club.

After dinner and dancing there was just one speech, setting a record for brevity.

"I want to thank everybody for your contribution," Mike said, "and your hard work, and loyalty. I'm also announcing a bonus and profit sharing plan for employees to begin immediately.

"MATTHEWS ENTERPRISES, INC. will also grant an automatic salary increase for any employee who turns in a record of educational course work designed for self-improvement or work enhancement. You're a great team. I hope we have a long association together."

Privately, Jane and Mike initiated planning with their attorney firm to establish a foundation for their personal benevolent giving program. To begin with, they settled on a scholarship program for first year college or trade school students.

"How about having our very own first year student, Mike?" Jane just slyly slipped the question into their quiet time at dinner one evening.

"Jane! you're not kidding me, are you? I know you've missed a period."

"No. I went to the doctor today, and he's reasonably sure I'm pregnant. And Mike, I'm thrilled. I want this baby very much. As you know I'm in between contracts, so I plan to tell my agent not to book me until after the baby is born. I'll probably just retire then, except for an occasional commercial which I could shoot in Miami."

Mike was in ecstasy.

"Just think, a child. Me a father."

He couldn't wait to call Bob and his parents.

"What are you thinking Jane," he asked, "a boy or girl?"

"Oh, I would like a little girl, but I'll settle for an ornery little kid like you were, Mike, as long as he's healthy!"

"Sweetheart, now we've got to take extra special good care of you and get that nursery ready."

The next months flew by for Mike. He was so turned on by the thrill of becoming a father, and the challenges and accomplishment in his business. New personnel were being added, and he exercised the option on the one hundred additional acres of land.

However, for Jane time understandably dragged. In addition to her discomfort, Mike could tell she missed New York and her career.

"Why don't you fly up there and visit Ashley," he suggested. "We certainly can afford it. I'll miss you, but I would think that would be fun for you. See some friends, go to some plays. You might even enjoy doing some shopping for junior."

"I'd like that, Mike. Maybe you could join me for one trip."

"Let's plan on it. I'd love to celebrate an anniversary of

our springtime in New York."

"They did just that. Had a nostalgic time revisiting some of their favorite places. Jane managed two other visits. It performed magic for her morale.

Fortunately, Jane's health was perfect and she appreciated the conveniences they could afford, as well as patterns of cooperation they agreed on for their marriage. They had a cleaning person once a week., and Mike shared in the household chores.

Knowing that special times in a marriage just don't happen, Jane and Mike also set a goal of trying to have evening dinner as often as they could. If they ate at home, instead of going out, frequently Mike would bring something home from the deli.

This was an intimate time. Telephones answered strictly by the recorder. No interruptions. No business discussions.

This was their private time for personal communication, and they vowed that as much as possible they would strive for this goal as a family when children were included.

Jane and Mike also came to some other agreements. Jane would manage her own bank account, not just for the home and living expenses, but for herself personally.

They also decided that at least one evening a week would be their special evening together, even after they had children. They talked about priorities, and agreed that the marriage came first and a child or the family second.

Jane, wisely, made arrangements in advance for a very reliable lady to be with the baby one day a week so she could have that day for herself. Mike also said that he would enjoy some private time with their child, so during those times Jane could also do her own thing.

What a fantastic thrill it was the night that Jane gently shook Mike awake about one AM.

"Mike, I think it's time. The contractions are coming close together. My overnight bag is packed. I think we'd better head for the hospital."

"I'll call the doctor, Jane, and we'll be on our way."

It was a long tough delivery, and Mike was a typical father. Felt so helpless. Stayed in the room as long as they allowed him to. Smoked a pack of cigarettes in the waiting room.

Finally it was over and Mike was ushered into Jane's room by the nurse. Jane, though exhausted, looked as beautiful to him as ever.

Cradled in her arm was their son.

"Jane, are you OK?"

It was just a whisper, but there was a big grin on her face.

"Yes, I'm so grateful, and very proud. Michael Charles Matthews meet your son Scott Michael."

They had agreed on the name for a boy. Their choice for a girl was going to be Teresa Jane.

Chapter 15

It's A Boy! . . . It's A Girl!

"How does one prepare for parenthood," Mike wondered? "Read books? Take courses? Talk to other parents? I suppose all of the above helps. Actually, there is no substitute for experience."

Jane was a devoted mother. Her dedication was inspiring to Mike. He took occasional turns at diaper changing and bottle time, but it was Jane who was the pro.

In no time, it seemed, Scott was walking and saying his first words. It was about that time Jane and Mike made a startling discovery. The books were right about the "terrible twos".

The inquisitive mind—the relentless determination to explore—perpetual energy during waking hours. Then so innocent and sweet, cuddled with a blanket, at night and nap times.

Jane and Mike planned to have a second child in about two years. They reasoned that Jane could concentrate her mothering on two almost as well as one and they thought a playmate for Scott would also be wise.

This time, they definitely hoped it would be a girl. No way! They kidded about Scott being such a strong personality that he got his order in first for a brother.

A brother it was—Dane Charles. As beautiful a child as any parent could hope for. And so different. More placid. Almost never crying. Patient for his bottle, and very soon sleeping through the night. Content to fit into his brother's "grown-out-of-hand-me-downs."

"Aren't we the luckiest parents alive?" Jane whispered as she and Mike stood with arms around one another in the boy's room at night. The little twosome were long gone into dream land.

Something happens to a man when he becomes a father, Mike discovered. He is proud. Afraid. Grateful, but also in awe of the enormous responsibilities.

Thus, Jane and Mike began thinking about parenting goals.

One weekend evening, while having a private dinner at the club, Jane suggested, "Why don't we talk about our objectives as parents. We could try to formulate them in writing. I'll start."

"Wonderful, Jane," Mike replied. "Let me get a piece of paper and pen from our waiter, and we can record our notes. What should be number one?"

"Above all," Jane began, "I would hope our children will feel loved without being smothered and over controlled."

"I agree, Jane. I remember some of the lessons I learned from a hunting mentor, when I was a boy. As he and I stood quietly in the woods watching, the wood ducks pushed their young out of the nest when they were ready to fly and face the world. 'There, Mike,' my friend said, 'is one of the most perfect examples of parental love in nature.'"

"I hope we can be good teachers for our children," Jane responded.

"Hopefully, we have learned something about life, Jane. Subconsciously, I find myself praying that we can take the best knowledge of past generations and apply it to the present."

"At least you got to know your parents, Mike. My parents have been gone now more than half my life."

"I know how rough that was for you Jane. In my case, my parents struggled with being poor. It was totally beyond their control.

"I do hope that our children can be more comfortable materially than I was."

"But not spoiled," Jane added. "And not take possessions for granted. Not identify things exclusively with happiness. Learn to be grateful, to share and care about others."

"I couldn't agree more with you."

"Here's another suggestion for our list, Mike."

"In order to have even a remote shot at our ideal, I believe our children should learn to work, not only play. To deprive them of this opportunity would be terribly selfish I feel. So let's vow, Mike, that we will help them to stretch for high accomplishments, and take the pride in achievements."

"Perfect. I've been thinking about another important goal, Jane. I think we should help our children learn to know themselves. Their own very personal uniqueness. Acquire a deep feeling of self esteem, without attitudes of bigotry or superiority."

"So important, Mike. I agree. I also think we need to be good listeners for our children. I hope that we can help them feel secure in talking with us about anything, without being criticized or condemned, but understood."

"Agreed," Mike replied. "We've got quite a list to live up to, don't we?"

"I'd like to suggest one more," Jane added. "I'd like us to help our children to discover their right of freedom of choice. Somewhere in my reading about parenthood, I recall this statement: 'The chief responsibility of parenthood is to assist your children in becoming self-reliant.'"

"I hope we can accomplish our goals," Mike replied. "At least have a good win-lose record."

A very down to earth realization which fatherhood gave Mike was a sense of economic responsibility. The need to make money to pay for clothes, doctors, dentists, toys, sitters, books, lessons, sports equipment, college tuition, cars.

So, without a break in stride, following the birth of Dane, Mike plunged with increased zest into his business.

Approval came through for the one hundred acre plat. It was divided in approximate equal thirds between high density residential, medium density and single family homesites.

The high density plans were nearing completion for twin ten story towers of luxury condominiums overlooking the ocean. Architects were also working on plans for villas and townhomes—some with direct access to the intercostal.

Mike's Marketing people were constantly working with clients on custom homes.

Grading, utilities, and magnificent security type landscaped entrances were almost completed. A marina on the inland waterway was on the drawing boards. Lots were being staked for the homesites. Marketing goals and graphics, together with models, were all set.

The management division of MATTHEWS ENTER-PRISES, INC. did a fabulous job of managing rental units. Not only were they achieving about ninety-eight percent occupancy ratio, but they were carrying out the corporate credo of fair and generous service to people.

Home buyers and renters knew that any list of complaints or repairs could be discussed in person with a staff member assigned to their area. The discussion took place in a friendly, living room like atmosphere of one of the models over coffee, cokes and cookies.

Any sense of foreboding and tension was simply removed. The clients knew they would be treated fairly, and problems corrected rapidly. Bonuses were paid to subcontractors and their crews for repairs done well and on time. The client was telephoned, as a follow up, to be sure the problem was resolved to their satisfaction.

By the time MATTHEWS ENTERPRISES, INC. was five years old, accountants informed Jane and Mike that they had a net worth of around eight million dollars. Mike couldn't comprehend that, but insisted that their contribution to the private foundation and bonuses for employees be proportionately revised.

Jane and Mike also increased their church pledge, and when a violent hurricane struck the panhandle, Mike had his crews help the homeless rebuild their houses.

He was on the Board of the State Contractor's Association, and was able to organize a commitment of time and services, without charge, to the project.

Mike's commitment to community service also included board memberships with Rotary, Chamber of Commerce, church and country club.

Jane managed the foundation.

"Do you realize," she informed Mike, "we have granted freshman scholarships to fifty college students. What would you think about having a party, over the Christmas holidays, for as many of them as can attend?"

"Wonderful idea. I wish we could do it in our own home. But of course it's not big enough, so why don't you work with the club. We can do it there."

It turned out to be a gala affair. Parents were also invited, and Jane and Mike agreed it would be an annual event.

"Next year what would you think, Jane, of having our party in our own new home? I recently bought some land which has access both to the ocean and the channel leading to the intercostal. There's an acre there which would make a fabulous homesite. How would you like to begin working on plans?"

"Mike, are you kidding? How would I like it? I would be on cloud nine. I know the site. I love our home now, but I've been paging through some of the architectural magazines. I have a lot of ideas to run by our architects.

"And, Mike, there's another reason I'm thrilled about a new home. I think there's a good chance I'm pregnant again. We've been trying for one more, you know. This time I know it'll be a girl, and then, as we said, no more pregnancies. No more birth control pills for me to make me fat. A vasectomy for you, which you said you wanted. Just sex for fun!"

"Jane, that's wonderful news. I hope it'll be a girl. Then I agree. The vasectomy for sure, and nothing but sex for fun.

"Just plan enough bedrooms in that new house for the three children, maybe a guest house and even separate quarters for a live-in couple. The lady could help with the children, meals and cleaning. The husband could be qualified to supervise gardening, lawn care and get a captain's license to run the big boat."

"What big boat?"

"Well, I wasn't going to say anything yet, but I have my eye on a fifty footer for the ocean to go along with our small sailboat and the twenty foot runabout for the intercostal. We'll go look at it together."

"Mike, you're going to spoil me."

"No chance. You're too solid, Jane.

Mike did sense of late, that Jane needed something more stimulating than caring for small children.

He knew she missed the stage. She had joined a local theatre group. Helped raise funds for a center for the performing and creative arts. Participated in a couple of local plays, and directed another. She had also been giving a few private acting lessons.

Mike also felt that working on their new home could fill a creative need for Jane, and it did.

The pregnancy was verified—by two months. Just seven months to design and build their home. That meant priority had to be ticketed by all departments of the company for the owner's next residence.

With three weeks to spare, the home was finished, including landscaping, pool, security and private dockage. It was spectacular. Six thousand square feet plus the guest cottage, and caretaker's quarters.

The Matthews' home won the top State Contractor's 1958 design award in its price class. It was featured on the front page of the HOME section of both the Miami and West Palm newspapers. It was also chosen for a prestigious garden club's benefit tour.

The views of the ocean and channel were fantastic. There was a central, all weather controlled atrium with plantings, small trees and a spectacular view of the sky—the perfect blues, the angry storm clouds, the beckoning moon and glistening stars.

Off the master suite was a library-office. Mike vowed to spend more time at home now.

Some mornings, as the first glow of the sun peaked over the rim of the sea, he thought, "This is perfection. This is pure tranquility. Perfect beauty.

"I am surrounded by those I love. I am generously paid to do something which is so much fun. And now, having a third child! Hopefully, a girl miniature of Jane."

It was a girl. From the moment she arrived, Teresa Jane became the princess of the Matthews family.

Chapter 16

Boats - Mansions - Millions

Scott and Dane finally arrived at an age, nine and seven, when Mike felt he could clearly communicate with them on a one-to-one basis. They were also old enough to get into trouble.

There were a few hair raising incidents. Like the afternoon he was working at home and was supposed to be watching the boys. Dane was napping, but Scott suddenly was nowhere to be found.

Mike got a little panicky. Checked first the pool and then the ocean beach. No Scott. Next ran to the intercoastal dock. Bingo!

He noticed the inflated rubber dinghy was missing off the cruiser. Sure enough there was Scott, with one of his neighborhood chums, paddling down the waterway.

Fortunately, he was able to catch up with them and tow them back with the inboard before they got out into the big water.

"Where were you planning to go, Scott?"

"Miami," he calmly answered.

"Oh, that's quite a trip. You know how long it takes us to get there in the big boat, don't you? And you know you aren't supposed to go out without an older person."

"Well, Dad, my friend is ten."

"Oh boy!" Mike thought. "Memories of my escapades including my winter trip down the river on an ice raft."

Dane contributed his parental scare one day when he was only seven. Jane and Mike woke up early one morning and realized he was gone. The live-in maid hadn't heard him leave. Neither had Scott.

Fortunately, the frantic neighborhood search was quickly over. Dane was decked out in his cowboy outfit—complete with boots, hat, six-shooter holster set—sitting on his little suitcase at the corner bus stop.

"Hi, big guy," Mike said, "going on a trip, huh?"

"Yup."

"Where are you headed, Son?"

"I'm waiting for the bus to take me to Disneyland."

"There was no questioning where his sons got their spirit of curiosity and love of adventure," Mike realized. "There would be much more to come," he knew.

Like the time Scott awakened Jane and Mike in the middle of the night because Dane wasn't feeling well. They knew he had a cold, but when they found him so limp and groggy that he seemed almost unconscious they were really worried. Especially, when questioning Scott, they found the aspirin bottle on the dresser half empty.

"But, Mom and Dad, I wanted to help make my brother well."

"How many did you give him?"

When he held up both hands twice they made a fast dash to the emergency ward for a stomach pumping.

Scott and Dane were inseparable friends. They spent hours playing together. Once in awhile there was the usual tiff between brothers, but it never lasted long.

Their insatiable curiosity and creativity had its hazardous side, however. What one couldn't think of the other could.

One day Mike discovered them in the workshop off the garage. They were covered with paint, and having the time of their lives stirring and mixing.

"What are you up to, boys?"

"Oh, we're getting ready to paint our bedroom a different color."

They would have too, or tried, if Mike hadn't discovered them.

Jane and Mike really got a kick out of an incident on one of their vacation trips. They left four year old Teresa with their live-in couple, and flew to Bar Harbor, Maine where they had spent their honeymoon.

They leased an Airstream mobile home and camped at Acadia National Park. The boys insisted they also have a small tent which was also located by the campfire.

They had a ball together—days at the cove beach— evenings at the ranger programs or roasting marshmallows. Early one morning Mike found their sleeping bags empty. He didn't bother Jane, because he couldn't imagine they could have gotten far.

But there are miles of trails in the park. For some reason or other, Mike followed his instincts and headed up the trail to Cadillac Mountain.

Fortunately, he came on a young couple headed down. "Did you happen to see two boys on the way up?"

"Sure did. They were having a great time, talking and swinging their canteens. We thought they looked a little young to be out on their own."

In no time Mike caught up with them. "You really gave me a scare."

"Why? We're just going for a hike to the top of the mountain."

"Well, why don't we go back to camp now and make breakfast on the campfire. Then tomorrow, if you'd like, all four of us can pack a lunch and hike up to the top. Your mother and I would enjoy that. You know we'd rather you didn't take off like this without telling us first. Would you do that after this?"

"Sure, Dad. We just didn't want to bother you."

"It's never a bother, Scott and Dane.

"I've got an idea. Since you seem to love camping and hiking why don't we plan a real camping and fishing trip for next year—maybe just the three of us guys. Would you like that?"

"Would we ever," Scott answered.

All year long Jane kept telling Mike how the boys talked about plans for the fishing trip. At night after dinner when Mike had to go out for meetings, Jane would say goodnight to Scott and Dane. She would see their maps and brochures of camping and fishing spots.

"Do you think Dad will really take us?" Dane would ask.

"Of course he will. He's excited about going, and now that Teresa is almost five she and I are doing fun things together too."

One of Jane's "fun things" with Teresa turned out to be a Walt Disney movie and ice cream soda afterward at the local drug store soda fountain.

Teresa, who since birth had been such a cheerful, petite, adorable little lady, had a tantrum in the drugstore. She plunked herself down on the floor blocking the entrance to the store.

As Jane told Mike the story, this charming gentleman came by, after finishing his purchase, and wanted to leave. He looked down at Teresa and smiled.

"Sweet little girl, could you move just a little so I can open the door?"

Whereupon Teresa glared up at him and said, "F...k you!"

"Wow!" Mike thought, when Jane told him about it, "which of her brothers taught her that?"

"Gotta keep your sense of humor when you're a parent," Jane reminded him.

The Matthews family became a very closely knit, bonded circle of love during those early years. Holidays, birthdays, Mother's and Father's Days, first day of school, last day of school—almost anything special—was a cause for celebration.

Jane and Mike also managed to hold, with few exceptions, to their family dinner times. These were almost sacred times when all members of the family took turns serving and cleaning up.

Conversation was confined to sharing happenings of the day. Asking questions about anything. Sharing jokes, c talking about exciting events coming up.

Friday dinner times were the family weekly meetings. Each one took turns being the moderator. The moderator could do it any way they wished, but there was a time limit.

One evening when it was Teresa's turn she brought a coloring book to the table. She opened it to a picture of a golden Cocker Spaniel.

"Family," she said, "it's time for a pet. What would you think of one like this? Her name is 'Taffy'. All in favor say 'I'."

The vote was three to two - only because Mother and Dad didn't get their hands up as fast as the children. They were looking sideways at one another wondering what the other was thinking.

But then Jane said, "Teresa, I think Taffy would be a happy addition to our family. What do you think, Mike?"

"Great, I'll make the vote unanimous. There's a beautiful spot on our property for a dog house and kennel. How about if I have our building people get to work on it?"

"That would be fine, Dad," Teresa responded, "but I was thinking Taffy could sometimes sleep in my room. I wouldn't want her outside in the storms."

"Certainly not. Taffy will be welcome in our home, and in your room, Teresa."

So it was that Taffy became the first of a long procession of pets in the Matthews' family. They ranged from puppies, to kittens, a pet snake, rabbits, hamsters, and eventually horses.

Jane and Mike purposely used their pet's sex life to help introduce the children to their own sexuality. Whenever one of the female pets was in heat, and the Matthews family was ready for a litter, they made an excursion to the vet to witness a breeding session.

Growing up in the small town of Lakeville, Mike was aware that farm children usually had a healthier, natural attitude to sex than city kids. Witnessing the breeding helped the children feel natural about sex and ask questions. Whatever they were, Jane and Mike answered them factually with right words like penis, vagina and intercourse.

Jane purchased an excellent visual slide presentation on sex for children. She felt very strongly that sex education was first the responsibility of the home, not the church or school.

The slides gave a relaxed opportunity for a family discussion. The presentation helped the Matthews children to understand the correct biological terms and functions of sex. It aided them in feeling good about their own sexuality, and helped them know that, among all of life on this planet, human beings are special. Sex, for humans they learned, is not only for procreation, but pleasure.

But along with this pleasure, comes responsibility such as love, tenderness and respect. Ideally, it should result in parenthood only when two people are prepared to be good parents.

Jane and Mike also sought to help their children avoid a guilt trip about masturbation. They spoke of various forms of birth control and the shared responsibility of both male and female in their choices.

Jane tried, as time went along, to help Teresa understand how an unmarried teen could cope with an unwanted pregnancy. She knew she could discuss it with either one of us.

The Matthews family shared its first sorrow together over their first and most adorable pet, Taffy. It was several months after she came to live with them that Jane took the three children and Taffy in the car to the local shopping center.

Somehow, the moment the car door was opened, Taffy slipped the leash and made a mad dash for another dog in the lot. Tragically, the children and Jane witnessed Taffy unavoidably hit and killed by a car.

Mike was at the office. His secretary knocked on the door, and rushed in, which she usually didn't do. She always used the intercom. He took one look at her face and knew there was something troubling her.

"There's an urgent call from your wife, Mike. I think you'd better take it right away."

"Mike, Taffy is dead. Run over by a car. Can you come. We're at the shopping center."

He could hear the children sobbing along with Jane. "I'll be right there. Is someone helping you?"

"Yes. The lady who hit her. It wasn't her fault. She helped carry Taffy into the car. Mike, the children want a funeral. Please hurry."

Mike broke every speed law on the way home. The family was huddled around Taffy's body on the lawn overlooking the ocean. Dane had found a small piece of marble in the garage, which had been part of an old lamp base.

"Will this be OK for a grave marker," he asked?

"Sure, Son. Let's use it along with a nice box I have in the garage. We'll build a grave for Taffy right here overlooking the ocean."

The five of them, wiping away tears and holding one another, walked slowly to a spot near a flower bed. Scott and Dane took turns digging the grave, and then they all helped cover over the box and put the sod back with the marble marker.

"Dad, will you say a few words?" Scott asked.

"Yes, Son."

Mike found himself remembering that day in Montana when he conducted the funeral for the drifter who committed suicide. He said much the same thing as then.

"Do you see this georgeous flower I picked from our flower bed? And look at the beautiful gulls soaring over the beach? You remember the story Jesus told about God loving the lowliest flower of the field and bird of the air. Remember then that he said 'God loves us just as much and maybe even more.' So as we say goodbye to Taffy it's wonderful to know that God cares also about Taffy and how we'll miss her."

Scarcely had Mike finished, when over the cadence of the surf, Teresa started singing:

"There is a green hill far away, beyond a city wall, where the dear Lord was crucified. He died to save us all."

"That includes puppies, doesn't it Dad?" she asked.

Mike was so choked up he could hardly answer.

"Yes, sweetheart, I'm sure it does, because nothing really ever dies. It just changes. Like the flower seed we put in the ground. It doesn't die. It changes into this beautiful flower."

"You mean, Taffy will change?"

"Maybe. Just like you and me someday, Teresa. For the better."

Within a week the Matthews family added Taffy II to their parade of pets.

It was time for the camping-fishing trip promised to Scott and Dane.

"What would you think of inviting Uncle Bob Mackay to join us?" Mike asked.

"Oh, would that ever be neat to have Uncle Bob along," Scott answered. "Then we could fish out of two boats and catch more fish. Uncle Bob doesn't have any boys, does he? Just girls. We could show him a real good time."

After dinner that evening, Mike called his friend.

"How are you doing buddy? I know you're working too hard as always. But the school year is almost over, and you can take a little time off. How would you like to join my boys and me for a week of camping and fishing?"

"Mike, good to hear from you. Sounds like a great idea. I think I could get away about the middle of June. What's the plan?"

"The boys and I were thinking we'd fly to Wisconsin and say 'hi' to my folks. We could meet there and stay overnight. Rent a station wagon and head for the wilderness canoe country in northern Minnesota. They have outfitters where we can lease all our equipment—canoes and backpacks. They also sell the licenses, bait and food. What do you say?"

"You can count on me. How about June 15th, that's a Friday. That way I can be gone two weekends. Please say 'hi' to the boys, Jane and Teresa for me. I'll see you then."

The arrangements were completed in no time. Jane, Teresa and Taffy II saw the campers off at the airport. This was the boys' first airplane ride. They were sky high in more ways than one.

It was fun for the three of them to see Grandma and

Grandpa again. They were beginning to show their age, although Dad was swimming his mile a day at the local "Y".

On a visit to Florida, Mike had introduced his father to golf. For Christmas they had given him clubs, bag and a pullcart.

Reverend Matthews was infatuated with the game. Played once a week on a little nine hole course. Mrs. Matthews walked with him and held the flag stick when he putted.

Mike was up before anyone else the morning they left for the canoe area. The coffee was perked and he had some juice and toast on the table when his mother joined him.

"You're very happy aren't you, Michael?" Mrs. Matthews said.

"Yes, Mother, life couldn't be better. Right now are 'the good old days' for me. Jane and I are very much in love. We have a wonderful family, and of course my business is better than I ever dreamed it would be. We're very lucky."

"I'm very proud of you, Michael. You know that. I'm especially pleased to see you and Jane sharing so much of yourselves and your blessings with others. You've almost convinced me that you're involved in a high calling from the Lord. It must not be easy to be a good Christian businessman.

"It's a challenge every day, Mother. But that's the most rewarding part of my business. The money is secondary."

"Do you ever think about being a minister? I haven't given up, you know."

"I suppose there are times when I think about it. Usually when I visit a church, attend a wedding of one of my employees or a funeral, and listen to the minister.

"Not to put anyone down, but some of them are poor communicators. They mean well. They're sincere and devout, and are probably good on a one-to-one basis but their sermons leave people blank. They're so rote, mechanical, uninspired and dull.

"Sad to say, I have to agree with you, Michael. There's little uplift for the spirit. Little feeling of encounter with God."

"Yes, Mother, at those times I think about it," Mike added.

Just then an avalanche crashed down the stairs in the form

of two hungry boys. Dad and Bob soon joined them, and after one of Mrs. Matthews' marvelous breakfasts they were on their way.

The trip through pine forests, and past hundreds of lakes took all day. They left the outfitters about nine AM the next morning and paddled and portaged until four PM. Some of the portages were just a rod or two. Others were almost a mile. It was exhausting, but the boys held their own.

They set up camp near a cove on a small island. All the right things were done about their food supply, like securing the pack on a high, small branch so the bears couldn't get at it.

There was just time for a quick jaunt around their little island. Bob and Mike showed the boys how to rig their rods with leaders and a jig. Then they were off to catch their first genuine shore dinner—Walleye Pike from the nearly ice cold water so pure they could drink it.

Scott and Dane each caught one and in no time they had enough for dinner.

The fish weren't large, about a pound and a half, but so delicious fried in the black iron skillet with Crisco and cornmeal over an open fire. Afterward, they talked about cleaning fish, sharing cleanup time, where the garbage was buried, and the place you went when nature called.

Everyone was bushed. But what's a camping trip without an evening campfire? They just had to have a couple of roasted marshmallows, try to find the big dipper and make their fishing bets for tomorrow. Who was going to catch the first, the largest and the most fish. The winners would be excused from meal cleanup one time.

Bob and Mike had a fabulous time with the boys. The fishing was excellent. Only one day of rain when they played poker in the tent. The meals were gourmet, and they saw bear, moose, deer and otter.

The largest fish was hooked by Scott, a twenty-three pound Northern. He almost fell out of the canoe when Bob netted it. But the picture of the four of them ready to break camp with Scott holding his fish was proof as to who caught the biggest fish.

Bob caught the first, and Dane the most, counting the babies they threw back. Mike took first prize running the motor.

Though there would be other Matthews' fishing trips, the four of them agreed this first one would be the most memorable.

Jane and Mike also managed a trip or two per year alone.

They acquired a condo at Hilton Head, and frequently enjoyed a few days there for quiet seclusion. They also enjoyed major trips over time to Europe, Spain, Mexico, Hawaii and the Bahamas.

During these trips their live-in couple, who were almost like family, took care of the children. Once in awhile Grandma and Grandpa also stayed at their home.

It became more and more difficult to plan family trips. The boys were playing Little League baseball much of the summer. They were also active in school football and basketball.

Teresa was the proud owner of an Arabian jumper. Much of her free time was devoted to grooming, lessons and horse shows. Every time Teresa came home from the stable, the boys would hold their noses.

"Teresa," they would say, "you smell like shit."

She knew it was good natured kidding.

The Matthews clan was very supportive of one another. They cheered one another on at every event they could attend.

Jane continued working with the local theatre, and played golf and tennis at the club. Beyond business, the family and community service projects, Mike struggled to maintain a single digit handicap in golf.

However, family trips were a high priority. They enjoyed the time of closeness, exploring, adventuring together. To facilitate these opportunities, the Matthews invested in a motor home.

The boys still preferred to pitch their tent by a campfire when they hit the state and national parks. But the motor home was ideal for roadside lunches, a game of catch, a side trip hike to a special historical site, and their own comfortable beds.

They covered the state of Florida from the Keys to Fort Walton Beach in the panhandle. Had a fabulous time on the Early American history trails through Boston and Washington D.C. Twice toured Maine, Vermont and New Hampshire.

Their longest and most exciting excursion was to Disneyland. Teresa was so hyper she couldn't wait to get there. They'd only been on the road a half day when she asked: "Are we almost there?"

The children must have gone on every ride at Disneyland at least once. Jane and Mike agreed, "You just haven't lived until you've seen Disneyland through the eyes of your children."

The West was such a thrill. Especially after all the westerns on TV westerns. They covered the giant Sequoias, the Grand Canyon, Yosemite, Zion, Bryce Canyon, Yellowstone and the Black Hills.

They made a stop in Wisconsin for a breather with Grandma and Grandpa, then headed for home via New Orleans and the Gulf highways.

Their last night before arriving home, as they were parked in a state park, they shared feelings about the past month. Sure there had been a few tiffs, but they didn't last long.

Around the last embers of a campfire, they shared their choices for the number one thrill of the trip.

Teresa was first, "Disneyland and all the rides, and Mickey Mouse," she said.

Without hesitating, Dane said: "The bears and buffalo in Yellowstone."

"I guess it's my turn," Scott continued, "I wish I could have two, because I can't make up my mind, but I guess I liked Yosemite and the mountains best, because I would like to climb mountains someday."

"Do you want to be next, or last, Jane?" Mike asked.

"You go ahead, I'm still thinking."

"OK, my biggest thrill was spending time with you, Jane, my wife, you kids and our feeling of closeness."

"OK, now mine," Jane said. "It was the majesty of the Sequoia trees. I felt very humble in their presence. Just thinking about the centuries they have stood in the forest. Sentinels pointing to the sky. Before we say goodnight, I'd like it if we could hold hands and join in a little prayer."

"OK, Mom," Teresa added. "Let's hold hands everybody."

"Almighty and loving God," Jane began, "we are so grateful for our wonderful country. Thank you for peace and freedom. Help us to find ways to share this blessing with others. Thank you for our beautiful trip together. Help us to grow from our experiences of this trip and always to love one another. Amen."

"That was nice," Dane said.

"Thank you, Jane," Mike added, "and now let's hit the sack. It's off for home and back to work tomorrow."

Chapter 17

Matthews Enterprises, Inc.

MATTHEWS ENTERPRISES was flourishing.

More apartment complexes were built. The management division now operated over five thousand units. A few buildings with the best locations and view were converted to condominiums. This also proved to be exceedingly lucrative.

Through their own condo at Hilton Head, Mike got on the trail of a spectacular mile of ocean front. He was able to purchase this property, subject to suitable feasibility studies, for a luxury condo building. The purchase agreement was also contingent upon plat approval. It took a year, but it turned out to be a credit to the serenity and beauty of the island.

When it was finished, Jane and Mike sold their condo and took over the penthouse of their own building for their occasional retreats.

MATTHEWS ENTERPRISES was also asked to do a complete residential, commercial, retail development at Fort Walton Beach in the northern panhandle. This turned into almost a five year project, including a million square foot regional shopping mall.

About this time, Mike's marketing personnel informed him that the company was being made a test case, to see if they would sell to blacks.

The issue of racial equality and freedoms—on buses, public buildings and the right to vote had been fermenting in America since Martin Luther King became the leader of the blacks in 1955.

It was now ten years later, and following a demonstration in Selma, Mississippi, congress had just passed "The Voting Rights Act" guaranteeing equal rights at the polls.

MATTHEWS ENTERPRISES had three higher bracket single family home projects going. The developments were just underway. Lots were expensive and the homes very elegant. There were association by-laws and deed restrictions as to size, style, and construction material allowed.

There was one black family ready to sign a purchase agreements in all three neighborhoods. Obviously, this could effect the tone of the neighborhood.

If white home owners would not accept black families as neighbors, millions of dollars could go down the drain.

Mike asked his marketing manager, "What are we waiting for? We don't have a choice. Legally, but most importantly ethically and morally, let's do what's right."

He asked to meet the three families personally. He called and made an appointment with each one at the model show-rooms, and asked if they had children to bring them along.

Mike brought Scott and Dane also, and after introductions, said:

"Welcome on behalf of MATTHEWS ENTERPRISES. I want to tell you we're happy you've chosen us to build your new home. It's long overdue that we human beings of different races and colors learn how to be friends and live together. I believe that's the way it was intended to be.

"One more thing, I can't wait to tell my trades-people that you're moving in. About a third of my crews are black and I think they build a darn good home.

"As of tomorrow, I am going to see to it that at least one of my building superintendents is black. I'm also going to promote other blacks in our management and marketing divisions to supervisory positions.

"If everything doesn't go well during the building of your home, please call me directly. Tell your friends about this neighborhood, and let's see if together we can make it one of the most attractive, serene communities in the state."

The three projects proceeded without a hitch. In the following months, Mike made a point of driving through the neighborhoods. Though they were outnumbered, there were black kids playing with whites. Mike learned that some black and white neighbors had become the best of friends.

For many years these black families also became Mike's good friends. Jane and Mike received Christmas cards from them, and at their annual gala holiday celebration, staged for new home owners, they were present.

Mike thought back to those early days of his business venture when he wrote his credo. The goals of treating people with equality, fairness and generosity, beyond payment received, was inherent in their application of fair housing, and not just a fuzzy ideal. He wasn't self-righteous about it; but it made him feel good and sleep well nights.

Early in Mike's business career, Dan Adams had taught him that there can be no such thing as status quo in a business, anymore than there is in life.

There are constant changes, and new opportunities. The minute a business grows complacent and shirks research and development—keeping abreast of what's new—the downslide begins.

For months, executive staff meetings had been discussing the proposition of syndicating various properties. Possibly also purchasing others, and building new projects such as apartment complexes and shopping centers for syndication.

The tax laws were favorable to limited partnership investors. The fees and capital gains for the general partner could be lucrative. All partners could share in the write-off of depreciation, in addition to a share of mortgages, interest payouts and real estate taxes.

If the project was managed properly, well located and constructed, and leased effectively, it was a win-win situation.

Mike's team decided to begin with one of their apartment complexes which was only nine years old and always 98% rented.

One of their marketing brokers went through the stiff academic training to obtain a principal's license. The company was then eligible to become a broker-dealer, and was licensed by the National Association of Security Dealers.

The attorneys did all the legal work and prepared the prospectus for the private offering. With the track record and reputation of MATTHEWS ENTERPRISES, INC., it took only ten or twelve weeks to raise five million dollars.

With these funds, the old mortgage was paid off, and the buildings were now owned by the general and limited partners. The company also experienced a sizeable capital gains and cashflow from the sale to the partnership.

Normally, the partnership would hold the investment approximately seven years while the property appreciated substantially. But in this case, the value soared so quickly that they elected to sell after three years.

The company had nothing but happy investors, because they had experienced something like a 34% annual internal rate of return on their invested dollars, after taxes.

After discussing the program further with his colleagues, Mike authorized them to proceed both in acquisitions and construction for syndicating purposes.

However, they developed some very rigid, conservative guidelines with respect to location, quality of building, demographics of the area, percentage of leveraging, and write-off for tax purposes.

They had a fundamental agreement that these projects had to be financially profitable even without tax write-offs.

Mike's real estate holdings were pyramiding. Jane and he were now informed that they had a net worth somewhere in the thirty million range. It was almost scarey —the preacher's kid who had grown up in the depression. Sure, they worked hard, but so did many other people who barely had enough to eat.

He didn't feel guilty, but sometimes he felt bored. Although he was turned on by the challenge of ethics in business and numerous benevolent programs, his main satisfaction and pleasure was the time Jane and he could spend together, and participate in the growth and development of their children.

Both boys were in high school. Scott at sixteen was a junior and fourteen year old Dane, a freshman.

It was a thrill for Jane and Mike to attend their games. They both played football, basketball and baseball. It was entirely their choice. Of course they knew their dad had been an athlete in high school and college and was a nut about sports, but they were never pressured to be active in sports. The choice was theirs. They knew their mother and father would have been just as proud if they had chosen to play the flute, or write poetry.

Teresa was winning her share of ribbons with her horses. Now she had two of them—one to show and jump, and one just to take care of, talk to, and ride for fun.

It was obvious that she had her mother's creative talent. Instead of the performing arts, she expressed her talent in brushes, paints and easels. Her first showing in a local gallery took place when she was only twelve.

These were not easy times to be parents, however. Certainly not easy to be teens. It was 1969—generation gap time in America. The beginning of popular use of drugs, and the horror of Vietnam.

It had been back in early August, 1964, that an American destroyer on "intelligence" patrol in the Gulf of Tonkin off the Coast of Vietnam, was supposedly attacked by Vietnamese torpedo boats. Two days later, it was reported that another American ship was fired upon. President Johnson immediately ordered reprisal air raids over Vietnam.

So began an era of American history which led to the death of thousands of American young people, and left deep scars on nearly every family in the United States.

Mike had become rather well acquainted through their governor, with Vice President Hubert Humphrey during his days in the senate. It had been Mike's privilege to introduce him as the speaker at a state contractor's convention. On several occasions Mike had visited with him in his office about housing legislation.

It was through Mr. Humphrey that Mike had met the Speaker of the House whose private opinion held that the White House was using the Gulf of Tonkin incident as an excuse to escalate a full scale war.

In spite of voting for the Gulf of Tonkin Resolution to retaliate, it was common knowledge in Washington that many legislators, as well as military leaders, felt misled by the executive branch.

They were supporting the President publicly, but over a few beers at night, they acknowledged that this started as a civil war. The Vietnamese attack was like using a BB gun to destroy a tank. They hadn't even hit the U.S. ships. But Americans were led to believe that this was another of the old domino theories, namely: "If we lose in Vietnam, we lose in Thailand, Laos and Cambodia and then lose face in the Philippines and all over the world. Next, the Communists are at our shores."

"Bullshit," Mike thought.

This was also the response of many of U.S. leaders in private. They really felt that America needed to bring the conflict before the United Nations, stop bombing North Vietnam and support an Asian solution to what was primarily an Asian problem.

As parents of two sons who potentially could go to Vietnam, Jane and Mike were intimately affected. No family escaped. There was a torrent of unrest, dissension, peace marches, fear, violence.

While brave young Americans were fighting and dying, some were defecting to Sweden or Canada. Others were conscientious objectors.

There was a very real generation gap—a rebellion against authority, and what many young people saw as a worship of materialism and a facade of hypocrisy by the middle age generation.

Teenagers were labeled the "Hippy Generation." Their trademarks were long hair, ragged clothes, unbelievably loud shattering rock music, and sometimes communes with gurus and drugs.

Jane and Mike were aware that their three children experimented with pot and booze. They talked about it together. Fortunately, they had no addictions or excesses.

There was an unlocked bar in the Matthews' home. It was

customary in the family to have a toast on special occasions. Jane and Mike took the position that wine and liquor was available in this culture. They would rather have their children grow up feeling they had a choice, because that's what they would do anyway.

At home, and on the boat, they saw their parents have a drink with moderation. The children appeared to respect that. The boys, of course, during school sports time, were in rigid, absolute abstinence. Otherwise, there were times on their motor home trips, or hunting and fishing outings, when they would have a beer together.

The Matthews family did have one pact that had worked. The deal was, as time went on and the kids got older, if they were ever in a position where they had too much to drink, or were riding with someone who had, just call.

It was agreed, it didn't make any difference what time of night it was. Either Jane or Mike would come and get them. No questions asked, and no reprimand.

The kids were right about this generation being guilty of generalizing. Mike would sit in the men's grille at his golf club after a game, and listen to fathers bemoaning their long-haired hippy sons who had no gratitude for their luxuries and how hard Dad worked.

Finally, one day Mike couldn't stand it any longer.

"What's the matter with you guys? Do you want to talk about your pranks, your drinking, your escapades when you were a kid? Just because a boy has long hair doesn't make him a hippy. As far as gratitude is concerned, have you taught your kids how to work? Or have you just given them everything so your ego would feel good? Furthermore, as far as long hair goes, I predict within ten years all of you will have longer hair and half will have mustaches and beards."

"Are you kidding?" one of them shot back. "Not me."

Actually, he became the first.

Scott and Dane, as well as Teresa, had been taught to work. Very early in their lives they each had their duties. They kept their own rooms picked up and beds made between weekly cleaning lady visits. They knew how to fry an egg and work the washer and dryer.

An allowance had been agreed upon, with extra for special chores like cleaning the boat. They had their own bank accounts, and took pride in spending their own money for special things, including gifts at birthday and holiday times.

As they grew older, both Scott and Dane had jobs, between sports, in the summer. They helped clean out town homes, apartments and residences during construction. Later, they were trained by the marketing people to hand out literature and guide visitors through models.

When it came time for cars, the deal was agreed on that they pay half and Jane and Mike half. They also worked out what was considered fair split for college costs. When it came to sports equipment, like skis, the parents paid, unless they wanted two or more of something.

Teresa also seemed to enjoy learning to work. She got a job at the stable helping groom horses. Later, she helped on special days in the models, as well as filing in the office.

The late sixties still were tough times emotionally for the Matthews. Scott, particularly, was affected. He was on the threshold of college, and philosophically, a deep thinker.

Mike and Scott had many long talks—out on the boat alone or sometimes having lunch together, just the two of them.

"Dad, as you know, I'm opposed to the Vietnam war. I took part in a peace march at school the other day."

"Yes, I know. You have a right to do that."

"I love our country and prize our freedom. You probably don't like my hair getting longer. I guess it's just one of the badges we're wearing to let the older generation know we don't agree with everything they do. That's mainly what it is."

"I know, Scott. Your hair doesn't bother your mother and me, as long as it's clean."

"Don't worry, they wouldn't let me play sports if it was dirty. What's really disturbing is the possibility of having to go to Vietnam. I've decided I can't do that. I'll file for Conscientious Objector and serve the country in another way."

"I don't blame you, Scott. I understand your decision, and we'll support you. You have a right under the laws of our country to do that. It'll be tough, because it goes against the grain of what seems to be patriotic at the moment."

Scott continued his own personal war against war. Especially after an amazing incident on one of his college selection visits.

He had been offered a football scholarship at several schools. One of them was Princeton where Uncle Bob taught. Scott invited Mike to accompany him as he toured the campus and met the coaches.

The second evening Mike had dinner with Bob, his wife and two daughters while Scott went out with some of the team members. Scott's evening almost turned into a brawl.

They stopped for a couple of beers and ran into two or three students from South Vietnam. They got into it pretty good. The Vietnamese were studying at Princeton. They were from wealthy families. Their parents had been able to "buy" them out of the country so they wouldn't have to go to war.

That did it.

"You gotta be kidding," Scott and his buddies said, "you're studying here, enjoying our freedoms and our country while we're dying over there to protect you. And you can buy your way out? Forget it. You can take your country and stick it up your ass."

The next day there was a loud, long, boisterous peace march in front of the president's office building. The TV cameras showed up. On the six o'clock news, there was Scott and his pals waving their banners and whooping it up. One of them gave a very sensible, articulate explanation of what had happened the night before.

Before Scott and Mike headed for home, Mike had a long personal talk with Bob. He sensed something was wrong. He thought maybe Bob might be ill.

They were still in the habit of jogging. So they went out in the morning—threw the football around for awhile, and then jogged by Bob's office building.

"Mike, why don't we catch our breath for a minute. Let's

go into my office. I'd like to ask you something."

"Good, I also want to see what new books you've added to your library. You know I like to read a good contemporary book on theology now and then."

"Mike, I'll get right to the point. We've known each other a long time. You're my best friend. We don't see each other often, but when we do it's like it always was."

"You've got that right, Bob."

"I'm really in a fog. In addition to my professorship, I've been active on the executive committee of my national church body. Now they have asked me to consider the nomination to be its president."

"I knew it! Didn't I always say you'd make it to the top, Bob? Take it. You're just what the church needs."

"That really isn't the only issue, Mike. I've been attracted to a woman faculty member. I think I'm in love with her. She's married and has children. She's younger than me, and says she loves me and wants to divorce her husband and marry me."

"I'm listening. It's heavy, but not unusual. Keep talking."

"The irony is, Mike, I love my wife. I always have, and still do. She doesn't know about this. Nobody does. I'm sure of it. But it's tearing me apart. I can't study or write or lecture decently. I'm losing sleep and I've started drinking too much on occasion."

"Have you sought counseling or therapy, Bob?"

"Yes. I've been getting into New York regularly to visit our church headquarters. I've been seeing a good clinical psychologist on the staff of one of our churches. She tells me I am going through mid-life crisis. She's helped me a great deal, says if I do the right thing it will pass."

"I want to know what you think, Mike."

"I can empathize with you. It happens to many of us. I've been fighting some of the same feelings without the affair."

"We're doers, Bob. High achievers. We've driven ourselves all our lives to reach, to grow, to develop, to pursue. We're perfect examples of the poet's philosophy: 'A man's reach should exceed his grasp, or what's a heaven for.'"

"You are so right, Mike."

"Now, we come to that time of life when the chase can seem more important than the catch. Sometimes that applies to the woman in our life also, Bob.

"It can be true that two very wonderful people, who were exactly right for one another at one time, are not for another time. It's possible for two dynamic people to develop in different directions, not parallel lines. When that happens, there are times when it can be better for both of them to go their separate ways."

"But that's not the case with my wife and me, Mike. I'm sure of it."

"Your counselor probably told you, Bob, and I've read it as well, that recent medical research has turned up the possibility that certain chemicals are secreted by the brain at our age which might contribute to a crisis time just like menopause for women. The first thing you should do, immediately, is have a thorough physical."

"That's what the clinical psychologist also said."

"Do it. Don't put it off. Be sure to exercise every day like you're doing now. Dump the caffeine. You'll sleep better. Take a vacation. Get away for a while. Come down and see us. We'll take the boat out and do some deep sea fishing. Cut down the booze. Anything to help the emotional side of this crisis."

"It all makes good sense. But when you're in the middle of your dilemma, as you know, it seems there is no way out."

"You're so right. But as far as the sex thing is concerned and the affair—as long as you and your wife are happily married, the other woman is just one last fling of your manhood to see if you can still make it.

"It's a classical pattern. Get away with your wife, Bob, alone. As long as you still love one another, you don't want to kick away all those priceless years."

"Thanks, Mike, as usual it's so great to talk with you."

"It's mutual. Take's one to know one. You've helped me many times, and I'm sure I'll need you again.

"One last bit of advice, Bob. Take that nomination. Don't

get caught up in a guilt trip. Break off the other relationship as quickly and quietly as possible. No need to tell your wife or anybody else.

"You're going to be OK. The new job will be a fabulously different challenge for you. The national church body will be lucky to have you."

Chapter 18

Open Door to U.S .Senate

Scott decided to accept the football scholarship from Princeton. He proved to be an excellent lineman—a pull-out guard on offense.

Unfortunately, it was during only his second collegiate game that he drove his helmet into a would be tackler and sustained a career ending concussion.

His contact sport days were over. But so was the possibility of his being drafted for Vietnam. Naturally, Mike thought of his football injury and how at another time, and a different war, he was kept from the military.

Jane and Mike flew immediately to New Jersey when they got the news and visited Scott in the infirmary.

"Mom and Dad," he explained, "I'm not that disappointed about not being able to play anymore. Not only because I won't have to be concerned about the draft. There's a more important reason.

"I never told you this, but my senior year of high school I wanted desperately to quit football and go out for the class play. I was captain of the team, you know, and was talked into staying on the team by my co-captain."

"That's interesting. You could have shared that with us," Jane replied.

"I'm really turned on by plays, poetry, and novels," Scott continued. "I think I would like to be a writer. I had that great class in writing as a senior in high school and now I've got a super freshman English teacher of creative writing."

"We couldn't be more happy for you, Scott," Jane responded. "I'd be grateful if one of my children loved the creative or performing arts as much as I do."

"As far as being drafted and Vietnam," Scott went on, "now I know I can just stay in school. I guarantee you, though, I'm going to continue my peace activist role. You taught me, Mom and Dad, to stand up for what we believed to be right. So that is what I hope to do in as effective and rational way as possible."

Meanwhile, Dane was winding up his junior year of high school and corresponding with colleges. His top priorities, for the moment, in a college were: (1) a strong reputation for undergraduate preparation in the field of architecture and (2) accessibility to a major ski area either in Vermont or Colorado. Skiing had become Dane's top sports interest.

Jane and Mike had a terrible scare over Dane in the fall when he had an accident with his motorcycle. His best friend was riding with him, when a Volkswagon full of teenagers made an abrupt left turn directly in front of them. Both boys flew over the car when they hit.

Fortunately, they were wearing helmets. They were skinned up badly and knocked unconscious. But Dane's worst injury resulted in the tendons in his right hand being severed when his arm went through the side window of the car.

Jane and Mike were playing golf at the club that afternoon. They were called off the course, and got a police escort to the hospital. They immediately gave the orthopedic surgeon permission to do microscopic surgery.

Miraculously, all the severed tendons were repaired, and Dane's hand healed A-1 except for a slight crook in his little finger.

Though he had to pass up football one season, it didn't hurt either his skiing or baseball abilities.

Darling Teresa was no longer "little" Teresa. She continued to win blue ribbons with her horse. Collecting pets, stretching canvases and painting much of the time, she was a daring adventure seeking junior high student.

She demonstrated that one evening when Jane and Mike were at some friends home for dinner. A call came from Teresa. She obviously wasn't where they thought she was. The background noise on the phone was a giveaway. But she made no attempt to fake it.

She asked for Mike, so he took the phone.

"Hi, Dad."

"Hi Sweetheart, what's up?"

"Well, you see I went along with these older kids to this music bar. There's this real cool rock group here."

"I can hear that, Teresa."

"How did you get in? Didn't you have to show an I.D.?"

"Yeah."

"Well, how did you manage that?"

"I hope you won't be too mad at me, Dad, but I used Mom's driver's license."

"You used Jane's driver's license?"

Later it seemed funny, but not at this moment.

"You mean, Teresa, you took your mother's license out of her purse, and you got by with that?"

"Yeah, I guess they didn't look at it very close."

"They must not have. Thanks at least for calling, Teresa. Your mother and I appreciate your letting us know where you are. We've talked about stuff like this. Have you had anything to drink?"

"Just one beer. I don't really like it too much. I'm OK. I'm fine. Don't worry Dad. The guy that's driving has his father's car and he's very careful."

"Tell you what, Teresa. I'll make a deal with you. Since you called, enjoy the music. Don't have anymore beer and be home by midnight. OK?"

"Could you make that twelve-thirty, Dad?"

"Why?"

"Because, the group doesn't want to leave until twelve and it'll take about a half hour to get home."

"OK, Teresa. That's a deal, but one more request. If there's any doubt at all about the driver having too much to drink will you call us?"

"Yes, Dad, I will. Thanks. Goodbye."

When Mike returned to the group at the host's dinner party the group wondered if everything was OK.

"Everything's fine. Teresa just had a question. I'll tell you about later, Jane."

Jane gave Mike plenty of heat as they drove home.

"How come you didn't check with me first, Mike, before telling her she could stay. I'm disappointed. I can't believe you'd be so liberal with your daughter. You certainly were harder than that with the boys."

"You're absolutely right, Jane. I should have called you to the phone. It all happened so fast, and I was dumbfounded. I didn't think too clearly, I guess. Imagine? Using your license? At least, she's got an ingenious imagination.

"Well, she'd better not use it that way again. I feel we should ground her for a week through next weekend."

"OK, Jane. You're right, and I apologize. I know we've always tried to handle these things together."

"I'll talk to her when she gets home, Mike. And I forgive you.

"You are a wonderful father. Not perfect of course. But neither am I. What do you suppose is going to happen next?"

"Next" turned out to be a phone call from the local chairman of a political organization in which Jane and Mike were active. He was a member of their club, as well as Rotary and their church.

"I was wondering, Mike, if you would be willing to meet privately with our screening committee. We would like to talk to you about accepting a nomination for the U.S. Senate come fall."

Mike was totally flabbergasted. At a loss for words. Ever since the United States Information Agency appointment fell through he had given no thought to public service.

Finally, he managed to say, "Thank you sir. It's an honor to be considered. I've never thought of myself in a position like that, but of course I'd be delighted to meet with you."

There followed several weeks of soul searching about his career future—about his philosophy of vocation. Jane and Mike talked far into the night on many occasions.

"Did this feel right?" they wondered. "Were we ready to move and leave all this? Were we prepared to spend a full year campaigning? And then, how about if Mike didn't get elected?"

All of these questions were on his mind as he walked into the imposing board room at party headquarters. There were at least fifteen people around the table. Mike was warmly welcomed, and then the questions started.

"Mr. Matthews, your name has been submitted to us by many people from different economic and social levels of our community. You have a lot of friends and admirers. We assume your presence here today indicates that you would give a nomination serious thought?"

"Yes, it's an honor, and I can assure you I will weigh it carefully, if I prove to be your choice."

"You know, of course, that the rigors of campaigning are strenuous. How is your health?"

"Excellent, as far as I know."

"We'd want a physician's report. Would that be OK?"

"No problem."

"How about your business? Could you be away for a year during the campaign? Is that a problem?"

"Not at all. I have people who can take over."

"You realize that the party is prepared to compensate you financially at the level you are used to during this year?"

"No, I didn't know that. I don't mean this facetiously, but that would be neither necessary or possible. The party might go broke. We could make some arrangements on that."

A light hearted snicker went around the table at Mike's comment. It seemed to lighten up the meeting.

"Mr. Matthews, there would also need to be a full disclosure on your part of your holdings—audited financial statements, for example. Any opposition to that?"

"No, I have no problem with that."

"Also, if you ran and were elected you would need to turn

over the operation and control of your business enterprises to a trust. There must be no question of a conflict of interest. Could you do that?"

"Yes, I'm sure I could live with that."

"How about a full security check? We would need to put you through a complete FBI clearance. Any objection?"

"No, I've been through that once before. I know a little bit about what that's like and I would have no objections."

"Now, we need to ask about Mrs. Matthews. How do you think she would respond to the grind of campaigning and being a senator's wife. We'd rely on her to be by your side and be supportive, you know."

"Ladies and gentlemen, I can't speak for her. But she knows I'm here, and I think she would understand and accept her responsibilities. I wouldn't go into this without her support. That's the way our relationship is, but I can assure you that if I am nominated she would be an asset to the campaign in every way."

"Now, Mr. Matthews, for our final question, do you see yourself being able to support, President Nixon. We expect him to reelected."

"Frankly, I might have a problem with that. I don't believe I could support Mr. Nixon in everything. I have to be honest. I think he is brilliant and very knowledgeable politically. But sometimes he seems to come across as too aloof and imperial for my taste."

"Could you expand on that briefly?"

"I think he tends to surround himself with a very close knit, almost secretive group. They seem to be bright but some of them don't appear to me to have much class or talent. To be truthful with you, some of them appear to follow the philosophy of winning at any cost. They seem to believe that nice guys finish last."

"I couldn't support that, if it's true. I would do my very best to be a conscientious senator, representing the best interests of our people and our country after careful study and debate of the issues."

"Mr. Matthews, the party and this committee wouldn't

expect you to vote with the President on every issue. That's why we have our system of checks and balances. Why our nation needs sharp, successful, intelligent people like you in government.

"Thank you, sir, for meeting with us today. You've been very patient and candid, and we appreciate it."

"How long do I have to consider this?"

"About two weeks. Will that do? We'll need to make our decision then. Our chairman will call you."

It was a difficult, stressful couple of weeks. In addition to the major career decision, Mike had been putting off action on a promise he had made his parents.

Reverend Matthews was approaching seventy, and wanted to retire. Of course he and Mrs. Matthews had little or no money. A pittance of a clergyman's retirement income and social security. They had never made enough to save anything.

Mike had introduced Dad to a classmate of his from the seminary who was the senior minister of a large church in Portland, Maine. Reverend and Mrs. Matthews had visited with him and fallen in love with the area. Now an invitation came for Reverend Matthews to serve part-time as a visitation minister. He was to visit hospitalized members and elderly "shut-ins."

It was a perfect situation. Reverend Matthews would be paid a part-time salary. He could do what he loved best. To share kindness, understanding and love on a one to one basis. Mrs. Matthews was also elated. She loved the scenery, the coastline, and spectacular fall color season of New England.

Just one problem. They needed a home. The church promised them a housing and car allowance as part of Reverend Matthews' compensation, so that would help.

They had also insisted on signing legal documents naming Mike trustee, guardian and executor of their affairs.

The first thing Mike did was fly to Portland, where he arranged to meet his parents. They spent a fast paced day purchasing a lot. For the first time in their lives they could look forward to owning their very own cozy home instead of living in a parsonage. By the end of the week Mike had some of his crew on the job getting the permit and overseeing the excavation and footings.

Reverend and Mrs. Matthews were able to occupy the home in ten weeks. Jane and Mike arranged to have flowers and champagne delivered and the formerly ultra conservative elder Matthews shared a toast with Jane and Mike via phone to celebrate the happy milestone in their lives.

Mike's trip to Portland, coming as it had during his difficult decision time on the senate nomination, turned into a fortunate circumstance. He used the trip as an opportunity to exercise a couple of his guidelines for decision making: (1) Get away alone for some quiet reflection. (2) Seek the advice of at least one close friend.

He called Bob. He was living now in Jersey and officing in New York. His mid-life crisis was over. Bob and his wife were very close and enjoying all the exciting new things happening to them.

Bob was president of his national church body.

It took a few minutes for Mike to get through the switchboard to Bob's personal secretary. When the sugary voice said: "Good morning, sir, may I please tell Dr. Mackay who's calling?"

Mike felt the devilish urge to do something he'd always wanted to do. He answered "No, thanks."

There was a painful silence. She was at a loss for words then she put him through.

"Dr. Mackay," Mike began, "my name is Mr. Charles. I'm in New York for just a day or two and would like to meet with you, if you could spare the time, sir. I belong to one of your church's parishes."

"Thanks for calling, Mr. Charles."

"I've been a heavy contributor for years, and have just come into a sizeable amount of money. I would like to visit with you personally about where I could put it to the best use."

"Of course, Mr. Charles. Normally, I would refer you to our special gifts director. But I would be happy to meet you personally. Could we have lunch tomorrow? Where would you like to meet?"

"I'm staying at the New York Athletic Club for just this one night. How about meeting me here at noon tomorrow. Just ask for me at the desk."

Mike was elated that he pulled off his prank. He figured it must have been his fake high nasal pitch and the handkerchief held over his mouth that fooled Bob.

Nevertheless, he had the time of his life the next day, watching from the lounge area. As Bob walked to the reception desk asking for Mr. Charles, Mike quickly sauntered up behind and tapped him on the shoulder.

"You looking for Mr. Charles, sir?"

"Mike! You son-of-a-gun. What a prank! You've got one coming now for sure. But what a treat to see you. I'm going to order the most expensive lunch on the menu and you're buying."

"I'm happy to see you haven't lost your sense of humor, Bob. If only some of your fellow dignitaries could hear about this story."

"You wouldn't."

"That depends. Let's have lunch. I need to talk to you. This time, I'm the one who needs help."

As usual, talking things out with Bob helped immensely. He enabled Mike to sift out the negatives and positives of the senate nomination possibility. He verbalized the enormous challenges and honor of being asked to run for the Senate. He helped Mike identify some of his political beliefs. He aided him in sorting out how Jane and he would be affected in their lifestyle, as well as demonstrating vocational code of ethics in the political arena.

By the time Mike's plane landed in Florida that evening, and Jane met him in the terminal, he felt it was clear what he should do. The two of them reviewed the subject again over dinner.

The next day he also spoke with the boys and Teresa.

After sleeping on his decision overnight, he telephoned the committee chairman.

"Sir, I want you to know how much I would like to have

a voice and a vote as a United States Senator. I have a keen interest in vital issues like disarmament, peace, ecology, housing, education, and racial equality.

"We're seeking a nominee of your caliber and dedication Mr. Matthews," the chairman said.

"I would like to work on programs for the elderly, the farmers and anti-drug and crime efforts," Mike continued. "I feel deeply about making a stronger effort to curtail the fiscal deficit and runaway bureaucracy and taxes."

"Couldn't agree with you more."

"I believe much of our international relations philosophy is arrogant and mired in the stone ages of the domino theory."

"You're probably right Mr. Matthews."

"Nevertheless, Mr. Chairman, I have reached the conclusion that I must decline your generous invitation. The timing is not right for me.

"I'm disappointed. Could you tell me why?"

"There are three principle reasons," Mike said, "which I trust you'll respect.

"One, I truly find that I could not give Mr. Nixon the kind of support you justifiably expect from your senator. Second, I promised to be totally honest with you. I could not run against the Democratic incumbent from this state. As a matter of fact, I like him. He's a friend of mine, and I believe he is doing a credible job.

"Three, political wives in Washington seem to be a sorority of a kind of nameless sisterhood. They seem to lose their identity and sense of individuality. The political environment in Washington, I am told, is still in the age of Blackstone, the commentator on English common law. He said when two marry they become one, and he is the one. Jane and I are not comfortable with that type of relationship.

"For these three reasons I am unable at this time to accept your gracious offer."

"Our entire state committee will be disappointed. But we certainly do respect your candid and careful evaluation. Maybe next time."

This was one of the toughest decisions Mike had ever had

to make. But after it was over, he felt good about it. Knew he made the right choice.

Scarcely was the senate decision history, however, when a registered letter marked "personal" came from Bob.

The minute he opened it he was plunged into another difficult decision time.

Dear Friend Mike,

I can't begin to tell you how much it meant to me to see you again. We've meant a lot to each other since the day we met on the campus of the seminary.

You've helped me through some tough moments; and now I'm grateful I could be of help to you in making your big decision.

Mike, I'm going to give you a shot at one more major choice. When you explained to me that you felt the time was not ripe for you in the Senate, I thought "maybe the time is ripe for Mike to enter the ministry."

Remember those beautiful poetic words we read in the original Hebrew from Ecclesiastes in the Old Testament?

"To everything there is a season, and a time to every purpose under the heaven: A time to be born, and a time to die; a time to plant, and a time to build up; a time to weep, and a time to laugh; a time to mourn, and a time to dance; a time to cast away stones, and a time to gather stones together; a time to embrace, and a time to refrain from embracing; a time to get, and a time to lose; a time to keep, and a time to cast away; a time to rend, and a time to sew; a time to keep silence, and a time to speak; a time to love, and a time to hate; a time of war, and a time of peace."

Maybe it's time, Mike. Think about it, buddy. I've said it before, and I'll tell you again, you have a lot to offer. You'd make a heck of a minister.

I know you've literally been an outstanding minister in each of your three vocations, but now perhaps the time has come to share your talent with the church.

Times are changing, there's more intellectual and spiritual

freedom within the organized church. I'm convinced there is a fit for you, Mike.

You and I and God know you're not a blind conformist. You're a maverick. A free spirit. An entrepreneur of the soul.

Although it's been twenty-five years since seminary, I know you're an avid reader. You've probably read more contemporary publications on philosophy and religion than most of our clergy.

You've often said you didn't feel adequate to be a minister. Now you've got twenty-five years of gathering life maturity. Three careers and twenty years owning your own company.

You've also been critical, with reason, of organized religion.

Why not make a contribution from "inside" rather than criticizing from the outside?

As your best friend, and in my official position as president of our church body, I invite you to join us. I know you'll weigh your decision carefully.

Yours in friendship,
Bob

"Wow! That's quite a letter," Mike said to himself.

He read it three times before slipping it in the top drawer of his desk. He didn't even mention it to Jane when he went home for dinner. Later she told him she wondered why he was so quiet.

Chapter 19

Challenge of a Lifetime

Mike slept very little that night. Conflicting reactions to Bob's letter were chasing one another through his mind. The next morning he called Bob.

"Good morning. Bob, you really got my thinking out of the starting blocks with your letter."

"Good. Glad to hear it. You're giving it consideration then."

"I have to, coming from you, Bob. My biggest hurdle is not the issue of turning over my business or leaving all this affluence we're used to. Jane and I were willing to leave that behind when we considered the senate nomination."

"I sensed that, Mike, when we talked about your possible senate career."

"There may be a problem though, as there was with the Washington setting, with Jane coping with a minister's wife role. I also need to sift and sort out my personal religious convictions—reidentify my own inner spiritual self—and relate it to the state of the church today to see if there is indeed a possible fit."

"Right on, Mike. Go to work. I'll be thinking of you. This might be one of the greatest challenges you've ever faced."

"No question about that," Mike replied.

"But I know you," Bob continued "you'll have fun wrestling with the challenge and come out with a plausible conclusion which you can live with. Just don't tell your mother. You know she'll go directly to the commander-in-chief in her prayers and you won't have a chance."

"You're right. No, of course I won't be consulting her. She's too biased. If I have any further questions, Bob, I'll call. Otherwise, I think I'm going to summarize my thoughts in writing, in a type of 'position paper'."

After sharing Bob's letter with Jane, and having a number of long talks together, Mike recorded his reactions on dozens of note sheets over the next several days. He wrote notes while driving, between appointments and at night when he couldn't sleep.

About a week later he wrote his criteria for acceptance of Bob's proposition, should that be his decision. He labeled it "Position Paper". It stated the following:

(1) I recognize that around the world there are thousands of spiritual leaders performing an effective service to individuals, communities, churches and society in general. Frequently, their work is unappreciated, unrecognized and under supported.

Many of these men and women are well educated, devout, dedicated and in some cases very talented. It could be an honor to join their ranks.

By contrast there are rascals and renegades wearing the cloak of the spiritual leader, and they aren't all on TV. They deceptively manipulate people. Cause them to question noble, basic values and replace them with inauthentic ones. Their message frequently is one of hell, wrath and vengeance, not love and mercy.

Often they are charismatic and appear very sanctified. Actually, their message is treacherous, false and spiritually hollow. Frequently, they meet people at the point of their greatest vulnerability, when they are troubled, disturbed, insecure. They come at them with a Las Vegas type of Jesus, promises of instant dissolution of all problems, followed by the big shakedown for money.

Obviously, I don't want any part of these renegades. If there is such a thing as an unpardonable sin, people who misrepresent God and profit from a distortion of mind and spirit—these are the ones committing the unpardonable sin.

In between the two extremes there is a third type of representative of religion. They are pious, sincere and devoted. Unfortunately, they are also incompetent, joyless, rigid and negative. They proclaim a drab, dismal, uninspiring system of beliefs and living which is irrelevant to our contemporary human situation.

In the case of the Christian religion, it is questionable whether they are reflecting the dynamic, exciting invitation of Jesus of Nazareth who said, "Come, and follow me . . . The Kingdom of Heaven is within you."

I would choose not to be one of them.

(2) However, it would not be my objective to spawn another sect, adding to the already confusing maze—each one, unfortunately, claiming to speak for the one true God.

In fact, I would not want to assume the role of speaking FOR God. I question whether anyone ever has or does speak exclusively FOR God. It would be enough of a humbling honor to attempt to speak ABOUT God—to relate to our humanness God's truth, love, and creativity as revealed now and through the ages within and around us.

(3) Consistent with this position, I would try to avoid pomposity in the form of labels and uniforms. I would choose not to be called "Reverend" (because who is?). "Mister" would be preferred. I would like it best to be known as Mike. I would choose not to wear the clerical collar or the robes. At the most, I would wear a choir robe during a service.

I would choose not to use a pulpit, which to me is a symbol of setting myself apart and isolating me from my fellow worshipers. A lectern on the front platform of the Church would be preferred.

I would wish for no one to think of me as being above others or on a pedestal. It would be my hope that though striving for excellence, parishioners would recognize that the only thing at which I am perfect is being imperfect.

At sermon time I would like the listeners' perception to be that I am speaking WITH them not AT them.

(4) It would also be my wish that every worship service

would be a highlight of the week for each participant. In the fifty to sixty minutes people come together the overwhelming mood should be: "We are in the eternal loving presence of God."

I would hope that the setting, music, words, silence, and prayers reflect a pageantry of awe, mystery, majesty, healing and new vitality of spirit. Worshipers should be moved at least to as much depth of feeling and wonder as they are when listening to a great symphony. Standing in the presence of a magnificent glacier. Watching a prize play.

A church service should be orchestrated by its leader to inspire participants to a mood of communion with God. It should be relevant, positive, uplifting, joyful. Each person should be able to leave with at least one powerful idea as an aid for spiritual growth and living during the week.

Irritating intrusions into the reflective, meditative, inspiring mood should be eliminated, such as: ridiculous, repeated standing and sitting sequences like "jack-in-the-box" times; intermissions for announcements (people can read the bulletin); the commercial for the offering (appropriate offering boxes at exits can perform the same function).

Finally, with regard to the worship experience in a church, it is my opinion that the Church needs to take a page out of the marketing experience of America's supermarkets. Worship opportunities, other than Sundays, should also be offered at key times during the week rather than haranguing people for not showing up Sunday mornings.

(5) In order to accomplish the objectives of number four above, it might be necessary to eliminate the use of certain archaic hymns and prayers which at best are poor poetry and bad translations. It would also be necessary to rewrite some lesson plans, and conduct rigorous volunteer teacher training, for religious education classes.

(6) It would be my preference to be a minister in a city setting with a potential outreach to a variety of economic, social and racial strata. I would also prefer working primarily with children, teens, working age singles, and young to middle age marrieds.

(7) If number six above necessitates starting a new congregation from scratch, I would be pleased to do that. It would also be my desire to personally fund, anonymously, through the outreach division of the church, the start-up costs of such a new congregation.

It would be expected, subsequently, that this congregation be self-supporting—including, for their own integrity, refunding the start-up loan to the church body.

My income would be no more and no less than the average salary. I would have nothing to do with handling the finances of the church, other than sharing goals and motivation for giving. I would also not live in a parsonage, but own my home. Such home would be unpretentious, compatible with the neighborhood served, but large enough to entertain groups of church members.

(8) I would expect that my various business ventures would be placed in trust, and managed apart from my personal involvement, during the period of my service to the church.

(9) In keeping with my philosophy of "vocation", as being a calling from God, I would populate my staff primarily with non-ordained personnel.

They would be professionally trained and skilled in such areas as administration, financing, education, counseling, youth leadership, music and the arts, child care and service to the aging.

(10) Though some of my personal theological and doctrinal positions do not fit some of the orthodox views of the mainline church, I would pledge not to deliberately disturb the beliefs of parishioners which might clash with mine. I would expect, however, to be able to encourage free inquiry, intellectual and spiritual freedom, and the ideal of unity in diversity.

In conclusion, I would expect to be interrogated by an ordination review board of the church. Since my theological bent is more in harmony with a Thoreau or Emerson's Universalism than the church organization in question, I would have no problem with a decision against my ordination, should that occur.

Jane was the first person who read Mike's "Position Paper." She had several good suggestions.

"Would you consider," she asked, "adding something about my role as a minister's wife? In many of the churches I have observed, the wife is cast in about the same role as the senator's wife, a nonentity, an afterthought, an appendage standing in the shadows of her husband. She is expected to be impeccably pure, supportive, and no opinions of her own. I don't want to lose my identity, Mike."

"You're absolutely right, Jane. I'll add that to my statement and make a special point of it when I talk with Bob."

"I think it would be very important," Jane continued, "to continue our family dinner times, as frequently as possible, for Teresa's benefit as well as our's. I would hope, Mike, that you and I could have our one night a week privately away from the business of the church."

"I agree, Jane, we should pledge that we'd continue to get away for a day or two whenever we could. Also, I feel if you would like to develop interests or a career of your own, like returning to the stage, you should feel free to do so."

"I need that freedom of choice, Mike. And I have one more suggestion. I don't know if you want this as part of your written statement, but if you decide to do this are you going to say anything in advance about how long you would be willing to be a minister? Your pattern has been to live in career cycles. Do you see yourself staying with the church until you retire? If not, do you think you should say something?"

"I think that's an unknown, Jane. But you've raised a good point. I don't think I should put anything in writing. I can't see myself taking an ordination vow requiring a lifetime commitment."

"How about having one of our family meetings, Mike, and let the boys and Teresa express themselves?"

"Good idea. I do want to involve the children. I value their advice, and besides they will be effected in varying degrees."

"Scott will be a junior in college, and Dane will be starting his college career a year from this fall," Jane continued, "so the change won't effect them as much as Teresa. However, with Teresa just starting high school this might not be such a bad time for a move. But let's give them a chance to express themselves."

Scott was coming home for the weekend, so it was agreed to have a family conference Sunday before he went back to school.

Jane asked that the kids have advance time to form an opinion, so Mike had copies made of his paper and gave it to them Friday evening before they all took off with their friends.

The meeting Sunday was very emotional. Teresa was the first to speak. "What am I going to do with my horses and pets? I can't give them up."

She was beginning to get choked up.

"How about if we make arrangements for one horse," Mike said "to be shipped and boarded wherever we move, and keep one of your dogs and the cat? Could you live with that, Teresa? And then find a wonderful home for your other horses and dogs here? You could visit them periodically."

"I suppose so, Dad. But what about my friends? I'll be so lonely starting high school in a new school."

Jane responded to this tense issue: "We know this would be very difficult for you, Teresa, to say goodbye to your friends. But your very closest friend is a girl you spend most of your time with. How about if we could make arrangements for her to visit, and you to go back to Florida frequently? She could also visit at our condo at Hilton Head when we're there."

"As far as high school is concerned, that's the beginning of a completely new adventure in your life," Mike added. "We have to learn to handle these changes. But you make friends so easily. I'm sure within a few weeks, you'd be having a ball."

"You're probably right, Dad."

So far Dane and Scott had just been listening. "What are you thinking, Dane?" Jane asked.

"Well, I'm really proud of you, Dad, that Uncle Bob would want you to be a minister. That's a big honor, just like it was to be asked to run for the Senate. I've been doing a lot of thinking since you gave us your statement. I think your words are well thought through."

"Thanks Dane."

"I was wondering, though, if there would be any chance for me to stay here and finish high school. It's my senior year coming up, you know. What about the Adams' home? Do you think they'd let me stay with them? John and I are in the same grade and good friends. I could visit you as often as possible."

"I think that's a good possibility, Dane," Mike responded. "What do you think, Jane?"

"Naturally, we'd miss you terribly Dane, and watching your ball games. But we could visit here occasionally too. I think Dan and his wife might welcome that idea. It would be one of the first things we'd check into if your dad decides to do this."

"I suppose we'd have to sell this beautiful home, huh?" Dane added.

"Yes, we would," Mike replied, "We'd all miss it, but we would keep our place at Hilton Head and move the boats up there. Also, if you boys wanted to, you could still have a job summers with my companies here."

"Scott, you look very thoughtful. What do you have to add?" Jane asked.

"I agree with Dane, Dad. It would be an honor and you'd make a heck of a good minister. I'd go to your church. If this works out you don't know where it would be, do you?"

"No, I don't Scott. As implied in my paper, I would like it to be in or near some major city."

"Speaking of a city, Dad, I'm going to transfer to Boston University. Maybe you could live there. I want to go into some phase of writing, and Boston U has a good creative writing department."

"Could you specify with Uncle Bob," Dane chimed in, "a general area of the country you would prefer?"

"Yeah, that would be neat," Teresa added, "we all like to ski, and you and the boys, Dad, like the lakes and mountains of New England. Mom likes New York and Maine. Could you get a church somewhere around there?"

"Probably, Teresa. Grandma and Grandpa also live in

Portland, so we could visit them once in awhile. Why don't I tell Bob that as a family we'd prefer some city area in upper New York, Massachusetts or Pennsylvania? How does that sound?"

"I think we'd all vote for that, Dad, if you decide to do this. How do you feel about that, Dane?" Scott asked.

"I like that idea. There are dozens of good universities in the East with a reputation for good architectural schools. We'd be reasonably close to Stowe and Stratton Mountain, Vermont. Also we'd probably have non-stop airline connections back here to Florida when we wanted to visit. Yeah! I'd like that."

The family conference closed on that note, with everyone agreeing that they'd try to be positive in exploring this possible new adventure. Jane and Mike promised to speak with Dan Adams about Dane living with them for his senior year if the decision was made to move.

After editing the position paper with the comments about the role of a minister's wife, and the Matthews families' location preference, Mike expressed it off to Bob.

Two days later Bob telephoned.

"I liked your paper, Mike. Superbly thought through and worded. I don't see a major problem, especially with your preference to start up a new congregation. If you would go into an older, traditional congregation there could be some conflicts. But this way you should be able to achieve all of your criteria."

"It's important that I do, Bob."

"How do you want to handle the screening for possible ordination, Mike? Do you want to do it before your final decision?"

"Definitely. I could do it as soon as you can arrange it," Mike replied.

"OK, I'll get to work on it immediately. You know, Mike, that the elected review board of five members is augmented by two of my appointees. I can tell you now, one of them is going to be the clergyman you counseled way back there in St. Paul when you were with Bradshaw Associates. The clergyman told me about your helping him, and how much he appreciated your confidence. He's retired now, so I'm sure he'll accept the appointment.

The second appointee is going to be your father. What do you think?"

"You devil, Bob. I think you're stacking it."

"That's my privilege. I'd like to make this as simple as possible, Mike. What would you think of your writing a short statement of your position theologically using The Apostles' Creed? I could distribute that to the review board in advance."

"I'd be happy to do that. I could have that to you in a few days."

"As you know," Bob added, "that's the oldest and briefest doctrinal statement of the organized Christian religion. I know from our many talks in the past that you don't agree with some of the traditional orthodox vocabulary or interpretations of that statement. But I think the majority of the board will vote for your ordination based on the way you explain yourself."

"I'll get to work on it, Bob. By the way, you also have my permission to share a copy of my 'Position Paper' with the review board members, if you wish. I assume it will be held in confidence?"

"Yes, it will."

"Good, Bob, I'll talk to you in a few days. Meanwhile, I'll be doing my own reviewing of my decision if I'm approved."

Mike's review included an in depth analysis of some of his personal religious beliefs in relation to The Apostles' Creed. He wrote it out so he would have the words in front of him.

"I believe in God the Father Almighty, Maker of heaven and earth, and in Jesus Christ his only Son our Lord, who was conceived by the Holy Spirit, born of the Virgin Mary, suffered under Pontius Pilate, was crucified, dead, and buried; he descended into hell; the third day he rose again from the dead; he ascended into heaven, and sitteth on the right hand of God the Father Almighty; from thence he shall come to judge the quick and the dead. I believe in the Holy Spirit; the holy catholic Church; the comm   of saints; the forgiveness of sins; the resurrection of the body; and the life everlasting. Amen."

Mike followed Bob's suggestion of writing a brief capsule of his religious beliefs, as measured against The Apostles' Creed. He addressed it to: The Ordination Review Board, as follows . . .

"Gentlemen: You will quickly see this is not intended to be an exhaustive summary of my religious faith, or a detailed explanation of The Apostles' Creed. I am only intending in this statement to capsulize my opinions as they may vary from a traditional interpretation.

"At the outset, I would like to go on record as admitting: 'I DON'T KNOW,' as to many of the dogmas of Christian Theology. This may seem like a terrible admission to you; but it is one that I must make, and feel that all clergymen should acknowledge.

"When I say 'I Don't Know,' I mean, of course, that I am not in possession of absolute, exclusive knowledge. I am not using the word 'know' as it means to perceive, to have understanding, or to be aware. I am using the Greek derivative as it means 'to have direct cognition of.'

"It is my observation, from nearly half a century of exposure to the Christian Church, that to give the impression of knowing everything about God gets ministers into a peck of trouble.

"For example, very soon they actually seem to believe they know everything. Their parishioners believe it. Then the minister is expected to have the final answer to every subject, and he or she is in real trouble. There is a tremendous stress factor. The guilt trip can also be devastating when it becomes apparent that a weak or wrong answer to a question has been given.

"It is deplorable, in my opinion, when a minister develops an inflated ego and thrives on the adulation of parishioners who actually believe their minister can say or do no wrong.

"How much better to admit: 'I don't know', when one does not know for sure. This is one of the first things I tell my marketing people in business: 'When you're selling a property, a home, a townhouse, an apartment building or an idea to a city council and you aren't certain about the answer to a question, don't pretend or manufacture a reply, just admit, 'I don't know;' but I'll work on it and be back with the best answer I can discover.'

"I have personal difficulty with the anthropomorphic designation of God as 'Father.' I do not choose to visualize God as male or female. In a culture aspiring for equality between the sexes, it is a mistake, in my opinion, to cast God as either male or female.

"There are so many shabby images of 'father' in this world—fathers who are cruel, deserters, liars, drunks, addicts, wife beaters — that it is counter-productive to label God as 'father'.

"I personally think of God as an eternal, intelligent, personal, caring presence permeating the universe and indwelling all of life, including 'everyman'.

"The word 'only' I must omit from my personal use of the Creed, as it relates to the identity of Christ. I believe that Jesus Christ was son of man and son of God. I believe God, the Creator, incarnated Jesus of Nazareth, as God indwells every person. In Jesus' life, I believe he allowed more of the divine to encompass his awareness.

"Perhaps it would be more accurate for me to say that I believe Jesus of Nazareth allowed God to permeate his being more fully than most other humans to date on this planet. Just as there are in human history, phenomenal genius personalities in music, art or science so Jesus possessed exceptional gifts of Divine Spirit.

"Unquestionably, Jesus was a master of religious principles. His teachings and followers have dramatically effected the course of history over the past 2000 years. Faith in his teachings, as recorded in the Gospels of the New Testament, and the continuing vitality and energy of his being, are still revolutionizing people's lives. He is light and hope and motivation for millions. Music, art, literature and drama in the western world are still being influenced by his teachings.

"Further, I hold that the language 'conceived by the Holy Spirit, born of the Virgin Mary,' is unnecessary to my faith.

"It is highly probable that the phrase is partially reflective of an attitude toward sex during the time period when the Creed was written.

"To me, a sexual relationship between man and woman is intended to be a beautiful, pure act of love—a gift of God. It does not diminish my image of the greatness of Jesus when I think of Joseph and Mary being his real earthly parents.

"Understandably, Jesus went through 'hell' as the Creed says. However, I don't find it necessary to think of 'hell' as a place, anymore than 'heaven' must be a place rather than a condition.

"When a person is deserted by his friends, that's hell. When an individual suffers excruciating pain, descends into the dregs of human experience, feels totally separated from God, loses a sense of hope, is tempted to give up all faith—that is hell.

"To me it is irrelevant whether Jesus transferred from death to life on the third day or the fourth or tenth. If we believe in an eternal Creative Presence permeating all of life, there is no such reality as time; and there is no death—only change.

"As the Creed declares, I believe Jesus exists, as do we, forever, and dwells in and with God. His life, to the degree it is accurately recorded, is a standard of spirituality against which we can be measured. To that extent we are judged by his ideal.

"I do not find it necessary to be anthropomorphic and visualize Jesus as a 'Judge' wielding a gavel in a planetary courtroom.

"I surely do believe in an ecumenical and universal church as a communion of believers. Sadly, it is not 'holy', however. The organized followers of every religious leader in history have not always lived up to the ideals and principles of the founder.

"Tragically, bureaucracies of religion sometimes forget

their source, lose sight of their origins and betray their founders. Do we really think that Jesus of Galilee would recognize his 'church' today, accept it as his and feel at home in its fellowship?

"I am aware that one of the questions I will be asked by the ordination review board is: 'If you are approved, and if you should decide to enter the ministry, what is your basic, underlying reason for doing so?'

"In the interest of time before the review board, I would like to summarize my reply in this paper.

"I have a strong sense of the need for spiritual vitality in our society and the world today. I believe in the sanctity of the family, the dignity of mankind, the equality of all people before God.

"I believe in a God who is creator, loving, fair, kind, personal, positive, joyful. I believe that an awareness of God's presence within and around us creates an incomparable sense of serenity and peace.

"Experiencing and feeling this causes one to wish to share this mystery, this wonder, and miracle with others. The only question is how? Thus far in my life I feel it has been my privilege to share the power and presence of God through several different careers.

"I am sad and appalled at the many self-appointed counterfeits of religion in our world. How many thousands of people are there whose lives could be enriched by being set free, not only from ignorance, but distortions of the truth and misinformation?

"It is conceivable that, as 'there is a season and a time to every purpose under the heaven,' perhaps it is time for me to accept the challenge in a more direct way, to help set free those who are in bondage.

"Gentlemen, I look forward to the opportunity to review this question with you.

"In summary, this paper contains the thoughts which go through my mind when I read the words of The Apostles' Creed. I remember that this statement was, of course, not composed by the twelve apostles, but by a group of early church leaders who constituted one of the first councils of the movement of Christianity. They wrote the words for their time as they perceived the apostles' credo.

"In this contemporary setting of 1972 in America, and according to my personal spiritual beliefs, I would choose to phrase the words this way:

I believe in God Almighty, Creator of heaven and earth, and in Jesus Christ son of man and son of God, who was born of Joseph and Mary, suffered under Pontius Pilate, was crucified, and buried; he descended into hell; he rose again from the dead; he ascended into heaven, and dwells in the presence of God. I believe in the Spirit of God, the ecumenical, universal church, the communion of fellow believers; the forgiveness of sins; the resurrection and the life everlasting. Amen."

Chapter 20

Passing the Test

Prior to the meeting of the review board, each member was mailed Mike's position paper and credo. Bob called after reading the statement on the Creed.

"I think you're in, Mike, if you want to be. There may be three members who will have a problem with parts of your doctrinal statement. But it's my opinion that the vote will still be at least 4 to 3 in your favor."

"You should know," Mike replied. "I have mixed feelings. The truth is it wouldn't fracture me if I were not approved. I'm very happy with my life right now. The business is going well, and we just started a huge new venture."

"Oh, what's that?"

"We're getting into the highway hospitality business. My vice president for research and development talked me into beginning a chain of lower priced, first class motels without the frills."

"Sounds like a dynamite idea. Especially with all the freeway traffic and tourism in your part of the country."

"Besides, and most importantly, my family seems very happy. Jane gets restless now and then for a more challenging career interest, but we're very close in our marriage. Teresa, Dane and Scott all seem to have it together."

"How about you, Mike? I sense that you might be ready to reach for a new dream, something more exciting than a new chain of motels. You know what you and I used to talk about in some of our late night seminary sessions: 'Choose your dreams carefully. They have a way of coming true.'"

"I know, Bob, I'm going to tread carefully on this one. It could be the toughest and most important decision of my life. I appreciate your call. Let me know when the meeting date is decided."

"I will. You know sometimes the board doesn't require a personal appearance. Maybe they'll pass on this one based on the statements you've written. Of course, in order to be ordained it's required that the candidate have an assignment to a parish."

"Yeah, how about that? Where are you thinking of assigning your old buddy? Death Valley?"

"How about the Badlands? You and the rattlers. Seriously, my first choice for you is an area on the outskirts of Boston," Bob said. "How about that? Our old girl chasing, beer drinking territory."

"Yeah, actually we didn't have much time for chasing during those years and about enough money for one beer a piece.

"But Boston, you say. That sounds fascinating. Could make a difference to my family and my decision. Scott has transferred to Boston U. It's close to excellent skiing. Jane would be close to her friends in New York. It would be convenient to visit my parents in Portland, and it would also be an easy commute to Florida."

"I feel you would be an excellent fit for the intellectual, social and age mix of people there, Mike. The area is growing rapidly. Of course I'd let you pick the exact location. With your years of experience in demographics and choosing sites, you're the expert on that."

"Bob, did you deliberately plant all these exciting possibilities in my brain? Sure you did. But that's your job, and you're good at it. I've got to run now. Got tons of things to do. Thanks again for your call. See you soon."

Mike's days were jammed from six a.m. to at least midnight. Jane saw to it that they still took time for their usual morning swim in the pool. They also had another family conference over dinner centered on the possible move. On a scale of one to ten, Mike was given eight in the overall reaction to Boston.

Even Teresa was more up when she learned that she could be close to some horse boarding areas as well as great art museums and galleries. Jane also was fascinated by the prospect of being closer to metropolitan cultural centers.

It was essential for Mike to take some time to be alone. He craved the luxury of solitude for his decision time. He needed time to cleanse his cluttered mind, to let shafts of spiritual light into his soul. He needed to allow his business cares to recede into the background momentarily so he could reflect on this enormous possible change of direction.

Typically, he could think and be alone best walking the beach or taking the boat out on the ocean—watching the sunrise, feeling the spray in his face, fighting the winds, sensing the surge of power in the engines.

Other mornings, before any normal golfer was on the course, he would throw his light bag over his shoulder and head out, hitting two balls around the course. He found some of his best spiritual therapy on the golf course. He thrived on the challenge of the game.

"It's like life," he thought. "Just the course and me. No one to blame for a bad shot except me. Likewise, when playing well, knowing I did it. Listening to the mating calls of birds. Observing alligators and turtles basking in the sun by the ponds. Watching the flowers grow. Monarchs dancing on their stage, and sometimes in the pelting rain and ferocious winds thriving in being soaked and overcoming."

Often times he would think, "This can be infinitely better than going to church when the service is abrasive and the sermon lousy.

"Better ponder this, Michael Charles Matthews, if you are thinking of going into the ministry."

Ponder it, he did! Sometimes awakening during the night and taking pen and notebook on the nightstand to hastily scribble notes so he wouldn't forget come morning.

Mike's mother also called. He expected she would.

"Dad has always shared everything with her," Mike recalled, "so I knew she would read my papers mailed to the review board."

"Michael Charles, I'm so proud," Mrs. Matthews said. "You've made me indescribably happy that you're at least thinking about the ministry. I told you that you were destined, didn't I? Oh, I know I'm not supposed to say that. I too have changed. Hopefully grown through the years. I realize now it's your choice, not mine. How are you, Son?"

"Fine, Mother. The Matthews family is doing some hard thinking. When the time comes, I think I'll be ready with the right decision, Mother. How are you and Dad? I know you've had some arthritis, and Dad's wearing hearing aids plus he's having increased hardening of the arteries problems.

"Speaking of hearing aids, Mother, have you heard the one about Sam, the senior citizen who went to his ear doctor?"

"No, I haven't Michael."

"Well, he went to see his ear doctor. 'Doc,' he said 'I can't hear well and my hearing aid quit working.'

"'Let me take a look, Sam. No wonder, you've got a suppository in there.'

"'Goodness' Sam replied, 'I wonder where I put my hearing aid?'"

"Oh, Michael! I'll have to tell your father that one.

"Seriously, Michael, you know we're enjoying our lovely home that your company built for us. Dad swims everyday also. He just got a YMCA award for being the oldest 'miler' in the swim club. That means he has to swim at least a mile a day for five days a week."

"That's super, Mother. And what do you do that's interesting?"

"Oh, I'm busy all the time. I love my garden and flowers. I knit and crochet, and you know how I love to cook. Dad likes to have me go with him sometimes when he visits the sick and shut-ins, and I like helping bring cheer and sharing the love of the Lord with those who are lonely and in need."

"I remember how you love to do that, Mother."

"Remember too how I would leave a note in the kitchen for

you after school when I was out with yourfather. I listed your daily duties after you'd had the one cookie and glass of milk I set out. But I knew you had a second cookie, Michael. You didn't fool me for one second. Did I also tell you I knew you were smoking your Dad's cigars in the loft of the garage?"

"You're kidding? You didn't know."

"Oh, yes, I did, but I didn't tell your father. One of the only secrets I ever kept from him. Well, I'd better let you go. I've got things to do.

"We're packing for a short trip up the coast of Maine. We take a picnic basket and then buy a fresh lobster on the docks when the fishing boats come in. They boil it in salt water and seaweed, and we find a place on the rocks to have our lunch. Believe it or not, we top our lunch off with a glass of wine."

"Good for you, Mother. You and Dad are surely getting modern, aren't you?"

"I suppose so. You know what else we enjoy?"

"No, Mother, what?"

"Remember all those movies we wouldn't let you kids see in the theater?"

"Do I ever! Mother, you wouldn't?"

"Yup! Your dad and I love to watch some of them in the evenings on the TV set you gave us. You know what? Some of them are really good. Sorry we were so straight-laced."

"Don't worry about it, Mother. I've forgiven you for that ages ago. I'm just pleased that you and Dad are enjoying life. You deserve it. I love you both very much."

"Thank you, Son. I've got to run. Good luck and God bless you on your decision. Goodbye."

Bob's call came two days later. Mike was out examining one of the new motel sites when his office put him through on the car phone.

"What's up, Bob? Is the decision all made?"

"No. The review board would like to meet with you personally, Mike. That's good news for me because it means they haven't turned you down. Could you be here day after tomorrow at the church headquarters office at 10 a.m.?"

"I'll cancel whatever I have scheduled, if necessary. I'll be there," Mike replied.

He asked Jane if she would be willing to make the trip to New York with him. "We can stay in one of our old haunts, The New York Athletic Club," he said, "and you can renew some of your old friendships, if you like, and do some shopping. Maybe we can work in a play."

"You know I'd love to go. I'll make arrangements with our caretakers so Dane and Teresa's needs will be taken care of while we're gone."

On the plane Jane reached over and took Mike's hand. "Mike, this has been a trying time for you, hasn't it?"

"Yes, but it's been exciting too. No dull moments in the Matthews' household are there?"

"That's right. You've made your decision, haven't you, Mike? I feel it. I know you have, and it's 'yes', isn't it?"

"Yes, it's what I want to do at this stage of my life. All those years in college and seminary when my friends were dying in the war, and I tried to enlist . . . tried the chaplaincy as a side door when I couldn't pass the physical . . . all these high adventure years of thrilling, challenging careers . . . now I feel Bob is right 'there is a time', and it's now that I have something to offer. I wasn't ready after the seminary. The task was too awesome. I needed to grow, to live, to learn."

"A church would be lucky to get you, Mike."

"Thanks. As you know, Jane," Mike continued, "I love children, young people, the new generation. If I can put a burr under a few saddles, as Teresa would say, to change a few lives for the better . . . if I can open some windows, stretch a few minds, sweep some cobwebs out of a few souls (mixing metaphors, aren't I?) and undo some distortions of religious ideas sold by a few counterfeiters and hucksters, I will be satisfied."

"Mike, I know you will do all of that." You have my love and my support. You know that."

"I do know that, Jane. I couldn't begin to move into this new arena without your approval. I love you very much. I couldn't choose to make this move if I felt it would be harmful to our relationship or the children."

"There's just one thing I need to tell you, Mike," Jane added. "I too have wrestled with this decision. It represents an enormous change for me also.

"I don't know if I'll be able to handle the traditional role of a minister's wife, Mike. If I find that I need breathing room, if the parish role becomes too suffocating for me, I would like to have the freedom with your approval to develop my own career interests."

"I think that would be wonderful, Jane. I don't have any difficulty with that. The children are older. We'll only have Teresa at home. Are you thinking of something related to the theater?"

"Yes. I've been thinking of getting back into acting. It's in my blood. It could be repertoire theatre, or off broadway either acting or directing. What do you think?"."

"Jane, you'd have my complete blessing. Sounds exciting." I would just hope that we wouldn't be separated for prolonged time periods."

"Same here, Mike. I'm sure we can work something out."

The conversation was interrupted by touch down. They had traveled light so there was no waiting for baggage. It didn't take long to commute to the Athletic Club, and Mike was on his way to the church headquarters' building.

He enjoyed seeing his dad again. They gave each other a hug as they walked into the board room. Everyone was genuinely cordial, and Mike got a warm feeling of friendliness from the group.

"Mr. Matthews," the chairman began, "we've looked forward to meeting you. Thanks for coming. As Dr. Mackay has informed you, we have all read your thorough and thoughtful papers. Well written by the way. You have a gift for lucid, articulate expression."

"Thank you, sir," Mike replied.

We have discussed in depth our response," the chairman continued, "and I asked each member of the board to submit, in advance of your coming, any questions which the board member would like me to ask.

"Actually, there are only four. I would like to raise them with you now, if that's acceptable."

"Please let me hear them, and I'll answer them to the best of my ability," Mike responded.

"Mr. Matthews, it appears that you hold a position on the outer edge of the classical theological interpretation of the Trinity. Is that true?"

"Yes, that is correct. Although I would qualify my reply, as I have in my paper, by also saying 'I don't know' for sure. I am not the first, nor will I be the last, within the family of the Christian religion who cannot fully subscribe to the catechism's definition of 'Trinity'."

"Would you care to elaborate, Mr. Matthews?"

"Yes. I believe, as I have stated, in God's Presence, and Power revealed in Jesus of Nazareth. I believe he is therefore Divine. But I believe others are also, though not at the same level. Furthermore, I believe God's Spirit permeates the universe . . . me, you, 'everyman,' every aspect of creation."

"You would hold a position close to Ralph Waldo Emerson. Is that correct?"

"Yes, I would say so."

"Thank you, Mr. Matthews.

"Are there further questions from the board on this subject?"

Since there were none, the chairman went on. "Given your viewpoint on the doctrine of 'Trinity' the board would like to ask: 'How would you reconcile your expression with the Church's standard baptism liturgy for a child?"

"It would be my preference," Mr. Chairman, "to vary the wording slightly to read something like: 'I baptize you in the name and in the spirit of the one loving creator God and his son, Jesus Christ'."

"Thank you, Mr. Matthews.

"Now, one of our group asked me to raise the following question: We understand your objection to using male gender words like 'Father' with reference to God. However, one of the oldest traditional prayers of the Church comes from the New Testament . . . the words of 'The Lord's Prayer'. Would you not use the salutation 'Our Father'?"

"I could use 'The Lord's Prayer' as traditionally recorded", Mike responded. "For our times and our culture I would prefer if it began 'Our God', or 'Our Maker', or 'Our Creator'. But I understand the Hebrew and Aramaic culture in which Jesus lived made it very natural to refer to God as 'Father'. It would never be my presumption to write a new version of this beautiful prayer."

"I guess I couldn't argue with that," the chairman responded. "Now, unless there are further questions, the final one submitted to me was this: 'What would you anticipate might be your reaction if an individual wanted to join your parish who claimed to be a fundamentalist convert and a 'born again Christian'?"

"It would be my guess, Mr. Chairman," Mike replied, "that even though as you surmised, I do not fit into that style of religious expression, I would answer something like this: Welcome, friend! Be assured, that if this is a church home you feel at home in, we are happy to have you. It would be my hope that you will be treated with courtesy, love, and respect even though your spiritual expression may be different than others.

"Conversely, we would expect to be treated by you with the charity of I Corinthians 13. You remember the words: 'love suffereth long, and is kind; love envieth not; love vaunteth not itself, is not puffed up, doth not behave itself unseemly, seeketh not her own, is not easily provoked, thinketh no evil; rejoiceth not in iniquity, but rejoiceth in the truth; beareth all things, believeth all things, hopeth all things, endureth all things. Love never faileth; but whether there be prophecies, they shall fail; whether there be tongues, they shall cease; whether there be knowledge, it shall vanish away.'"

"Well put, Mr. Matthews. Do you have any questions you would like to ask us?"

"None that I can think of at the moment."

"If you would be so kind then as to wait in the reception room we would like to summarize our reactions, take a vote and report to you in a few minutes."

"Thank you, gentlemen," Mike said. "I'll look forward to your decision. You've been most gracious."

All of a sudden it hit Mike what was at stake. Here he was forty-nine years old, an entrepreneur worth millions, successful over the years in several careers, a recipient of two graduate degrees and many corporate and personal honors; yet he was feeling like a school boy sitting in the outer office of his eighth grade principal waiting to see if he would be expelled.

"It is a good experience, humbling, stimulating," Mike thought.

In approximately ten minutes the door opened and the chairman invited him back.

"Mr. Michael Charles Matthews, son," (it was his father speaking and there was a bit of mist over his eyes, but he spoke proudly and clearly) "this ordination review board has invited me to announce to you our decision. We have voted to invite you to join the clergy of our church body. We hope that you will accept our decision as a positive encouragement in weighing your choice. If it is negative, we will understand. If it is positive, we will be extremely pleased."

Now it was Mike's turn to be choked up. After what seemed like minutes of silence, he rose to speak.

"Dad . . . gentlemen, this is a highly emotional moment for me. So I prefer to stand as I say what I would like to express to you.

"As you know, Bob Mackay has been my closest friend for almost thirty years . . . since seminary days. He is the one who said: 'This might be your time, Mike, to express your sense of vocation as a minister.'

"You also know, of course, that I grew up as a preacher's kid, not always exemplary I confess. It's a honor to meet with you today and have my dad announce your decision to me.

"You have read my 'Position Paper'. You know my commitment to a philosophy that all of life is a vocation, a calling from God. With all due respect to each one of you, I don't believe the position of the ordained clergy is automatically a loftier vocation on God's list than others.

"However, I have made my decision. I told Jane, my wife, what it would be as we sat in the plane on the way to New York. I have turned my mind and soul upside down, inside out and back again. My decision is to accept your invitation and go to work as soon as possible developing a new parish outside of Boston. How long . . . for how many years . . . Bob knows he will need to leave that up to me. But I assure you, gentlemen, I will give it my best shot for as long as it seems right to me."

Bob was pacing the reception area waiting for our meeting to end. As Dad and Mike came through the door, arm in arm, he could sense the outcome.

"It was 'YES', right? Congratulations buddy and welcome to the team. Now there's someone waiting for a call. I promised your mother she'd be one of the first to know. Why don't you use my office?"

Mrs. Matthews was ecstatic. She was so excited she even forgot to call him Michael Charles.

"This is the happiest day of my life, Mike" she said. "Now I feel like Simeon in the New Testament when he saw the Christ child brought to the temple: 'Lord, now lettest thou thy servant depart in peace, according to thy word.' I can't wait to attend your first service and ordination. When will it be?"

"Probably in September, Mother. You and Dad will have a reserved seat. That's for sure. You take care now, and we'll stay in touch."

There were dozens of pressing responsibilities requir-

Chapter 21

What On Earth Are You Doing?

ing attention before the Matthews could move to Boston.

Their home was made ready for sale. MATTHEWS ENTERPRISES was structured with new top management. There were boards and activities to vacate, and farewell parties to attend.

Nothing, however, was more important in the Matthews' household at the moment than junior-senior prom time for Dane. It was orange blossom, Hibiscus, orchid tree spring. Time for romance and celebration.

When Scott's prom dates had been announced it was generation gap, against establishment time, and Scott had not attended.

Dane's girlfriend was an adorable petite blond. The whole family loved her. Dane asked if he could use the Cadillac rather than his MGB convertible.

"Imagine, a teenager stooping to use a Cadillac?" Jane commented. "That's a switch."

"It's yours for the evening," they told him. "Are you double dating?"

"Yes, John Adams and his girlfriend are joining us."

"How would you like to have them over to the house first for some hors d'oeuvres and a glass of champagne?" Jane asked.

"Sounds great, Mom."

"Also, if you'd like you could have dinner at the Yacht

Club before the prom. I believe the prom's at the Country Club?"

"Thanks Mom. That would be special."

Jane and Mike were one of the chaperone couples. Periodically, they'd sneak a look in the ballroom.

Jane was all smiles. "Look at that handsome son of ours dancing with that adorable girl. Can you believe he's ours? Never in my wildest dreams did I think I'd be the mother of three such wonderful children. I have to admit Dane's my favorite, though. Don't tell anyone. Aren't we lucky, Mike?"

"We sure are. We're fortunate in so many ways, and this is one of those most memorable moments in our lives."

For the grand finale sweetheart dance, each chaperone was escorted to the dance floor by their son or daughter. Mike watched with pride as Dane danced with his mother. They did some rock and then some cheek to cheek.

Before closing the evening with a final dance with his girlfriend, Dane escorted his mother back to Mike. "She's all yours, Dad," he said. "It's your turn."

"I love you, Jane," Mike whispered in her ear as they danced to a waltz requested by the kids.

"I love you too, Mike. What a romantic evening!"

The next day major changes began. Attorneys and accountants completed the arrangements for putting the Matthews' business in a blind trust. It was made clear that the Matthews were going to live on the minister's salary, with the exception of educational trust funds for the children, a home in Boston, and holding on to the condo at Hilton Head.

In addition to a car for Jane, Mike kept one of the company cars equipped with CB, telephone dictating equipment and a flip-down writing table in the back seat. He intended to continue his practice of creative time management and productive work while being driven around the city by an executive assistant.

Jane and Mike decided to hold off closing on the sale of the home until early fall. It was felt this would give the children and Jane an opportunity to make an easier adjustment for the move.

Scott and Dane wanted to earn as much as they could working for the company. Teresa could enjoy her friends, painting, and time with her horses, as well as finding a good future home for one of the horses and two of the dogs.

Jane, it was agreed, would commute back and forth during the summer, as would Mike less frequently. It was his plan to decide first on the sites for the church and their home. He intended to begin work immediately and occupy an apartment until fall.

With the help of a demographics firm, Mike had frequently used, he quickly settled on a twenty acre site for the church. Bob gave his immediate approval. The site had a gorgeous pond and marsh on it, some trees and enough land for an expanding campus type of church plant allowing for growth.

He located a lot for their home in a new development far enough away from the church to provide privacy. They could have a pool and be surrounded by equivalent value homes and a good mix of different ages, including teens.

Jane and the children flew to Boston and gave their approval. They also helped pick out a temporary apartment for the summer.

Since Mike had committed to donating anonymously the initial investment of property and first church building, he had no trouble getting approval from the company trust to send a company architect and construction foreman to Boston to begin work on both the church and the home.

The primary objective for the summer was to lay the ground work for the opening of the new church in the fall.

Part of Mike's agreement with Bob was that he would personally replace the usual start-up funds for the church with his private donation covering the initial salary of two full time people: (1) A combination executive assistant and driver, (2) A trained visitation person with proven marketing skills to canvas the immediate territory of the new parish, distribute brochures, and organize volunteer telephoning of prospects.

The promotion included: a series of direct mailings; professionally designed signage and advertising in local papers, sometimes a visit by Mike door to door cold calling with follow up telephoning, and a major first class announcement of the first fall service mailed to each prospect.

Within two weeks he filled his two key positions with skilled, experienced people. Emerson Theological Seminary recommended a dynamic young man who had grown up in Boston, spent one year at the seminary, and then decided to join the marketing division of a large local firm. Mike felt fortunate to talk him into joining him.

Mike's driver and executive assistant also was native to the area, and knew the tangletown of Boston backward and forward. This proved to be a necessary assist for his efficiency.

She was a middle aged wife and mother of a teenage daughter. She was positive, pleasant and responsible. She was also college educated, and Mike felt ideally suited to this key position on his staff.

Before launching their promotion for the summer, Mike asked that the three of them meet on the site for the new church for a few moments of prayer. They held hands, as Mike spoke these words:

> Loving spirit of God bless this place.
> Inspire us with compassion, faith and
> enthusiasm. Help us to tune in to your
> will. Assist us in being sensitive to the
> spiritual needs of people as we invite them
> to join hands with us in this new church. Amen.

The summer was dramatically different for Mike. He worked from his apartment, telephone and car. The days were full, beginning with an early morning jog or bike ride, replacing his usual swim.

Between the three of them, Mike figured they rang about two thousand doorbells. The pertinent family data of those who were prospects for the new congregation was recorded. There were hundreds of follow up telephone calls.

Mike's evenings were reserved for appointments with those who indicated a desire to be included in the first service and religious education classes.

The two building sites were on Mike's route each day. He got a kick out of meeting with the construction foreman, and helping coordinate scheduling and quality control. There was no doubt that their home would be finished by September first, and the initial church building by the end of September.

This was different than building hotels, shopping centers and apartment buildings, Mike realized. He was reminded of his neophyte apprenticeship with Dan Adams twenty years ago. Here he was a beginner again, and there were times he was desperately lonely—for Jane, Teresa and the boys, his business associates, their ocean front home and the country club.

It was also a drag sleeping alone. Mike missed the touch of Jane's hand, their satisfying sex life, a goodnight kiss. Jane and he talked on the phone almost every evening and he found solace in her visits to Boston or a quick trip for him to Florida. Often he wondered: "What in the world have you done? Are you sure this is for you?"

Somehow he always came back to the same conclusion: "It appears to be right for me. Keep at it. These are the humdrum days, the monotonous, the routine before the greater adventure—like the training time for an athlete, the laboratory for the scientist, rehearsal for an actress, campaiging for a president."

Mike also did a lot of reading. Books had always been like friends to him. He usually had three or four going at a time. Before going to sleep at night or at lunch or dinner alone, he always read a chapter or two. Fortunately, he had learned to speed read, so it was remarkable how many books he could get through in a year.

Mike's reading menu was varied. He loved well written contemporary novels, biographical and historical books, poetry, philosophy, upbeat self improvement works and books on economics and business. He even read an occasional western or novel of intrigue and mystery.

Mike learned so much about life and people this way. Oftentimes when he finished an autobiographical book and put it away on the shelf he felt he had lost a best friend. He also loved good movies and plays, documentaries and sports on TV.

Much of his reading that summer resulted in files of ideas, notes and quotes for future speeches and sermons. More than ever now, he realized what a demand there would be on his time for speaking. With the high standard he had set for himself, he knew it was imperative to be prepared. So he even began to outline first sermons, especially the initial one for the new congregation's opening service and his ordination.

Mike was on the phone frequently with Bob also. If there was ever a time when he needed encouragement, it was now.

During one of their talks, Bob said: "As soon as possible locate an outstanding individual or couple, who will be members of your church, whom you can trust implicitly as a personal friend. As you know, the life of a minister, surrounded constantly by hundreds of people, can be very isolating."

"I know, I remember my dad and mother feeling that," Mike answered.

"You've counseled ministers, Mike, on this very subject. But now you're going to experience it yourself. A part of my difficulty when you helped me through my mid-life crisis was this intense feeling of loneliness and isolation coupled with the phantom of a departing youth."

"Yes, we all sooner or later are haunted by the phantom, aren't we?"

"The alienation caused by popularity can be worse, Mike. It's a paradox. There can be a deep feeling of melancholy and loss of intimacy in the flip side of fame. The more widely known you become, the less you may be known as a person and the more as an object."

"How true," Mike agreed.

"You will be adored, revered and sought after," Bob continued, "yet live in a world of strangers, casual contacts and endless meetings. You have said, Mike, that you don't want to be on a pedestal; but it's inevitable. They will put you on a pedestal, in their own minds. So for somebody as sensitive as you are, life could become a prison. I don't want that to happen to you."

"Thanks, friend," Mike replied. "What do you advise? You spoke of locating an individual or couple I could feel very close to."

"That's perhaps more important than anything, Mike. It's like having a therapist. You can let your hair down. You can say anything you feel deep inside. Share your secrets if you wish. Kick up your heels once in a while. Have some laughs, maybe a drink or two. You will not be judged, condemned or criticized. "It's a fact, Mike, that people in the public spotlight— including doctors, clinical psychologists, counselors—need their own private counselors."

Bob's words were prophetic. During the summer Mike met the husband of his driver and executive assistant. Immediately, Mike knew he had found not one confidant, but two.

Jack and Maria Stewart were both natives of New England. That was in itself important for Mike, because it helped him avoid some blunders in relating to the legitimate idiosyncrasies of some New Englanders.

Early on he learned that Jack and Maria shared his "Emersonian" bent of religious beliefs. Jack was a man of superb judgement, widely known throughout the city and state, and trained as a journalist, newspaper and TV man.

He now was a senior partner in the largest advertising and public relations firm in the city. He was a genius communicator, and was of tremendous help in introducing Mike to key community, business and political people. His assistance in preparing brochures, advertisements and connections with newspaper, TV and radio was invaluable. He also loved to fish and play golf.

Jack and Maria introduced Jane and Mike to an excellent public golf club where they could play for much less money than a private club.

Jack and Maria's friendship, saved Mike many times from the pit of despair, alienation and loneliness. Teresa also found a friend in their daughter, Sally, who was her age and loved horses almost as much as she did.

On a much more mundane, practical level Jack accepted

the appointment by Bob to be the first president of the congregation. He arranged for an attorney to draw the required articles of incorporation.

Since a name was required before filing the articles, Mike decided on "PRINCE OF PEACE COMMUNITY CHURCH."

He also coordinated the appointment of first officers to be trustees of the financial management of the new congregation.

Mike, as written in his position paper, had one implicit rule regarding this congregation and money. At no time would he touch the cash, the offerings or the check book.

The finances would be handled exclusively by officers of the church, and the books audited by a reputable CPA firm.

He would recommend budgets, be responsible for providing the inspirational leadership and advise on fund raising techniques for securing necessary funds, but that's where his involvement would end. Relative to his personal income, he was to be treated on a par with the senior minister of other churches of similar stature and size.

It was an impossibility, as well as undesirable, to hide the fact that this new clergyman was independently wealthy, and came from a successful background in business.

Already there were news releases in the Boston Herald. As a result, Mike had been invited to join the Metropolitan Ministerial Association, Chamber of Commerce and Rotary.

As far as his own finances were concerned, it was necessary for his self-respect to be honorably paid for services rendered. Conversely, it was vital to this congregation to pay its way, to be responsible stewards, to see to it that its generosity was commensurate with its vision and its faith.

By fall all promotion and logistics for the first service and ordination ceremony were in place. Both the church building and the Matthews' new home were completed. The home in Florida was sold, and the family resettled and ready for the big weekend. Scott kept his own apartment with friends near Boston U.

Dane was living with the Adams family in Florida for his senior year, but was excused from football practice for the weekend so he could join in the festivities. Teresa had met the

Stewart's daughter and was beginning to feel at home. Mike's parents were house guests, and Bob was flying in for the dedication of the church building and site, the inaugural service and Mike's ordination.

It was launch time for the second generation Matthews Man of The Cloth.

The first service at PRINCE OF PEACE COMMUNITY CHURCH was a celebration.

Both Matthews families were in the first pew. There were over two hundred and fifty people present. The overflow section was jammed with folding chairs, and the children's nursery was full.

At Mike's request the dedicatory ritual and ordination were abbreviated so the service wouldn't be dragged out. He wanted time for those who wished to remain for the potluck dinner afterward in the social hall.

In spite of the twenty hours or so spent on his sermon, which became his minimum preparation time, Mike was tense. He had delivered hundreds of speeches at business conventions, service groups, and commencements, but this was different.

He felt it was because he felt the awesome responsibility of representing spiritual truth clearly, positively, joyfully, briefly, and with a single dynamic idea which could be of help to people during the week.

True to his "Position Paper" Mike stood at a lectern dressed in a business suit. The title of his sermon was: "WHAT ON EARTH ARE YOU DOING?"

He delivered it without notes or manuscript. He wanted to maintain eye contact and communicate as though it were one-on-one.

"Good morning, and welcome to this first service at PRINCE OF PEACE COMMUNITY CHURCH.

"Early one morning, many years ago, when I was a boy of about ten, my sister Judy and I set the alarm for five o'clock and slipped quietly out of the house.

"Our destination was the chicken coop. It was depression time, and my parents raised chickens for eggs and 'finger lickin' fries and roasts.

"My sister and I were fascinated by the egg laying process. We were determined to sneak into the coup and figure out how it was possible for these birds to produce their large white eggs.

"We had just crouched down where we could get a good view of the nests, when the door swung open, and there stood my mother in her robe. She'd gotten up early to bake fresh rolls and get the breakfast started. She couldn't find us in our rooms, so she went looking.

"'What on earth are you doing?' she shouted. 'You get back in the house. Right this minute.'

"'WHAT ON EARTH ARE YOU DOING?' That question has stuck with me from a philosophical point of view ever since.

"This is a Sunday of firsts . . . first use of this building, first worship service together, my first sermon as a minister.

"In preparing, I thought it appropriate to reread Jesus' first recorded sermon called 'The Sermon On the Mount'—it's been called that because he spoke the words on a spiritual retreat atop a high hill in Galilee.

"The words in his sermon which seemed appropriate for our first day together were these: 'Seek first the Kingdom of God and his righteousness, and all these other things will be added unto you.'

"He was talking about the supreme 'first' of life. A major life purpose . . . a principle priority. Putting spirituality and God at the center of our lives.

"WHAT ON EARTH ARE YOU DOING?

"Some of us put other things first. Power, money, fame, popularity, possessions, addictions, pride, ego, fun. It's not easy to put God first.

"Especially, to keep the first in balance with what is second, third, fourth.

"Jesus talked about the other priorities also. He said (to paraphrase): 'You shall love the Lord your God with all your heart and mind and soul. This is the first and greatest commandment. The second is related to it. You shall love your neighbor as yourself.'

"There is the balance. Of course we need a good self image. It's essential to have self-esteem if we are going to connect, relate, share love with others.

"We are multifaceted beings. We are made up of dimensions other than spiritual, such as social, recreational, mental, creative, sexual. To achieve wholeness and worthwhileness, we need all the dimensions developed and in balance.

"To be an absolutist in any one of our human dimensions is to dwarf our noble identity. For example, it's possible to have such an inward, dull, distorted expression of religion that it scares people away from the real thing.

"I like what more and more doctors at the Mayo Clinic are saying to their patients. My development company frequently staged investment seminars at the Clinic, and I recall after one of our sessions one of the physicians said to me: 'We tell our patients that one of the secrets of good health and happiness is balance in four areas: a sense of work, a sense of play, a sense of love, and a sense of worship.'

"There's the balance, but putting the spiritual first is not easy. There are, however, many different ways we can try.

"For sure, you don't have to be a minister, or work for the church. You can work on an assembly line, be a college student, strive to be a worthy parent, run a company, raise crops, work at a computer or a typewriter, pump gas, fly airplanes, serve food, wash dishes.

"I spent twenty-five years in several other vocations than the ministry. I felt that each one offered a way of putting God first.

"WHAT ON EARTH ARE YOU DOING?

"In order to be a seeker of the Kingdom of God first, I think we not only need balance, we must recognize who we are.

"I have a name, but that's not who I am. I have a social security number, but that's not me. I have a phone number and street address, but that's not my full identity. I have titles, degrees, honors associated with my name, but that's not the whole me. I have a financial statement and a resume but that's not me. I have a special set of fingerprints, a certain gait to my walk, a unique sound to my voice, but that's not me.

"I have a body with a certain color of eyes, height, weight, clothes size, but that's not me.

"The Bible, and most other religious writings of the centuries, agree that we are not only physical.

"We are created in the image of God. There is a supreme dignity and divinity potential about us. We are unique among all of life on this planet. We are indelibly linked to the Infinite and Eternal . . . the Kingdom of God.

"The spirit, love and power of God, like a spark of cosmic energy, is within us and at our center . . . albeit dormant, suppressed and unrecognized by some of us.

"I am fascinated by a news story which appeared in 1932 about a Cleveland laboratory discovery. A researcher by the name of Dr. George Crile, announced that he had discovered in the heart of every cell tiny centers of energy he called 'hot points' or 'radiogens' with temperatures of from 3,000 to 6,000 degrees—some as powerful as those emitted by the sun.

"Think of it! He was saying that within every cell of our body burns the fire of the sun, and a small counter- part of the stars.

"WHAT ON EARTH ARE YOU DOING?

"What is your major life purpose? Do you have a great dream? Have you discovered and accepted your fantastic real worth?

"When former Dwight Eisenhower retired to his farm at Gettysburg, reporters asked him, 'Why are you spending so much time restoring this property?'

"He answered, 'I want to leave one place better than I found it.'

"Are you trying to make this world a better place to live? Do you believe that we are not landlords on this earth, but caretakers?

"Do you understand that the true measure of a life is not its duration, but its donation?

"Could an epitaph someday be written about you, as it was for a dynamic seventeen year old who died prematurely? They wrote on his tombstone that 'He Lived All His Life.'

"I would love it if that could be said about me. 'He Lived All His Life.'

"What do you suppose your epitaph will say? 'Died at thirty-five, buried at sixty-five?'

"WHAT ON EARTH ARE YOU DOING?

"Think of all the enduring, genius accomplishments by some of our fellow humans on this planet.

"One discovers a cure for polio. Another writes a great book or symphony. One excels at open heart surgery. Another walks on the moon. One gives life for racial equality. Another walks among the poor, the homeless, the ill and impoverished. One creates magnificent paintings, or buildings. Another writes and produces dramatically moving plays. One breaks the world record in the Olympics. Another devotes life to molding the minds and lives of children.

"WHAT ON EARTH ARE YOU DOING?

"I have always liked this old legend from the construction industry. I used it often in motivational speeches to management and labor leaders in my business.

"A traveler wandered past a giant construction project in Mexico City. He paused to speak with some of the workmen.

"To one working with chisel and saw he said, 'And what are you making?'

"He replied, 'I spend my days sawing and chiseling beams.'

"To another workman, who was mixing cement in a trough with a hoe, the traveler said, 'What are you doing?'

"He responded, 'I spend my days mixing cement.'

"To another man, straining at lifting a heavy load of bricks, the traveler said, 'What is your task?'

"He replied, 'I spend my time day after day laying bricks.'

"The traveler then passed a stoop shouldered elderly man with gnarled fingers and blistered hands. He was clearly just a common laborer hauling debris and sweeping up refuse.

"'And what do you do?' the traveler asked.

"The old gentleman raised his head, and with a proud infectious smile replied: 'Sir, I am building a Cathedral.'

"WHAT ON EARTH ARE YOU DOING?

"You too can build a cathedral within and around you, if you have your priorities and balance in focus; because the dignity, divinity and eternal power of God is within you."

The first weekend as a "ministerial" family in Boston was a real high.

Dane's friend, John Adams, joined the festivities. Scott had some of his friends at the service, and Teresa appeared to have a fast start on a lasting friendship with Sally Stewart.

Jane and Mike enjoyed having Bob and the elder Matthews as house guests. The first service, followed by the old fashioned, get acquainted potluck dinner was rated a huge success. Mike's two assistants had worked very hard to coordinate all the arrangements.

The only blemish on the weekend was the noticeable slowing down of Mike's father. He talked to his mother about it, and she said she was also concerned. He was getting very forgetful due to hardening of the arteries, and his hearing had not improved with the hearing aid. She felt he should not be driving anymore. Mike asked that he be kept updated regularly on how he was doing.

Naturally, it was a let down when they saw everybody off at the airport, including Dane and John.

"Don't worry about me, Mom and Dad," Dane said, "I'll be OK. John and I have a good time together. Football is going well, and I'll do well in my senior year classes."

"We know you will, Son, but we'll miss you," Jane replied.

"I'll miss you too, but the time will fly by so fast until you all come down, as we planned, for the homecoming football game."

"We'll be there," Mike said, "and I know I'll be so busy getting things rolling here that the time will pass quickly. Then there'll be Christmas when we're going to the Vermont ski slopes, and before we know it you'll be graduating. Take care now, Son. I love you very much."

The days did fly by, as they do when a person is turned on, busy and happy. Jane was eagerly into her plans to get back into acting.

From the opening service there were dozens of visitor registration cards requiring follow up visits and phone calls. Even with the assistance of two competent staff people, Mike set as one of his goals to visit personally in every home of a new member planning to join the church.

This set a high demand on his time. At least three evenings a week he was scheduled for six to eight half hour home visits. He couldn't have accomplished this without his executive assistant, Maria.

Between stops at homes, he studied personal data cards on the family acquired from a prior visit by his assistant. It was tiring but worth it. Mike said to himself "that all too much of our lives are spent in a depersonalized society. It seems to me that the place we bow in worship on a common level before God ought to be where the minister at least knows our name."

At the church door after a service, he was able to greet each person by name as they shook hands and wished one another a good week. His executive assistant always stood behind him with either a note pad or pocket recorder. Maria was his alter memory to remind him the next day who had an ill family member, who wanted to join the church or was a new mother in the hospital. These people received a visit or a call from Mike or a volunteer during the week.

At least one evening a week he had a full schedule of counseling appointments at the office. Without fail, Maria was in the outer office greeting people and ushering them in. It was Mike's way of holding, as closely as possible, to a time schedule.

More importantly perhaps, his counseling training had taught him that when the appointment involves a woman or teenage girl it is imperative to have an assistant as close as a concealed buzzer button—which he had.

There were times when Mike needed to cope with being told that the lady he was counseling was passionately in love with him. Other times he shared empathy and advice with wives unfulfilled in their marital sex life. There were occasions of a teenager molested by a parent or older relative.

There were also those in shock over the loss of a loved one.

Others just needed a friend or advice for a job, college or career decision. Frequently, there were the marriages on the rocks or the post divorce shock.

"How pleasant it is, by contrast," Mike thought, "when I counsel with a couple deeply in love and preparing for marriage."

Very quickly his conviction was underscored that one of the principle hazards of being a minister is failing to recognize that one doesn't know everything. Often he had to say simply, "I don't know, but I'll help you find out if I can."

In these cases he developed a network of referral professionals with whom he felt comfortable. But he also vowed that as soon as funds would permit there would be at least one full time counselor on the staff.

Mike enjoyed working closely with Jack Stewart in developing the graphics for the church. A logo, stationary, calling cards, pew cards for visitors, Sunday bulletins artistically and creatively done. A parish newsletter at least once a month. Weekly mailings to visitors and newcomers to the community. Tasteful greeting cards for births, hospital stays, loss of a loved one, career changes, graduations and especially birthdays.

Everyone has a birthday. It was so easy for Mike, again with help, to sign the cards placed on his desk each week. Most often he wrote a short note wishing the celebrant God's love and peace during the coming year.

Meanwhile, there were three hundred individuals ready to join this fledgling church. At five o'clock Sunday afternoons Mike was holding membership classes. He also asked people willing to teach in the childrens' Church School to attend.

The young man on Mike's staff, who was doing such a good job with visitation in the community, had worked diligently preparing for the first Sunday of classes. The promotion included direct mail flyers and arrangements for bus service for certain neighborhoods.

The first Sunday of Church School was like an invasion. The social hall was jammed with classes.

"It's a good thing the fire marshall didn't attend," Mike thought.

"They had teams of volunteers with endurance, politeness and Christian charity. There were no mishaps and everybody seemed to be caught up in the spirit of joy and celebration. The morning was topped off by the children releasing several hundred balloons labeled PRINCE OF PEACE COMMUNITY CHURCH".

That evening, Jack and Maria, Jane and Mike got their heads together at the Stewart home over a light meal and glass of wine. It was decided that they needed to go to two services immediately and two sessions of the Church School. They also agreed there would be a brief chapel service Thursday evenings for those who preferred that weekly worship time.

Since all the boards and church cabinet hadn't been formed yet, they unilaterally made the decision. With a call for volunteers, and the help of Jack's firm, the necessary publicity and logistics were completed on time.

It turned out to be imperative, because the next Sunday the church received three hundred inaugural members. Nearly everyone at the two services stood for the reception ceremony.

Now began a relentless procession of meetings . . . committee meetings . . . meetings to form committees . . . organization meetings . . . trustee meetings . . . church cabinet meetings . . . fund raising meetings . . . staff meetings.

Mike thought, "Corporations get bogged down in meetings. Large, active parishes are worse."

The meetings he liked best were the teen meetings. He enjoyed helping the kids plan their youth council, their weekly mixers, parties or trips. It was fun dreaming with them about the day they would have their very own youth center in the complex of buildings. Mike knew that very shortly he would need a full time professional on his staff to guide this youth program.

In addition to the meetings, there was always next Sunday's sermon to prepare. It was always necessary to be one week ahead, because the topic for the next Sunday was printed in each Sunday's worship folder.

Frequently, Mike was putting finishing touches on the sermon at midnight Saturday night with a five a.m. alarm setting to commit the manuscript to memory.

There were also classes for which to prepare. Speeches to write for business groups, community organizations, service clubs and college chapel services.

He was beginning to feel harassed by the strain and pressure. Missed the beautiful home on the beach. Wished he could take the boat out for a day of fishing on the ocean.

Mike also found that the public course wasn't as conducive to a fast, relaxing round of golf as the private club they'd belonged to. Jane and he talked about trying to get away for a couple of days at Hilton Head, but all the airport and commuting time didn't seem practical.

In an unexpected way Mike did get away, but it was no pleasure trip.

His mother called. Between sobs she managed the sad news. "Son, your father is in the hospital."

"What happened, Mom?"

"He had a severe stroke. It's affected his hearing, his memory, his mind. He doesn't recognize me. He thinks I'm somebody else. There's a blank stare in his eyes. It's so sad."

"Mother, I'll make arrangements immediately to come."

"You will? If you could get away for just a day it would mean so much to me. I don't know what to do. Should he go to a nursing home? Is there a chance he might get better? I don't know."

"Try to get some rest, Mother. I'll get the first plane possible to Portland and take a cab to the hospital."

Fortunately, Jane was not involved in a play at the present time, so she could be home with Teresa. In a matter of minutes Mike communicated with his two staff people and Jack. All bases were covered for the next couple of days in the church program.

He found his dad's condition just as it had been described. He didn't know Mike. Thought he was his younger brother from the old country. Tears were running down his cheeks. He had no pain, but it was obvious he had some very deep feelings of unhappiness. He couldn't hear at all, but he could speak.

"Please, get me out of here," he kept repeating. "I don't like it here I want to go home."

After conferring with the doctor and his mother, it was agreed he'd be best off in a nursing home. Mike located one owned and operated by a marvelous church group.

The superintendent, nurses and aides were models of sincere gentleness and tenderness. Mike felt he had discovered true sainthood. There was an extra bed in the room where his mother could stay overnight. The home was spotless, comfortable and inviting.

The specialists attending Reverend Matthews told Mike there was very little chance for improvement and almost no possibility of return to normalcy. After calling his sister, who now lived in California, Mike exercised the power of attorney and executor-trustee status his parents had given him, and signed the guarantee of costs.

He also made arrangements to take over their social security and medicare receipts and make the payments on all their bills.

"I'll call you at least twice a day, Mother," Mike promised. "You'll be OK, and we've got Dad taken care of the best we can. Remember those words you used to repeat to me from the prophet Isaiah: 'Those who trust in the Lord shall renew their strength; they shall rise up with wings as eagles; they shall run and not grow weary; they shall walk and not faint.'

"This is a time, now Mother, for you to draw on that strength."

"I know, Son. I shall. Thank you."

It was only a week later that Dad's physician called and told Mike that Mrs. Matthews had also just suffered a devastating, crippling stroke. It had happened during the night at the nursing home when Mother got up to go to the bathroom. She had fallen, and fortunately was found shortly thereafter by a nurse, and taken by ambulance to the hospital.

Mike's mother was paralyzed on one side, and her speech was totally gone. Jane joined him for the return trip to

Portland, after making arrangements for Teresa to stay with Sally.

His mother's mind was clear as a bell. That was apparent as we walked into her room. Her eyes were brimming with tears as she reached out to touch them with her one good hand. Fortunately, she could communicate by nodding her head. They also encouraged her to print messages with her left hand now that her writing hand was paralyzed.

"Mother," they asked, "would you like to be in the same room with Dad?"

She immediately nodded, "yes".

"The doctors tell us," Mike added, "that for the present they can't do any more for you here. The nursing home has an excellent therapy service so we'll have the hospital move you to Dad's room today. You know we'll keep in close touch with your doctors and therapist, don't you?"

Again, Mrs. Matthews nodded "yes".

It was a desperately sad moment when Jane and Mike said goodbye to his parents after making all the arrangements for their comfort that they could. Mike realized that a chapter in his life was over. The odds were high that his parents would never again return to their beautiful little home which they cherished so much.

Now it was back to the demands of a rapidly growing church for Mike. Back to work with the added pressure of his responsibilities and concern for his parents. He called the nursing home each day, and after getting an update from the head nurse, he would have her put his call through to his mother just so she could hear his voice.

Knowing how much his mother liked to read, he suggested the grandchildren take turns sending cards and notes to her. Once every two weeks he managed to fly in for an hour visit or so before heading back to the airport.

However, Mike's visits with his dad were now pretty much of a blank because more and more the elder Matthews' mind was living in another world.

Chapter 22

My Brother Is Dead!

Frequently, drifting off to sleep time turned into a hand holding, conversation time for Jane and Mike.

Such was the case upon returning one night from a nursing home visit in Portland.

"We have been so lucky, haven't we Mike?" Jane said. "We've had twenty-one wonderful years with no serious tragedy to deal with in our family."

"You're right, Jane, we have been very fortunate."

"I know you're feeling badly about your parents," Jane added, "but we know it's inevitable that they will be leaving us someday. It was tougher for me when my parents died, because I was so young."

"Yes, and my parents have lived a very rich, full life and have been very happy together," Mike responded. "I just hate to see them suffer though. I know they're being well taken care of, but for their sakes I hope they don't have to stay in the nursing home very long."

"Have you had a chance to call Judy about no more emergency ambulance trips to the hospital, and not being hooked up to life support equipment?"

"Yes, and she agrees with me. No more artificially prolonged existence when there is no hope of recovery. Just the best of care and comfort. I got a letter off to the doctor about this as he requested."

"We have so much to be thankful for, Mike," Jane repeated. "Just think we have three wonderful children. I'm so proud of them, and next week we're going to have a real homecoming in Florida with Dane. It's the big homecoming football game, and Dane has a date afterward for the dinner dance with his favorite girlfriend."

"Yes, and Scott is going to be able to get away from his classes to join us."

"And how about Teresa? She's so happy here. She asked, you know, if Sally Stewart could go with us, and Jack and Maria said 'yes'. We'll be staying with the Adams' in their guest house. We'll have a chance to play golf at the country club and go for a cruise on the ocean past our old home. It'll be so much fun. I miss our friends and the life style we had."

"I know, Jane," Mike agreed. "I'm looking forward to getting away too. My lay assistant will handle the services, and I've convinced Jack Stewart to take the sermon time. He's going to talk about 'Ethics in Business'. The church will be in good hands while we're gone."

The October homecoming date finally arrived. There was a welcome celebration at the airport. Balloons, flowers and a colorful banner: "WELCOME MATTHEWS FAMILY". Dan had even hired a singing telegram girl with a guitar to serenade the arrival in the terminal.

There were so many good friends present. Dane and his girlfriend, the Adams' family, young people Jane had worked with in acting classes. Many of the executives and office-marketing staff of MATTHEWS ENTERPRISES INC. — some of the kids Mike and Jane had helped through college— friends of Scott and Teresa, and fellow golfing couples from the club.

There was a lot of hugging and kissing. Then it was off by chartered limousine for the Adams'.

The five festive days, Thursday to Monday, seemed too few. The weather was in the low 80's and sunny, with almost a full moon at night.

Jane and Mike got in eighteen holes of golf. Spent a gorgeous afternoon on Dan's boat. Walked the beach by their old home. Renewed dozens of old friendships. And Dane's football game ended dramatically in a 7 to 6 victory over their arch rival.

Teresa and Sally had a ball with fellow high school freshmen, and Scott, Jane and Mike joined chaperones at the homecoming party. Dane was particularly proud to have one dance with his mother.

Mike even sandwiched in a meeting with the corporate C.P.A. firm, and the executives running the company. That was the only disturbing element in an otherwise perfect relaxing time. Some of the MATTHEWS ENTERPRISE hotels were doing badly, and required sizeable infusion of capital.

Otherwise it was an "Alice in Wonderland" vacation. Jane and Mike slept in Sunday morning, which was a real treat. No last minute sermon preparation or multiple services to get ready for. Just a pleasant morning swim and lounging in the sun by the pool with the Adams until brunch time.

The girls were still sleeping. Scott was enjoying the whirlpool. Dane and John Adams joined the group for some fast laps, and then announced they had an errand to run.

"We have to take this .22 rifle back to the guy who owns it," Dane announced. "It'll only take about fifteen minutes. We'll be back for brunch."

"What's the hurry with the rifle?" Mike asked.

"Well, you see," John replied, "we've been doing some target practice back in the woods, and the rifle is part of an antique collection of our buddy's grandfather."

"Yeah! We didn't really get permission to borrow it," Dane added, "so we'd like to get it back before he notices it's missing."

"OK, see you later."

"Mind if I join you?" Scott asked.

"Please do," John replied.

"Dane, why don't you get the .22," John said. "Scott and I will bring the car around and pick you up out front."

Off they went dripping wet, a towel over their shoulders and downing a glass of orange juice from the poolside cabana bar.

It was about ten minutes later that Scott was back. Mike

took one look at him and sensed immediately that something was wrong.

"What is it Scott? I thought you left."

"Dad, could I see you a minute alone?"

"Sure, Son."

Mike followed Scott into the kitchen where he took hold of his arm and said, "Dad, you better sit down."

"What's the matter?"

"Dad, Dane is dead."

"What? No! He was just here. He can't be. What are you talking about?"

"Dad, I can't believe it," Scott sobbed. "My brother is dead."

"Where is he? What happened? Please tell me."

"He's in John's room. I'll show you. John and I waited out front in the car for a few minutes, and when Dane didn't come I went in to get him. I found him on the floor with the rifle lying beside him."

"Scott, we've got to call an ambulance. Maybe it's not too late. Show me where he is."

Scott took Mike by the hand and they ran to the other end of the house. There he was, lying on the floor, just as Scott had said. John was holding his hand just staring into space.

Mike quickly felt for a pulse and there was none. There was just a trickle of blood coming from Dane's mouth. It was only then that he saw the tiny hole in his shirt over his heart.

Mike reached for the phone on the desk and dialed the operator and asked for the ambulance, the paramedics, the police, the works. He was crushed. It was hard to think straight. He tried to figure out what happened.

"Where was the rifle, John?"

He seemed to come out of his shock long enough to reply: "It was behind the drapes."

"Oh my God! It looks like when he reached for it the trigger caught on the webbing of these heavy knit drapes. Someone must have left a shell in the gun. Dane has always been so careful with guns. He and I went to gun safety classes together.

By this time both Scott and John were on the floor by

Dane's body sobbing their hearts out. "If only I had come in to get the gun instead of Dane," John cried. "It's all my fault."

"No, John," Mike tried to assure him, "it was an accident. It's not your fault."

Mike realized he had to get hold of himself. He didn't know how to break the news to Jane and Teresa, but it had to be done.

He ran back to the pool. By this time Teresa and Sally were up, and the Adams and Jane were enjoying the sun. Mike asked Teresa to join them for a minute, and knelt down beside Jane. Holding Teresa's hand and with his free arm around Jane he said, "Jane, remember the other night we were talking about how lucky we have been in our family. Well, now we're going to have to be real strong and help one another, because our son Dane is dead."

"No! No! It can't be! What are you saying? Where is he?"

Teresa let out a scream and Mike thought Jane was going into shock. Fortunately, the Adams took over as they half carried the girls and Jane toward the bedroom. They insisted on seeing him, and Mike did his best to mumble through an explanation of what happened.

By this time the medics and police were arriving, and Jane was given a tranquilizer. Dan shepherded everyone to the cabana while Mike went over the sequence of events with the medics and police leading up to finding Dane.

Since a gun shot was involved, the law required a police and coroner's report. The two young officers arrived at the same conclusion Mike had as they carefully measured distances, the angle of the shot, took fingerprints and interviewed Scott and John.

They wondered why no one had heard the shot, but understood as they noted Mike's reply about the huge size of the home. How far away they had been and the fact that all interior walls were sound treated.

As they carried Dane's body away, Mike felt numb. Devastated, drained, emotionally bankrupt. Already the anger, resentment, disbelief and pain of grief were setting in, and he knew that Jane, Scott and Teresa were feeling the same.

He also knew the days ahead were going to be tough, but he realized this was a time to draw on the support of "the everlasting arms" of God's love . . . to learn . . . to survive . . . to grow . . . to attest to the grace, the strength and validity of their spiritual beliefs.

Mike also sensed that he would need to be strong not only for himself but for his family. Somehow, as he took a few deep breaths and tried to be calm, the miracle of the flow of energy beyond himself began.

From deep within his memory came the recollection of words by the poet Gibran:

"Your children are not your children.
They are the sons and daughters of Life's
longing for itself.
They come through you but not from you,
And though they are with you, yet they
belong not to you."

Remembering these words enabled Mike to breathe a prayer of gratitude for the eighteen beautiful years shared with Dane. He also reminded himself that Jane and he were blessed with another fantastic son, and wonderful daughter, still with them who needed love more than ever.

There were all the arrangements to make. Thanks to the Adams family and a mortician friend and fellow Rotarian, all the routine details were taken care of. Jane and Mike were able to get some rest in between talking to friends who came to the house or called.

Dan telephoned Bob Mackay who agreed to take care of the "memorial celebration" as the family chose to call it. He also spoke with Jack and Maria Stewart in Boston who assured him that everything would be handled smoothly at the church.

The day of the service came all too swiftly. As a family they held a private conference and agreed on how they wished to memorialize Dane. They agreed that so many funeral services were almost barbaric with open coffins and reviewals.

They decided to have a private grave side family meditation with only the four of them and Bob present. This to be followed by a memorial at the church where Dane's graduation picture and selected mementos would be displayed on a simple table at the front of the church, with four bouquets of flowers—one from each of his family.

At the request of Teresa, the Matthews made one last minute change in their memorial plans. "I have to see him once more," Teresa said just before they left for the cemetery. "I miss him so."

Mike explained that Dane was no longer in his body—that his eternal spirit had moved on, but she persisted. So they went to the funeral home where the mortician opened the coffin for one last look at Dane's body.

"Please, Mother and Dad, I would like a little lock of his beautiful black hair."

"OK, sweetheart."

Mike's mortician friend was gone just a minute to get a scissors. He carefully snipped a lock of Dane's hair and gave it to Teresa. Then the coffin was closed for the last time.

Bob opened the family graveside farewell to Dane with the words of the twenty-third Psalm. Then as a surprise to Jane and Mike he read two poems, the first by Teresa and the second by Scott.

Teresa's poem read:
> "His entity perceived
> The omniscient circumference of life
> While watching a bird's shadow in flight
>   across now covered mountains
>   on his way down;
> Calculating the stars for ancient man,
> I watched as he shot a bird
>   and found
> The question of how life began.
> He could have stayed in this time
>   to see me hold his hand.
> He could have stayed in this time,
>   and sketched the falling leaf
> That made Galaxies shine."

Scott's poem was next. I learned later that he had stayed up most of the night composing it.

The sun slept and the earth shivered,
Clouds brushed against the sky
Sprinkling raindrops across the lawn;
Birds soared and floated toward the sheltered bay.
Peace stilled the ocean and bonded the shores
Blanketing the frigid forms beneath.
Sealed now in the vault of contentment, time's
     brother
Whispers life's beauty in muffled echoes.
Vivid memories of Dane locked,
Fondling the pages of our past
And etching scribbled symbols on our souls
Into memorial statues of his love and joy.
More fragrant are the flowers that will blossom in
     spring
And kiss the sky good morning in friendship
To the warm winds that caress the laughing waves;
And soon will they splash again upon the beaches of
     our lives."

Jane and Mike closed the graveside meditation by whispering together, as best they could, the ancient Hebrew benediction, which as a lad Mike had heard his father give so often:

"The Lord bless you and keep you. The Lord make his face shine upon you and be gracious unto you. The Lord lift up his countenance upon you and give you peace."

The memorial service at the church was a celebration of Dane's brief life. The sanctuary was packed. There were over a hundred of Dane's classmates present. The class president announced that their 'year book' would be dedicated to Dane.

One of his coaches gave a tribute, saying: "I did not have the privilege of having a son, but if I had I would have been proud to have a son exactly like Dane."

All of Dane's teachers were present, as well as friends of Jane and Mike from all over the country. Ashley Martin came to be at Jane's side. Mr. Bradshaw from St. Paul was still living, and escorted in a wheel chair by his son. The president of Jefferson University and Emerson Theological Seminary were there, as well as several of Jane's producer friends.

Mike's parents, of course, were unable to be there. In fact they had decided not to tell them about Dane's death. They felt that no good purpose could be served by adding to their own troubles.

It was especially supportive to Mike to have Jack and Maria present from the fledgling congregation. Bob had asked him to say a few words.

"Pastor Mike," he began, (that's what he called him in public), "Jane, Scott and Teresa, I'm not often at a loss for words, but I am now. I just want to say from your friends at our new community church that we love you. We care about you and share your sadness. We feel awfully lucky to have you as our minister, Mike. Take your time about coming back. Hang in there! We'll be thinking of you in our prayers."

It was very moving to have Mike's best friend, and now president of the national church organization, serve as their spiritual mentor at the service.

He began his message by saying:

"My dear friends, the Matthews, and all of you who grieve today because you miss this fine young man, Dane, I want you to know I share your grief.

"Jane and Mike, I knew him almost as long as you did. Your kids all called me 'Uncle Bob'. I have never had a son of my own, so it was a special joy to share in the hunting, fishing and skiing trips with Dane.

"Today is a reminder that life is full of tragic accidents.

"Two cars crash on the highway. A home catches fire in the night. A child drinks a toxic liquid by mistake.

"We are together today because of such a tragic accident, and our hearts are heavy.

"I have been called upon to say something meaningful as we honor Dane's memory. This isn't easy. The last thing I would want to do is give the impression that there is an easy answer. Therefore it is with real humility that I say anything.

"However, I would like to share with you four things this sudden accident has taught me.

"First, I am reminded of the need to love one another.

"How intricately our lives are woven together. We go about our routine daily rounds thinking so often of just ourselves. We are so often blind to how many people are influenced by what we say or do.

"Then a tragic accident like this happens and we are jarred into awareness of how important one life is. We are reminded how urgent it is to show compassion.

"One of you seniors who are here today, Dane's close friend, summed it up best yesterday when you got up to leave after visiting with the Matthews family. You said, 'I guess all of us now must love one another a little bit more.'

"The second lesson I have learned is to be more thankful.

"It's so easy to take the glow and luster of everyday things for granted.

"I was especially made aware of this when I read one of Dane's English papers which his family shared with me.

"It was entitled: 'Moving Time', and it describes his feelings when leaving his room for the last time as the family moved. At first he was saddened as he looked at his empty room and thought of leaving it.

"But then he says, 'I remembered all the memories secreted within these walls, and as I closed that door for the last time, I was no longer sullen and depressed about losing something, but happy and grateful for all the good as well as painful experiences which that room left in my memory.'

"This is our challenge—to be happy and grateful for all the good as well as painful experiences of life, because they can all help us to grow, learn, achieve, be grateful.

"The third insight which has come to me from this accident is the need for everyone of us to develop a faith, a lifestyle, a basic philosophy with which we can face life.

"This is a lifetime project for all of us. It doesn't come easily. But we need the kind of faith that is deep enough to go to the depths of despair without surrendering and enables us to endure the turmoil, the sorrow, the confusion of life.

"It must also be broad enough to encompass the feelings, the hopes, the aspirations, and 'everydayness' of life. We need this so we can keep going and live in a world where things like this tragedy do happen.

"We need this kind of faith because it helps us to learn how to live without a final simple answer to experiences like Dane's sudden death.

"And this is the final lesson I have learned: When everything is said and done there is still a great emptiness.

"It is now that we need to bow before the mystery, the awe, the nonrational wonder and say: 'God! God help me!'

"We need to feel, at the depth of our being, the underlying arms of acceptance which gather up and enfold you and me and Dane, and promise the adventure of another lifetime.

"May our love be greater, our hearts more grateful, our understanding broadened, and our faith deepened because of this wonderful life."

There wasn't a dry eye in the church when Bob closed the service by inviting everyone to the Adams' home for refreshments and a sharing of friendship. But in addition to the tears, there was the feeling of a radiant, uplifting vitality and energy filling the church.

There must have been two hundred people coming and going in the home, by the pool, on the lawn. Each one tried valiantly to share some encouragement. With some it was just a handshake, a pat on the shoulder, a smile.

No matter. To those who were stuck for words, Mike simply responded:

"Comfort for grief comes in other forms than words. Sometimes it's just being silent, but being there, and being willing to be a good listener when a grief stricken friend feels like sharing the pain and sadness. So thank you from all of us."

Chapter 23

A Minister Talks to Himself

Mike knew getting back into responsibilities at the church was going to be extremely difficult.

Again, Jack helped by having his company mail a simple note to each member sharing the news of Dane's death.

Included was the announcement of the topic of Mike's sermon for his first Sunday back. It was called: "A MINISTER TALKS TO HIMSELF".

Both services were packed. "Good morning good friends," he began. "Thank you for your cards, greetings, calls and shared love. Thank you for sending Jack and Maria Stewart to be by our side. Jane and I, Teresa and Scott appreciate your kindness and concern.

"For you visitors here this morning, let me just briefly explain. Our family had a wonderful mini-vacation at our former home in Florida. It was our son Dane's homecoming with his final high school football game, dinner dance and reunion. Sadly and suddenly our vacation ended in a tragic accident resulting in Dane's death.

"Because we just returned, time didn't permit me to prepare a formal, structured sermon, I'm not even beginning in the traditional manner with a Biblical text, although I will leave you at the close with a favorite verse of mine.

"You might find this to be more meaningful than the usual sermon. Because it's very private and quite personal. I know there are many of you who have gone through tragedies in

your life. The odds are that there will be more of them for all
of us.

"Ministers need to gather solace and strength for sadness
and trouble too, you know. We aren't immune from struggle,
pain, bewilderment and grief. There are times when we, like
you, are at our wit's end. Don't know where to turn.

"That's the way I felt after my son died. I asked myself,
'How am I going to handle this?'

"I had to answer at first, 'I don't know.'

"But then help started coming from friends, from you,
from Bob Mackay, President of our National Church body,
and my best friend. But most of all help came from the
spiritual energy within, which I attribute to God, and my
family—Jane, my wife, and Scott and Teresa, my son and
daughter.

"We have always tried to have a weekly family conference.
After Dane died we talked several times as a closely knit
family. What I have to share with you today comes from what
we said to one another, and what I have been saying to myself.

"I also realize that what has helped me the most did not
come from a book at the seminary. I gradually learned it as a
kid clawing my way out of poverty. Struggling to make a
living. Competing in sports, and fighting to stay on top in the
fast lane of the business world.

"I have been remembering three people especially who
taught me how to handle adversity. One was a tackle on my
college football team. In every game he went up against guys
taller, stronger, heavier, but he always won the battle because
of his incredible fortitude and determination.

"The second person I remember is also from my sports
experience. I was in the finals of the third flight of my golf
club. My opponent was a legendary golfer and good friend.
He also had only one arm. But he beat me with a birdie putt
on the eighteenth hole. He too taught me something about
how to handle adversity.

"The third person I am remembering was a business
colleague. Charlie was one of my attorneys. He'd had crippling polio as a child, but he never gave up. He only weighed

about a hundred pounds. He walked with a giant limp. Every breath came with intense struggle and pain.

"Eventually he married a beautiful woman and had three children. He was an outstanding success in his profession. I never saw him without a smile on his face. He donated his time and energies to one charitable event after another. He was a hero to hundreds of people.

"After I thought of these three people, who met adversity with courage, grace and honor, I really started talking to myself.

"'Mike,' I said, 'these people had what you could call the three 'D's': DECISIVENESS, DETERMINATION, DEDICATION. They DECIDED to make a commitment to overcoming a problem. They pursued their objective with almost a fury of DETERMINATION. They exhibited a DEDICATION which would not let them feel sorry for themselves or quit.

"A second thing I learned from these people, which I know I need, and so do you, is to 'LISTEN TO YOUR BODY.'

"It's so essential for us to be physically active, get regular exercise, have a hobby, get the right amount of rest and sleep and practice good dietary habits.

"My mind and spirits are so much improved after hiking, biking, swimming, golfing or skiing.

"A third message I started feeding back to myself was: THERE IS NO MAGICAL GRIEF PILL. At least there is none which works permanently.

"There are fake remedies which will temporarily dull the pain. Like hiding behind a mask—holding it all inside. So when your best friend says, 'Mike, how're you doing?'

"You say, 'Oh just fine.' When you're really churning inside and can't share it.

"Or, you can get a temporary fix by soaking up sentimental trash. There's plenty of that around. Like the sympathy cards which say: 'He's not dead. He's just away.'

"Bull! He's dead. But it's possible to deal with it courageously and with peace and honor.

"But not by getting on a merry-go-round of activity or self-indulgence. Not by creating a make believe world with drugs and booze.

"I have said to myself, 'Mike, there is no magical grief pill that works. It's a fact that you must go through each stage of grief and deal with it: the hostility and resentment, the anger, the depression, the feelings of you could have done more. Walk carefully through each of these stages and you will learn, grow and overcome.'

"A fourth source of help is to cultivate a habit of SEEK-ING THE SILENT, SERENE, EMPTY PLACES.

"I recall a statement from one of my English classes in college. Samuel Coleridge, the poet, said, 'The silence sank like music on my heart.'

"I need some private time alone just for me . . . time for meditation, wonder, dreaming. I have felt it hiking in the mountains by a glacier, on the ocean in a storm. Absorbing a sunset on the beach. Playing a solitary round of golf on a beautiful course. My aloneness was my peaceful companion. It walked beside me calming me and affirming my faith and hope in my silence.

"A fifth message I have been giving myself is to CUL-TIVATE THE ATTITUDE OF GRATITUDE. I cling so fiercely to the belief that God and his power, wisdom and love permeates the entire universe.

"We can't see, touch or feel this presence in the conventional sense, any more than we can the oxygen we breathe, or the air waves which bring us sound and pictures. But of this I am sure. When I start thinking about the reasons I have to be grateful I feel the energy, strength and peace of God flowing into my being.

"I also, in this mood, cannot feel depressed. Think about it! When we're grateful it's impossible to feel sorry for ourselves.

"A sixth part of my talk to myself has been, LIVE IN THE NOW.

"At the reception following Dane's funeral one of my friends came up to me and said, 'Mike, I never know what to say on occasions like this, but I feel like telling you this. It might be of some help. I never had a son. You've had two, and although you have lost one of them you enjoyed sharing eighteen wonderful years with Dane and you're privileged still to have Scott.'

"How right he was! Don't whine about the loss and the hurts or wallow in the past. Live in the now with appreciation for the joys of today.

"A seventh part of my message to myself is REACH OUT TO OTHERS.

"The best instant therapy for me when I am down is to visit a patient in a nursing home or the hospital for crippled children. I come away so revived, and again so grateful, that I can be of help to someone who can use it.

"I need to remind myself constantly, however, that help is a two way street. Reaching out to others involves opening yourself to someone who has the ability, the concern, the understanding and the desire to be of help to you when you need it.

"My final message to myself these past days has been, KEEP AT IT. Don't give up. Don't quit. Stick with it. Continue to dream. Hold on to hope.

"There is that bittersweet reward which I experienced as an athlete. After the sweating, the straining and training comes the joy of accomplishment. Maybe not first place or the championship medal but the satisfaction of achieving the best which could be done at this time and this place.

"My father taught me this. I recall one of his sermons on New Year's day. He spoke about the illness, the sufferings, the catastrophes which he had witnessed during the past year in the lives of some of his parishioners. And then he said, 'I propose a toast to you for just enduring. Not always being radiant or positive, but just hanging on and surviving.'

"So I say to myself, KEEP AT IT. Think of all the nameless achievers who have done that. Even some who became famous have succeeded by plugging along and refusing to give up.

"Imagine, with all his success, it was Albert Einstein who said, 'I know from my own experience, my painful searching with its many blind alleys, how hard it is to take a reliable step, be it ever so small, towards the understanding of that which is truly significant.'

"It is the one step which is important. And then another and another. Like Tchaikovsky said about his creating great music, 'ever since I began to compose I have tried to be in my work just what the great masters of music—Mozart, Beethoven and Schubert—were in theirs; not necessarily to be as great as they were, but to work as they did—as the cobbler works at his trade—by daily work.' The result was something colossal, because he kept at it.

"My friends and dear members of my family, this is what I propose doing.

"And here is the Biblical text which I promised would be at the end of my talking to myself today. These are favorite verses of mine which seem especially appropriate.

     "Though I walk through the valley of the shadow of death, I will fear no evil; for thou art with me; thy rod and thy staff they comfort me.

     Thou preparest a table before me in the presence of mine enemies; thou anointest my head with oil; my cup runneth over.

     Surely goodness and mercy shall follow me all the days of my life; and I will dwell in the house of the Lord forever."

Chapter 24

Having The Time of His Life

The first Christmas after Dane's death was filled with nostalgia for the Matthews.

Fortunately, it was also very busy, especially for Mike. The church was growing so fast that now there were three services and three sessions of children's church school each Sunday morning, in addition to a Thursday evening service.

There were three children's Christmas pageants, divided by age groups, and two separate choir concerts so the growing numbers in the congregation could have an opportunity to attend.

Mike also spoke at three candlelight Christmas Eve services.

It was obvious that there would be a need for additional building facilities more quickly than anticipated. Happily, financial support through pledges and giving was at a commendable high level. As a result, the building committee started working at a stepped up pace with architects on the second stage of their three stage plan.

This addition was to include class and meeting rooms, nursery facilities, daily child day care provisions, offices, a youth center and full size gymnasium-auditorium with locker rooms and a major kitchen facility.

Plans also included a live-in caretaker apartment, storage for folding chairs, tables and stage equipment, as well as a prayer chapel which could be open twenty-four hours a day.

The gymnasium-auditorium, with its stage, was to serve the multiple functions of worship services, concerts, pageants (all with portable seating), social events and dinners in addition to a recreational facility for the youth center. The target was to have this expansion completed within one year.

This first Christmas the congregation sprung a gala surprise party on the Matthews. They had learned about their plans for a ski trip to Vermont over New Years. Since Dane's death, however, Jane and Mike had decided not to go back to Stratton Mountain which had been Dane's favorite, but to go to Switzerland.

Plans were completed to take John Adams along. He was so depressed over Dane's death they felt this would be helpful for him. Teresa invited Sally Stewart also.

Just before they were to leave the congregation had the surprise party. They rented the gracious ballroom of Jack's country club. Festivities included a buffet dinner, caroling, and a brief program followed by dancing.

As the finale to a wonderful evening Jane and Mike were presented with a gift of money to pay for their ski vacation. It was a heartwarming experience for the Matthews' family. They each spoke their words of thanks in their own way, but everyone agreed Teresa put it best.

She said, "I really miss my brother. We were so close, but you have helped fill the empty place with your kindness and love. Thank you, and we'll be thinking of you when we're in those beautiful mountains close to God."

Before they left, Mike had one final responsibility. It seemed to him that his father was not going to last much longer, so he went to Portland to visit his parents for Christmas. Mike told his mother that they were leaving for Europe. In case Dad passed away while they were gone, he assured her all arrangements were made for the service.

She, of course, would be unable to attend the funeral but Mike told her that Bob would lead the service if he could not return in time. He also said the cost of airline tickets from California for Judy were covered.

Saying goodbye to his mother was traumatic for Jane and

Mike and the children. They were all in the room. Reverend Matthews was under heavy sedation.

Though he couldn't hear, as far as they knew, Mike wanted to convey a message to him.

"Dad," he began, "We love you. Thank you for being such a kind father and gentle, loyal husband. Thank you for teaching me many valuable lessons. Thank you for working so hard to provide for us.

"And now as we say goodbye we want to read together one of your favorite Bible verses, from Psalm 100: 'Make a joyful noise unto the Lord, all ye lands. Serve the Lord with gladness: come before his presence with singing. Know ye that the Lord he is God: it is he that hath made us, and not we ourselves; we are his people, and the sheep of his pasture. Enter into his gates with thanksgiving, and into his courts with praise: be thankful unto him, and bless his name. For the Lord is good; his mercy is everlasting; and his truth endureth to all generations.'"

Mike's mother could not speak, but she could hear, and she responded with a smile. She motioned for the pencil and paper by her bed which she had been using to communicate.

Slowly and proudly she wrote with her good left hand; "God bless you, Michael Charles Matthews. I told you one day you'd be a pastor like your father. You were born to be a servant of God."

"You never gave up, did you Mother," Mike answered. "We'll be with you in spirit, and Judy will come when you need her."

They took turns giving her a kiss on the cheek as they left the room for the airport limousine and Switzerland.

They had a fabulous vacation. The weather was perfect, and Scott and John found the deep powder challenging. They also found some nordic girls attractive, because after the first day they showed up only for dinner before they were off to the most popular disco.

The second evening a call came from Judy. The inevitable had happened. Reverend Matthews had passed peacefully away. She told Mike not even to try to come back for the funeral. She knew that goodbyes had been said before leaving. She assured them that Mother was holding up well, and the services were in good hands with Bob.

It was only six weeks after the Matthews returned that Mike's mother joined her husband. She was laid to rest next to him in a beautiful cemetery overlooking the ocean off the coast of Maine.

Mike and his family felt it was a fitting memorial place for two of America's pioneers who had given so much love, not only to their children, but to hundreds of others who were lonely, hungry, poor and spiritually in need.

It was quickly apparent that Mike had a growing giant on his hands with this new congregation.

Every Sunday there were dozens of first time visitors. People were coming from all over the city. Valiantly, the staff struggled to keep up with the mailed welcome greetings and follow up visits to homes.

With Jack's help, and under the leadership of the staff member in charge of visitation, neighborhood block areas were organized. Volunteers were recruited and trained to make a prompt and courteous call at the home of visitors.

From the smaller more intimate neighborhood arenas evolved a closeness, opportunities for personal spiritual growth and service sometimes missing in larger churches.

From the neighborhood connection there flowed a steady stream of talent for the choirs, teachers in church school, counselors for teens, participants in ladies service groups, nursery and child care attendants, Sunday morning parking supervisors and ushers, leaders of adult study and prayer groups, helpers to count and record Sunday offerings, volunteers for the singles group and men's club.

The list kept growing. Every participant in any activity of the church was also asked to report to the church office the name of a person facing a crisis of illness, divorce, loss of a job, a death in the family, a new child born or any other circumstance which might be helped by a visit with a minister or counselor.

In order to keep his fingers on the pulse of this myriad of activities, Mike designed an organizational chart and formed a minister's cabinet. The plan was structured so Mike could delegate each division to an assistant as staff could be added.

He realized additional staff was an essential priority. By the time the building addition was completed, he wished to have in place a full time professional lay person in the areas of: music and drama; religious education; youth center and administration.

These positions to be followed by additional secretarial help, professional counselor(s), and assistant ministers as needed.

Mike wrote job descriptions for each position. He also wrote a personnel policies and practice manual, and presented them for approval to the church cabinet. With only slight modifications, and subject to availability of budget dollars, his proposal was approved.

One of Mike's favorite activities was the men's club.

Jack and he had discussed this subject at length. "Don't you think it's true, Mike," Jack would say, "that a majority of American men have abdicated their role in religion and church life to children and women?"

"Yes, that's true. Why do you think it's happened?"

"Well, for one thing," Jack continued, "as you know from your corporate experience, men are constantly kept on edge and challenged by their career. There's a lot of stress there."

"True," Mike replied, "but ask any mother with children and a high powered husband and she'll tell you she also knows all about stress."

"OK. Then why is it that we men usually go for diversions in other directions than a church? We're into sports, hobbies, service clubs, fraternal groups, country clubs, and maybe once or twice a year we'll reluctantly opt for church. Why?"

"For starters, Jack, we have to admit the service may not be uplifting and the sermon boring. I wouldn't go either under those circumstances. I could get more inspiration from a walk in the woods, a good book or a game of golf."

"You are so right," Jack replied. "Fortunately, we don't have the problem of the dull services. But there has to be more we can do to fill the spiritual vacuum in men's lives."

"This is my dream," Mike responded. "I would like to see a men's club in our church be the most dynamic men's group in town. I'd like to see the program and companionship be so stimulating, informative and inspiring that the guys couldn't wait for the next one to happen. They would change their schedules, if possible, to get there."

"How are you going to do that?" Jack asked.

"With your help, and other men in the church who are interested," Mike said. "Let's kick around some ideas like these: a first class 6:30 dinner meeting once a month; hold it on the best night of the week to catch the most men; let it be something the guys hit on their way home from the office; begin promptly and end no later than eight o'clock; have a brief social period with cheese, crackers, soft drinks, coffee first.

"I agree with you so far, Mike."

"Then with your help, Jack, we print and mail some classy promotional literature, schedule the absolute hottest and best speakers available in the city and state. This might be a senator, the governor, a leading radio-sports-TV or education personality. Limit the speaker to twenty minutes with fifteen for questions, and close the meeting. Guys that wish to stay and talk for awhile may, and the rest can still have the evening with their families or their briefcase homework. How does that sound?"

"Sounds great!" Jack replied. "I'll get to work on it. And a couple of more ideas I'd like to throw in. I'd like to see something really special as an opener in the fall. Then I think the men's club should help with the teen and youth center program, and form a couple of bowling and softball teams for the city park leagues."

"How about a super fishing weekend trip at the close of the season? Wouldn't that be great?" Mike added.

"I promise you, Mike it's done."

And it was done! The first dinner meeting was attended by almost a hundred men . . . an attendance which swelled to five hundred through the years.

Season tickets were sold to build up a treasury for speaker fees and sponsorship projects. The men's club became the envy of every service club and church group in the area, including the ladies organizations which served the dinners.

Mike personally had fun attending, because he had little or no responsibility other than advisory.

He also wound up being a pitcher and leading hitter on one of the softball teams.

A fishing weekend of the men's club resulted in a holiday for Mike. A chance to renew one of his favorite sports, and become better acquainted with men of the church. The twenty minute sunrise shore service on Sunday and the shore lunch, before packing for home, proved to be everyone's favorites.

These were stimulating and rewarding days for Mike. The varied multiplicity of his responsibilities was at times staggering, but exhilarating.

He spent hours each week with the architect and contractor in an advisory and quality control capacity on plans for the new building. He was involved in a search for personnel to fill staff positions. The Sunday services were on radio once a month. Occasionally Mike was asked to appear on TV.

His sermons were taped and typed each week. One volunteer office person was kept busy two days a week sending out requested copies. Frequently, he was asked to repeat a sermon.

As a result, he inaugurated a "favorite sermon series" for one month in the summer. The response was amazing. On those summer Sundays attendance held up as well as during the rest of the year.

Mike also said "yes" to an invitation to serve on the board of the City-wide Ministerial Association. Because of his business background he was asked to be on the board of a major bank, as well as one of the principle construction firms in the area.

"Pastor Mike," as some people referred to him, was living a fascinating, demanding, challenging life in his role of A Man Of The Cloth.

Chapter 25

Storm Clouds

How fragile the balance between tranquility and turmoil!

One moment serenity. The next strident stress, struggle, strife.

All the more reason, when a single moment, a day, an experience is beautiful, to relish it, absorb, enjoy, hold it as long as possible.

It might be the best, the last, the only one of its kind, never to return. The stuff of which "the good old days" are made.

It seemed to Mike that two ominous storm clouds were hovering on the horizon at the moment. One appeared to be threatening his business. The other his marriage.

The profit and loss statements crossing his desk from Florida were looking bleak. The trustees, watching over the MATTHEWS ENTERPRISES, INC. noted warning flags on numerous fronts.

Several of the hotels were running in the red, and in need of capital infusions. Conversion of apartment complexes to condominiums was drastically behind schedule.

A one hundred million dollar diversified development, intended by the CEO and board to heal the cash flow crunch, was stalled on the shelf of inertia, incompetence and broken promises by city planning commissions and councils.

There were other circumstances beyond the corporate executives' control contributing to the downturn.

One of them was unanticipated escalating interest rates.

However, as usual when a business runs into trouble, a few bad decisions had been made.

One of them was in the area of demographic forecasts. The company being used to analyze expansion trends and consumer needs for hotels, condominiums and retail-office space had just plain goofed. Major litigation was pending on that front.

In hindsight, some poor choices had been made in choosing joint venture partners. A few of them were running scared and not coming up with major capital commitments as needed. Some of the financial institutions dealt with for years were turning skittish about honoring credit lines.

The downturn was correctable, but unfortunately Mike's hands were tied. Legally, and by choice, his personal leadership was limited to an advisory capacity.

Of much more concern to Mike was the cloud hovering over his marriage. He had sensed it coming since the decision was made to join the clergy and move to Boston.

Jane and Mike had allowed other priorities to keep them from their minimum one night a week out by themselves. Their sex life, and intimate conversations at sleep time, were neglected. Their family dinner talk times were also suffering.

Teresa got them back on track with a major attention getter. It was a Friday evening and Mike had scheduled three meetings at the church. Jane was in New York auditioning for a new off-Broadway production.

Mike called Teresa to see if she'd be OK for the evening.

"I'll be fine, Dad," she said. "Sally and I are going to MacDonalds and maybe a movie. I'll be home early."

She was home early, but not by design. Mike got home about 10:30 as the phone rang. It was a state trooper. "Mr. Matthews," he said, "I've just had a talk with your daughter, Teresa."

"Is she OK? Anything wrong?"

"Well, that depends. Yes, she's OK," he replied. "We interrupted a beach beer party at one of the kids' favorite spots on the river. When I came on the scene they all ran. Then one of them came wandering back to my squad car. It was your daughter."

"What happened?"

"I'll give her credit, Mr. Matthews. Her car was there and she had some beer in the trunk. 'Young lady,' I said, 'we've got you cold. You're too young to be drinking, and I could haul you in. But I have to admire your guts for coming back. Why did you do that?'"

"What did she say?" Mike asked.

"Well, she just kind of shrugged her shoulders and said, 'I knew you'd find out I was here, because it's my car. So I thought I might just as well face the music now. Besides I don't want to cause my parents any more problems than they already have.'"

"Then what happened?"

"I told her I was going to let her go with one stipulation. She was to drive straight home, which she was fully capable of doing since she'd only had a half a can of beer. And then she was to tell you what she was up to and let you handle it. I told her she was to call me after you'd talked, and if I didn't hear from her by Saturday morning, I would come and see you."

"Thank you, sir. What is your name, and where can I reach you?"

"Your daughter has that information, Mr. Matthews. Judging from my impression of her attitude she'll be home shortly and talk with you."

"Just then Mike heard Teresa's car drive in, and sure enough she came right into the kitchen where he was sitting.

"Dad, I've got something to tell you," she began.

"Fine," Mike replied. "Should we go out and sit by the pool and have a coke or something?"

"OK. Would you rather have a beer? You've had a long, busy day."

"No, but let's take this bag of popcorn along. I managed to skip dinner again."

They'd no more than settled in the chaise lounges when Teresa plunged into her story. It was essentially the same Mike had just heard, though of course he didn't let on that he knew what was coming.

"Teresa, I admire you for handling the situation the way you did," Mike said. "Thanks for keeping your promise to the trooper. You're lucky you ran into a man with such human qualities. My guess is that he may have some teenagers of his own. Now, how about talking about the future and why you felt it was necessary to go to the beer party."

"That's just it, Dad, I did want to go. The majority of the kids go to beer parties. I want to be with my friends. It's important to me to be accepted and liked. I know it's illegal to drink at my age, and I wasn't planning to get drunk, just to have fun."

"Aren't there other ways to have fun?" Mike asked.

"Sure. I love my horses and I'm winning a lot of blue ribbons jumping. Sally and I also have a blast sleeping over at one another's houses after a movie. I am really enjoying my painting. Did I tell you I've been asked to enter one in a display at the local bank, and my teacher said someone wanted to buy it for $300?"

"Wow! That's terrific, Teresa. Congratulations!"

"You know what, Dad? Why I really went to the beer bust tonight?"

"No, tell me."

"Well, I was lonely. It's no fun all of a sudden being the only child after all those wonderful years being around two brothers, even if they did bug me sometimes. Scott has his own place at the university so we don't see him very often, and I miss Dane. We used to have those family talks one night a week at dinner. Why did we stop that? Why can't we keep doing that? Sometimes I feel so alone. I know I'm only one, but I am one, and I am important. You keep telling me that."

"You're right Teresa," Mike replied. "It's not fair. I'll take the blame. Let's begin over again next Friday at dinner. I'll talk to your mother about it. Meanwhile, you'll call your trooper friend? And no more beer parties until you're older. OK?"

"OK. Thanks Dad. I love you."

"I love you too, Teresa. I'm grateful we can be open with

one another. Since we're talking now, let me ask you about your long term plans for the future. Have you thought about a career or what you'd like to do after high school? You'll be a senior next year, you know."

"I've thought about it some," Teresa replied. "I think I'd like to be an artist. Maybe go to college at Florida International University. They have an excellent art department."

"Sounds wonderful, Teresa. Your mother and I would be thrilled to see you do that."

"Besides being a painter," Teresa went on, "I think I'd like to teach grade school children. Art can be so much fun for them, to create things, express their inner feelings in color, texture, form and beauty.

"And by the way, Dad, I'm looking forward to the new youth center at church. I think the kids will go for that. It'll be a place just for us where we can hang out. Do you suppose we could have some art classes for kids at the center? I'd like to help with that."

"I accept! I'll personally see to it that the center includes art classes."

"By the way Dad," Teresa continued, "I miss Mom when she's away. Why does she have to be gone so much? I know she wants to get back her acting career, but couldn't she do that here in Boston? I know she also likes to go to Hilton Head. But to tell you the truth, I wonder if you two are getting along OK. It seems like you aren't as close as you used to be."

"You may be right, Teresa. Perhaps we haven't been paying as much attention to our relationship as we used to. Thanks for the reminder. I'm a little bushed now, so see you in the morning. Try not to be on the phone all night with Sally."

"I won't. Goodnight, Dad."

The next Friday evening was a highlight for the rejuvenation of the Matthews' family conference. Scott decided to come home for the weekend, which pleased all of them, not least of all Teresa. Barbecued hamburgers poolside was the menu. It was even warm enough on the gorgeous May evening to go for a swim.

Each member of the family had something happy and positive to share. Jane was in a good mood. She was elated about her audition. She was also looking forward to a visit with some of her friends at Hilton Head.

Teresa couldn't wait for school to end for the summer so she could be officially a senior. She was also excited about landing a job at the stables where her horses were boarded. She would be helping to groom and exercise other horses.

Scott talked about a student charter flight from the university to Europe. They would land in Frankfurt and be on their own for two months. He hoped to visit Germany, Switzerland, France, Italy, Greece and Spain. Two of his best friends were planning to meet him in Rome for the latter half of his trip.

"I've got a great idea Dad," Scott announced. "Why don't you take a couple of weeks while Mother is at Hilton Head and join me. Teresa can stay at Stewart's with Sally. It would be good for you to get away, and we could have a great time together."

"Yeah, Dad, that would be good for you," Teresa chimed in. "You have some vacation time coming don't you?"

"Yes, I do. Maybe I could work that out Scott. I've got my new staff people all set I think, and the new church building should be completed on schedule for September. I'd love to spend some time with you in Europe, Scott. Thanks for asking. Maybe we could even do some mountain hiking. Notice I didn't say 'climbing'. I'll leave that to you. I hear you're getting pretty professional on some of those New Hampshire White Mountains with your friends."

"I enjoy the challenge and testing," Scott replied. "It's a thrill to reach your goal against tough odds. The grandeur of the mountains is awesome. But Dad, you and I could just do some back packing like you and Mom used to do."

"What do you think about my going, Jane?" Mike asked.

"Mike, I think it would be a once in a lifetime opportunity for you and Scott to enjoy one another and get better acquainted. Let's talk about it some more this evening. You and I made a date, you know, at one of our favorite lounges overlooking the bay."

Teresa and Mike exchanged knowing glances before they scattered for the evening—Teresa for a movie, Scott for a date and Jane and Mike for some intimate alone time.

The lounge was on the top floor of a luxury hotel. Jane and Mike were ushered to a window view table where the sky was a golden treasure of spectacular cloud formations and magnificent sunset.

They ordered a glass of wine as the last sliver settled beneath the horizon.

"Here's to us," Jane said as they touched glasses. "You seem in a rather pensive mood tonight, Mike. What are you thinking?"

"Oh, I was thinking how beautiful this moment is. How good it is to be here with you."

"I was happy we had our family together this evening," Jane responded. "We've been neglecting some important priorities."

"I agree. I also feel a distance growing between us, Jane, in the past few months. I know Dane's death has been especially devastating for you. I wish you could talk about it. I sense you're holding it all inside. Like hiding behind a mask."

"I guess you're right, Mike. It was so unfair, so sudden. No warning. One minute he's here, and the next he's gone. It's so final. You're right. I can't accept it. I'm angry. I hate the powers that be, God or whatever, which allow tragedies like this to happen. I know all the rational answers, like: it's been going on since the beginning of time; others have gone through far worse experiences; we should be grateful for the years we had with Dane; we're lucky to have other children. But I miss him. I can't help it. You have been able to work your way through grief. I haven't."

The torrent of words poured out, and it was good for Jane.

"It's good for you to express yourself," Mike said. "I know you are aware as well as I am that nobody can get you through this but yourself. Help and guidance is available, but ultimately it's one of those lonely roads where you choose your own way, and reach out for the hands of help offered to you.

"I understand that Mike. But it's one thing to know and another to do."

"It's good to see you making an effort to get back with some of your friends," Mike went on. "A dependable, supportive, good listener friend can be the best therapy in the world."

"You're right," Jane replied, "and you know what? Beyond Ashley in New York, I don't have one exceptionally close friend, except you. I think I started to shut the door on intimate relationships when my parents were killed. I felt the shock and the loneliness so deeply. Subconsciously, I think I began locking out the possibility of letting anyone get close to me again so I wouldn't be hurt. But then I met you, and we had the children. Life was so beautiful until suddenly I lost my son."

"You are such a fiercely independent person, Jane. All of us deserve our privacy, our individuality, our aloneness. But I believe life is a wasteland, a bleak, arid desert without close friends. I only have two besides you, Bob Mackay and Dan Adams. I have hundreds of acquaintances, outer circle friends; but I'd trust my life with these two."

"I like them too, Mike. Many times I wish I could open up, but now I'm afraid. I don't want to get hurt again."

"Maybe it sounds corny," Mike added, "but I believe in what the poet said, 'Better to have loved and lost than not to have loved at all.'"

"I know, and I'll try, Mike. I'm aware of all the statistics about marriages going down the tubes after a common tragedy. I don't want that to happen to us."

"I don't either," Mike replied. "I promise I'll do my best to be patient. I can be a good listener when you feel like talking, or if you wish I can recommend a top-notch counselor."

"Not for now, Mike. I think going to our retreat at Hilton Head with Ashley and a couple of other girls will be good for me. And, by all means, I think you should do whatever you have to do to rearrange your schedule to spend a couple of weeks with Scott in Europe. He needs you too, you know. He has his own pain and his own life ahead of him. You are important to him."

"I know that's true, and I'd love to spend a couple of weeks with Scott in Europe."

"Poor Mike, you're so important to so many people. I don't know how you hold up."

"I have to admit being a minister is more of a grind than I imagined," Mike replied. "Despite all the counseling I did to minister friends, who came to see me when I was in the business world, I wasn't prepared totally for the stress. The hours and pressures are enormous in this type of a rapidly growing church with fast paced, multiple offering of programs and services.

"Isn't there some way you can slow down, Mike?"

"I don't know how. It's like being on a nonstop merry-go-round," Mike said. "There's no quitting time unless I get out of town."

"But you were super busy running your companies, Mike. How is this different?" Jane asked.

"I can put my finger on the answer to that question very easily," Mike replied. "It's the constant, relentless flux and flow of swift emotional changes from minute to minute, week to week."

"I think I know what you mean, Mike. But explain."

"I know I'm mixing my metaphors, but it's like being on an emotional roller coaster with perpetual ups and downs, peaks and valleys. One moment I'm sharing the joy of a new baby in the family. The next I'm called to a home where a husband is threatening his wife with a shotgun.

"In one twenty-four hour period I'm deep in creative thought and study preparing for the next sermon or speech. Swiftly, I move to the emergency ward of a hospital where a member lies shattered from an automobile accident.

"While at the hospital I will visit a child with Multiple Sclerosis. I return to the office to settle a problem with a staff member.

"I rush to the chapel to conduct a wedding for a beautiful young couple whom I've been counseling. Then it's back to my office to meet with a couple who are having marriage problems.

"On the way home for a quick supper and a pittance of family time, I stop at the youth lounge to say 'Hi' to the kids and make sure their advisors are on duty.

"After three or four evening meetings or appointments, I go to bed bone tired only to have the phone ring. It's the young man I've been meeting with at AA. He's at a bar, incoherent and drunk."

"Mike, have you ever thought you might have made a mistake by going into the ministry?" Jane asked. "Maybe it's not for you. I hate to see you so stressed out. It affects me too, you know. I feel the backlash of your fatigue, your frustrations."

"I'm sorry about the spin-off, Jane. But it's understandable. As for your question, I feel I made the right decision."

"You're used to being in control," Jane continued. "When there was a problem in your business you solved it. You didn't have to go through umpteen committees. When your company needed more money you sold something, beefed up your marketing program, created a new development, took on a joint venture partner or used your credit line. In the church you're always scrounging, cutting corners, pleading, motivating members to share their blessings so they can be blessed more."

"But, Jane, I love what I'm doing. I don't feel I made a mistake. I believe I belong here for this time in my life. I have something to give. It's part of my dream, and it's going to be so much smoother when my new staff members come on board this fall. I'll be able to delegate so much more."

"I hope so," Jane replied.

"I'll just have to learn to cope with the emotional roller coaster ride," Mike continued. "You see, it's so much more of a problem for me than some ministers because I have such high standards of performance. I'm committed to excellence. I believe the church and religion needs to be relevant to the contemporary NOW. I have my own ideas of how this should be accomplished. I'm not willing to settle for secondhand performance whether in the pulpit, the nursery school, the youth center, the music and arts program, counseling or the administrative-financial needs of the church."

"You're right, Mike," Jane added. "You wouldn't be happy doing anything halfway. I guess you'll just have to work at coping with the emotional ups and downs.

"Sometimes I wonder though, if you care too much," Jane added. "Get too intimately involved with people's spiritual needs and problems. You're not God, you know. You're just a human being."

"Maybe I do allow myself to get too involved emotionally, Jane."

"It's one of your great qualities that you're not a phoney, Mike. You don't put on any pretenses. That's one of the reasons so many people are attracted to you. But remember, Mike, you're not a guru. You vowed not to put yourself on a pedestal. If people put you there because of some role model or past cultural conditioning, that's their problem. Keep on being yourself, Mike."

"That's quite a speech, Jane. Thanks. Let's have another glass of wine and talk about where you're coming from. You said you feel the backlash of my emotions."

"I don't know where to start, Mike. Yes, I do feel the spin off from your emotions. I know for you it's 'lonely at the top.' But in many ways it's more lonely for me."

"Tell me how you feel, Jane."

"Well, remember when you were asked to consider running for the senate?"

"Yes."

"Remember what I said? I told you I didn't want to be a second class citizen as a senator's wife. A non-entity. A nothing. Just walking in the shadow of my husband."

"I remember, and I agreed."

"I also expressed the same feelings when we talked about your going into the ministry," Jane continued.

"It's happening, Mike. I'm not blaming you. It's just the way it is. You're on center stage. I'm not even a supporting member of the cast in the eyes of many church members."

"That's a bummer, Jane. I'm sorry you feel that's the way it is because you are my best ally."

"But I feel I'm just supposed to look charming, not cause any stir, be a perfect example of motherhood and sainthood, not get involved in controversies, be placid. I can't continue do that, Mike."

"I understand what you're saying, Jane. Is there anything I can do to change the situation?"

"No. Not really. In time maybe, but I think the system is too entrenched to change fast enough for me. That's one reason I'm spending more time trying to reactivate my acting career. I enjoy it so much. It's a challenge for me, and I receive tremendous satisfaction from performing. I need to do something creative or I'll go nuts."

"You have my full support, Jane," I replied. "I do miss you very much when you're away, and so does Teresa. But if it helps make you happy and fulfills your needs we'll handle the home front while you're away.

"I've also noticed that when you get back after one of your trips you're not as depressed as you were."

"I know. I'm sorry, but I feel depressed a lot," Jane replied. "There are times all I feel like doing is sleeping, and then again many nights I stare at the ceiling because my mind won't shut off. My doctor says I may be having the beginnings of menopause. He prescribed valium for me."

"Oh, Lord, Jane! I didn't know he did that. I think that drug is dynamite. I've seen it destroy people, especially taken with a drink or two. I wish you wouldn't take valium. There must be other medication or therapy which would be better."

"I'll look into it," Jane added. "My goodness! Look what time it is? We'd better be getting home. It's time for Teresa to check in. What a beautiful evening this has been. I enjoyed the conversation, Mike. Look at the lights of the city. I love this place. Can we have one slow dance on our way out?"

Holding each other, and gently moving to the strains of the combo playing, "The First Time Ever I Saw Your Face," made everything feel better, for the moment.

Chapter 26

Is Your God Too Small?

Europe for Scott and Mike was better than could possibly be imagined. No schedule. Staying in bed and breakfasts. Greeting each new morning with "what should we do today?"

They met in Frankfurt the day after Scott's chartered student flight arrived. They rented a car and took off clutching cameras and paperbacks: "Seeing Europe for Ten Dollars a Day."

The goal was strictly adhered to until their last night together when Mike insisted they splurge at a luxury hotel near the Roman Forum.

Meanwhile it was hand laundry at night, continental breakfasts, famous art galleries, ancient cathedrals, walled villages, tour bus rides, gorgeous corner flower stands in Amsterdam, the Copenhagen Gardens of Tivoli, the Roman Colosseum, and the stark, joyless streets of East Berlin behind the barbed wire.

What a fabulous, once in a lifetime opportunity, after walking the vineyards overlooking the Rhine, to sprawl on a grassy slope with wine, cheese and a loaf of bread! No deadlines. Just talking, father and son, one man to another. Spontaneous sharing.

It was here that Scott talked to Mike about his career and graduate school plans. "I'd like to go to New York, Dad," he began. "I've decided I would like to pursue a Ph.D in humanities at New York University. Ultimately I would like to be a professional writer. What do you think about that?"

"I think it's great, Scott. I've always told you to follow your dream and do what seems right for you."

"I know it's going to be tough financially for a while," Scott continued. "I have some money saved from working for MATTHEWS ENTERPRISES, and I intend to get a part time job in New York. I'd really like to try getting work as a teaching assistant. I remember you always told us any post-graduate education would be our responsibility, but I was wondering if you and Mom would be able to help me if I need it."

"I'll talk with your mother about it when I get home, Scott. But I'm sure we'll be able to do something. As you know, your mother and I are living strictly on the salary from the church. Your mother is beginning to have income again from her career, but that's entirely her own.

"However, when I turned my business over to the trustees, there were a couple of funds set aside in escrow for Jane and I to administer. One was for upkeep of our family place at Hilton Head. Another was a college educational fund for you, Dane and Teresa. Now that Dane won't be using his, I am sure we can divert part of that for your graduate work. Just count on it, Scott."

"Thanks so much, Dad. And now I have a surprise for you. Tomorrow we're going to stay in a youth hostel just outside of Lucerne. My friends told me to be sure to stop there. I'm sure you'll enjoy it."

It was a thrill for Mike to share this experience with Scott . . . to mingle with other tourists where the oldest guest, other than Mike and the host couple, was twenty-five. After a help yourself supper at picnic style tables, and pitching in to help clear and wash dishes, they sat on the floor and talked and sang with students from around the world.

Their singing took on nearly operatic proportions later on in the trip in a rathskeller in old Vienna. Everyone locked arms with new friends from East and West swaying to the beat of a rock group on stage.

Then they shifted into old and new favorites including, for the Americans present, "Mine Eyes Have Seen The Glory of the Coming of The Lord."

The crescendo rivaled the shouts and cheers of a superbowl crowd each time the number of a patron's ticket was called to appear on stage. If the "lucky" ticket holder could down another stein of beer without stopping it was half price time on the house for everyone.

Scott and Mike agreed that Switzerland was their first love. They had skied some of these awesome mountains. Now Scott wished he'd brought his climbing equipment, but in lieu of his climbing alone, Mike joined him one morning for a couple hour hike on a well marked trail.

They crossed a meadow with its contented milk cows and their tinkling bells. Walked through a silent forest, gradually working their way up, talking all the while, and absorbing the songs of birds and the fragrance of wild flowers. Before they knew it a couple of hours had turned into three, and they were above the tree line, scarcely aware they were still climbing.

Soon they ran out of trail, and were walking over and around the rocks and boulders left by an ancient glacier. Mike's old tennis shoes were suddenly not adequate for this kind of footing. Scott wasn't much better off.

They were also aware that the sun was now straight overhead. It felt like about 90 degrees and they were dripping wet, thirsty . . . and hungry.

Scott said, "Stupid us! We didn't even bring a pack with a canteen, because we were only going to be gone a short time."

They finally stopped to rest and Mike said, "Don't you think we'd better turn around and head back."

"I've been thinking the same thing, Dad. But guess what? I'm lost. Isn't that a joke? Me, the mountain climbing student. I have no idea where the trail is, and no compass."

"What do you think we ought to do?" Mike asked.

"Well, I figure we're up about ten thousand feet," he answered, "and by the position of the sun I think we should head south."

So they headed in the direction Scott was pointing.

Mike was getting a little concerned, but he had all the confidence in the world that Scott knew what he was doing. So they silently struggled on. It was mid afternoon now, and at least they were moving down, sometimes slipping, sliding and almost crawling to keep from turning an ankle on the rocks.

Suddenly in the distance they saw their first fellow human on this trek. Another father and his son. They frantically screamed and waved until they got their attention.

"I can't remember when I've been so happy to see someone," Mike said to Scott. "They'll get us back on the trail."

Well, that proved to be wishful thinking. They spoke nothing but French and couldn't understand a word of English. But somehow through the gesturing and desperate sound of voices they sensed the Americans were lost, and they pointed in the direction they should go.

It was an hour later that Mike and Scott picked up a trail. It was a different trail from the one they had started on, but it didn't matter.

A few moments later, Scott who was leading the way began shouting and laughing.

"Look, Dad, do you see what I see? It's a woman with a bunch of girls. They're dressed like Girl Scouts. Sure enough, they are Girl Scouts. Now we are safe. We'll just follow them down."

So they did. It was about six o'clock when they got to a road and found a small fruit and soft drink stand. The proprietor and natives standing around thought they were nuts as they gulped down a full six pack of coke and ordered more.

Mike said goodbye to Scott in Rome. Accompanied by two of his university friends, Scott went on to Greece and Spain and Mike headed for home rejuvenated for the months of work ahead.

It was gratifying for Mike to be welcomed with genuine enthusiasm by church members and staff. His new lay staff members were officially installed as Ministers of Education, Music and Drama, Youth and Business Administration. They blended well with the other staff members already in place: Minister of Visitation, Administrative Assistant, various office personnel, and his most important aide of all—Maria Stewart, his driver and executive assistant from day one.

By early fall, the second phase of the building facility was complete. They devoted six weeks to a "shake down cruise" adjusting to the new spaces and expanded programming. There were now over five hundred children in Sunday morning church school. The youth center was busy seven days and evenings a week.

It was wonderful to see teenagers enjoying their new center. At various times they could be found in the lounge chatting, sipping a coke, playing pool, watching TV, listening to music.

Others were in the library or the gymnasium shooting baskets or playing volleyball. Teresa's art studio classes went over big. The participants came in all sizes, colors and creeds.

There were no requirements that they be members of the church. Just treat their facilities with respect.

Phenomenally, the Minister of Music and Drama began a Saturday morning "Choir School" for elementary and high school ages. He trained the volunteer teachers, wrote much of the curriculum and exuded the joy and enthusiasm of the best religious music, art and drama—past and present.

The quality, fun and exuberance of his program was contagious. Church members couldn't believe what they were seeing. This young man who had a Ph.D. in music, specializing in choral music and organ, was a genius. Parents couldn't believe what was happening either.

Kids pleaded to join choir school on Saturday. By the end of the six week trial run, there were almost three hundred of them, divided now into a morning and afternoon session.

There were also eight different choir groups covering all ages, a church orchestra and plans for a major drama production for Christmas.

Although the gymnasium, doubling now as sanctuary,

seated about a thousand people, it was apparent by dedication Sunday that they would need two services and two sessions of church school.

Dedication Sunday was a happy celebration. Nearly five hundred new members were welcomed. Between services hundreds of children released helium filled balloons which were imprinted with the words: "God loves you —Be happy!" followed by the name and address of the church.

By prearrangement through Jack Stewart, one of the cities' major TV stations covered the happening, including interviews with several children.

As preannounced, the subject of Mike's sermon was: "IS YOUR GOD TOO SMALL?"

"Imagine for just a moment," he began, "that you are standing on the shores of the Atlantic. You are feeling the awe and wonder of the ocean's vast, enormous power. You are moved deeply by its mystery, splendor and beauty.

"You hold in your hand a tiny test tube, and you stoop to fill it to the brim with the ocean's water. You look at the test tube and ask yourself, 'how many times would I have to fill this to empty the waters of the ocean?'

"The answer, of course, would reach almost into infinity.

"I feel something like this about this sermon today. Imagine ... trying to capture the mystery, the transcendent energy, the infinite cosmic order and presence of the universe in a few understandable words?

"Many years ago when I was at the seminary, I made a pledge to myself that if I ever became a minister I would not presume to speak FOR God; for this, I believe, is the ultimate presumption.

"I vowed, however, given these circumstances today, that I would attempt to share my feelings ABOUT God.

"Jesus said, 'The Kingdom of God is within you.' I believe this.

"So in order to speak about God means we need to listen to the joy of the universe, the melody of our own souls, the transcendent presence within us.

"I have only one purpose today. It's not to give you simple answers, but to stretch your mind and cause you to think.

"I don't wish that you abandon a faith which for you is satisfying and adequate. But I challenge you to dare to explore . . . to begin a new spiritual adventure.

"You could find it fulfilling and liberating.

"We humans have been trying since the beginning of life on this planet to identify and describe God. We have used myths, legends, allegories, and titles trying to box God in to a definition.

"We have called God Zeus, Father, Yahweh, Allah, Mother of the Universe or the Man Upstairs.

"Ask a child in our Western culture to describe God and you will probably get the answer: 'An old man in a long white robe with a beard.'

"In our frenzy to describe God we have even at times created a portrait of a celestial monster, who would say for example in the Biblical tradition: 'Thou shalt not kill.' But in the next verse, 'Go into Cana and destroy all the Cananites.'

"The fact is that the system or theology which presumes to have found the ultimate truth about God is wrong . . . because God can't be contained in a CAPSULE of definitions. God is beyond names, systems, forms.

"I like the words of the Hindu's Sanskrit which says: 'He who thinks he knows, doesn't know. He who knows that he doesn't know, knows. For in this context, to know is not to know. And not to know is to know.'

"Amazingly, however, the transcendent, absolute infinite presence of God dwells within us.

"This, I believe, is what the major religious traditions mean when they say, 'we are created in the image of God; and what Jesus meant when he said, 'The Kingdom of God is within you.'

"God is like a sphere without a circumference whose center is everywhere, including within you and me. All the best human compassion, love, brilliance, intelligence, creativity, honor, truth magnified into infinite proportions—is God.

"Anything less . . . any attempt you might make to put God

in a CAPSULE, and YOUR GOD IS TOO SMALL.

"I also believe YOUR GOD IS TOO SMALL if you attempt to confine your God to a single CULT or CREED.

"Picture for a moment an expedition of visitors to our planet from a far out solar system. By our time-space measurements, they have been with us for about a year.

"They are about to leave with their report about this strange civilization when one of their group insists their assignment is unfinished.

"They have thoroughly studied all phases of human existence and knowledge. It has been noted that no matter what our language or color of skin, we humans all subscribe to a common order in fields of mathematics, physics, chemistry, engineering, etc.

"However, in the one area of our development, which our visitors hold to be the most important . . . the spirtual . . . our differences and disagreements are dramatic.

"They note that we have religious orders and systems in the thousands. Each one claims to be the best, unique, the only true religion. Each one professes the only contact with the one true God.

"The various cults not only passionately defend their theological positions, but they fight over them.

"It is noted by our earth visitors that millions of humans have been killed in 'holy' wars. The wars are still going on, despite progress in education, inner value systems and mutual respect and compatibility.

"Our visitors decide to stay for another year in an attempt to understand this phenomenon. For all I know they are still here.

"It's a fact. We are still trying to confine God to a cult.

"We draw lines between the 'in' group and the 'out' group. If people don't wear our costume—if they don't pray the way we do—they are branded heretics or pagans.

"The lines are drawn not only between hundreds of religions of the world, but between the brands of Christianity.

"Not that everyone has to march to the same drummer. I

believe the transcendent mystery of God can be experienced and expressed in a variety of ways.

"I recall some graduate studies I took in Ecumenical Theology. The term 'Unity in Diversity' was commonly used in my classes to describe religious compatibility.

"I like that. Because I believe any attempt to institutionalize God, to blueprint God, to reduce the awe and mystery to a single code or creed and OUR GOD IS TOO SMALL.

"Finally, I would add that when we have a mental image of God as a kind of CELESTIAL COMPUTER our GOD IS TOO SMALL.

"What do I mean?

"The computer image portrays God as having everything preprogrammed. Capriciously, God pushes the buttons which snip the golden threads of lives and events.

"This view of God really causes me to cringe . . . when I hear pious, well meaning phrases like: 'his time was up, so God took him.'

"Not right! No way! If for no other reason we are in God's image. Remember? Among other things this means we have choice. We have freedom.

"We live in a universe of fellow human choices and circumstances beyond our control. Fortunately, through meditation and prayer we can reach deeply within ourselves and draw on the presence, the power of God to endure, to overcome, to cope when crises come. But it is my belief that God is not a master computer preordaining our lives.

"Nor is God the computer of the universe keeping track of our every move—recording every act, every thought, keeping score, giving us pluses and minuses.

"This image causes us at times to try to strike a bargain—to bribe the Deity. For example, have you ever said: 'God if you'll only give me another chance; if you'll only make me well; if you'll only get me through this mess, I'll be true to you forever?'

"I do believe a record is kept and penalties paid for evil, but I think they're kept in our own computer, our own mind and soul. Indelibly the record is there, and at some time and some way, in this or other lifetimes, there will be a settlement. But to carry in our soul the image of God as a master computer is to have a GOD WHO IS TOO SMALL.

"Focus instead on the image that God is the ultimate mystery.

"Celebrate with gratitude and wonder that we are related to the Cosmic Order of things . . . that we are created in the image of God.

"Applaud with thanksgiving that we can have a feeling of the presence of all creation within us . . . that we belong to all the universe, and this presence within us is very much alive.

"Sing this hymn of our tradition with a new zest today as we close our dedication service:

> 'O Lord my God! When I in awesome wonder
> Consider all the worlds Thy hands have made;
> I see the stars, I hear the rolling thunder,
> Thy power throughout the universe displayed.
>
> Then sings my soul . . .
> How great Thou art!
>
> When through the woods and forest glades I wander,
> And hear the birds sing sweetly in the trees;
> When I look down from lofty mountain grandeur
> And hear the brook and feel the gentle breeze
>
> Then sings my soul . . .
> How great Thou art!'"

Chapter 27

Crisis Time

In quick succession, the Matthews family had several opportunities to test the endurance of their spiritual fortitude.

Teresa had Sally over for dinner one weekend evening before going out with friends.

"Dad and Mom," Teresa began, "Sally would like to talk to you about something."

"OK. You've got the floor, Sally," Jane replied.

There was a long pause. It was apparent to Jane that something heavy was bothering Sally.

She started crying, so Jane said, "It's OK, Sally, we're all friends, and you're like a member of the family. You can share what's bothering you."

"Well, Mr. and Mrs. Matthews, I'm in big trouble. I don't know what to do. I'm pregnant."

Now she was sobbing, and Jane moved over to console her.

"Everything will be all right, Sally. We'll help you work something out," Jane assured her.

"But what can I do?" Sally asked.

"You haven't told your parents yet?" Jane asked.

"No. I don't dare."

"I told her," Teresa added, "that should have been the first thing she did a couple of months ago. But she was afraid to."

"Could you help me?" Sally asked. "Could you talk to my parents with me?"

Jane glanced at Mike and caught his nod, so she answered, "Sally, of course we'll help. But when we get together, and after we've broken the ice, I think it's very important that you tell them in your own words. I know I would rather have Teresa tell me if it was she who was pregnant, or whatever the problem was, rather than hear it from someone else. Your folks won't be happy, but I'm sure they will stand by with support and understanding because they love you."

"Are they home this evening, like right now?" Jane asked.

"Yes, I think so."

"Then why don't I call and invite them over for a cup of coffee with us," Jane said.

Fortunately, the Stewarts were free to join them, and Jane and Mike were able to help the three of them over the first hurdles. As anticipated, Jack and Maria, though very disturbed, expressed support and love for their daughter.

They also talked about the options— abortion—have the baby and give it a home—have the baby and offer it for adoption—or raise it as a single parent.

After an hour or so, the Stewarts opted to return to their home to pull things together, and try to reach the right decision for the three of them.

As it turned out, they decided, because of the term of the pregnancy, to let Sally give birth. She stayed for five months at a nearby social agency's home. She was able to visit her own home and complete her senior year of high school with a tutor, and graduate with the class.

The impression among her peers was that Sally was away as an exchange student for the balance of the school year.

Sally's crisis, however, gave Jane and Mike an opportunity to discuss birth control and alternative choices with Teresa.

She, in fact, began the discussion the evening after the Stewarts left. "I surely don't want to face what Sally is going through," she said.

"You don't have to," Jane responded. "The choice is yours. You control your body. You don't have to have casual, indiscriminate sex with any boy."

"But what if you really like a guy and you get turned on? What do you do then. It's not easy," Teresa said.

"I don't know for sure if Jane agrees with me," Mike said, "but I think she does. I think If you really care about a guy, and it's mutual, and you have love and respect for one another, you are going to be involved in passionate physical situations. If that leads to sex, I think you have that choice if it feels right for you. But then I think you both need to be responsible. Part of being responsible is not to have a child at your age or have a pregnancy force you into a wrong marriage.

"I agree," Jane said.

"OK. Does that mean I always make sure I have a condom with me?" Teresa asked.

"Perhaps. But why shouldn't the guy be responsible for the condom, Teresa?" Jane responded. "Why should it always be the woman who is supposed to be responsible?"

"I agree," Mike added. "But if you're in a relationship where you are going to have sex with some regularity, I'd rather we help you get the pill prescribed for you, if you preferred."

"Yes, for sure," Jane added. "And if you should ever get pregnant at this stage of life, I would much prefer that you get an abortion by a legitimate doctor in a qualified clinic. As you probably know, Teresa, the Supreme Court has ruled abortion to be legal in a hospital or clinic. That was three years ago in 1973."

"Please, Teresa, know that you can talk to us," Mike added. "We will always try to help you. Again, remember it's your body, and your choice."

"Thanks, Mom and Dad," Teresa replied. "I really appreciate this chance to talk with you, I'm grateful, you're so helpful and understanding. So many of my friends can't talk with their parents about any of the really important things."

Jane and Mike were still congratulating themselves on the opportunity to relate to Teresa in an intimate, meaningful way, when the next test of their durability in crisis was tested.

Scott, without his usual telephone call, appeared at home

one weekend. He hadn't been home for a several weeks. He'd been very busy with his senior year at the university, writing his dissertation, plus holding down a part-time job. He looked terrible—very pale, and thin."

"What happened to you?" Mike asked. "You were brown as toast when you got back from the Greek Islands. Have you had the flu? Or do you just need some home cooking?"

"I don't know what's wrong," Scott replied. "I feel weak and tired which isn't like me. I checked in to the student health service and they wanted me to go to the hospital for some tests. They thought I might be anemic or something. But I thought I'd rather come home and see our own family internist. Is that OK?"

"Well, of course it's OK. We'll make the appointment immediately," Mike answered.

The appointment was made. The tests taken, and then the report. Scott was diagnosed as having A-Plastic Anemia. The physician recommended that he be hospitalized immediately.

It was a grim situation when he talked to the three of them in his consultation room.

"Scott has one of the worst cases of this disease I have ever seen," he said. "I'm telling it like it is, because I firmly believe the patient's own attitude and immunity system must be an important ally if there's to be any chance of recovery."

"What is A-Plastic Anemia, Doctor?" Jane asked.

"It's a disease of the blood, akin to Leukemia, but not a malignancy. The body's manufacturing of blood suddenly goes goofy and no longer produces white cells which serve as the first line of defense for the immunity system. Without these cells even a common cold can kill a patient."

"What is the treatment?" Scott asked.

"Immediate isolation in a sterile situation in the hospital. Only immediate family allowed to see you and then never without surgical apparel including a mask. The same with physicians and nurses, and absolutely no person near you with any upper respiratory infection. We begin transfusions right away. You might have as many as one a day. There may be hormone shots also, and as a last resort a bone marrow transplant."

"Doctor," Mike asked, "how long will Scott be hospitalized and what is the prognosis?"

"I can only answer the first question by saying, a long time," the doctor replied. "The second question is a toughie. To be honest with you, in all the medical journals I've been able to get my hands on there have been just a handful of patients who have survived."

"Oh, no!" Jane exclaimed. "It can't be. What about the bone marrow transplant, and what caused this to happen?"

"Jane, I have to level with you," the doctor said. "The transplant is a last resort. It usually has to come from a sibling which would mean your daughter if she's compatible, and the truth is there is no guaranty it will work."

"Oh, no!" Jane repeated. "I can't handle this."

"As to what causes this form of anemia to happen," the physician continued. "Usually it's exposure to something toxic. It could be lead paint, even breathing lead in a room from paint on the walls. It could be toxic water or toxic fumes from a cleaning material. We don't know for sure, and everybody doesn't succumb to the toxic exposure. It depends on their particular immunity system at the time—just like a response to a virus."

"Well, Dad and Mother," Scott said, "we'd better get on with it. The sooner we start the better. This is my battle. I'll need all the help, love, support and prayers you can give me. Don't worry, Mom, I'll make it."

Four months into Scott's hospitalization there was no sign of improvement. He had received approximately sixty transfusions.

Friends, including hundreds of members of the church had registered as donors on the waiting list. Scott, had the worst case of A-Plastic Anemia ever recorded at Massachusetts General Hospital.

One member of the family had been to see Scott every day during the restricted visiting period. Jane had attended all of Scott's classes and taken lecture notes. As a result, and by special arrangements for exams, he had kept up with his classes and would graduate if he recovered. It looked very bleak. The verdict about the success of a bone marrow transplant from Teresa was shaky.

"Dad, I can't handle this situation any longer," Scott announced one day during Mike's visit. "I'm fed up with being a guinea pig. I've had doctors studying my case from all over the world. I feel like a statistic. Could I please go under the care only of our own doctor, and be moved to a private hospital. I believe it would make a big difference to me."

"I'll look into it immediately," Mike replied. "I'll talk to our doctor and let you know what he says."

The decision was to move. "Your son's attitude, peace of mind and personal comfort are so important with this disease," the doctor announced.

Two weeks later, as the Matthews sat down for dinner, a call came from the doctor's office. His excited voice on the end of the line was giving the best news the Matthews had heard in a long time.

"I can't believe what I'm seeing," he exclaimed, "Scott's blood test today has suddenly righted itself. His body is starting to produce white blood cells in normal numbers again. If this keeps up he'll be one hundred percent by the end of the week."

Mike let out such a loud cheer that Teresa and Jane thought he'd gone goofy. He told them what the doctor had said, and Jane grabbed the phone.

"Doctor, when did this happen? Just today? Thank you! Oh thank you!"

"Don't thank me, Jane. Thank God, because this is a miracle."

"If the count gets back to normal, will it stay that way?" Jane asked.

"I believe it will. I think your son will be as healthy as if he'd never had the disease. He should take it easy for awhile and get his strength and weight back, but otherwise he should be OK."

"Mom, ask when we can see Scott" Teresa chimed in.

"We all want to know when we can see Scott, Doctor."

"How about in thirty minutes, about as long as it takes you to get here."

There had never been a happier meeting of the Matthews family. Scott was beaming from ear to ear. He had been the first one to be told.

"I knew I was going to make it," he said.

"When did you begin to feel things turning around? Did they change your medication?" Mike asked.

"Whoa! One question at a time. No they didn't change anything. But I did. When I made the move to this hospital I decided I wanted to get well. I mean I concentrated with fierce determination every waking moment. My subconscious was working while I slept. I set my mind on overcoming this disease."

"That's tremendous, Scott. You're talking about what medical science is calling a physiology of optimism and self-healing."

"Absolutely. I felt myself drawing on the creative energy within me," Scott continued. "I practiced deep intense meditation and prayer. I believe I felt a higher power flowing through my body. I didn't try to bribe God or offer to make any bargains. I had this deep feeling that either way it would be OK. I believe that the power of God within me, and the support and love of my family and friends, energized my immunity system until I got back on track. That's what happened, I believe. It was a miracle."

Thanks to Jane, the family shared in another miracle—Scott's graduation. They felt Jane should also have received some type of sheepskin for all the classes she took, the notes, the book reports which made the celebration of Scott's graduation possible.

Unquestionably, Jane had been on a high taking the university courses. Her contribution gave her a renewed feeling of worth and importance. Despite the worry and strain, it had been gratifying to Mike and Teresa watching her vitality and energy at work.

Now, unfortunately, they were seeing her slide back into her valley of depression. She became listless. Slept more than normally. He could also feel their drifting apart. Early mornings together jogging, bike riding or swimming were getting fewer and farther between.

Jane was also reading more, which Mike hoped would be helpful. It seemed to him that she read every new self help book on the best seller list. But they only added to her confusion. For two reasons, Mike felt.

One, some of them tended to offer a lot of cheap, easy solutions to complex problems. Two, "how to" formulae were frequently conflicting, and the valid principles weren't assimilated. She didn't put them into practice in her daily habit patterns. Consequently, much of her reading contributed to a sense of guilt.

The only time Mike felt Jane's enthusiasm peak was when she took off for New York for another audition, fulfilling a contract for a role in a play or a TV commercial. There were signs then of a return to her old buoyant, positive self.

Jane also exhibited a joyful bounce in her step while guiding Teresa through senior prom time and high school graduation. Reluctantly, Teresa had agreed to a date with a patient suitor whom she thought of as a brother.

Her hesitation, Jane learned, was due to a long distance love affair blossoming between her and John Adams, Dane's best friend. They were both making plans to attend Florida International University, Teresa in Fine Arts, and John in a pre-architectural major.

It was exciting for Jane to join her daughter in a college clothes buying expedition. Who was more giddy was difficult to tell as Jane and Teresa left for Florida in Teresa's first new car of her own . . . Jane to help Teresa get settled in her off campus apartment . . . Teresa to begin her collegiate career.

At the same time, Scott moved to New York to pursue his graduate program and part-time teaching fellowship at New York University.

Suddenly the nest was empty, and Mike felt the haunting tinge of loneliness.

"What is it going to be like," he wondered, "to celebrate holidays, anniversaries, birthdays without the family circle complete. He knew he'd miss the weekly conferences. He understood there would be the potential of new horizons of fascinating experiences, but he couldn't help but feel the hollow emptiness of an era which was over.

Meanwhile, during all of his own personal family transitions and struggles, Mike was intimately involved in the crises of individuals in his church.

He regularly attended Alcoholic Anonymous meetings. Space in the church was donated for meetings, close to a kitchenette where there was easy access to coffee and cokes. The recovering alcoholics set a new record for consuming coffee, cokes and cigarettes.

Obviously, they were leaning on an alternate addiction while scrapping a more devastating habit. "God bless them!" thought Mike. He was accepted as friend, chaplain and counselor. Many nights he'd get a call to help one of them make it sober through the night.

It was especially frightening to Mike seeing the growing numbers of teenage candidates for treatment, both for alcohol addiction and drugs. More and more of his counseling appointments were with parents who didn't know where to turn with a son or daughter hooked on drugs or alcohol.

Fortunately, he had been able to recruit several members of the church who were professionally trained as counselors. They donated their time as resource persons.

An experience Mike found especially repugnant was dealing with the parents of an only child, a teenage girl who was very active in the youth center program. In classes he taught he noticed she was unusually withdrawn and shy.

At dances and parties she would be by herself. She never went on the fun weekend biking, camping or cross country ski trips. Mike joined the other counselors in trying to help her open up.

Finally, after one of Mike's classes, she asked if she could talk to him. They went into his office where she completely fell apart and began sobbing. After getting her calmed down, she told him the whole sordid story.

Her parents were nudists. Every weekend she was forced

to join them. She was repulsed by the whole experience. She couldn't buy the indoctrination program that nudism was nature's best teacher—especially after she was fondled by her own father.

At her request, Mike had several private sessions with her parents. They finally relented in their insistence that their daughter participate in the nudism. It was a joy to watch the girl gradually come out of her shell.

Mike found it especially tough emotionally to deal with situations of violence. There were suicides and stabbings, not only among the minorities . . . the Hispanics, Blacks, and disenfranchised and poverty stricken members of the church.

One day Mike was called to the intensive care section of a local hospital. One of the wealthiest, most successful young men of the church had been stabbed the night before in his sleep by an emotionally disturbed wife.

She had returned from a night on the town totally drunk. Later her teenage son found her dead in her car with the motor running and the garage door closed.

Always Mike personally felt the pain and sadness of his parishioners' tragedies. It was his wish to be a messenger and vehicle of the compassion, concern, and power of God . . . sometimes by just holding a hand, being there, a promise of hope, a word of empathy and encouragement.

No tragedy placed a greater challenge and strain on Mike than the young corporate CEO in his church who was responsible for a highway death on one of his business trips. He was not a heavy drinker, but he'd had two beers with lunch and fell asleep.

His car crossed the median, and plowed head-on into a small car killing a young wife and permanently injuring her husband.

The judge gave him five years in the state prison. His wife and young daughter were suddenly without a husband and father. But the other young woman was dead and her husband a paraplegic.

Mike visited his church member once a month. He was exposed to every grim experience of being a prisoner including forced homosexuality. He worked in the broom factory. He was a model inmate.

When his turn came up for parole, Mike met in advance with the parole board. He knew one of its members very well as a social worker. He even went to the capital and talked to the governor whom he had also learned to know on a personal basis.

Mike felt this man had paid his debt before the five years were up. He was deeply remorseful. He would never drink and drive again. He was not in need, it seemed to Mike, of more rehabilitation.

"Why not parole him?" Mike thought.

But nothing he could say or do shortened his sentence. He served his full five years.

Mike visited with his wife several times a month. Fortunately, she held up. Got a job, and gently guided her beautiful daughter through a difficult time.

Their family reunion after five years was memorable. The man got a new job. A happy family relationship was restored, and they became Mike's friends for life.

Chapter 28

Whispers of Thanksgiving

Mike's need for a friend was never more critical than the day he opened a certified letter from the chairman of his corporate trustees. It announced that MATTHEWS ENTER-PRISES, INC. had filed for bankruptcy under Chapter Eleven.

Mike felt temporarily devastated. How could it happen? A few short years ago he was worth millions. Now apparently it might be gone.

If the company couldn't be successfully reorganized, the bankruptcy court would take everything except personal possessions. This included two cars, the home, the condo at Hilton Head, Teresa and Scott's educational fund, and the foundation account dedicated to assisting college freshman.

Everything could be lost . . . the apartment complexes, condominiums, land, hotels, and the corporation itself.

Fortunately, nothing was owed the IRS.

"How could it happen?" Mike wondered. "I thought I had left the company in good hands. The choices of people heading the different divisions felt right at the time.

"True, there have been warning signals," he reflected, "a tightening market, escalating interest rates, some question-able decisions."

Mike called Dan to see if he could throw any light on the reasons for the collapse.

"Mike, I was just about to call you," Dan said. "I'm so sorry. I just read the story in the morning paper. It seems unfair. You worked so hard, and now are doing so much for others. What can I do to help?"

"Dan, it's good just to talk with you," Mike replied. "Right now I'm in shock. The worst part is the hardship all those employees will go through in losing their jobs."

"Leave it to you, Mike, to be concerned about others when you're the one getting zapped the hardest. Tell you what! Let me make a few phone calls and see if I can get any inside information which might help us to salvage the company. I'll call you back in about thirty minutes."

In less than a half hour Dan was back on the line. "Not a lot of consolation, Mike, but I did get some information. I learned that the last hundred million dollar development proved to be the culprit. If it had succeeded it would have bailed out everything and doubled the net worth of your holdings. It was a good gamble."

"Why didn't it work, Dan?"

"Three factors, as far as I can figure out," Dan replied. "The city council changed its mind—actually went back on its word, according to your attorneys. The council cut back on square footage allowable in the mall, and reduced the number of floors in the office tower. No way could the project be profitable with those cutbacks."

"What else happened?" Mike asked.

"The firm which did the demographic studies, predicting area growth and present and future market numbers, plain fucked up, Mike, (excuse my French). The coup de grace was dealt by that S.O.B. financial institution your people were working with. They could have restructured the financing and extended the leverage period with a balloon at the end. That would have saved the project. After all the years you've made money for them, they chose to call the note immediately. I understand they recently went through a management shake up and the new leadership could care less about loyalty to long term faithful clients."

"Any good news, Dan?"

Mike was feeling a little better now. A bit giddy but getting his equilibrium back.

"Yes, I believe there is some good news," Dan answered. "The attorney appointed as the bankruptcy trustee is someone I know and can work with. At the appropriate hearing I am going to make an offer of something like twenty-five to fifty cents on the dollar for some of the MATTHEWS ENTERPRISE properties. If I can swing it, and leverage the purchase, I can salvage some of your holdings and keep a major share of your employees in place. I believe we can also reorganize your company over time."

"Thank you, Dan. It means everything to me to have a friend like you. At the moment I feel like such a failure. I can't think of anything I've failed at before. You and I were raised that way. We have pride. We're achievers."

"You're so right Mike. It's been drilled into us from childhood that men don't fail."

"To go bankrupt is like fracturing our masculinity," Mike continued. "I feel as though I've contracted some horrible contagious disease. I feel I should go into isolation and hide someplace."

"Screw it, Mike! You know better than that. You're not a failure. Look at all your accomplishments. This is a temporary dip in your financial worth only. You can come back. Some of the leading corporate and professional men in America have gone through bankruptcy. That's why our forefathers designed laws providing for an honorable alternative to debtor's prison."

"I know you're right, Dan."

"Don't let me hear another word from you about being a failure, Mike. Do you know how much some of the wealthiest men in America would give for your kind of success in terms of self-worth, peace of mind, a legacy of lasting influence for good in this world? They'd swap their entire bankroll for what you have. You have your health, a brilliant mind, a fabulous reputation, the respect of friends and colleagues, a wonderful family and work which is inspiring and gratifying."

"I know Dan," Mike replied. "Thanks for reminding me, and for being the kind of friend you are. Wow! That was quite a lecture you gave me. I should have you come up here and speak in my church some Sunday."

"No, that's not my bag," Dan replied. "But I'll tell you what I will do. I'll be your go-between with the bankruptcy trustee and your attorneys, if you wish. I'm sure, with the power of attorney properly in place, you won't even have to go through the trauma of appearing. I'll see to it your accountants and attorneys handle everything."

"Thanks again, Dan. Let me know if there is anything more I need to do."

There was so much more Mike needed to do. But not concerning the bankruptcy.

Millions of net worth was lost, but restructuring worked, and thanks to Dan, Mike was able to cope with the trauma of the economic losses.

The continued growth of the church multiplied Mike's responsibilities and challenges. By the fall of their fifth year it was necessary, despite the size of the new facilities, to have three services per Sunday plus the one on Thursday evenings.

The variety of activities and programs under the coordination of the staff was proceeding successfully. However, there were two remaining personnel gaps. Mike felt the need for a full time trained counselor in addition to the professional volunteers from the membership.

He also felt two additional ordained personnel should be added—an older experienced person to assist in the visitation of hospitalized or otherwise traumatized persons—a younger ordained individual, preferably female, to assist in all pastoral responsibilities including preaching.

Since Thanksgiving week was rapidly approaching, the traditional time for reviewing budgets and receiving pledges of gift support for the coming year, Mike presented a proposal to the finance committee for these two new staff additions. To his surprise it was tabled.

Even Jack voted to table, and then explained his reason.

"Mike, our top financial priority this year is to increase your income and benefits if pledged giving permits. We intend to provide a substantial salary increase which you've been turning down in previous years. We also have an increased budget for books and periodicals in the church library for your use. After you finish reading them they become a permanent part of the church collection.

"That all sounds terrific, Jack," Mike said.

"We also intend to provide a discretionary fund under your sole jurisdiction," Jack went on, "for individuals you encounter who are down on their luck. We know you've been using your own funds for this in the past. Finally, we want to increase your annual time away from the parish from four to six weeks. We recognize the value to the church that you have time for graduate work, reflection and rejuvenation. Therefore we also have decided that after each tenth year a full time clergy or lay minister is with us there will be a fully paid sabbatical year.

"Goodness! I'm overwhelmed, Jack."

"By the way, all conferences or seminars attended by you," Jack continued, "where you do not receive an honorarium for being part of the program, will be paid by the church.

"We're aware of the unfortunate economic problem of your company, Mike. We feel badly about it, and would like to put our money where our mouth is, so to speak. We've done our homework and know that you're lagging behind what other clergymen serving similar size churches are receiving. That was our deal when you came here. Remember? End of discussion. This is our decision."

"Well, for once I don't know what to say" Mike replied. "Be sure to get that in the minutes, Jack I appreciate your consideration very much. But let me make a deal with you. I think you know I would rather have more help to do a better job of serving the community and members of our church than an increase in salary.

"However, since you've made it clear there's no room for debate on the issue, how about an alternative amendment? If our growth in pledged giving increases enough to support fifty percent of the salaries for two more staff people, would you approve my proposal on the basis of increased giving from membership growth during the year?"

"Mike, you don t give up do you?" Jack answered.

"Turning to the other finance committee members Jack put the question. "Those in favor say 'yes' and against 'no'.""

It was unanimous. Mike's proposal was accepted.

Before the meeting adjourned Jack asked, "Why do you prefer having an ordained woman on your staff, Mike? I'm curious. Like to hear your answer. You already have several women on your team: the Minister of Education, my wife Maria, your executive assistant, several ladies in the office."

"Happy to answer your question," Mike replied. "It's important, I feel, that we have balance on the church staff, including among ordained personnel. I believe the words of the Apostle Paul are absurd: 'let women keep silent in the churches.'

"Obviously women have ability and intelligence at least equal to men. If a Ghandi and Thatcher can lead a nation women can also be leaders in the clergy.

"Though women are equal, I believe they are also unique, not only biologically, but in temperament, feelings, emotions, sensitivity. Whether this is due to nature or nurture in our culture, I don't know, but I believe it's true. With all the mothers, single professional women and teenage girls in our church, it seems to me they deserve a woman of the clergy who speaks their language, to whom they can go for guidance spiritually if they choose."

"Well put, Mike," Jack responded. "I'm sure we all agree, but we needed to hear your reasons so we can also give valid answers when we're asked."

The days before Thanksgiving week launched the period of pledged giving support at PRINCE OF PEACE COM-MUNITY CHURCH. Mike spent many hours lobbying in offices of corporate executives who were church members. He made dozens of phone calls to members he considered to be centers of influence in the parish.

Through the monthly newsletter each member had an opportunity to read his column outlining the staff proposal and its conditions of financing.

The evening before Thanksgiving, Mike offered three identical half hour vesper services. He called them "WHISPERS OF THANKSGIVING."

Following appropriate music, he shared this meditation with the families attending:

"Most of us have experienced the feeling of life caving in on us.

"We felt desperate.

"We thought there was no possible way to carry on-overcome.

"The situation seemed hopeless.

"When faced with emotional and spiritual bankruptcy, I have learned that there is one therapy worth trying. It can work miracles, and we can initiate it ourselves.

"The secret is: instead of screaming anger and frustration, whisper a prayer of thanksgiving.

"Why not try it?

"To make a God-connection we don't need to call information, or dial a number.

"Our words do not need to be theological or fancy. In fact we don't have to use words at all. Just our thoughts and feelings focused on God as we perceive God.

"Why not try it?

"Say, for example:

"God, it's been a while, and I'm no expert at this; but I need to communicate with you.

"I'm told that you are compassionate, and I believe it. I'm told you created us humans in your image, and dwell within us. If that's true, then you've made it easy for us to communicate. So I'll try.

"God, I've been told I can talk with you in a Cathedral, a Shrine, or the Church up the street. But these are not the only places.

"You are equally approachable:
On a walk in the woods.
Viewing a sunset.
Climbing a mountain.
Sitting at a desk.

Washing dishes.
Operating a farming tractor.
Working an assembly line.
Floating a canoe downstream.
Flying an airplane.
Driving back roads.
Listening to a symphony.
Reading an inspiring book.

"Just so I am willing to be quiet.
Concentrate.
Listen.
Be frank.
Open.
Aware.

"God, some say that I can talk with you best by kneeling. Others say to take slow deep breaths, fold my hands and bow my head.

"But I have learned that these are not essential.

"Posture is not the key, but a mood of reverence.

"God, I am told that I can tune to your frequency by setting my mind on the channel of thanksgiving—not petitioning or bargaining.

"It seems to work, because already I am feeling better.

"Closer to you.
Empowered by your strength.
Encouraged by your love.

"It's true! It's impossible to feel down or sorry for myself at the same time I am concentrating on my reasons for gratitude.

"Thank you, God.
I feel very small.
Lost.
Hurt.
Helpless.
Afraid.
Weak.

"So my prayer may just be a whisper, but I have a feeling you'll hear me. I just want to try to say how much I appreciate the treasures I take too much for granted.

"Dear God, I thank you for my home. It's comfortable, inviting, and shared by people who love me.

"I am grateful when they are patient with my faults; forgiving when I am weak; encouraging when I fail; respectful of my need for privacy; buoyant on holidays with celebration and laughter.

"Thank you too, God, for my family. Past and present. Concerned parents, brothers, sisters and grandparents who have loved me, shared my dreams, and contributed to my cherished memories.

"I am grateful also for the privilege of parenthood. Sons and daughters . . . the feeling of pride in their successes and hope for their fulfillment.

"Thank you also, God, for friends. Someone I can trust. Who accept me for what I am; offer loyalty and support; share with me their secret needs.

"I am also grateful, Dear God, for health—mentally and physically. How fortunate I am not to have crippling pain! How privileged I am to have an alert mind, and the skills and endurance to pursue adventure and excellence!

"Thank you too, God, for work. A job which is challenging, interesting, creative. What a privilege to get up in the morning and feel needed! I am grateful for the chance to return to the world a dividend of something worthwhile.

"For now, God, there is one more gift for which I would like to say 'thank you.'

"I am grateful for faith . . . faith in your transcending presence revealed in:

> Echoes of your teachings.
> The majesty of the universe.
> A passing parade of spiritual masters.
> The still, small voice within.

"Now, Dear God, I would like to sign off with just one petition.

"I need your help to be more sensitive to some of the people around me . . . who don't have the comfort of a home; the support of family; the loyalty of friends; the joy of health, work and faith.

"Help me never to get so wise that I cannot cry in the face of poverty, pain and loneliness . . . So sophisticated that I cannot take the hand of a child . . . So busy that I miss the highest priority of what is infinite and eternal.

"As you have touched me, Dear God, while I have been reaching inward, help me to reach outward and touch those who weep and wail . . . Shout their sounds of bitterness. Moan with mourning and pain.

"Help me to offer a hand to those plagued by the demons of fear, cruelty, addiction. Who stare from behind barbed wire. Are born in places where I wouldn't want to be caught dead. Live in an X-rated world. Whose nightmares come in the daytime. Who go to bed hungry, and cry themselves to sleep.

"God, help me be aware.

"Help me to express my thanksgiving in action.

"And not only in far away places, or ways that make headlines.

"Help me to start by:

> Welcoming a stranger.
> Looking up a forgotten friend.
> Keeping a promise I've tried to forget.
> Offering a kind word, a smile, a listening ear.

"Thank you, God, for listening today.

"I no longer feel desperate.

"I know now I can overcome.

"If, like breathing, I tune in to this connection in the daily rhythms of my life.

Mike was on cloud nine when he received the finance committee's report following Thanksgiving week. The pledged goal was met. He had the green light to fill the two critical staff positions.

For the time being, he now felt comfortable with the number and quality of the staff. Including the full time custodial couple, there were sixteen people entrusted with leadership in this congregation of three thousand . . . and growing.

Chapter 29

A Real Shocker

Mike was at his den desk preparing for a chamber of commerce speech in a posh suburb.

His subject was "DOES IT PAY TO BE CANDID IN INTERPERSONAL BUSINESS RELATIONSHIPS?"

He was in a pensive mood. Reflecting about superficial, automatic language in greeting associates in the competitive fast lane of business.

"How's it goin'? we ask. How're ya doin'? What's new?

"Glibly we throw out the idiom of our greetings! How easily and frequently we respond with lies and exaggerations.

"Just fine, we say. Or, Nothing's changed! Everything's great. Couldn't be better.

"Maybe it's true, but the odds are it's all a fabrication," Mike recognized.

"The truth is we may be hurting and aching something fierce ... in the pits ... on the verge of despair ... nearly spastic over incredible, sudden reverses. But we still answer: 'Nothin's changed ... everything's fine.'

"The fact probably is that everything's changed, because nothing ever stays static. Plus the person asking the question doesn't want to hear the long, boring answer anyway unless the individual is an intimate friend."

This was Mike's train of thought when he opened a special delivery letter from Jane's New York apartment address.

Dear Mike,

I love you. I need to begin my letter this way rather than signing off with these words.

I do love you very much, and always will.

Our years together have been full to the brim with adventure, struggle, tragedy, happiness.

Ever since Dane's death I have been on the skids emotionally as you know. I have tried so hard, but I'm still bitter and I have to work this out my own way.

With respect to the church . . . I've attempted to be the perfect minister's wife, but I can't. Something within me won't let me settle for life in the shadows as number two.

We're both aware that over these past six years or so we have drifted apart. I don't think it's more one person's fault than the other. We've both tried.

But we've both changed, and our circumstances have changed. As you've said so often, "nothing remains constant."

We have grown, but not in parallel paths. We could stay together, but I don't think it would be fair to you, and maybe to me.

So, my darling Mike, I have decided to pursue a divorce and set you free. Our children are grown and well on their way. you have your work which you love, and I now have mine again which I also enjoy.

I hope my decision will not come as too great a shock. I'm sure you felt our paths converging to this fork in the road. Try to understand, Mike, and be my friend for life.

I remember way back there when we first fell in love, you used to say to me: "Love can be whimsical and temperamental. It may come as mysteriously as a gentle breeze to caress you and disappear without warning.

"When it comes, accept and enjoy it, and when it departs cherish its memory. Love is life's greatest experience because it brings us into communion with infinite, divine presence; and it's influence on your life is forever."

I don't want anything from you materially, Mike. We can even use the same attorney. But now that I have decided, I'd like to do it as soon as possible. Please call me after you've

read this if you wish, and we can talk further on the phone.
                    Fondly forever,
                    Jane

    Mike was numb. Crushed. Shocked. But not completely surprised. Jane probably was right. They both knew it was coming.

    Mike had opened the letter almost frantically with a sense of foreboding.

    He sat staring at the picture of the two of them on his desk. The letter fluttered to the floor. He picked it up and re-read it . . . and read it . . . and read it again.

    By this time tears were flowing. It was a beautiful letter, really. Reflecting pathos, dreams, hopes, and love.

    Mike found it impossible to accept. Their marriage had been so good in many ways. So much better than most. On a scale of one to ten, it would deserve about an eight.

    "It just can't be over," Mike thought. At least I'm not going to give up without another try."

    Even though it was late, he dialed Jane. Her phone rang only once.

    "Hi Mike. I knew it was you . . . hoped it was. Now you'll think I'm psychic. You read my letter."

    "Yes, Jane. We're all psychic in a way I guess. I wasn't totally surprised. But I'm sad, and I miss you."

    "I miss you too," Jane replied, "but I feel this is the only way I can find my way at this stage of my life. I don't want to do anything to hurt you, Mike, but I have come to the conclusion that this will be the best for you as well as me."

    "Perhaps you're right," Mike answered, "but I can't give up so easily. You know I've always agreed with your stand on women's rights to equality and individuality. We've had such a good life together. We've shared a lot. We've gone up and down so many peaks and valleys. Can't we give it another try—maybe go to an experienced, capable marriage counselor?"

    "I've been doing that on my own, Mike. In fact I've been seeing the woman counselor on your staff, and she's terrific.

You've got a good one there. Her conclusion with me is that you and I will eventually be better off going in separate directions."

"Life surely has some strange twists, doesn't it?" Mike added. "Here I am devoting a major vocational chapter in my life to a spiritual vocation. Almost every week I touch the lives of people with a shaky marriage, and here I am on the verge of divorce."

"Mike, don't get down on yourself, now it's my turn to help you stay on an even keel. I'll be home day after tomorrow. We can discuss then which attorney to consult, and work out the arrangements which will suit both of us best. Take care now. I'll see you soon."

Even though it was past midnight, Mike felt he had to talk to somebody. So he called Bob Mackay and got him out of bed.

"Bob, it's Mike. Sorry I woke you, but this time I need you."

"Let me grab my robe," Bob replied, "and get to the phone in my study. Hang on a minute. Better yet, let me call you right back."

"OK. I'll be here."

Seconds later the phone rang. "What's up?" Bob asked.

"I just got a letter from Jane. Bob, she has decided she wants us to be divorced. Remember, I told you I was afraid this might happen."

"I'm sorry, Mike. Do you want me to catch a plane for Boston tomorrow. I'll reschedule some meetings if I can be of help."

"Thanks, Bob," I replied. "I appreciate that, but I just need a friend to talk to. I'm afraid it's final. Jane has her mind made up. She's been through counseling. In fact she's been seeing the professional on my staff, who agrees divorce would be best for both of us."

"I think the world of both of you, Mike. You know that. You helped save my marriage once. I'd do anything to help you now if I could."

"Jane is coming home day after tomorrow, and we'll have

a chance to talk then," Mike continued. "I'll keep you informed, Bob. Meanwhile, though, I wonder if we do go ahead and have the divorce what is the protocol prescribed by church headquarters regarding divorced clergy staying in church service?"

"Don't concern yourself with that," Bob replied, "I would handle that. We've come a long way. In situations where there is no blatant affair on the part of the ordained person, and a conscientious effort to preserve a good marriage, the clergy are encouraged to remain where they are. It's also usually contingent on the congregation expressing that wish through its church council or cabinet."

"That sounds reasonable," Mike responded.

"In your case, Mike, I would personally schedule a meeting with your cabinet to relieve you of any awkwardness. So don't waste a minute thinking about that."

"Thanks again, Bob. We've shared so much, haven't we, since that day back there on the seminary commons when we met each other on the passing and receiving ends of a football.

"One of these days we'll have to go on a fishing trip together or maybe I can take a few days off and come to New York for one of our old fashioned 'bull sessions'. It would be fun to include Scott also."

"How's he doing?"

"Great," Mike replied. He's getting a Masters in Creative Writing, and also teaching part time at New York University He's been able to see Jane quite a bit, and that's been good for both of them.

"He's also made some contacts with an agent and is working on his first book. He'll be ready for a leisure break soon."

"I'll give him a call," Bob said. "Maybe he and I can have lunch next week."

"Bob, I've got to hit the sack, I've got an early morning meeting and you need to get back to sleep. I'll talk to you soon."

The next day Mike telephoned Scott and Teresa. Both of them were more aware than he anticipated of the drifting apart

in their marriage. He sensed their genuine feeling of understanding. They both thought it was most important to do what
we thought was right for them, rather than be concerned about
their reaction.

Teresa was especially helpful. "Dad, please don't feel like
you and mother are failures," she said. "The quality of a
marriage is not measured by the number of years two people
are together. You've had a beautiful relationship, and you'll
always be friends.

"I know you're right Teresa."

"Don't worry about Scott and me. We love both of you,
and always will. You are both dynamic, creative people.
Maybe it's time for Mother to take off on a different road.
You'll be OK, Dad. Please call me if you get lonesome."

There were many lonely days after the divorce was final.

When Jane returned from New York they had many long
talks before filing, but always came to the same conclusion.
Mike even suggested that after one more year he could leave
the church and go back into business.

However, it was clear that Jane's decision was final, and
not exclusively tied to her frustration as a minister's wife.

The day of the final hearing and the decree was filed they
had a quiet lunch at a favorite restaurant. The next day Jane
moved to her apartment in New York.

Mike sold the home and bought a small townhouse. The
capital gains from the house as well as the Hilton Head home,
was put into an income producing annuity for Jane.

The divorce caused a telephone chain reaction among
church members. It also made the newspaper with the caption:
"Prominent Clergyman and Wife are Divorced. "

Jane and Mike had been called by a reporter and agreed to
an interview. Since Mike had become well known in the city
as the senior minister of a large church, they felt it was best to
share the reasons for the marriage dissolution.

Astoundingly, the article brought a flood of calls and cards
empathizing and wishing them both well. It also nearly
doubled requests for Mike's services, and that of his counseling

staff, for appointments related to troubled marriages.

There was never a doubt that the congregation wished him to remain. It wasn't necessary for Bob to meet with the cabinet. Their decision was unanimous that Mike stay.

Suddenly he was single again, and he hated it. He missed Jane's companionship, the fun things they did together. Their intimate talks, trips, mutual love, sexual relationship.

Mike ate most of his meals on the run. His refrigerator contained a bottle of ketchup and a coke. He got to know every fast food restaurant in the neighborhood. Once in awhile he would accept an invitation to share a meal in the home of a church member, but most of the time he was too busy.

As time progressed, there were many well meaning couples in the church who tried to introduce Mike to a divorced or widowed friend. Once in awhile he agreed to a date . . . a movie, dinner, a concert or play.

He had a strict rule, however, no dates with a church member. Most of the dates turned out to be boring. The widows seemed intent on snaring a husband, and the divorcees were obsessed with hostility and anger from a previous marriage. Mike could sense it within ten minutes of their meeting.

So for the most part he devoted himself to his very busy life at the church: guiding and coordinating the staff; classes for teens and new members; attending a constant procession of meetings; preparing for each week's speeches, lectures and sermons as well as delivering them; regularly visiting the youth center and choir school activities; keeping his counseling appointments.

Mike loved the rare private times to read a good novel, attend a concert or play, see a good movie, go for a long walk on a nature trail, take a bike ride, go for a swim, or his favorite pastime—play golf. It was important to him to listen to his body and stay in good shape with regular exercise and stimulating, mental diversions.

As a result he was rarely ill. Hardly ever had even a cold. All the more reason Mike thought of it only as a nuisance when one day he came up with a sore throat. It turned out to be a corker.

"But no reason to see a doctor," he thought. "I'll just suck on lozenges, and in a week it will be gone."

In a week or so it was gone, but several weeks later, while biking, Mike became suddenly dizzy and unusually short of breath. He felt his heart racing.

"No problem," he thought. "Just age and the exceptionally hot, humid day."

But when the discomfort persisted, he jumped in the car and headed for the doctor's office.

He happened to be in and saw him immediately. After examination, he asked, "Have you been ill with anything, even a cold?"

"I just had a sore throat," Mike replied.

"I can't be sure, Mike, and I'll want you to see the cardiologist in this building, like right now. But I think that sore throat was a virus infection, which has settled in your heart, causing a severe rapid and uneven beat, and maybe some damage. That's why you're short of breath and dizzy. I want you in the hospital immediately."

"Doc, I don't have time to spend time in the hospital right now," Mike said. "Can't I just see the cardiologist? He's down on the second floor isn't he?"

"If you value your life, listen to me, Mike. At least stay overnight. There are other tests, x-rays, cardiograms we need, stress tests, and they're so much easier to do here in the hospital."

"OK. But let me call my office first."

Mike got Maria on the phone. "Listen, I've been feeling a little punk lately," he said. "Nothing serious. I'm having a physical and the doctor will find it easier to complete his normal tests faster if I stay overnight in the hospital."

"Are you OK, Mike? How come I didn't have this in your schedule book? Did you forget it? That would be just like you," Maria chided him.

"Yes, I'm OK and I did forget it," he fudged. "Please, this is private. Don't say anything to the staff or anyone else. I'll be in later tomorrow."

The next day he received a grim verdict.

"Mike, I've got to level with you," the doctor began. "The cardiologist and I agree. You did have a viral infection. It has quite severely damaged your heart to the point that you're down to about seventy percent efficiency. It's called cardiomyopathy."

"What's the treatment?" Mike asked.

"We can do an electric shock therapy procedure directly into the heart. In some cases this will restore the heart to an even beat, thus preventing progressive damage. The only problem with this procedure is that the results may not last, and it could be fatal."

"Oh! That's exciting," Mike replied. "What are the odds?"

"About fifty-fifty," he answered.

"Let's skip that for the moment," Mike said. "What other treatment is there?"

"We can put you on several daily medications such as a form of digitalis, plus a blood thinner to protect against blood clots and heart attacks, as well as a prescription to aid in the elimination of liquid build up in your system."

"What else is involved? Will I have to slow down, or change my routine?" Mike asked.

"Yes to a degree. But you can continue your work, and certain forms of regular exercise. But everything you do should be done sensibly."

"What does that mean?" Mike asked.

"Specifically, watch the balance in your life. Don't drive yourself to outer limits. When you play golf, for example, ride or walk with a caddy. If the course is hilly, ride. I would advise no running such as jogging or playing tennis. No more downhill skiing, only cross-country in moderation, and daily walks. Reasonable, recreational bike riding is OK also."

"What about corrective surgery?" Mike asked.

"We're beginning to perform some miracles with open heart surgery," the doctor replied. "But that won't help you, nor would a pacemaker. Actually only a heart transplant would solve your problem completely. That's a future possibility."

"Meanwhile, I continue on the daily medication. Is that right?" Mike asked.

"That's all we can do, Mike, plus monitoring for additional progressive damage."

"What are the odds of that?"

"About fifty-fifty," he answered. "The truth is, on the average you can expect about five more years, Mike. If you're lucky, ten, and should you be an exceptional phenomenon, fifteen. Present medical history only records a handful of those."

"Thanks, Doctor, for being so frank with me," Mike responded. "I like that, because I can better deal with it. "I'm going to set my mind on being one of those fifteen year phenomenons."

"No question about it, setting your mind to it, taking the medication and living sensibly will help." the doctor replied. Your mental attitude, a strong faith and the love and support of others can have a positive affect on your healing and immunity system. Meanwhile I want to see you in ninety days . . . less if you feel worse."

Mike left the hospital with a whole new set of feelings. One of them was a vow of privacy. He decided he didn't want to have people fussing over him. He would follow the doctor's orders to the best of his ability.

Another strong emotion was a commitment of determination to be healed, or at least focus on not allowing the damage to progress.

He felt a calmness—a tranquility. He was grateful for his rich, varied and multifaceted life thus far. He felt that if this phase of life was over, it was OK.

But, on the other hand, there was so much yet that he hoped to experience and accomplish.

In this mood Mike recorded his thoughts in some lines of free verse which he called: A BREATH AWAY.

> The end of here
> always just one

breath away . . .
odds higher now
  parts deteriorated,
    moving on
      not my choice
unless human
  dignity done,
    creativity, growth . . .
only burden
  on others . . .
    a breath away?
      worth reflection
need to stretch
  my purpose . . .
    am rich in love
      family, friends,
could it continue
  for a time
    would give me joy . . .
either way,
  not death
    but life.

He tucked his poem away without showing it to anyone.

A year later he reread it as his doctor announced: "You are one of the lucky ones, Mike. The damage appears to be halted. I don't think it will progress further. Your heart muscle is enlarged because of working harder to do its job, but right now it looks like you, and that dynamic congregation of yours, may both have bought some time."

"Great news!" Mike replied. "I was confident this would happen."

"We'll check on you every six months, Mike. Continued good fortune!"

Chapter 30

Older? Smarter? Wiser?

Mike was fifty-six going on thirty-five. In spite of aging on the outside he didn't feel old on the inside.

Therefore, he was flabbergasted when he received an invitation to speak at the banquet for his fortieth high school reunion banquet. He did a double take on that number forty.

"They must have made a mistake," he thought. "How could it be forty years? But it was, '39 to '79."

The reality hit him a few days later when he was called by the president of Jefferson University.

"Do you realize how many years it's been," he began, "since you graduated and returned as Vice President of Development? My predecessor told me what a great job you did."

"I'd have to stop and figure out how long it's been," Mike replied. "Can you believe it's really been thirty-six years?"

"Mr. Matthews, the University has never forgotten what you did for us. We're still receiving dividends on your contributions."

"Thank you, sir."

"I'm also happy to inform you," he continued, "that the Board of Governors and faculty has opted to confer on you an honorary doctorate degree at this year's commencement. You have also been elected to fill an unexpired term on our Board. We hope you will accept and be with us for commencement."

"Thank you again," Mike replied. "That is a real honor.

I'm looking at my calendar, and yes I will plan to be there. It so happens that the date is just a few days before I am scheduled to speak at my fortieth high school reunion."

"Good. The timing will work out well for you then."

"Incidentally, could you tell me if Mr. Bradshaw is still living?" Mike asked. "I've lost track."

"No, he passed away last year after a long illness. It's a shame no one told you. I realize the two of you had a lot of respect for one another."

"Yes, I would have liked to see him again."

"We'll look forward to your visit then, Mr. Matthews. It's been good talking with you."

The trip back to St. Paul, and the small Wisconsin town of Mike's early teen years, was a pilgrimage of the spirit. He decided to use part of his vacation, take his time, and drive.

It was a delightful experience to enjoy the leisure of the countryside, small charming towns and bed and breakfasts along the way. He stopped at Niagara Falls, took the car ferry across Lake Michigan, and visited the Door County peninsula where he had a day of fantastic fishing.

On the return drive, Mike planned to visit Mackinac Island, Sault Ste. Marie . . . and take the trans-Canadian highway through the national forest to Montreal. Then back down through Vermont, New Hampshire and home.

The trip was filled with nostalgia. Mike's emotions really ran high when he walked across his college campus, revisited the football stadium, a few of his professors still living and several of the buildings he had been responsible for getting built.

Receiving the honorary degree was special, and Mike really got choked up while touring the old student union where he and Jane had first met.

His kaleidoscope of treasured memories was really set to spinning at his high school reunion. He had never been back for a reunion before and didn't know what to expect. So he didn't set his hopes too high, because he realized it could turn out to be a dud.

But it was far from disappointing. The three day weekend was an "Alice in Wonderland-Sentimental Journey." The committee had done an excellent job. In advance they had mailed a copy of the class picture, and a capsule biographical sketch of each classmate.

The alumni stayed at a lovely resort motel on a tournament class golf course. When they registered they received a plasticized name tag with their high school picture on it. What an assist that was sorting through the branding iron lines and wrinkles of aging.

Mike was amazed at the turnout. Eighty-five were in their class. Twelve had passed away and three could not be located. Sixty were present, plus spouses.

It was a thrill for Mike to revisit his old home, find it still standing and restored. He toured the remodeled church where his father had been the minister, the football field and tennis courts where he had played, the factory where he worked, the hardware and drugstore where he was employed. He also drove past his first serious girlfriend's home, and hoped Sara would be at the reunion.

The reception cocktail party and dinner was the most fun Mike had experienced in a long time. The golf tournament was played on a fabulous spring day, and won by Mike with a 77.

There was an afternoon picture taking, getting reacquainted, reunion-cake-cutting social at the country club. He was also invited to three of his classmates' homes over the weekend. They had stayed in the community all these years.

These were all never-to-be-forgotten pleasures for Mike.

But the best for him was a visit to a nursing home where he discovered his childhood fishing and hunting mentor, Steve Woods. He was living out his last years there. He was alone in this world, his wife having died several years ago, and no children.

Steve didn't recognize Mike when he walked into his room. But the light of recognition brightened on his face when Mike said: "Hello Steve. I'm Mike, the kid next door, whom you taught to fish and hunt. Remember me, Steve?"

"Mike . . . are you really Mike? Sure, I remember. But I haven't seen you for so long. We've got to wet a line again. Can you go with me?"

"Of course I can, Steve," Mike replied.

But he knew Steve wouldn't remember. His Alzheimer's disease permitted him spurts of memory in the long term, but for the short term . . . forget it. He was emaciated. Shrinking away. But what a joy for Mike to see his spark of life light up when he said:

"Remember that first time you took me rabbit hunting? I had my first own shotgun bought with money I'd saved. We hid in a thicket, and your hound brought the rabbit right by us just like you promised he would."

"Sure, I remember," Steve answered.

"I haven't seen you in forty years, Steve," Mike said, "but I'm here for a high school reunion, and when I learned you were here I wanted to visit you."

"That's so nice, Mike."

"I've wanted to tell you all these years, Steve, how much you meant to me when I was a boy. You were a real friend. I looked up to you. You taught me how to hunt and fish. But I learned so much more from you about life . . . about how to enjoy the woods, a sunrise through the mist, the quiet waters of our favorite lake, how to learn from nature and appreciate the beauty and luxury of our earth. I came here to say 'thank you, Steve, and God bless you.'"

They were both misty eyed when Mike put his arm around Steve and said "goodby".

The speech at the dinner dance was a challenge. Typically, the preliminaries dragged. The title of Mike's talk, printed on the program, was: "OLDER? SMARTER? WISER?"

He began by saying:

"This reunion has really been a nostalgic trip for me. I hope you've enjoyed it as much as I have. One more time . . . let's lift our glasses high and drink a toast: 'Here's to you, committee, our thanks for a fabulous experienc

"Now, I can hear some of you saying: 'Do we have to listen to this guy? A preacher? Stuffy, long-winded! This program has lasted long enough. Let's get on with the partying and dancing.'

"I don't blame you if you're annoyed, but let me make a deal with you.

"My deal is similar to the one I get at a fast food restaurant in my neighborhood. These words are printed on its menu: 'If your meal doesn't arrive in ten minutes, it's on us.'

"My deal is if I'm not finished in ten minutes, and you don't walk out of here with at least one stimulating thought, I'll personally refund the cost of your dinner.

"Yes, I am a minister, and having the time of my life at it. And some of you know I've also had several other careers. So, tonight I'm reaching into my past for one of my brief business-executive, motivating type of talks.

"OK! Let's set our watches. I've got ten minutes.

"OLDER? SMARTER? WISER? Let's look at each one for two minutes.

"First OLDER . . .

"When I look at you I see bulges, wrinkles, thinning and graying hair not present on your picture name tags. Can you believe I haven't even begun to describe the guys yet?

"Sure, we've gotten older. But I agree with Maurice Chevalier who observed: 'Old age is not so bad when you consider the alternative.'

"All my life I've tried to follow a motto which I abbreviate with the word PEP. It stands for three dynamic life attitudes: POSITIVE, ENTHUSIASTIC, PERSISTENT.

"I have found that when I've been able to live by this motto, I may have dramatic changes outside, but inside I remain alert, creative, productive and happy.

"I agree with Cicero who wrote: 'The fact is that old age is respectable just as long as it asserts itself, maintains its proper rights, and is not enslaved to anyone.'

"OLDER? Yes, but how old is old? Age is not in the eyes of the beholder. It's in the eye of the individual wearing it. If we don't feel older within, we'll remain youthful to the end.

"How about SMARTER?

"You be the judge. We've seen a lot of changes since '39. Buck Rogers has come true. We've walked on the moon. We pay two dollars and fifty cents for a hamburger when we used to pay twenty-five cents. A nickel coke has turned into a buck.

"We've really gotten sophisticated with our sexuality. The "F" word is now slang. R and X-rated movies are openly available.

"Basketball teams now score a hundred points or more a game. We sometimes had games ending fourteen to ten.

"We wear contacts and can have almost guaranteed instant cataract surgery. Mothers are in and out of the hospital in just a couple of days with a new baby. We can have hip transplants. Soon it will be hearts and brains.

"Just think of the buzz words we've added to our vocabulary. We talk about spaced out, state of the art, data bases, cost effective, impacting, software, modems, holistic medicine.

"We use words like 'cool' which has nothing to do with temperature, and 'punk' which has nothing to do with lousy, and 'straight' which doesn't refer to a line.

"We go to Europe, Mexico, the Caribbean, and the Far East in hours by air, when it used to take days by train or boat. We do complicated math problems in seconds with a miniature calculator.

"Yes, I'm sure we agree —

"Surely, we have grown SMARTER.

"But have we grown WISER?

"We won World War II. A quarter century later the victim seems to have become the victor. GM and Ford are being threatened. Japan and Germany are threatening to take over the car market. They're outproducing us in most electronic fields. They appear to be on the way to outstripping us in quality, efficiency and value.

"I'm reminded of the old saying attributed to the Pennsylvania Dutch, 'Too soon old, too late schmartz.'

"We are older, smarter, but are we WISER?

"We can send probes to Mars and Venus. We have

sophisticated weapons. We can press buttons and destroy a nation or our globe. Our national debt is soaring.

"But we can't cure the common cold or elm disease, or dedicate ourselves to solving the ozone problem, the threat of acid rain, wild life extinction and water pollution.

"Are we WISER?

"Do we produce and read more good books? Do we have a greater appreciation of enduring art, great music and theatre? Are we doing a better job of caring for the homeless, minorities, the disenfranchised, our poverty stricken brothers and sisters in ghettos?

"Are we more tolerant than we used to be of people who look different, don't wear our uniform, share our politics, or worship as we do?

"Have we learned that being truly alive requires a daily effort in some rewarding and worthwhile activity? Do we know that a healthy, active mind grows better with age and use?

"Do we believe with Robert Browning that 'the best is yet to be'? Do we understand what it means to be created in the image of God? Are we satisfied with our spirituality?

"OLDER? Yes . . . SMARTER? Probably . . . WISER? Maybe.

"Now, my ten minutes are up. I'm going to conclude with a verse we recited the day we graduated. You see I cheated. I really didn't remember it for forty years, but I looked it up.

"Remember how our class advisor worked so hard helping us to clearly enunciate these words?

> God—let me be aware.
> Let me not stumble blindly down the ways.
> Just getting somehow safely through the days,
> Not even groping for another hand,
> Not even wondering why it all was planned,
> Eyes to the ground, unseeking for the light,
> Soul never aching for a wild-winged flight,
> Please, keep me eager just to do my share.
> God—let me be aware.

God—let me be aware.
Stab my soul fiercely with others' pain,
Let me walk seeing horror and strain.
Let my hands, groping, find other hands.
Give me the heart that divines, understands.
Give me the courage, wounded, to fight.
Flood me with knowledge, drench me in light.
Please—keep me eager just to do my share.
God—let me be aware.

"So long good friends! See you in ten years for our fiftieth."

Driving home to Boston Mike reflected on what his pilgrimage of the spirit had meant.

Thomas Wolfe's famous words came to him, "You can't go home again." Of course he knew what Wolfe meant. We can't relive the past. We can't do over again what's been done.

However, Mike felt it was extremely helpful for him "to go home again," in spirit and memory. He rediscovered part of his roots. He found it enjoyable and revitalizing to remember what it was like to be a child and teenager.

He agreed with Carl Sandburg who said, "People are what they are because they have come out of what was."

In "going home again," Mike experienced a comfortable feeling of shelter and safety. He felt a kinship with former classmates. There was a warm feeling of love among them, and Mike discovered from the past some of the answers to the puzzles of the present.

Chapter 31

Bridal Letter From Dad

At this stage in the development of his church, Mike had one major concern. It was shared by his cabinet and staff.

As they grew bigger they wanted to be sure also to become better. According to their sense of purpose this meant primarily to be an effective channel in helping satisfy the spiritual needs of the individual.

They wanted the worship services and study groups to be as effective as they could be.

Were they relevant? Were the contents and presentations of sermons and study courses vital, and on target to human contemporary needs? If not, what changes should be made? What topics would members prefer?

Is this church missing crucial areas of service, internally or in its outreach in the community? What about the time schedule of program events, as well as worship services? Could the use of the plant be improved? Should the final projected expansion of the sanctuary be considered now? How can the congregation better assimilate new members and help them feel at home?

What do members think of the music, art and pageantry ministry of the church? How do they evaluate the youth center and religious education program for children and teens?

What about the counseling services? How about auxiliary programs such as the men's club, women's social and service groups, the young adult and singles club, visitation teams or

neighborhood groups? Are they effective? If not why not, and
how could they be improved?

Mike was thrilled at the response to his suggestion that a
task force be formed to guide this study. Each division of
interest and mission of the church was represented. The Task
Force numbered nine, but with all its subcommittee members
there were over one hundred individuals involved.

Jack Stewart and his public relations firm helped develop
an effective questionnaire which was mailed to each member.
Follow up phone calls were made to those who delayed
returning it. Through this conscientious effort ninety percent
of the members responded.

The Task Force chairman had results tabulated and fed
into a computer. A detailed written report was presented to the
cabinet, and a highlight summary to each member. The entire
project took six months, and proved extremely worthwhile.

Basically, the evaluation of the church, its staff and
program, was positive. Mike was given sermon subjects that
members would like repeated as well as some suggestions for
new topics.

The staff received creative ideas to assist new members to
ease into the life of the church. They learned that a majority
of members thought the sanctuary should be built in a year or
so, and were willing to pay for it.

The report also proved to be an effective performance
review for the staff—something Mike did annually before
recommending salary increases. Consequently, the staff felt
closer to members as they learned how they could fine-tune
efforts to meet the spiritual needs of each individual.

A monumental result of the questionnaire was an increase
in volunteer participation and leadership. Almost seventy
percent of adult members were now involved in at least one
activity or mission of the church.

One of the results of the self-analysis, which Mike liked
best, was the beginning of an annual Youth Sunday and also
a Layman's Sunday.

The Youth Sunday services were conducted from beginning to end by high school and college students. Sermon time

was shared by two or three different young people at each of the three services.

Layman's Sunday followed the same pattern with women and men of the church conducting each service. It was a special treat for Mike to listen to people of various ages and cultural, racial, religious and economic backgrounds talk about their growth spiritually and how it made a difference in their lives.

He came away from these special Sundays with a feeling of celebration.

"Life," he thought, "is looking good for Michael Charles Matthews, after a number of rocky detours."

No sooner said than Mike was confronted with a heart-breaking crisis.

Without warning, Maria Stewart died from an aneurysm. Suddenly a close friend, counselor and staff leader was gone. No chance even to say goodbye.

Jack and Sally were in shock. Mike was devastated, as were hundreds of Maria's friends.

At the memorial service, Mike wished to pay tribute to Maria in a special way. So he decided to address his tribute personally to Maria, feeling that Jack and Sally would thereby also find solace and strength.

On the printed memorial folder, his eulogy was entitled:

"TRIBUTE TO A GRAND LADY."
    "I salute you . . . Maria Stewart . . .
    and thank you.
    I think of you in the present because you live.
    You are here with us.
    You exist in the now.

    You live . . .
    Not only in our memories . . .
    In indestructable atoms and molecules . . .
    Or on a far flung galaxy of stars . . .
    Not only in the eternal bliss of a celestial
        kingdom . . .

Not only in the ongoing genes inbred in daughter
and future generations . . .
You live . . .
Through the lives of your friends and colleagues.
In the continuing inspiration and energy of those
with whom you worked . . .

I know what you meant to me. You were my 'daytimer' . . . my right hand . . . my calming friend . . . my 'mother superior.'

There is a beautiful truism in the New Testament which fits you.

Paraphrased, it reads: "Greater love has no person than this, to lay down one's life for a friend."

Maria, you did this daily.

In the process, as always happens, you did not have less, but more.

Your contagious qualities multiplied: cheerful, caring, positive, loyal.

Whatever enduring value was achieved by those you served was enhanced by your gallant, glowing personality.

In the caressing breezes of God's infinite, loving spirit, I hear . . .

Echoes of solemn silence and prayer . . .
Whispers for help born in agony, pain, grief . . .
Triumphant choruses of song . . .
Spontaneous laughter of children . . .
As the shadow of your presence lengthens, I see . .
Mystical encounters with transcendent Deity . . .
Miracle moments of healing and transformation . . .
Romantic moods of two lives pledging love . . .
Serenity flowing from the discovery of one's
best self and brightest dream.

This is why, long after the halls and walls of PRINCE OF PEACE COMMUNITY CHURCH have returned to dust, the pyramid of your influence will be building.

I salute you . . . Maria Stewart . . . and thank you.

It was a happy, fabulous day when Mike received a call from Teresa.

"Dad," she announced, "you know I'm graduating in June. I just found out today it will be magna cum laude."

"Fantastic, Teresa . . . congratulations. You deserve it. You've really worked hard."

"Thanks Dad."

"What are your plans now?" Mike asked.

"Well, I'm continuing with my painting. I've won firsts in a number of shows and am carried by a couple of galleries. I've also been offered a position as an art therapist in a small private hospital here in Florida. They specialize in treating teenagers whose lives are all screwed up from drugs or parents who've given them everything but love. I'll probably take that job for at least awhile."

"I think you'd be outstanding, Teresa. You helped a lot of kids here in the youth center program."

"Now for the big news, Dad! John and I are getting married."

"Teresa . . . when? Is that ever exciting news. Have you told your mother yet? Where are you planning to have the wedding?"

"One question at a time, Dad. As far as when, it will probably be in August. I want to adjust to my new job and John will be starting work on his architectural degree in September. We'll get settled in at a new apartment, probably one of the projects you built. Then we'd like to be married by you and Bob in the chapel of your church. We'll have to set a date soon, I know, because it's in use so much. Is that OK?"

"It sounds fabulous. Teresa, this is one of the happiest moments of my life."

"Oh, I forgot to tell you," Teresa continued, "yes, I just got off the phone with Mother. We keep in close touch and she's just as happy as you are about our plans.

By the way, John and I would like a very small, informal wedding. Sally will be my maid of honor and Scott will be John's best man. Of course Mr. and Mrs. Adams will be there, and we'd like Jack Stewart to attend. That's it. I think we'd like to write our own vows, if that's OK with you."

"That sounds wonderful to me," Mike replied. "Let me know the date as soon as you can, I'd love to come down for your graduation too."

"I hope you can, Dad. I'll talk to you soon. I love you. Take care."

As Mike hung up, he thought of the swiftness of the passing parade, and the joys which Teresa had brought into his life.

That evening he shared with her some of his feelings in a letter:

Dear Teresa,

I cherish my memories of you. The day you were born was sunrise and spring. You gave your father the incomparable thrill of having an only daughter.

You were the brightest star in your mother's sky. Your brothers teased and taunted, but behind the mask of nonchalance they bubbled with admiration and pride.

I remember your childhood . . . the sparkle in your eyes, your ever ready giggle, your leap into my lap, the tight clasp of your arms around my neck.

Your first valentine to me was cut with your own scissors, and crayoned with the words, "I love you Daddy."

How can I forget your love of things soft and furry . . . like puppies, ponies, kittens and hamsters.

You were ecstatic over all things delicate and beautiful . . . like buttercups, violets in the woods, a pair of earrings, a pretty new dress.

I remember your growth into girlhood . . . your reach for independence and womanhood. Dolls were replaced with records, horses and skis . . . easels, brushes, canvases . . . teen parties and cars.

There were adventure trips to Disneyland, Hilton Head, Acapulco and Switzerland. How about your first art exhibit, your first sale of a painting.

You inspired me with responsible hours working in our

youth center. Your friends knew they could always count on you.

Suddenly, the day came when you weren't Daddy's little girl anymore. You were off and running on your own quest for selfhood. You took me seriously when I said, "The main goal of a parent is to help children become self-reliant."

I admired your courage, perseverance, determination. You braved loneliness, hurts, a few dead end streets.

You kept at it . . . studied and worked . . . sifted and sorted, and learned to know yourself . . . who you wanted to be.

You set values and goals in tune with the infinite creative force within you, which some of us call God. Through it all you became my friend, occasional companion and sometime counselor.

Now you are about to commit your deep capacity for love in marriage. You know, my beautiful Teresa, that your mother, brother and I support you with our love and prayers.

May this mystical expression of love be a mutual commitment of giving, trust, respect, loyalty.

I wish for you continued growth in your individuality as you share one of the most exhilarating of life's experiences . . . the love relationship between a man and woman.

Your Dad

When Teresa received the letter they had another long talk on the phone. It concluded with their agreement that Bob would handle the service up to the point of the vows. Then he would give a brief talk and lead them through their vows. Teresa also told Mike that Jane had arranged with one of the church's serving groups to handle the reception.

The trip to Florida for commencement was fast but fun. Scott and Jane were also there. It was a thrill for all of them when the name of Teresa Matthews was announced as an honors graduate.

It was also enjoyable for Mike to visit with Jane again. She seemed happy, in control of her life. She was doing some directing now, and spoke glowingly when she shared the news that she was going to be remarried at Christmas time.

"Congratulations and a happy future, Jane," was Mike's response to her announcement after the graduation reception for Teresa.

"Thanks, Mike. I know we'll always be friends," Jane replied. "I hope your future will include another mate also. I'll always treasure our good times. The very best to you, Mike."

The time raced by to August and the day of Teresa's and John's wedding. Jane had made arrangements for the flowers. The chapel had never looked more beautiful.

Mike didn't know if he was going to be able to control his emotions as he walked up the aisle, but he made it. Teresa squeezed his hand when it was his turn to answer the question he had asked others hundreds of times: "Who gives this woman in holy matrimony?"

After Jane and Mike answered "We do," Mike switched roles and began his talk:

"Dear Teresa and John . . . what a thrill it is for all of us to share the magic of this celebration with you.

"We're here to tell you that we care about you, are happy for you and wish you lifelong happiness together.

"One of my favorite verses from the Bible reads: 'now abides faith, hope, love, but the greatest of these is love.' This thought is included in many of the major religions of the world.

"I'd like it to be the theme of my talk with you today. Its message is very simple, but also profound. It's saying that love is the most powerful energy force in the world.

"It's saying that one day after we have mastered the power of the wind, the waves, the tides, gravity and the sun . . . then, as a wise philosopher predicted, 'if we will harness the energies of love, for the second time in the history of this globe we will have discovered fire.'

"Love is powerful. It is able to change loneliness, hopelessness, emptiness into happiness, feelings of self-worth, purpose in living through companionship with a mate whom you love.

"But love is also fragile. It's as delicate as a spring butterfly. It must be nourished gently, carefully.

"I remember the cartoon portraying middle-aged George. Every three years he comes running into the court house with his marriage license waving in his hand. And the clerk tells him each time, 'No, George, I keep telling you that it's your drivers license which needs renewal, not your marriage license.'

"Oh, but it does! Our marriage vows do need to be renewed. Otherwise we move so quickly from being soul mates, to merely roommates, and finally just cell mates.

"How do we renew our marriage vows? What gives us the best chance of staying happily married?

"Through the years I've been collecting my own list of ten guidelines which I think help keep marriages renewed. I'd like to share my list with you.

"1. People who remain happily together frequently repeat to one another a trilogy of three words: 'I need you' — 'Please forgive me' — 'I love you.' They believe these words are as important as touching.

"In other words, I'm saying that successful lovers aren't like stoic, introvertive Scandinavian Lars who loved his wife so much he almost told her.

"2. People who remain happily together are also physically affectionate . . . like the couple I saw in church recently holding hands. I sensed that they felt touching was as important as talking.

"3. Couples who remain happy also express their love sexually. Their sexuality remains vital through the years, and it's mutually expressive of their caring.

"4. They also demonstrate their appreciation of one another with acts of kindness—sometimes just in little ways.

"I recall one young couple with whom I especially enjoyed my premarital counseling sessions. He was so attentive. Always opened the door, called her 'honey' and helped her with her coat.

"About six months after their wedding I happened to see them coming out of the supermarket. He was walking out front. She was pregnant and carrying the groceries, two bags, one in each arm. He marched straight to his side of the car, and when she fumbled trying to open her door, he barked 'What's the matter, you crippled or something?'

"5. Couples who remain happy also reveal themselves to one another. They don't expect their mate to read their mind. They share their inner thoughts, hopes, aspirations as well as hurts, angers and disappointments.

But I don't think they thrive on 'letting it all hang out.' In other words, they don't find it necessary to shout and scream. They are at least as polite and courteous to their mate as they are to a friend or associate at work.

"6. People who stay happily together offer one another emotional support in times of illness, difficulty and crisis.

"7. They express their love in material ways also. They share gifts, not necessarily large, expensive gifts. Sometimes just small, but thoughtful expressions of love.

"8. They also accept requests from their mate and put up with shortcomings. They recognize that neither of them is perfect. They do not try to dominate, manipulate, demand or control.

"9. They do, however, communicate. They feel free to express how they feel without being put down. They know they don't have to agree about everything. They respect one another's differences.

"10. Finally, happy couples create time to be alone. They know they don't have to be together all the time. They respect one another's need and right to privacy and separate interests. But they know it is important for continual renewal of their love to create times to be alone.

"These are my ten keys to keeping that powerful, but fragile, gift of love alive and growing for a lifetime.

"Teresa and John, we wish this for you. Good luck. Congratulations! And God bless."

Chapter 32

Is Life Fair?

For weeks Mike had been looking forward to the Sunday services following Teresa's wedding. Bob and Scott both agreed to stay over one more day. The plan was to have a three-way dialogue in place of the customary sermon.

The dialogue was to be repeated at the three services Sunday morning, and the recording of it played for the following Thursday evening service.

The subject had long been one of profound interest to Mike. He also learned from the replies to the task force's questionnaire that a high percentage of church members had a keen interest in this puzzler, namely: IS LIFE FAIR?

In other words, what about the problem of evil in this world? Why is there so much suffering? If there is an all knowing, omnipotent, loving God how can the cruelties, atrocities, hunger, pain, disease be allowed to exist?

Are these grim experiences punishment for sin? If so, is God some kind of a cruel ogre who uses one person controlled by greed and hatred to pull the trigger on another person who is an innocent bystander at a burglary?

Or why do some people appear to escape adversity? Why is it that saintly people can go through so much hell on this earth? Does God play favorites? Is God involved at all? If so, how?

IS LIFE FAIR? How can we reconcile good with evil?

Bob, Scott and Mike prepared for their dialogue over

a period of several weeks. They each wrote, and exchanged, a paper on the subject. There followed some fascinating three-way conference discussions on the telephone.

Since Mike was to be the moderator, he submitted an outline script for them to critique. This was followed by an edited version and a "dry run" rehearsal the Saturday of Teresa's wedding. It was agreed that they wanted to be free to ad-lib, without digressing too far from the script, or going past the time limit of twenty-five minutes.

Their "set" on the auditorium stage consisted of a "coffee table" and three casual chairs from the church lounge. They each wore lapel microphones.

The attendance response following several weeks of promotion proved to be outstanding. All three services were filled.

Mike began informally.

"Good morning. I hope each of you had as wonderful a week as I did. It was my joy to celebrate my daughter's wedding in our chapel yesterday. What a joy to wish those two young people the best of life on their adventure together.

"And now it is my privilege," he went on, "to moderate this three-way dialogue in place of the sermon today. For those of you who have not met my son, this is Scott on my left. Scott is completing his doctorate in creative writing at New York University, and completing his first book to be published soon."

"Directly across from me is my best friend, the president of our national church body, Dr. Robert Mackay. My children grew up knowing him as 'Uncle Bob'.

"We're going to talk about a question in which you have shown a great deal of interest. Philosophers have been puzzling this subject for centuries. Thousands of theological volumes have been written on this topic: IS LIFE FAIR?

MIKE: "I'll begin by admitting: 'I don't know.'

Bob is aware that when he invited me to leave my business and enter the ministry, one of my conditions was that I have the freedom to be frank on certain religious issues and occasionally admit 'I don't know.'"

BOB: "That's correct, Mike, I agreed with you. More clergy need to admit they don't know the final answer to every profound religious question instead of coming on like they are infallible. I have often said, 'It's the absolutists in this world for whom we need to have the greatest fear . . . the Napoleons, Hitlers, Marx's or any preacher down the block representing denomination X-Y-Z who claims: 'I've got all the final answers.'"

SCOTT: "It's refreshing to hear you say that, Bob. I think there can be several legitimate answers to our discussion question. For example, 'the answer may be different for me than you.' Or, 'what seems unfair in the short term may not seem fair in the long term' . . . or, the answer could be 'maybe,' or, 'I don't know yet'. A legitimate answer might also be 'NO' or it might be 'YES', or it could be simply 'you decide.'"

MIKE: "Do I understand you to mean that if we think of life only in terms of a time-space stage on planet earth and days-years in this lifetime, then we could have an incomplete perspective of what's fair and unfair?"

SCOTT: "Yes, that's partially what I meant. But I'd like to add something which might seem a bit academic to some in our audience today. I can illustrate what I meant by referring to one of the laws of physics.

"I'm referring to the law of polarity. Simply put, everything in our universe has its pair of opposites. And opposites are actually identical in nature. They differ only in degree. Or to change the metaphor, the opposites might be different sides of the same circle.

"Let me illustrate. The north and south poles are opposites—positive and negative. But they are also two extremes of the same thing. They differ only in their direction.

"Likewise, there actually is no absolute cold or absolute heat. They are only differences in degrees of the same thing. The same is true of light and darkness, because it's impossible to tell where one begins and the other ends. It's the same with high and low, hard and soft, big and little, slow and fast. The law of polarity explains these paradoxes, and everything in our universe is subject to this law."

BOB: "Therefore, you are saying that when we think something in this life is unfair, it might be that the final score isn't in yet, and what appears to be 'bad' might be 'good.'

"I can go along with that. I think that's a lesson my grandmother was attempting to teach me when I was a child. She had this Bible verse crocheted and framed on the wall of her kitchen: 'All things work together for good to those who love God.'

"As a boy I said to her one day: 'Oh, no, Grandma. That can't be true. How can it be? When I went out on my sled and hit a tree, and got a big gash on my chin, how was it that it was good? It hurt. It was painful. I have this big scar. That couldn't have been good.'

"Grandma just smiled and replied, 'Be patient, my child. Wait a while. Did you learn anything? Did it make you more careful next time? Were you better able to be sympathetic with friends when they were hurt?'"

MIKE: "Did it work that way?"

BOB: "Very definitely, in time. It was Carl Jung, the psychologist who said: 'It all depends on how we look at things, and not on how they are in themselves.' In other words, what appears to be kind and gentle is not always good; nor is rough always bad."

MIKE: "Bob, you're the theologian in this threesome. Let's shift our discussion slightly to the question: 'Does God cause pain and suffering, and is it punishment for sin?'"

BOB: "In my opinion the answer is emphatically 'no'. To take the opposite position is to paint a picture of God as a cosmic roller of the dice who capriciously doles out favors or demerits."

MIKE: "So, you are saying that pain and suffering have nothing to do with punishment or reward."

BOB: "That's my opinion. I don't believe, for example, in the cliche often expressed when somebody dies, 'his time was up,' or 'God took her to be in eternal bliss because she was so good.'"

SCOTT: "In other words, God is not the cause of such scenarios as these: A tornado destroys my house but not my neighbors; or, I'm in a plane crash, and I survive, but a friend sitting next to me burns to death; or, two equally talented people go into business. Both work hard . . . one is scrupulously honest . . . the other cuts corners, cheats here and there . . . but the honest one goes bankrupt and the cheater can't begin to count all the profit."

MIKE: "What do you say then to the honest victims of failure, the survivors of a crash, the relatives of the home destroyed by the tornado? What do you say to people who ask 'why me?' I face this question all the time in counseling sessions. Let me address the question to you again, Bob."

BOB: "I say it's chance . . . circumstance . . . an accident . . . tragic for the present perhaps, but still an accident. We live in a world of risk. We also have freedom to choose, and sometimes we can be the victims of other people's actions and choices. It's how we handle what happens to us that really matters."

SCOTT: "That's what Hindu karma means. The Indian religion teaches that we choose what type of person we will be in this life and any life to come.

"We can find all kinds of circumstances and people to blame for what appears to be misfortune, but in the long term what we are as human beings is our choice. . . one freedom no one can take away from us is to choose our attitude toward what happens to us. We can blame our parents for our weaknesses. Freud taught that. Or we can take the position of Marx and say suffering is the fault of society's upper class. But ultimately we are in control. We can blame circumstances beyond our control, or search endlessly for ways to explain, but the real issue is how we handle what happens to us."

MIKE: "I appreciate you saying that because, as you know, I went through a series of tough experiences . . . the loss of your brother, my son, Dane . . . the failure of a business empire . . . a divorce . . . an almost fluke viral heart damage. But, you know, it was after all this that an extremely successful man, measured by wealth, came up to me after a motivational speech I gave and said: 'You have no idea how I envy you. You have everything I've searched for and can't find . . . a magnetic inner peace and contagious vitality and happiness.'

BOB: "Let's talk about that for the final part of our discussion, the question of how we turn what appears to be a negative into a positive."

SCOTT: "I'll begin. I believe negatives become positives only when we quit looking for philosophical answers and search within ourselves. We need to find our own inner quiet place, our true center, the eternal force within, what Jesus meant when he said: 'the kingdom of heaven is within you.'"

MIKE: "I agree. It's what the Tibetan Buddhists mean when they refer to Nirvana. It's not a place but a condition, a state of mind and consciousness which can begin right here on this earth. But we have to be willing to make the pilgrimage, pursue the inward search, and recognize the prize when we encounter it."

BOB: "What you were saying, Scott, is that the inner tranquility and strength we seek can play tricks on us. It frequently has a sly way of slipping in by the back door. Often it comes disguised as misfortune or temporary defeat."

SCOTT: "How true! I believe failure can teach us far more than success. Enduring adversity can help us flourish in new ways. Overcoming setbacks can teach us how to go forward. In suffering a weakness we can grow strong. This is what the native Hawaiians believed, 'that no difficulty has any power over you unless you give it. Life in not a bad joke. Suffering can unlock the door to many answers. Trouble will enter life like a storm. Do not resist . . . there is a balancing power at work . . . your new self is about to be born.'"

MIKE: "I like what George Eliot had to say about this: "He was talking about this same paradox when he wrote: 'Any coward can fight a battle when he's sure of winning; but give me the man who has the pluck to fight when he is sure of losing . . . There are many victories worse than defeat.'"

SCOTT: "I like Edwin Markham's poem called Victory In Defeat. "Listen to what he wrote:

> Defeat may serve as well as victory
> To shake the soul and let the glory out.
> When the great oak is straining in the wind,

The boughs drink in new beauty, and the trunk
Sends down a deeper root on the windward side.
Only the soul that knows the mighty grief
Can know the mighty rapture. Sorrow comes
To stretch our spaces in the heart for joy.

MIKE: "Thank you for sharing that poem with us.

"Let me tell you a story which illustrates this poem so well. It's about a young man whom we'll call Joe. It's a true story, and I have permission to tell it. Only the name is disguised.

"Joe lived in this community . . . was born into poverty . . . never knew his father . . . his mother survived by working as a prostitute.

"By the age of sixteen Joe was an expert at street fighting, breaking and entering, and pushing drugs. He also had a girlfriend and baby.

"His temporary escape was to lie about his age and enlist in the paratroopers. He lived through the horrors of Vietnam. He became a combat photographer with a camera in one hand and a forty-five in the other. Joe received a captain's field commission as he produced films recording atrocities and carnage on both sides.

"His service career came to a quick halt when his body was torn apart by a land mine. He became a paraplegic . . . returned to an America fractured by confusion and dissent . . . He was married and divorced. Joe had every reason to be hostile and bitter, and he was.

"Then a miracle occurred. One of you invited Joe to this church. Over time he discovered the image of God within himself. He found his peace, and fulfilled his dream.

"Today he's a teacher. He doesn't make much money, but he's living his peace and purpose—teaching poetry, art history and photography at a college. He's also married to a wonderful young woman with two children. Joe has all the qualities we've been talking about. He gives so much to me when we get together a couple of times each month."

BOB: "I'd like to add a thought: I believe my grandmother was right after all: 'All things do work together for good to those who love God' . . . If we give them a chance and enough time.

"IS LIFE FAIR? Part of my answer is this amazing truth: We can consider ourselves privileged if we have experienced adversity, and not only overcome, but learned and grown. The reason is that there are dividends available, as from no other source . . . not from books, education, wealth or just getting older. I'm speaking of mellowness, togetherness, sensitivity, wisdom, a capacity for love and appreciation—an exhilaration for life.

"I think this is what the apostle Paul meant when he wrote to his friends of the first century in Rome (Romans 8:38-39): 'I am persuaded, that neither death, nor life, nor angels, nor principalities, nor powers, nor things present, nor things to come, nor height, nor depth, nor any other creature, shall be able to separate us from the love of God.'

"IS LIFE FAIR? — you decide!"

MIKE: "That's a good place for us to conclude . . . Let me capsulize the six main ideas on which we've focused: ONE, there can be several different answers to our question, such as 'yes', 'no', 'maybe', depending on the time-space perspective one has; TWO, the temporary answer of the short term may not be the permanent answer of the long term; THREE, what appears to be bad could be good and visa versa; FOUR, God is not a cosmic roller of dice dealing out punishment and reward; FIVE, we can only find the correct answer when we discover our true center, our quiet place within; SIX, the ultimate prize is not to blame or explain, but to seek the help of God in turning defeat into victory and adversity into happy, exhilarating living.

"My thanks to you Scott and Bob. Thanks to each one of you who have so patiently shared this discussion. We hope you have found something helpful for your personal spiritual quest."

The response at all three services was a standing ovation. This was a FIRST on Sunday morning at PRINCE OF PEACE COMMUNITY CHURCH.

Chapter 33

Life Goes On

Mike was reaching a crescendo of satisfaction and inner peace in his career as a senior minister of PRINCE OF PEACE COMMUNITY CHURCH.

There was a cohesive harmony and productivity among his staff.

Volunteers, and members, exuded a caring, dynamic thrust of spiritual purpose in the community.

The church now numbered approximately five thousand adult members. Once more it was necessary to have four services per Sunday. The final service was on radio.

Mike had been having a wonderful time as advisor to the building committee and architects designing the sanctuary.

The statement of criteria for this final building on the church campus was dramatic and specific. The feelings they wished to express were: an inviting spirit of welcome . . . moods of togetherness; happiness; reaching upwards . . . a sense of awe, beauty and sacred presence without being ostentatious.

They also wished to capture the dramatic views of the private lake on the property. They wanted esthetic exposures to natural light as well as effective use of artificial lighting.

The acoustics for both music and speaking were also top priority. Seating was planned for two thousand, and there would be two services per Sunday.

Blueprints and specifications were complete and out for

bids. Financing was in place. Mike felt the team of members and architects had done a remarkable job of achieving their criteria. Groundbreaking was scheduled for Palm Sunday, 1982, with completion about a year away.

The evening of Palm Sunday Mike had the surprise of his life. The men's club of the church staged a "This Is Your Life" party for him.

Scott, Teresa and John were there as well as the Adams from Florida, the Mackays, the presidents of Jefferson University and Emerson Theological Seminary, and a host of friends from his former company in Florida. It was a gala evening, complete with voices and pictures from the past to the present.

The committee even flew Mike's sister Judy in from California. He hadn't seen her since Dane's funeral, although they kept in touch by phone and greetings at holiday times.

A generous gift of money totaling over five thousand dollars was presented to Mike for use during his sabbatical year, beginning the week after Easter. He had been working for weeks with the cabinet and staff for a smooth transition during his absence.

After the hilarity, the kidding, and reminiscing were over, Mike did his best not to choke on his emotions and express his deep appreciation for this demonstration of love.

"How can I thank you?" he began. "How did you pull this off? You know I always have to have my fingers on everything that happens around here. Or I thought I did.

"Now I'm finding that with my sabbatical just a week away I'm not so important after all. Your leaders, your cabinet, you volunteers and my wonderful staff have everything under control.

"You probably wonder what I'm going to do for a whole year. Well, your gift is really going to contribute to many happy hours for me.

"I'm getting delivery next week on a motor home. I plan to hit the road with no commitment to a schedule. I would like to tour this wonderful country, particularly areas I haven't seen before.

"I'd like to visit with people in the countryside, the open plains, small towns, the state and national parks. I plan to do a lot of reading, and I have plans to do some writing.

"Now, I saved the best for last (I'm kidding).

"I plan to fish some of the most inviting waters of our continent . . . the trout streams of the Tetons, the ice-cold salmon lakes of Alaska, Great Slave Lake in Canada, and maybe even the waters off the Baja Peninsula.

"I would also like to play the best one or two golf courses in several states I visit . . . courses like Butler National, Chicago; Pebble Beach at Carmel; La Quinta in Palm Springs; Augusta in Georgia (I have a friend who belongs); Desert Forest in Carefree, Arizona; Bayhill Country Club, Florida. By the time I get back I should either be down to a three or four handicap or have donated my clubs to Goodwill.

"Thank you, good friends, for this fabulous party and generous gift. See you in church . . . next Sunday . . . it's Easter, you know . . . My sermon topic is 'LIFE GOES ON' . . . we'll all be able to gather together for the first time.

"Remember? Your church cabinet has rented the civic auditorium. We'll have just one service at eleven a.m. All choirs, eight of them, three hundred voices plus the orchestra will raise the roof with joyful song.

"The stage will be overflowing with flowers, and including our friends from the community and families and relatives, we are expecting about seven thousand people. See you then!"

Mike's family and friends were all booked in a hotel for the night, so he went home to his bachelor townhouse. In contrast to the emotional high he had just experienced, he was in a mellow, nostalgic, downright lonely mood.

He went for a long walk and thought about his "This Is Your Life" surprise. It wasn't hard to figure out why he was lonely.

His quad of life principals, which he had chosen to live by all these years, were in place . . . a sense of work, play, worship and love.

On a scale of one to ten they ranked an eight or nine . . . except the sense of love in his life. That was at about a five.

Family? Yes. Friends? Yes. Surrounded by people? Yes,
by the thousands.

Lonely? Yes.

Why?

"Here I am," he thought, "at fifty-nine years old, and
lonely. I'm living a full, exciting, meaningful life. Is my mood
just temporary? I hope so!"

He knew what was missing.

"It's time once more," he realized "to be open to a life
companion. Maybe my new journey will be a sentimental one
after all," he thought.

"In a whimsical mood he returned to his townhouse and
wrote:

> I miss . . .
>   a hug
>   when I've been away
> a goodnight kiss
>   cuddling in bed
>   a warm body
> next to mine
>   hand holding
>   anytime
> a lovemate
>   to share . . .
>   walks in the rain
> hikes in the woods
>   bike rides
>   symphonies
> plays
>   art museums
>   wine by the fire
> fragrance of spring
>   crimson of autumn
>   drifting snow
> frost on windowpanes
>   christmas lights
>   planning for trips
> sunsets in azure

beauty touches
    at home
jokes
    hopes
        dreams
tales of the day
    god talk
        whispers
of hurts
    failures
        betrayals
memory forging
    mealtime together
        parties with friends
I miss . . .
    saying
        'I love you.'

Now he knew how his Easter Sunday sermon was going to end. He'd been thinking about it and writing notes for weeks, but couldn't decide what the ending should be. Now he was sure.

He stayed up all night writing.

It was an April Easter. Bright, cheerful, sunny. The ushers estimated seventy-five hundred in attendance. The trumpeters, orchestra and choirs were magnificent.

Hundreds of daffodils, azaleas and lilies, going later to hospitals and rest homes, framed the simple lectern. It was a fantastic, electrifying moment for Mike, as he began his sermon.

"Good morning, good friends! A wonderful happy Easter Sunday to each one of you.

"Let all of earth and the heavens echo with the best news of all time. LIFE GOES ON!

"I'd like to begin by inviting you to listen to some lighthearted verses written by a friend of mine. These verses you children here today will also enjoy.

"After more than twenty-five happy years of marriage, my

friend's husband died from a heart attack while the family was on a ski trip.

"She was shattered with grief. Usually a bubbly, fun loving person she was now deeply depressed . . . no hope . . . no faith in anything, positive and good. But gradually, with help from counselors and friends, she lived through her sadness to write these happy words:

> I believe in fairies
> And I believe in gnomes
> And I believe in elves
> Who live in meadow homes.
>
> I believe in ghosts
> Who roam in people's halls
> And I believe in spirits
> Who lurk in ancient walls.
>
> I believe in pots of gold
> Sitting at the rainbow's end —
> That raindrops really can be tears
> Which cleanse and sooth and mend.
>
> I believe in clovers,
> And daisies really tell —
> And dandelions under chins
> Relay a message well.
>
> Santa Claus is real to me,
> And, too, the Easter bunny,
> Leprechauns do prance around
> All dressed up so funny.
>
> These are all so real to me,
> Extolled in books and song,
> They bring such joy and happiness —
> I hope that I'm not wrong!

"No, dear heart! You are not wrong. For you, and all of

us, LIFE DOES GO ON . . . because God lives we too live, NOW and FOREVER.

"This is the message of Easter. Those twelve scruffy, vagabond followers of the carpenter from Nazareth took this message to the world.

"They didn't have telephones, satellites or TV. They just walked and talked about what they had seen and heard. They went on a mission. They were dedicated to their pilgrimage and followed their dream.

"They told such puzzling, absurd riddles and paradoxes as: 'the first shall be last and the last shall be first; the meek shall inherit the earth . . . peacemakers shall be called the children of God . . . love your neighbor and your enemies as yourself . . . do unto others as you would have others do unto you . . . ask and you shall receive; seek and you shall find; knock and it will be opened . . . give and it shall be given to you . . . seek first the kingdom of God and all other things shall be added unto you.'

"Who ever heard of such a thing?

"Doesn't make sense, does it?

"But you know what? These absurd riddles revolution-ized the western world.

"The conqueror became the conquered. After three hundred years the mighty Roman Empire, which had crucified the man from Galilee, proclaimed his absurd, impractical ideas to be their official religion.

"LIFE GOES ON . . .

"There is life after life!

"Is heaven a celestial fantasy land on some far flung star? Will there be a reincarnation of the body in some distant galaxy? Who knows? Who cares? What difference would it make?

"I know one of the ancient Christian creeds proclaims a resurrection of the body. But that isn't the central message of Easter, that this poor body of ours goes on.

"The message is that because God lives you live . . . HERE and FOREVER.

"Death is not the end, as my friend discovered who wrote

the poem I shared with you.

Ralph Waldo Emerson put it this way: "It is a secret of the world that all things subsist, and do not die, but only retire a little from sight, and afterwards return again.

"I agree with those who believe that death is transition and change. Every one of the billions of our human cells, and every atom of matter, began as an intangible form of energy. All of life is energy, and it's a fact indelibly inscribed in this universe that energy and matter cannot be destroyed . . . nor can life be destroyed.

"Death is transition . . . a reblending with the infinite intelligence, energy and love with which we began . . . a moving on to some more perfect form than life on this earth.

"I share the faith of the poet Wordsworth who wrote:

Our birth is but a sleep and a forgetting:
The soul that rises with us, our life's star,
Hath had elsewhere its setting,
And cometh from afar.

"That being true, why is it that in our religious traditions we have so often treated funerals as grim almost pagan rituals. They should be celebrations.

"In nature when plants reach old age, we say they have ripened. When flowers burst into a bloom of fragrance and color, we say they have bloomed.

"Why is it then that when we reach old age we see it as deterioration, not as blooming or ripening . . . a beautiful fulfillment.

"I like the attitude of little Johnnie. He was only four years old. One day he looked up at his grandfather and asked: "Grandpa, when are you going to die? Are you looking forward to it? Are you going to take an airplane to heaven?'

"Grandpa replied, 'I don't know when I'm going to die, Johnnie, but if I take an airplane I surely hope there's no hijacker on it.'

"LIFE GOES ON!

"I think it's a certainty that when we do go on we take with us exactly what we were here.

"In other words heaven, or the ultimate transcendent spiritual consciousness, all major religions speak of, begins here or it doesn't happen at all.

"That's a pretty jolting reality isn't it?

"How do we find heaven here?

"The message of Easter says: Go on a quest—a pilgrimage—like the twelve friends of Jesus did. Search within yourself, because that's where the treasure is. 'The kingdom of heaven,' Jesus repeated over and over again, 'is within you.'

"Discover the image of God within you. Find the cosmic force which is part of you. Lay claim to the deepest purest dream of your heart. Then cling to it. Grow with it. Love it.

"But don't hoard it. Because (here we go again) it's one of those absurd paradoxes Jesus taught: Keep it to yourself and you'll lose it, but give it away and it multiplies.

"By all the laws of logic and arithmetic, it would seem that to give ourselves away leaves us with less of ourselves than we started with. But the miracle is that the reverse is true. When we give ourselves to somebody in pure and simple love we become for the first time our best and complete selves.

"So find ways to express your best self. Discover how you can share the beauty within . . . follow your conscience . . . hold to your dream no matter what your peers do, no matter what society says, no matter what family, friends, business colleagues follow. Hold to your dream.

"How do we do that?

"There is help, you know!

"For one thing, we can learn from the Masters who have gone before us.

"When we begin learning to read we don't have to rewrite the alphabet.

"If you wish to become an artist, you have a legacy to build on. You can learn from Michelangelo, Monet, Picasso . . . If it's music—you can learn from Mozart, Bach, Beethoven . . . If it's writing—you can learn from Dickens, Coleridge, Browning, Hemmingway . . . If it's science—you can learn from Edison, Einstein, Salk.

"When it comes to your spiritual quest, there's also help available from the Masters: Jesus, Ghandi, Moses, Schweitzer, Sister Theresa, Thoreau, Emerson . . . the list goes on and on.

"There is also help from Mentors.

"Find yourself, a qualified Mentor . . . someone you can trust, who has been there before you . . . demonstrated the cosmic connection . . . lived out the wisdom from infinite intelligence . . . cares genuinely about you.

"You don't have to make the same mistakes, take the same dead ends, follow the same wrong turns as others before you.

"There are Masters and Mentors to help you.

"Life does go on, and you may go way beyond the Mentors and Masters before you.

"The potential of the spiritual pilgrimage is limitless. Believe it! Hold to it! Follow it!

"Because . . . THE BEST IS YET TO BE!

"Now, my good friends, before we close this celebration of Easter, I have a personal message for you, our members.

"I have reached the end of ten years as your minister, and hopefully your mentor. They have been exciting, demanding years.

"Together we have worked and prayed, cried and laughed, worshiped and loved. Thank you for your patience, your support, your generosity.

"We have accomplished much together—measured not by numbers, or brick and mortar; but measured by the redemption and rejuvenation of people . . . of a single child, a teenager, a parent, a marriage, an executive, a single soul without hope.

"In many ways, hopefully for the better, we have gone beyond the mainstream of the traditional church, and you have accepted me as your MAVERICK OF THE CLOTH.

"Tomorrow I am leaving, not only on my sabbatical year, but to return my license and submit my resignation from the clergy as Dr. Michael Charles Matthews.

"I am not retiring. I hope never to retire because there are so many more challenges I would like to pursue as a lay person again.

...ne of you will remember me telling of my encounter ...n a spiritual mentor when I was in college who wrote this statement in one of his books: 'There are so many vocations in this world, it's a shame most of us miss all of them except one.'

"That idea sent me on a quest of living my life in several worthwhile chapters.

"This one has been the best. But life does go on for me also. When I began my career with you, I set as my private goal a time period of ten years. The ten years are up—so as difficult as it is to leave you, I believe it is time.

"In the years to come you will probably see little of me. Not because I don't care, but because I cherish your freedom, with my successor, to chart new trails without my intervention.

"During my sabbatical I'd like to do some plain ordinary loafing. Then I'd like to explore some learning ambitions of mine: perhaps take some courses in horticulture, maybe learn how to paint and play a guitar . . . do some writing, travel, read great books, absorb fine art, drama and music.

"Along the way I would hope to learn to know intriguing people, make more good friends, continue my involvement with my foundation for first year college students.

"Above all, I hope to pursue yet another vocational chapter in this lifetime.

"Now good friends, while the choirs sing their Easter benediction anthem, I will be taking my leave.

"I acknowledge I would not hold up well today greeting you at the exit.

"But I would like to leave this parting benediction with you:

> May the infinite patience and wisdom
>   of God take you gently by the hand
>   and aid you to . . .
>   Take your journey inward,
>   Sing your soul's sweetest songs,
>   Reach for your finest dreams,
>   Leave this earth better than you found it.